DISPLACEMENT

DISPLACEMENT

A NOVEL

RICHARD FORD BURLEY

PROSPECTIVE PRESS

P ROSPECTIVE P RESS LLC

1959 Peace Haven Rd, #246, Winston-Salem, NC 27106 U.S.A.
www.prospectivepress.com

Published in the United States of America by PROSPECTIVE PRESS LLC

TRADEMARK

DISPLACEMENT

ISBN 978-1-943419-85-2

G004

First PROSPECTIVE PRESS trade paperback edition

Printed in the United States of America
First printing, April, 2021

The text of this book is typeset in Alegreya
Accent text is typeset in Shift

PUBLISHER'S NOTE

CONTENT NOTICE

The following work deals with violence, illness, and loss of a family member, as well as sexuality and gender transformations which, while fictionalized, certain readers may feel are analogous to their own situations. The author has tried to treat these issues with care, and welcomes any feedback on these and other issues. Updated content notices and discussion can be found at richardfordburley.com/displacement

DISPLACEMENT

For all my beautiful misfits.

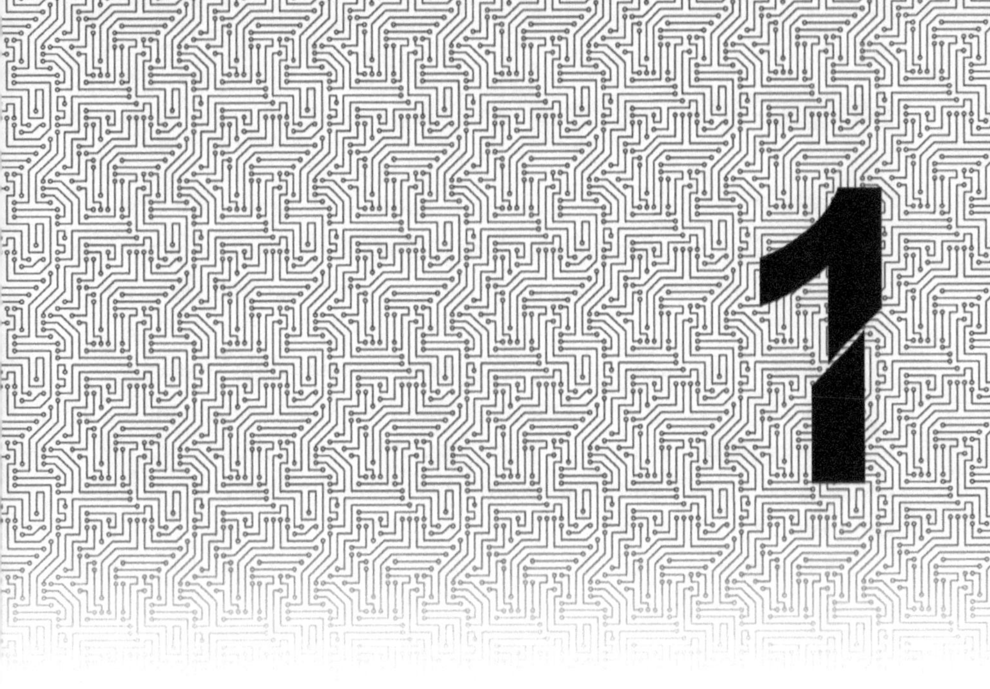

"**You cannot—possibly—be flat-out obtuse enough to think** you're going to get away with it."

Jamie's locker slams shut to reveal the girl behind it, her long black hair hanging straight past her shoulders and down her back, her school uniform a bit of a mess but within the academy's mundane regulations, her hand balled into a fist that's still holding his locker closed.

He grins.

"Why, whatever do you mean, my dear, sweet sister?" He steps back, opens the next locker over, and checks himself in that one's mirror, fixing a spike of electric blue hair that's starting to fray. He looks back at her. "I prerecorded the whole thing and ran it past the censors and everything."

"Censors—! Jesus, Jamie, it's not the White House press secretary, it's Miss *Evans*. She's older than death and she couldn't hear a seven-forty-seven if she were standing behind it on the runway as it spooled up for takeoff! She can't approve *anything*, and you, me, and most especially Headmaster McGuinness all know that. *That's why he said you have to run things by Amy first.*" She's got her arms folded and a look that could set him on actual fire.

Jamie sighs and steps up to her.

"Arms down."

"What?"

"It's killing me. Arms down." He unfolds her arms and puts them at her sides, before reaching up and fixing her collar and tie while he talks.

"*James*—" she says, looking up in exasperation while he works.

"It's Jamie, Lizzie, not James. Jameses wear boat shoes and salmon-colored polos; Jamies can wear whatever they feel like—which, by the way, I still have your skirt somewhere? Remind me about it sometime and I'll go digging."

"You still have that? No wonder I couldn't find it last week, thief," she says, still looking up.

"Yeah well, you can have it back. It didn't look as good as—well, *I* didn't think it looked—well the *point is*: only Patton calls me James." He stops, squints at the bowtie. "And for that matter he only *used* to call me that. Now he calls me 'And don't come back until you learn to show some respect.'" He does his best Billionaire Philanthropist J. Patton Goldmark impression as he speaks, then grins and steps back. "Better."

She sighs. "It was James in middle school."

"I didn't have a reputation to uphold in middle school, gorgeous."

"You don't have one here, either."

He ignores her. "If you're going to go with the boys' tie option at least practice tying one a little."

"Like you get a say when you're dressed like that—"

"Hey, you don't get to talk to me about *style*, sis. And anyway, the docs are 'black footwear;' the makeup, bracelets, and belts are 'accessories within reason;' and you can't blame *me* if the girls' pants just happen to look better on me." He smirks. "This is all technically allowed—"

"And you're going to get yourself technically *expelled*."

He puts a finger on his lower lip and looks up as if in thought. "Now wait, which one of us is currently on probation?" Last semester there had been an incident involving Lizzie, a certain unnamed redhead, and a shocking lack of clothing—well, a lack of clothing being *worn*—in her dorm room after hours. The only reason it hadn't been expulsion was that technically she hadn't broken any rules: it was officially only *boys* who weren't allowed in the girls' dorm rooms after seven.

She almost growls and Jamie steps back nervously.

"Look. You'd better run and get it before they—"

The speakers whine and crackle, followed by a peaceful, descending chime. Lizzie looks at him and sighs. "Now you're in it. Deep."

"Jamie Goldmark, kindly report to Radio Lab One at your earliest convenience."

The tones reverse, the speakers click off, and for a solid three seconds the loudest thing in the hallway is Lizzie's smirk.

"Oh, come *on!*" He stamps a foot, almost hops in frustration. "Of all the—" He puts his hands to his head. "It has to be *him?*"

Jamie bangs his forehead against the locker and leaves it there.

"Damn it, Lizzie." He withers. "McGuinness I could've taken."

Lizzie swivels and begins to walk off to class. "I'll tell Granger you're going to be a little late. She probably expects it by now anyway."

"Late? Try deceased!" He shouts after her. "I demand legal counsel! I have the right to an attorney!"

"Good luck with Jack!" She almost sings it as she rounds the corner.

He'd have better luck with Vlad the Impaler.

He's toast.

■ ■ ■

The red light's on, but Amy waves for him to come in anyway. She's smiling. He wants to run away, but instead he opens the door and walks on in. She's got rosy cheeks, chestnut hair, a great smile—if she weren't such a sadist, he might even be interested. He waves a little, but she's not looking. She's wearing headphones and throwing switches while Jack and Jules, sitting in the booth, toss a little banter back and forth between songs.

When she turns to face him, he realizes his hand is still halfway up and he pulls it down to his side. She pulls off the headphones.

"Hi, Jamie." Oh god, the tone. So sickly sweet. When it comes to Amy, the nicer she's being, the more violent your fate is likely to be. "What's goin' on?" she says.

"Eh, ah, hi, Amy." He's sweating. "How, uh..." He clears his throat. "Not much?"

"Mmmm." Like she's eating chocolate ice cream, or smelling fresh-baked cookies. "That's not what I heard." She says it almost lovingly.

He scratches the back of his head and looks up. Smooth. "Why, uh." He coughs. "What did you hear?"

She stands up and walks over to him. She puts her hands on his shoulders and looks him in the eyes. She smiles.

"I didn't hear anything at all. And I definitely didn't hear a pre-record of a certain punk rock show that very nearly made it to air. A certain show in which, in its single opening three minute and thirteen second—well, we'll call it a *song*, shall we?—there are fourteen instances of words banned on not just the school airwaves, but on any airwaves before ten PM, along with references to violence, illegal drug use, underage sex, sexually-transmitted diseases, and bestiality." She leans in even closer. "Do you know *why* I didn't hear something like that?"

Jamie clears his throat, and shakes his head.

"Because if I *had* heard something like that—just, you know, by chance—the person responsible would find themselves suddenly—miraculously, one might say—*missing*, and I—again, entirely coincidentally, you understand—would have started a collection of *human flesh trophies*. Do we understand one another?"

Christ, he thinks, she's still smiling.

He nods. There's no point in explaining to her that it's a classic punk anthem, so classic it was covered for decades by dozens of bands as mainstream as Metallica; that it was extreme on purpose, being written about the kind of people who always try to one-up each other; that it was banned on charges of obscenity and rounded up by the police when it was first released; and that it is therefore the *perfect freaking song* to begin a half-hour punk show on the theme of *censorship*.

And anyway, all that said, it's not even Amy he's really worried about.

A young man, serious and well-groomed, tall with dark hair and blue eyes, wearing the academy's awful standard green blazer so well it looks near custom-made, comes out of the booth and looks at Jamie having his *tête-a-tête* with Amy. This is John, Jack to his friends: top of the class in everything he studies, star of the academy's judo team, fluent in three—no, scratch that—*four* languages, and kind to children, lost puppies, and down-at-heel boys named James. He's Jamie's and Lizzie's childhood friend-slash-bodyguard, a combination of roles you needed to understand their family to fully comprehend.

"Uh. Hi, Jack."

Jack sighs and Jamie's cheeks go warm with embarrassment. He shoves his hands in his pockets and stares at the floor.

Amy backs off with an, "All yours," and sits back down, slipping her headphones on.

"Come on, Jamie," Jack says. He sounds tired. "Let's take a walk. Jules can handle the rest for today."

Jamie follows him out into the hall, and the door clicks shut behind them.

■ ■ ■

Jack doesn't say a word until they're out behind the building. It's early October and the air is starting to get a little cool at night, but just enough to turn the hillside into a sea of yellows and oranges. On a day like today you wouldn't even need a jacket, but a cute scarf might be nice. Jamie wishes he had one to bury his face in. Or maybe to weave a cocoon and hide in until whenever the heck butterfly season is.

"Jamie, I thought you were over this kind of thing." Jack leans back against the brick wall, the perfect picture of a young, clean-shaven Clark Gable, minus the cigarette. Jamie had tried to pick up smoking once in a mad fit of hero worship—kind of a Joan Jett meets Humphrey Bogart thing he'd been trying out—but Jack had talked him out of it, the way he's about to talk him out of his latest screw-up.

"What kind of thing?" He's got his hands shoved even deeper in his pockets than before. With anyone else he'd have said something like, "Come on, babe, it was a stroke of brilliance—I'm wildly misunderstood!" But instead he just stares at the ground, sullen. He hates that he gets this way. He can be charming around any human being alive. Anyone but Jack.

He gives Jamie a pained look. "Be serious for a minute, Jamie. They'd have thrown you out if Amy hadn't caught it."

"But—"

"I know what you were going for—the show was about censorship and you wanted to make it an object lesson. That's smart. You're a smart guy sometimes." He shakes his head. "But when dropping the F-bomb seven times and the C-word four times in three minutes isn't the most outrageous part of a song, you gotta think twice, kid."

He wants to say that Jack's the only person in the world he'd let call him 'kid,' but instead he just says "mm" and grinds his toes into the ground.

"Amy's not going to do anything about it. The show's gone and nobody's going to know it ever existed. The fact that she's willing to do that should tell you something about how bad this could have gone." He sighs a stream of white breath into the October air.

"I didn't..." He stares at the ground. "I figured they'd put me on probation and it'd be worth it since it proved my point."

Jack sighs again and stares at him. Jamie feels suddenly ridiculous in his metal spikes and blue hair, and desperately wants to go back to the dorm to change.

"They'd have expelled you, and probably canned AcademyOne for the whole semester."

Jamie's jaw nearly hits the ground. "You can't be serious. Shut down the whole radio program just for...what, a little swearing and ugly sex references?"

Jack nods. "Ever hear of the Jenny Q rule?"

Jamie hasn't, and shakes his head.

"Girl in her last year when we got here, Jenny Quincy, I think her name was. She tried a stunt like yours. It was a lot more mundane, of course. An unauthorized showing of some movie. *Girl, Interrupted*, if I'm remembering it right. Next thing you know there's an email apology in every student's inbox and she's gone back to wherever she came from."

"Actually, now that you mention it, that does sound a little familiar."

"Ever see a movie organized by students shown on campus?"

Jamie blinks. "Wait, are you serious?"

He nods. "That's the Jenny Q rule. Going three years on and you still can't get a movie shown without it having been seen start-to-finish by someone in admin. And since they're not keen on anything that's not on the approved national curriculum..."

Jamie crouches down and hugs his knees. This is why he doesn't like talking to Jack when he's done something wrong. Because if Jack thinks it was a bad enough idea to stop him, it was probably a really, fantastically, *epically* bad idea. He stares at the ground.

"Sorry."

Jack flicks one of Jamie's hair spikes, and, finding they're rubbery, tousles his hair.

"It's okay, kid. But damn, you still need a lot of supervision. What are you going to do when I'm not around next year? Your father will kill you if you get expelled, and then the great J. Patton Goldmark will come after me for not doing a better job of knocking some sense into his son."

Right. Jack's a year older than him and Lizzie. They'd all come here the same year, so he forgets sometimes. Jack's getting gone soon. That sucks.

"Probably get kicked out, I guess," he says.

Jack just looks at him in silence for long enough to make Jamie wonder, but he doesn't look up. "Don't," is all he says.

Jamie stays balled up, staring at the ground until he hears the door open and shut, and he's alone.

■ ■ ■

"A KitKat and some Pocky? That's what you call lunch?"

Lizzie plops herself down next to Jamie on the curb outside Mack's, the only convenience store within five miles of the academy. The place is so far from what he thinks of as civilization that he's pretty sure they had to pay someone just to put in a gas station.

"It's called comfort food, Gwyneth."

"Went that well, huh?"

He snaps off one of the little cookie sticks in his mouth and stares at what's left. "I miss the city." Back home, there hadn't been a week that went by without a local garage band or punk show down at the meeting hall, which an enterprising young punk or four could slip into through the side entrance for a small donation to the Steelworkers' Local 509. He used to laugh at all the money he'd given to unions over the years, a tiny bit of rebellion against his well-meaning despot of a father.

They'd formed a band of their own back then, played a dozen crappy sets, called themselves the Queer Young Punks—even managed to rope in Jack, who was about as queer as a vanilla Frappuccino but had taught himself to play a pretty decent guitar for the purpose. Back there, you could walk down the street and hear a dozen different languages, grab food from any country you wanted to, smile at boys, girls, enbies—whoever you liked. But things had changed, and Alice...after the 4/30 attacks in 2016, Patton had moved them out to the country.

Here, there are trees and well-manicured brick buildings and time-stamped campus leave passes and an overwhelming sense of *community*—of the 'enforced' variety. We Don't Talk About It is the name of the game. Hell, maybe it's the motto, he'll have to check the flag.

Sure, their old high school downtown had been pretty much perpetually on the verge of disaccreditation, it didn't have a radio lab or an arts center or tennis courts, and the ever-more-frequent protests had meant you couldn't always get to it on foot, but nobody had thought rainbows were subversive or that the one Korean kid in junior year counted as diversity. And he kind of hates tennis anyway.

But "back home" isn't even home anymore, he thinks, not without—

"I miss her, too," Lizzie says.

Ow. *Ow.*

"How do you do that?" he asks.

Alice. His twin. Neither of them wants to say her name.

"You're not as complicated as you think you are."

"Did I call you Gwyneth? I meant to say Sigmund."

"Yeah, yeah." She reaches over and takes a stick from the Pocky box and eyes it with suspicion. "And you seriously went with pink yogurt instead of chocolate? What is *wrong* with you?"

He doesn't respond for a minute; when he does, he's staring at the ground.

"Hey, Lizzie—"

"*Nope.* Nuh-uh. I know that tone. Not interested in that conversation right now—"

"Hear me out. Come on, you started it." His Docs have gotten dusty on the walk over, and he swipes at them with his fingertips.

Lizzie squints at him, lips pursed, then sighs. "Fine."

"About Alice—"

She closes her eyes and waits for him to say it.

"Do you think she would have..." he trails off. His hands are covered in gravel dust, and he wipes them on his shins. "You know what? I don't want to have this conversation either." He forces a laugh and stands up. "My bad."

She stands up too, stares at him, then punches him in the shoulder. Hard. He winces and rubs it, but his look is still apologetic. He turns away, facing the store window while he fixes his tie. He speaks quietly.

"You and Jack? You guys are pretty great."

She sighs. "Jamie—"

"Come on! I'm too young be a sad queen weeping into his junk food. Not my thing, you know?" He smiles, but she's not convinced.

"Plus, we're going to be late for chem," he adds.

She checks her phone and curses. They've got to get the passes back to the office first, too.

"We'll discuss this later," she says, and they break into a run.

■ ■ ■

Later, it turns out, has other ideas.

He's staring at a beaker with a little spinner in it, watching it make a teeny whirlpool in the clear solution, when he feels a light touch on his shoulder.

"Are you feeling all right? You're kind of spacing out."

This is Daisy—a tall and willowy brunette with Coke-bottle glasses, a kind disposition, and a habit of unintentionally wounding others. She's Jamie's lab partner this month.

"Also, you look a little, I don't know, flushed?"

He wipes some sweat from his forehead. He *is* feeling warm, now that she mentions it. He loosens his tie and undoes the top few buttons of his shirt. "Yeah well, if they hadn't turned the thermostat to ten million degrees, I think I'd be fine."

Daisy looks around.

"Maybe you should sit down for a minute."

He looks up from the experiment and at everyone else around the class. They're standing over their beakers, pouring in some green fluid and taking notes. More importantly, they're all wearing sweaters or cardigans over their shirts and looking pretty okay with it.

"I'm actually a little cold," she says.

"Well that's...weird." He sighs. "Watch this for a minute, I guess. I'm going to step out in the hall and cool off. Or warm up. Or...whatever." He shakes his head.

He almost makes it to the door, but then somehow he's falling, like his legs just won't respond. He tries to catch the door handle on his way down, to slow his rapid descent, but instead he stumbles an extra step forward and clips his cheekbone with it, to the accompaniment of blinding pain and flashing lights. From the ground he manages to twist sideways to peer through a field of stars and fireworks at the class, gone suddenly quiet, as Lizzie sprints across the room and mouths things at him he can't hear. Then everything goes dark.

■ ■ ■

Lizzie's always hated the smell of hospitals, the smell of disinfectant that never seems to cover up the things it's trying to hide, the offgassing of disposable scrubs and single-use plastics, and the sterile, un-eaten 'food' that never goes bad, shrink-wrapped and stacked on carts in the hallways. She's seen the inside of hospitals too many times.

And here she is again. Waiting for a doctor who never comes.

She gets up from the easy-to-clean plastic bench and walks back over to the nurses' station. She watches as the shift changes and all the staff are replaced by others, probably all students or recent graduates from the university the hospital's appended to, until there's no-one there who even knows who she is, let alone what she's waiting for.

"Hey, yeah, so—" she starts, trying to get a young nurse's attention "—hi. I've been waiting for a while to see a Dr. Mansfield? My brother's somewhere in here and they're not letting me in to see him, and I just want to know how he's doing."

A cloud of uncertainty passes over the nurse's face as she checks something on the computer, then looks up. "What's your brother's name?"

"Jamie," she says. "James Goldmark? He was admitted this morning."

"Oh, here he is. Mmm...no visitors—but of course you know that." Her gaze flickers across the screen. "Dr. Mansfield is the attending." She chews her lip. "Actually, it looks like he was just by about five minutes ago. I've got a digital signature here..."

Lizzie groans. "You've got to be kidding me." She puts her head down on the counter. "I've been waiting for him for over an hour."

The nurse's apology is forced to the background by the appearance of a familiar face walking down the hall. She stands straight and runs over.

"Pops!"

The silver-haired man smiles a quiet smile, his tailored grey suit looking typically immaculate as he approaches.

"Elizabeth," he says, giving her a long hug. "They called me the moment it happened. Where's John?"

"Downstairs. They wouldn't let him up this far. It's only 'family' allowed, apparently."

The man frowns and pulls out a phone.

"Sir?" comes a voice, as though the nurse has radar. "You can't use cell phones on this floor."

He closes his eyes as though to regain composure. "Young miss, when I had this hospital built, it was to a certain degree of specification. Cellular interference from phone use in the hallways isn't merely unlikely, it's essentially impossible."

She blinks. This is not the response she was expecting. "I'm sorry?"

"What's the name of this hospital?"

You can see the wheels turning in her head. To her credit, she catches on quickly. "Oh my god...you're Mr. Goldmark."

Lizzie hates this kind of thing, but she hides it well. Her father says nothing. An older nurse chimes in quickly.

"Mr. Goldmark, sir, we have a designated cellphone area just around the corner here, why don't I show you there?"

The great J. Patton Goldmark accepts this concession and walks off with a quick apology to Lizzie, who sighs and sits back down on the bench. She tries not to notice as the other nurses whisper to one another and stare over in her direction. She knows how it will go from here on in: doctors will miraculously appear every half hour on the hour, all courtesies will be paid, and everyone else in the hospital will have to wait.

That's how it was with Alice, too.

It's all happening again.

■ ■ ■

Jamie wanders into a kind of consciousness, his whole body on pins and needles, like ice crystals are forming, growing, and then breaking off or else shattering all over his skin, in a kind of constant crinkle and snap. He feels like he's drifting, falling through the bed in the white room with the white lights and the people in the white balloon-like suits. His delirium begins to reason for itself: if he's cold, then the white must be snow, and the men in suits must be from the Arctic. He's sliding on his back down a long, smooth hill that must, he knows, end in the vast and dark ocean—or else maybe he's on a sled, being pulled across the great frozen wastes by dogs at his feet.

But the splash never comes, and the dogs don't get tired, and he wanders back into the deep and dreamless sleep from which he came while the ice creeps its way into his skull.

■ ■ ■

Adopted, all three of them, almost four—Jack was a later addition. Lizzie still remembers the day when Patton had come in with the seven-year-old 'John,' even then too serious to be a 'Johnny,' the son of an old friend of his from some earlier military contract work before they were born. His father had trained him up like a little soldier from the moment he could walk, and it was only half-jokingly that Patton had started giving him an allowance to look after the others—an employment that had been formalized since. Jamie and Alice, always thick as thieves, had through sheer force of will molded Serious John into Marginally-Less-Serious Jack, and he'd lived with them on and off until his father had passed away on tour in Syria a few years later. After that, he'd moved in with them permanently, and to Lizzie it seemed like Jack had somehow decided that 'bodyguard' was a simpler role than 'friend.' Looking back, she almost thinks he'd started to open up again—and then they'd lost Alice, and they'd all gone back to square one.

And now, Lizzie thinks, they're about to lose another. She stares over at Jack, ever the adult, talking in hushed tones with Patton and a pair of unnamed doctors—part of the unending tide of helpful people who've shown up since her father arrived. Jack's posture is perfect, military. She imagines what she must look like, elbows on her knees on a hospital bench, hunched over and exhausted from worry. Like she might ooze into a puddle on the otherwise sterile floor at any moment. It's a hell of a comparison. It's been two days since Jamie collapsed. She hasn't slept.

"They're transferring him to a special care facility."

The voice is Jack's. Had she nodded off? She sits up to find him seated next to her on the bench.

"What?"

"They're taking him to a special care—"

"No, I heard you the first time. Where are they taking him? Have they said what's wrong? Is it like, like with…" *Alice*. She can't say it.

Jack shakes his head. "They don't know what it is, but it's not the same. Apparently he's lost all his hair, has a really high fever, lesions on his skin. They didn't say it, but you can tell it's bad, Liz. Hell, they thought it was radiation poisoning at first, but they can't find any traces of radiation anywhere, in him, his room, or anything. They've got him in lockdown because the symptoms are severe and they're worried about secondary infections. They say he's stable for now, but they have him in an induced coma, and they want to get him to the new place as soon as they can."

"Where?"

"North." His eyes are cold as he says it. "That part's the same." The same as where they took Alice. Where the next time they saw her was in photo montages on either side of a closed casket.

"Can we see him? They have to let us see him."

Jack shakes his head. "Mr. Goldm—your father will go with him for now."

Mr. Goldmark. Lizzie usually hates when Jack calls him that, but somehow the formality seems just about right this time. They're being shut out.

She wants to talk to her father, to demand that he let her come along, but he's disappeared down one of the hospital corridors, no doubt to bark more orders into his phone. She hangs there, suspended by invisible strings, waiting for someone to either move them or cut her down.

"So what are we supposed to do?"

Jack doesn't look at her when he answers, and Lizzie even thinks she sees his shoulders slump a little.

"We wait."

■ ■ ■

In the end, Jack is right: it is different than it was with Alice. Within a week Alice had gone, her body sealed away forever in the Goldmark mausoleum on the family's country estate. This time it's been four weeks, and they're saying Jamie's still alive, although neither Lizzie or Jack have seen him. Lizzie wants to say it's almost worse, being held in limbo like this, but every time she starts to think it she mentally slaps herself. It's always better if there's a chance he'll be back. Always.

She opens her locker and stares at the one next to it. At least she knows there isn't anything in there that could go bad. Jamie's preferences always leaned toward the vending machine rather than the fresh fruit option at the cafeteria. She feels a sudden twist in her stomach as she remembers scolding him for his unhealthy choices; he'd always respond that he was going to enjoy this life while he had it, and if that meant no time for apples then that was the way things were going to be. She grits her teeth and slams her locker, then nearly jumps when she realizes she's not alone.

"Liz," Jack says, leaning against the lockers on the other side of the hall.

"Jesus, how long have you been standing there?"

"You seemed occupied."

"Yeah, well. Maybe stoicism isn't everybody's cup of tea, okay?" The words come out more bitter than she'd meant them to.

"The new look's kind of familiar."

She pulls a lock of her hair out in front of her and stares at it. She'd dyed a streak of it something called "morpho blue" in the last week, giving it the unnatural sheen of a Peruvian butterfly. Her belt's got metal studs on it, and she hasn't worn a tie in a month.

"You okay, Liz?" he asks, calm like a Buddhist monk.

Of course she's not okay. How in *hell* could she be okay? How could anyone be *okay* in this situation? But she doesn't say it, doesn't say anything, just turns back to her locker and smolders.

Thick as he is, he seems to realize it anyway. "Sorry."

"Yeah well, it's fine," she says. "It's just some of us didn't go to military camp and learn to bottle it all up, that's all." She expects some kind of retort. Even Jack gets a little defensive when she pokes the right spots, and she's known him long enough to know where they all are. But it doesn't matter, he hasn't heard. When she turns to face him, Jack's giving his phone the thousand-yard stare.

"What?" she asks.

He closes his eyes before he speaks.

"He woke up."

■ ■ ■

"It is amazing. Really. I have never seen anything like it." The doctor—such as he is—is grinning, lab coat almost flying out behind him as he walks. He's a scruffy man with a vaguely European accent, long white hair, and glasses that might have been in style thirty years before the advent of the internet.

The walls of the private research facility alternate between bare concrete and glass-fronted offices, repeating over and over in an endless downward-spiraling hallway. Every few hundred feet or so there's another sliding door that requires another passcode before it hisses and trundles its way open before them. The whole place buzzes like a hive of white-lab-coated bees, and they draw ever more suspicious stares at each successive gate. Their guide, so excited by her brother's condition, rattles on, oblivious.

"To think a thing could effect such change in such short time, without killing the host? And to what end?" They stop at the next gate as he waves at a little camera before turning to face them. He's almost jubilant. "I mean, is it not, what do you call it, the *kicker*? Why would a virus or bacterium exist that would do such a thing?" He laughs. "We have no clue!"

"Do what?" Jack gets to asking before Lizzie has the chance to strangle it out of the good doctor. "You haven't told us anything."

"Well it is just—" the door hisses and he turns back as it starts to open "—you will see, you will see."

"But he's all right, yeah? He's fine?"

The doctor waggles his head back and forth, not a nod or a shake. "Yes. Medically, yes. The danger has passed. He—ah—is fine."

"What the hell does—"

"You will *see*." And with that he walks through the gate and into a door on the right. This one isn't glass, and leads to a darkened hallway with a long window acting as the only source of light. It's a one-way mirror, and they're in some kind of observation space.

Through the glass is a white room, lit from all sides by soft-glowing walls, floor, and ceiling, like some kind of 1980s sci-fi flick. In the middle is a medical-looking bed, an untouched single-serving of orange Jello sitting on a table serving as the only color in the room. Otherwise it appears empty. Lizzie looks at the doctor in expectation.

He half-laughs and looks a little embarrassed. "Sorry. Please wait." He pulls a headset up off a low shelf and talks into the microphone without putting it on. "Will the real Slim Shady please stand up?"

Lizzie rubs the bridge of her nose while the doctor snorts at his own joke.

There's a flurry of activity as a diminutive form pops up from behind the bed, grabs the Jello, and launches it at full speed at the mirror. There's a bang as the plastic bowl strikes the reinforced glass and globs of orange dribble down. Then whoever it was is gone again, back behind the bed, with an accompanying cry of, "Go to hell!"

The doctor lets out a noise that lodges itself somewhere between embarrassed and annoyed, then clears his throat and puts down the microphone. "Did you see?" he asks, back to enthused once more.

They're not sure what they saw. To Lizzie, it looked like the person in the room was blonde, petite, and most confusingly, female. The voice, too, had sounded like a girl's.

"You're sure this is the right room?"

The doctor frowns, then stoops and peers at their visitor badges, getting so close it makes Lizzie back up by instinct.

"Yes," he declares. "Yes indeed. The occupant of that room is James Goldmark. That is to say, your brother. Well, except—"

"Except that wasn't him." Jack is adamant.

"That wasn't even a *boy*," Lizzie says.

The doctor claps his hands, unable to control himself. "Precisely! Fascinating, no?"

"You're saying—"

The doctor grabs the microphone and talks into it. "Come now, do not be rude, your sister and—erm—"

"Jack."

"Yes, Jack, are here to see you." He looks around as if he's lost something, then finds a switch on the wall. "Here, here, I will turn on the lights."

Before anyone can react, the darkened observation hall becomes a lit one, the mirror transforming into just a normal pane of glass.

Lizzie and Jack watch in silence as an elfin face haloed with a tuft of short white-blonde hair pokes up from behind the bed and makes eye contact, then ducks back down in a hurry.

"Go away!"

"Can we—can I go in?" Lizzie asks, a look at Jack making a tacit agreement that one at a time would be better.

"Ah. Well. There do not seem to be any pathogens in the uh, but, ah. I do not think..." he trails off as he looks from Jack to Lizzie and back again, then sighs. "We will get you the moon suit."

■ ■ ■

The airlock hisses behind her, standing there in what feels like an inflated raincoat. It smells like the inside of a balloon. There's a loud clunk and the light on the door goes from red to green, and she finds the handle now turns. The door makes a sticky, rubbery noise as she pushes it open and into the well-lit cell.

She steps in, immediately aware of how alien the room feels. Standing there in a hazmat suit doesn't help. Jack nods at her through the observation window and she nods back. The doctor grins and gives her a thumbs-up. She waddles around the bed and looks down.

"Hey," she says.

The room's occupant is curled up on the floor behind the bed, knees hugged close, scruffy blonde head down.

"Hey."

Lizzie tries in vain to crouch down in the suit, but it wants to stay standing, and all she succeeds in doing is leaving the clear plastic window twelve inches above her face. The most she can do is sit on the edge of the bed, creaking with every move.

"How about sitting up here?"

"If I'm being honest, sister dear, I'd really rather not." The voice is small, childish. A little petulant.

Lizzie sighs. "Damn it, Jamie, if it really is you, then get your butt up here so I can have a look at you, okay?"

"You're not gonna like it."

"Just do it, doofus."

The little blonde pixie stands up and looks at her, and she gasps. Nobody says anything for a minute, while the girl that was her brother turns and flops down on the bed, facing away from the window, still slightly-mirrored from this side.

He looks like Alice. Not a little bit like her, not like her sister or something. Like *her*.

It takes a minute, but she finds her words.

"Jesus, Jamie, what did they do to you?"

"I can't even look." He waves a hand at the glass behind them. "They finally got the bandages off me and then they stuck me in here with a huge goddamn mirror. And now all I can see is her, only...it's me now. She's in the mirror and she moves when I do, and she talks when I talk. And my voice, it's so..." He looks at her, red eyes and lopsided smile. "I haven't showered in god knows how long, these damn scrubs are so thin they're probably edible, which is probably fine because the food is—" he waves his hands "—and my body...and the bathroom situation is...I—I mean it's...I don't—I can't...*Lizzie.*" A silent tear drips from an ice-blue eye down a porcelain cheek.

She tries to put her arms around Jamie but after a few awkward moments of shuffling to the *wrrp-wrrp* sounds of vinyl, they both start to giggle. Lizzie starts to sniffle and he grabs a tissue and starts wiping the outside of her suit.

"Here let me get that for you," he says. *Wrrp-wrrp.* Plastic pressing against her face, smearing a tear into a blurry patch. "Gee, it doesn't seem to be working." *Wrrrrrrrp.* "Maybe it's cause you're trying to talk to me through the world's biggest dental dam."

She snorts as he tries again, before she bats him away with flappy rubber arms, laughing and sniffling and fogging up the pointless little window of the suit. And then it doesn't even matter, and she's hugging her brother through the shifting plastic, blind as a bat, making all kinds of undignified noises. None of it matters, because whatever he looks like, Jamie's still Jamie and she's got him back, and she's not going to let him go ever, ever again.

■ ■ ■

In a room lit only by a green-glassed desk lamp, J. Patton Goldmark sits staring at the silent phone before picking up the receiver. He pulls a small card from his pocket and dials the handwritten number on it, listening for the now-familiar five-tone sequence on the anonymized line before speaking.

"Berolina has...been promoted," he says. "Denote as Princess going forward." He sighs, then continues. "Despite the change, I authorize continuing with the asynchrony campaign."

The voice on the other end responds.

"Yes, you could say that," he says.

He arranges the things on his desk as he listens. He adjusts some pens, three of them all parallel. Adjusts the angle of a closed laptop relative to the edge. He straightens a picture frame, then picks it up.

"Yes, I think unexpected and dangerous about sums it up," he says.

"I'm sure you are."

He leans back in the chair, still holding the photo. His grey suit and silver hair are immaculate.

"I won't say I disagree." He leans forward and puts the picture down. Three young people smile back from its surface, two men and a woman, all in their mid-twenties.

"Agreed."

He opens a drawer and pulls out a brown folder with a single sheet of paper inside, lays it on the desk, and picks up one of the pens.

"I'm signing it now," he says. He presses a button and a woman walks into the office, dark hair back tight in a bun, stilettos snapping on the marble floor. He pulls the receiver away from his mouth, closes the folder, and hands it to her. "Make sure this gets to accounting before the end of the day, please." She nods, takes the folder, and walks out. He returns to his call.

"Now that's settled, what's the prognosis—no, not the medical one." He leans back in his chair once more, eyes on the photograph. The faces stare back from its surface, their dark eyes still warm in the frozen slice of time.

"No, I don't suppose you do."

"Yes."

"Well I quite hope so."

"Mmm."

He leans forward and reaches out to the phone's cradle.

"As always."

He doesn't wait for a response, pressing down the hook and ending the call. He opens his computer and logs into this month's account.

An email is already in the inbox.

Confirmation

A493B46F7108C2A4EB80@gmx.com   just now (0 minutes ago)
To: me

Tunneling remains optimal. Will proceed with asynchrony campaign. Further involvement on your part will be requested if required. Otherwise will report when complete.
+15557204217

He notes the final digits on another blank business card before deleting the email and emptying the trash folder.

He closes the laptop and sighs at the absurdity of the routine; worse still is its necessity. He takes one more lingering look at the photograph on his desk before standing, straightening his clothes, and walking out of the office.

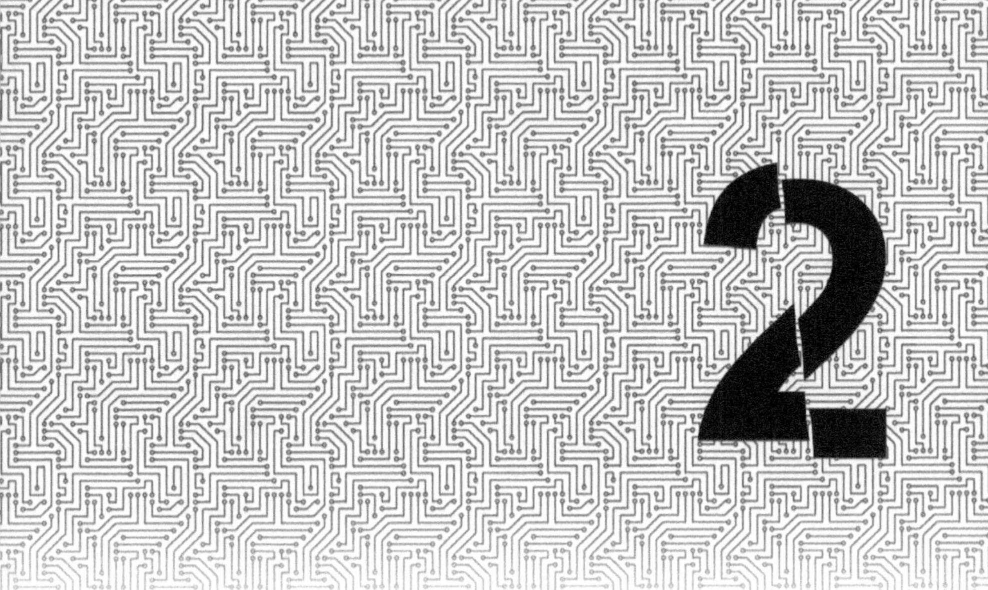

"**Well, I admit it's a little unorthodox, but I'm sure we can** accommodate your, ah—"

"Son."

"Right. Son. Sorry." A weak smile—disbelief and a little poorly-hidden impatience.

J. Patton Goldmark is sitting in the office with Headmaster McGuinness and a slowly simmering Jamie. He's kept the blonde hair boy-short but sans product and is wearing the school's boys' uniform, even though the shirt doesn't fit as well as it could in some areas.

"I'm a guy," he says, arms crossed, looking away. "I just *look* like a girl."

"Well, yes, but there is the matter of the other students in the dorms—"

Jamie snorts. "Well we wouldn't want to make *them* uncomfortable, now would we—"

"Leigh." Patton gives him a look that means *ease off*, using the new name they'd 'agreed' on. Explaining it as a transition would have been one thing, but a whole *face* change would, apparently, have been, 'A step too far,' as Patton had said.

Jamie Goldmark no longer exists; in his place is Leigh. As far as the school is concerned, Jamie transferred out due to medical issues a month ago, and Leigh just finished an 'alternative educational experience' abroad.

"You see the boys' dorm isn't really, ah, *equipped* to deal with, that is to say—"

"The communal showers? They have stalls. With curtains?" Leigh looks at his father. "Is he serious? How do you deal with other queer people then? Jesus, this should not be this much of a challenge." Of course he knows full well how they do—by closing their eyes and inserting their fingers in their ears.

Patton says nothing, but raises his eyebrows at the headmaster as if to forward the question on. After a bit of blustering and throat clearing the headmaster continues.

"Yes, well, there is a solution to this. We do have a few 'ensuite' style dormitory rooms, and while we typically reserve them for senior students who've taken on certain responsibilities within the dorms—perhaps we could make an exception." He produces a thin black binder from a drawer and leafs through it for a moment, before looking up and eyeing Leigh with suspicion. "You would need a second occupant—" he turns back to Patton "—how would your daughter Elizabeth feel about sharing with her, ah, brother?"

"She'll be fine with it," Leigh says.

The headmaster ignores him and waits for Patton to nod.

"Excellent," The headmaster says, noting something down in the binder.

"Then it's settled," Patton says.

Leigh's about to interject when Patton adds the words, "Isn't it?" and looks at him. The answer is clear.

"Ah, yeah." He sighs, reeling in his sarcasm. "Yeah, it's fine. Thanks for the accommodation."

Patton stands and gives the headmaster's hand a firm shake. "Thanks, Ed. I won't forget it."

If anything, this makes the headmaster more uncomfortable, which Leigh's sure is the point. Nothing makes you feel quite as guilty as a hearty thank you for barely and reluctantly rendered help.

"We'll see to the details. Why don't we have Leigh go to guidance to enroll in classes while I show you some of the more recent improvements to the campus?"

"Sounds great."

Leigh stands up. One hurdle down, another dozen or so to go.

■ ■ ■

"The girls' dorm?" Leigh is livid. "That makes about as much sense as the Sex Pistols's cash-strapped reunion tour!"

"What, you were expecting them to stick us in the boys'?" Lizzie is sitting on one of the two beds in the otherwise spartan dorm room. It's going to need some posters, stat.

"Well I'd have *preferred* it! I *am* a boy, and you don't even *like* boys, so I figured it'd be *fine*."

"Yeah, well, they're obviously having trouble with that first premise, and they *really* don't like to admit the second one here, so..." she half-squints at him, as if to finish the thought.

He closes his eyes and rubs his temples. "They're going to make me change in the girls' locker room, aren't they?"

"I'd bet on it, Jamie." She gets up and hugs him as she says it.

He sighs and walks to the bathroom. It's a bleak little affair, but it has its own toilet and shower, at least. He flicks on the light over the sink and stares at his face, familiar but not.

"Probably shouldn't call me that anymore, Liz." He opens his mouth and pushes his cheeks around. Alice had had freckles; he wonders if he'll get them too, once they let him go out in the sun. Right now, it's UV-blocking shirts and sun hats that make him feel like a southern belle—something about brand new skin and daylight not being the best of friends. He turns sideways and pushes up on his chest. "Not now I've got these, anyway." He frowns at them in the mirror.

Lizzie snickers. "Got what? You're flat as a board, bro."

His eyes widen as he puts on a show of wild offense. "How *dare* you say such a thing about my, uh...my knockers? Boobs? What do you call them when they're actually yours? Tits always sounded vulgar, but when they're this size maybe it's the right word."

Lizzie flops back on the bed, snickering.

"What?" He wanders over and flounces down on the other bed, which squeaks and bounces to a stop. "Boobs makes them sound, I don't know, big and round. Onomatopoetically speaking, of course." He turns on his side to face her. "I could still wear suspenders with these—thank god."

"A life without suspenders—a *true* tragedy."

"Fashion is *important*, Liz."

"Spoken like the most boyish boy *ever*."

"Mock all you like, philistine." He lies back and looks at the ceiling in silence for a moment before continuing. "I don't know...what even is a boy anyway? I mean, I've been reading things on the internet—"

"Beware the forums, young grasshopper."

"No, like, hear me out. I'm definitely not a girl, no matter what I look like now. I know that much. But I guess...I know I said hear me out, but now I don't know what to say."

After a minute, Lizzie speaks up. "What you want to be? That's up to you. Boy, girl, both, neither, anywhere in between or somewhere off to the side: you don't have to know right now, and you don't even have to pick if you don't want to. You're my brother—at least until you want me to call you something else, and then you'll be that. I love you, okay?"

"Okay, well, now you're just getting sappy." A pause, then, "I love you too, sis."

"And anyway, what you wanna call your new body parts is up to you, too, Jamie-lee." The corner of her mouth curls up the tiniest bit as she says it.

"Gee, *thanks*."

"I know someone who can teach you to strap 'em down...if you want." The lip curl has blossomed into a full-on mischievous grin.

He sits up. "What?"

"Maybe get you a little something to fill out those boys' pants, too."

"What? Scandalous!" He gets up and dives onto Lizzie's bed. "I'm scandalized!"

They both laugh until it fades into an easy silence, both of them lying there on the bed.

"Maybe," he says at last. "I don't know. It's weird, not having...I mean. You know. Sitting to pee and all that. And the breasts are...well, I guess small ones are okay."

"Wait till you get your first period. That'll be a riot." She's not smiling.

He stares into the distance, not saying anything.

"Oh, no...already?"

"Freaked the hell out."

Lizzie turns on her side and stares at her brother. His big attitude in such a little body. "I'm sorry I wasn't there to help. If it's any consolation, you get used to it."

"Yeah." He sits up and looks down at her. "But hey, at least I'm pretty."

"You *are* that."

"All the boys are going to love me."

"Oh *everyone* will love you."

"Damn right they will."

He sighs and stands up, wanting to say something else but unable to find the words. Instead, he takes a deep, cleansing breath and surveys the room one more time.

"Right," he says. "Guess we'd better get started!" He puts his hands on his hips. "Know any place we can get some vintage posters? I'm thinking Op Ivy to start."

Lizzie grins.

■ ■ ■

"Um, hi?" Leigh pokes his head around the doorframe and into the radio lab. Amy's sitting there with Jules, a fine-haired ginger boy, all freckles and smiles. Amy smiles, too, but there's something else in that look, a kind of suspicion. Jack, as Leigh's found to be more and more common since his change, is nowhere to be found.

"Come in, come in."

Jules pats a chair next to them and Leigh does as he's told and sits. He's toned down the punk a little—he's getting weird enough looks just dressing as a boy—and he's put a part in his white-blonde pixie cut for the interview.

Amy looks down at a clipboard. "So," she starts. "Jack's told us all about you, so just to fill you in a little, I'm Amy and this is Jules."

"Hey," Jules says.

"Hi," Leigh says, and waggles his head a little. So awkward being introduced to people you already know. Especially ones you've kissed. Augh.

"Jules and Jack swap off for the news in the morning and at lunch, Lizzie does one of our after-school slots, and my sister Tina, who's not here right now, does the alt-music hour after that—you probably haven't seen her around, she's a little...elusive at times..." She doesn't explain, but he knows what she means. He's pretty sure Amy mentioned once that her sister's autistic, but in terms of how that looks from the outside, all he's noticed is that she seems really quiet. "And we *used* to have someone to do the Tuesday-Thursday lunchtime slot." A shadow crosses her face, then passes. "How is your brother anyway?"

"Ah, he's...doing okay. He's not really himself these days." Understatement of the friggin' century, that one, he thinks.

"Well, we're sorry he's gone," Jules says. He probably means it, which is nice. "Do you think he'll be coming back?"

Leigh shakes his head. "It's, ah...no. No, it's not looking like it." Jules looks a little misty at that, and Leigh rushes to respond. "He's not, like, dying or anything. He's just, uh, it was agreed that this might not be the best place for him anymore..."

"Is this, you know, a Patton thing?"

RIGHT. He'd forgotten how much Jules already knew about his—about Jamie's relationship with Patton.

"Yeah."

"Oh...that's good, I guess," he says. "I...for a second I thought it, maybe it might've been, you know...a trans thing..."

Leigh's heart rate doubles—does Jules recognize him?—but he continues.

"Like, a thing to do with…because I know this school's not always the best place for us, and I didn't want it, you know…to have chased him away…is all." Seeing the look on Leigh's face he gets doubly flustered and starts backtracking. "Sorry, I don't mean *he* is, I mean, I thought maybe he might—well, but—more I thought he would've maybe mentioned…me?" Jules looks at him expectantly. "But then he didn't mention you, either." He trails off. "How about we pretend I didn't say any of that?"

Oh, Jules. Yes, Jamie would *absolutely* have mentioned you, you absolute darling, you. But Jamie did not *know*, because you did not actually *say*, and because Jamie is so self-absorbed that he never thought to *ask*. And now he feels kind of awful about it.

But also: 'us.'

He smiles as reassuringly as he can.

"It was definitely a Patton thing," he says. "And…I'm glad there's an 'us' here."

Jules smiles back.

"Well." Amy says, clearing her throat and reaffirming Leigh's belief that she literally already knows everyone's secrets and is forever and thoroughly unsurprised by any of them. "Tell him we miss him when you talk to him next."

And here he was thinking he'd topped out at his daily dose of shock—that was downright caring coming from her! He smiles again. "It's nice to know he made friends here. That hasn't always been, you know, easy for him." Talking about himself in the third person is the weirdest thing. Well, aside from everything else.

Amy rolls her eyes, making an unconvincing attempt to seem callous. "Yeah, sure, whatever. The little jerk had to go and get sick and leave us mid-term without someone to do the lunch slot." And then out comes the smile. "And that's where you come in, cherub."

Leigh swallows, almost audibly. With all the ups and downs in the conversation, he'd momentarily forgotten to wonder why he'd been summoned.

"How much do you know about punk?"

And all the tension that's been building in the pit of Leigh's stomach melts away in an instant. He relaxes into his chair.

"Punk?" He smiles. "I know a bit."

■ ■ ■

"A punk show!"

"What?" Lizzie's methodically working her way through folding a pile of laundry on her bed in order to get them into the inadequate drawer space provided by the school.

"*My* punk show! It had great ratings and—get this!—people came in to actually complain when it stopped! They want to start it back up again as soon as possible!" Leigh's pretty sure the grinning, hopping, and clapping isn't making him look any more like a boy, but for the moment he doesn't care. This is awesome.

"So?" She's focusing hard on folding her clothes, a scowl etched into her brows.

"Well, *duh*, kitten, I said I'd do it, of course." He stands beside her watching her futile attempts before hip-bumping her out of the way and taking over. She blinks and pops out of her trance while he works.

"That's great news," she says, and smiles.

"But really, though, did you never learn how to fold your clothes?" It's been about thirty seconds and he's already halfway through the pile.

She rolls her eyes and drops on his bed. "You're the domestic one, Jemmy-lee." He shoots her a look. "Jamie" has become "Jamie-Leigh" has become "Jemmy-lee." It'll be Jemmalee next. He just hopes it never progresses to Jimly.

"Hey, so you know this room's got a little kitchenette thing, right?" What they'd thought to be a second closet turned out to be hiding the world's tiniest fridge, sink, counter, and stove.

"Yeah?"

"I'll make you a deal. I will do your laundry." He looks over his shoulder at her before continuing. She's listening. "*All* of your laundry," he says, "if one day a week, you cook us dinner. Like, a real dinner. Something with actual flavor."

Lizzie grins. Back home she'd been a terror, throwing Patton's hired chef out of the kitchen up to three or four times a week, teaching herself to make steam-buns and curries and dumplings and pad thai— and testing it all on Jamie, Jack, and Alice.

"I mean, you've always been on at me about eating real food and stuff, so..." He trails off. The cafeteria menu is adequate, but a little lacking. When you're feeding four hundred students, the flavor palette tends to become a little...democratized.

Lizzie purses her lips and wanders over to the closet-slash-kitchen and steps inside. Everything's covered in a layer of dust and grease, and the fridge has been off for god knows how long. She frowns.

"Let's say I agree in principle. You gonna help me clean this up first? Just so we don't get, you know, cholera or something." She pulls a rusty nail out of the sink. "Or tetanus."

Leigh puts the last of the folded clothes into their too-small drawers and nods. "Counteroffer: you clean it, but I forage."

"Forage?"

"Kitten, if I'm going to have these lashes, I'm damn well going to make use of them." As if to demonstrate, he does the world's worst Jessica Rabbit, batting his eyelashes at her.

She just sighs at him. "I don't know what you're planning, but you're not going to succeed at it dressed like that."

He looks down, then back up at her. "What do you mean?"

■ ■ ■

"I look like a tart."

"That's what you were going for, isn't it?"

Leigh makes a noise like someone who's just touched something slimy. "Well, kinda..." He's standing outside the kitchen in a white knee-length dress with a little floral embroidery around the hemline, thigh-high white stockings, and one of his southern belle hats on askew. He wrings his hands as he looks around, afraid someone will see him. Thank god it's a Saturday afternoon and the building's pretty much deserted.

"But you know I think maybe using my newfound feminine wiles was a bad plan after all and maybe cleaning sounds like good, honest work of the kind that builds positive character traits and all those wonderful things Patton says I should be trying to do with my formative years and don't you think maybe he was right about some of that and... you know...maybe we should go back...to the room?"

But she's merciless.

"It'll be fine," she says.

"I think maybe I just got caught up in the excitement, and really I've underestimated how nice people can be, so I could just go in dressed more normally for me and just...ask for food like a normal person...? Also, where did you even get these?" He looks down at the—honestly pretty great—little white patent-leather shoes that complete the outfit.

"Old girlfriend left 'em behind. Glad I kept 'em." She just grins at him. "You look adorable."

"I feel a little like I'm in drag?"

"Well, you know what they say—we're born naked, and everything else is drag."

"This is what Jack is referring to when he says I let things get out of control, isn't it?"

"Self-knowledge is a valuable thing, brother dear," she says, sagely. Then she winks and shoves—*shoves!*—him into the kitchen and lets the door snap shut behind him.

■ ■ ■

He's standing in an industrial kitchen, all stainless steel and linoleum floors, rubber grip pads on the floor by the sinks, two giant pots of something bubbling away on a stove, and—in the midst of this so very *white* prep school—a handsome, thirty-something Black man in chef's whites and a paper hat staring at the sudden appearance of a ghost-pale five-foot-nothing sprite in her Sunday Best, looking very out of place.

He looks at Leigh. "Can I...help you with something?"

Leigh feels all the blood rush to his head. "Oh, I uh, it's nothing. I just. See my sister and I are sharing a room with a kitchenette...and um...getting proper ingredients isn't easy around here...especially spicy things...and...you know, without a car..." he trails off and stares at his shoes. This was a terrible idea. He's got half a mind to grab his frilly white hat and bolt.

It's silent in the kitchen except for the sound of whatever's in the pots.

And then it's full of the warmest laughter he's ever heard. It's an open-mouthed, unabashed, and *kind* laughter, the type of sound that turns the whole world a slightly rosier shade and puts everyone at ease.

"Well if that isn't the cutest damn thing I'll see all week. What's your name, girly?" He's standing next to Leigh now, or maybe even over him. He's so *tall*. Or maybe Leigh's just shorter than he used to be. He peeks up past the brim of the hat and tries to smile.

Girly? He twists his lips in embarrassment. "Leigh?"

"Everett." He holds out a hand. "Nice to meet you."

Leigh takes his large, calloused hand and shakes it. It almost envelops his own.

"Hi," he manages to say.

Everett smiles and walks back to the pots, giving them each a big stir. "You got guts coming in here and telling me you don't like my cooking." It's the kind of thing you'd say if you were angry, but he doesn't sound anything but entertained.

"Oh, but I didn't mean—!"

He looks over his shoulder at Leigh. "But between you and me, I don't get a lot of say when it comes to what I cook around here. Lily-white parents want their lily-white kids to have lily-white food—" he holds up his hands "—no offense, but I've never cooked so much bland meatloaf and mashed potatoes in all my life."

Leigh almost bounces back into his dramatic self. "Right? Augh, it's *killing* me. My sister used to make the *best* Thai curry you've ever tasted—well. You're, like, a chef and stuff, so maybe not the best *you've* ever tasted. But the best *I* have. And here it's all...I dunno. I mean there's only so much casserole a person can eat."

"Hey, don't forget stew," he says, not seeming to notice, motioning to the big pots.

Leigh smiles, finding himself more at ease. "Actually, I kinda like the stew...It's really, I dunno. Meaty? Savory?"

Everett gives him a conspiratorial grin. "Anchovies."

"What?"

"Secret ingredient."

"You're kidding. In beef stew?"

"Pureed and mixed in, adds just the right amount of buttery, salty, umami goodness."

Leigh grins. "Awesome."

Everett finishes stirring the pots, then looks around to see if anyone's watching before he motions for Leigh to follow him around the corner. He stops at a big stainless-steel pantry with a lock on it. He opens it to reveal shelf after shelf of spices and herbs, marinades and hot sauces. Leigh's eyes go wide.

"Jackpot..." he says, but not quietly enough for the chef not to hear. His laughter lights up the room again.

"You just said the magic word." He grabs a small cardboard box with a can of something in it and tosses the can onto the counter, passing the empty box to Leigh. "Hold this." He rummages through the pantry and starts throwing things in.

■ ■ ■

Lizzie's still standing outside the kitchen, tapping away at her phone when the door swings back open and Leigh emerges, cardboard box overflowing. Everett holds the door open to see him off.

"I can't thank you enough, Everett. Oh!" Leigh nods at Lizzie, who's stuck her phone back in her pocket and is looking a little awkward at the attention. "This is Lizzie, my sister."

The tall man nods. "Ah, so you're the sister who cooks, huh?"

"Uh, yeah." She nods.

"Lizzie, Everett. Everett, Lizzie." Leigh grins.

"My pleasure." He smiles and turns back to Leigh. "And hey, Leigh..."

Leigh turns around and cocks his head to one side. "Yeah?"

"You don't have to dress up like a girl next time you come visit—cute though it may be. Just come as you're comfortable, cool?"

Leigh goes four progressively warmer shades of red, coughs a few times, and is unable to respond before Everett winks and turns back to the kitchen, chuckling something about kids these days. Leigh stares at the ground, then thrusts the box out in Lizzie's direction.

"Don't say a word. Just take it."

Lizzie's grinning. "You. Were. Having. *Fun*." She takes the box.

"Shut up." They start walking. "He said there's a deli place about fifteen minutes past the gas station that'll sell us raw meat if we mention him."

"You were *enjoying yourself*."

"And we can steal veg from the kitchen whenever we like." He's ignoring her.

"Well, you look great."

"Shut *up*. I'm going back to the room and I am changing out of this ridiculous outfit."

"Cute though it may be."

Leigh mumbles something that Lizzie can't hear.

"What was that?"

"...cute though it may be." He might be smiling.

Lizzie's still grinning. "You know, far be it from me to take advantage of my poor brother's bizarre biology, but this is totally going to be fun."

"Yeah, well, don't expect this to be a regular occurr-*Aah!*" He stops in the hall.

Jack's standing there, looking at them.

Jack, whom Leigh hasn't seen in a week, staring at him wearing a white dress and stockings right there in the friggin' hallway. Of all the people on campus to be in that place at that time, it's him, in his judo uniform with a towel round his neck, just out of practice.

"Jai...Leigh?"

"Hi, Jack."

But it's Jack who looks uncomfortable. He *looks* more embarrassed than Leigh *feels*.

"What's, you know, going on?"

"That's a nice...ah, outfit."

"Thanks?"

Lizzie barrels through, her natural aversion to awkwardness carrying the day. "Well, that's all the time we have for *today*, folks. Come by tomorrow if you want some, uh..." She looks down at what's in the box. "How about curry?"

Jack's head turns so fast he almost gets whiplash. He stares at her, then at the box of ingredients, then separates each word with an almost visible space, "When and where?"

It looks like it's going to be three for dinner.

■ ■ ■

"The hell? Hey, Lizzie?" Leigh turns down the music he's been blasting all afternoon. He's sitting at one of the two desks that have been crammed into the room to accommodate dual occupancy. Everything's lit in soft tones by strings of multicolored Christmas lights they've strung up—not because it's just over two weeks to Christmas, but because it makes the place more festive. The plan is to leave them up year-round. He's peering at something on his laptop, back in his scrappy jeans and an ill-fitting Rancid t-shirt. "Come look at this, would you?"

Lizzie's been scrubbing the kitchen-slash-closet since they got back, while Leigh decorated the room—putting up a couple of posters that came in the mail in addition to the lights.

"What is it?" She wanders in, towel in hand.

"This email." He turns the computer and Lizzie hunches over it.

Information verification request

3E277B33DF294956CAEB@gmx.com   Dec. 7 (1 day ago)
To: me

Hello,
Please verify these vectors and inform me of any changes:
1. John Slade-Woodman (fWfFifmW2ifmF2)(live/running:6320@i6184)
2. Elizabeth Chelsea Goldmark (QN)(live/running:6077@i6184)
3. James William Goldmark (mfFcfWimfF2=>BN)(term:5926@i6127)
4. Alice Evelyn Goldmark (kQ)(term:4821@i5022)
5. Leigh Aiden Goldmark (BN)(live/running:56@i6184)

"What the hell...?"

"Right?" Leigh leans back in his chair.

"That's...us. Who's it from?"

"No idea. Some spam address. I was just cleaning out the filter when I saw it."

"What's all that stuff after our names?"

"Dunno. But I'm a little concerned that the phrase "live/running" doesn't show up after Alice or, you know, the old me."

"And that it does show up next to the three of us that are, you know, *alive* and *running*."

They stare at the message in silence until there's a knock at the door. They both jump.

"I'll get it," Lizzie says, and wanders over.

At the door is a girl who looks, well, to be honest, she looks like a tiny clone of Amy: rosy cheeks, chestnut hair. The difference, aside from the mini-me thing, is that she's so quiet she's almost perpetually fading into the scenery. Lizzie squints at her in her jeans and baggy flannel shirt.

"Hey, Tina. What brings you here?"

Tina, who's in ninth grade but looks even younger, peers sideways around thick-rimmed glasses and down the hall like she's being watched, then shoves out a crumpled piece of paper toward Lizzie and stares at the carpet.

Lizzie takes the paper, smooths it out and looks it over. It's a crappy, photocopied flier that looks like a ransom note gone wrong. It reads: QUEER YOUNG PUNKS OF THE ACADEMY, SIT UP AND TAKE NOTICE: BASSIST NEEDED FOR THE BEST PUNK BAND FOR A HUNDRED MILES. GIRLS' DORM 102, ASK FOR LEIGH. Lizzie blinks, reads it again, looks at Tina, then calls back into the room.

"Leigh?"

"Yeah?" His voice wafts forward from the half-darkened interior.

"I think it's for you."

■ ■ ■

"Aw, sweet! You play bass?"

Tina nods, perched on the very corner of Lizzie's bed.

"And you like punk?"

Another nod.

Leigh dives behind his bed and grabs a beat-up old four-string and hands it to her. "Show me."

She looks at him, then at Lizzie, then in the smallest voice imaginable asks, "No amp?"

Leigh shrugs. "No can do in the dorms, but we'll hijack something in the music department if you pass muster." He's grinning, he can't help it. Tiny Tina plays the bass? Leigh had played bass when he was Jamie, but he'd found that the new hands didn't work the way the old ones did. No part of his new body does things the way the old one did; it's like having to discover what you're good at all over again. And anyway, his new hands are way too small. Well, he'd thought they were too small, and yet looking at Tina...

She takes a moment—wrapping miniature hands around the large instrument and producing a fat, black bass pick from a flannel shirt pocket—and dives right in. As he watches, a transformation takes place: head nodding, hair hanging down in front of her, her fingers start to lope up and down the neck in the slow but steady rhythm of "Longview." She taps her foot as she goes, sliding into animation, upping the tempo, and transitioning into the opening of "Chick Magnet"—a little faster, a little more flourish, a lot more character.

Leigh claps. "Hey awesome! That's great—" he starts, but she doesn't stop, she just speeds up, left hand barely seeming to move fast enough, fingers becoming a blur on the strings as she transitions into the intro to "East End of the Bay." By the time she finishes a perfect recreation of the solo from "Maxwell Murder," practically channeling Matt Freeman while doing so, Leigh's almost falling off the bed. He's lying on his back giggling.

"That's *amaaaaaaaazing*," he says, sitting up. "You're AMAZING."

She's stopped playing and has her head tilted forward, hair hanging down so he can't see her face, but he's pretty sure she's blushing. She holds out the bass without looking, and he takes it and puts it back.

Leigh looks past her to where Lizzie's sitting at her desk, eyes wide and bewildered.

"So whaddya think, sis? Can we keep her?"

■ ■ ■

As the door closes Lizzie's masked expression gives way to open irritation. She holds up the flyer.

"Were you even going to *ask*?"

"What do you mean?" Leigh's too excited to sit still, bouncing around the room.

"A band. A *punk* band. You're putting QYP back together and you didn't even *ask?*"

Leigh looks at her, as her expression fades into straight annoyance. "But—wait, I was sure—you're *in*, right?"

"I don't know Jam—ugh—*Leigh*." She sits on the edge of her bed and looks at the flyer. "That was with *Alice*." Her voice nearly catches in her throat but she soldiers on. "With the old you. With Jack before he got all serious again."

"Jack's always been serious," he responds, deflating, but Jack had gone a little back to his old self after Alice. He sits on the edge of the bed, then draws his legs up to his chest and hugs them, suddenly unsure. "I just sort of assumed you'd be in." He rests his chin on his knees and looks down.

"I don't know, Leigh. I mean honestly." It's a thousand years ago, all that playing at being in a band. An old life where grades didn't matter, the future was theirs, where no one ever really died. "It's just so... ugh." It won't be the same, she wants to say, it's going to be a huge strain on everyone, most of all you. She stares at her brother, looking more like his new body than his old self. If clothes make the man, she thinks, then what does the body make? She looks at his face, bright blue eyes so much Alice and so much Jamie and yet neither, and sighs.

"I'm in, I'm in." She throws her hands up in the air.

"You mean it?" Leigh's got Jamie's grin again, and it's pretty much worth it just for that.

"Yeah, yeah. Just don't go signing me up for things without asking anymore, okay? It's not cool."

Leigh dives from his bed to hers and latches a hug around her neck. "You know who's the best sister in the world?"

"Yep." She lies there and lets herself be hugged. "It's me. I am. Don't forget it."

"Not a chance."

"Good."

"And who knew Tina could PLAY?" He sits up cross-legged on the bed.

"I'll admit it, pretty impressive."

"*Right?* And super cute, too."

She shoots him a look.

"What? I got a new body, not a new set of preferences."

"You already *had* the complete set. That's not the issue."

"Yeah, yeah, 'no dating bandmates,' fine."

Lizzie sighs. "Anyway, if you're not going to play bass, then…?"

Leigh jumps up on the bed, fully animated once again. "Get this: I'm gonna *sing.*"

She winces. It had been the one thing they couldn't get Alice to do. Jesus, this is a bad idea. It's like a goddamn time bomb. Leigh's still talking.

"You know, get a whole Joan Jett and the Blackhearts kinda vibe going on. I mean, slightly more masculine, but…" He motions down at his body. "Maybe not much more than slightly. And maybe you're right about the whole dressing the part thing. Not—" he quickly adds "—that I'm doing the dress thing again. Probably."

"Aw, but you looked so sweet." Lizzie tries a smile, and it comes naturally despite her misgivings.

"But maybe a little more fitted stuff…" He tugs sideways at his shirt, which has enough fabric for two of him. "And anyway, with you on drums and Jack on guitar—"

He notices that Lizzie's got a hand in the air, waiting politely.

"Yeah?"

"And you've asked him about this plan of yours, too, I'm sure."

"Wellll…"

"*Leigh.*"

"Not in so many words…?" He hops down off the bed and wanders back to a drawer, digs through the piles of new clothes all roughly his new size. Being Pop's kid sure has benefits, for all he complains.

She almost tells him, but she doesn't know what. About how Jack felt about Alice? About how whatever he does, it's going to be hard for all of them? At the least, she wants to tell him to be careful, because human beings are weak and fragile and even the best ones have flaws.

She wants to tell him not to get his hopes up, but she doesn't, and he keeps talking.

"But he'll sign on. I know it. You just wait."

Oh, kiddo...the things you don't know could fill a mountain of books. Enough to crush you flat.

Lizzie hopes to god they don't, and returns to cleaning the kitchen, leaving her brother to fantasize about being a punk band frontman, picking and discarding clothes until he's satisfied.

■ ■ ■

It's Sunday and the winter snow has finally started to drift from the grey skies that hang heavy over the academy's trademark green-shingle roofs. By mid-morning, Leigh's tried to get a jump on the day by doing the forty-minute round trip to get chicken for tonight's curry before heading to the radio lab for 'training.' From where the road cuts through the forest, the academy campus seems to mushroom up the hillside, red bricks sprouting between pockets of pine trees, all whitening with each passing minute in the falling snow. By the time he's halfway up the hill he's exhausted, his impractical but fashionably thin hoodie and bright orange cons are soaked, and the latter are probably leaching orange dye into his socks. He ducks into the rec-plex for a minute, hoping the squall will subside.

Standing in the heated entryway and watching the snow, he finds himself back in an old memory, of him and Alice, waiting out a summer storm. They'd sought refuge in a big concrete tube in an urban playground. That had been a Sunday, too, and they'd weaved their way past swing sets and too-low monkey bars to squeeze themselves into the nearest shelter. Out of the rain it had still been cold because of the wind, and they'd kept their minds off it by playing one of their favorite games.

The rules had been simple: read the other's mind. At first it had been a grand joke—Alice had seen something on TV about a pair of twins, some cartoon or something. They had superpowers and could talk to each other on the other side of the planet or whatever. But after a while he'd begun to feel like maybe they *could*. Maybe not tell what Alice was thinking exactly, but at least predict what she'd say next. He thinks she felt the same way.

"Me next," she'd said. Then she'd squinted at him hard, pinching her chin and pursing her lips, squinching up her freckled nose as though by tensing all the muscles in her face she could help the process along. Jamie had cleared his mind and was thinking of a sailboat.

"Ummm…" she'd tilted her head to the side. "Something wet."

"Hey not bad!" Jamie grinned. "Except that's pretty much everything but us right now."

"No, but like, something that's wet when it's not raining."

"Like a whale?"

"Was it a whale?"

"Nope."

"Then definitely not a whale." She grinned back.

"Let me try."

He rubbed his temples like he saw someone on TV do once and tried to conjure up whatever was going on inside his twin sister's head.

"A person," he said at last.

"Yeah, but who?"

"Is it someone…charming? Funny? Generous and kind? Someone who looks out for you all the time?"

Her eyes went wide. "Holy cow, James."

"I knew it! It's hard not to think about someone as awesome as me, isn't it?"

She smirked and tilted her head to the side. "Dork."

She hadn't been thinking about him. She'd been thinking about Jack. It hadn't been mind-reading; she'd always been thinking about Jack. To be fair, so had he, back then.

Things change.

That playground had become theirs over time. In the late evenings, they'd sneak off and squeeze themselves into their hiding hole, their secret base, away from Patton and homework and even Lizzie and Jack, who'd long since given up trying to find them when they wouldn't be found. Of course, Alice could get by just fine without the others—without homework, too, she was so annoyingly smart—while Jamie had always had to rely on the kindnesses of others.

He'd gone back to the park after she'd died, maybe half a dozen times before they'd moved. He'd sat in the tube, too small now and yet somehow too big and empty. He used to talk to her there, tell her about his days, about the boys and the girls and the drama and the boredom. He'd told her about Patton and Jack and Liz, and about himself, too. He'd said goodbye there, before the move. "Goodbye" and "goodnight" and "I'm moving on."

Now he sees her in every mirror, and somehow his goodbye seems premature.

He leans back against the wall in the rec-plex entryway and slides down it, pulling out his phone, catching her face in the reflection before the darkened screen lights up. The snow doesn't look like it's going to ease up, so he texts Lizzie to see if she'd maybe like to bring him a pair of boots and some dry socks. It's nice and warm in the entryway, and quiet, too. He strips off the sodden hoodie and stretches it over the radiator to dry. He wonders if there's any sports stuff going on. His phone buzzes with the answer.

Why don't you ask prince charming for his? Judo in the rec-plex Sunday mornings.

She's still in her pajamas and doesn't want to change, he can tell. He sighs, gets up, and wanders in. Maybe he'll just sneak into the locker room and steal them.

He wanders down the hall and puts his ear to the door: nothing. Good. They'll probably be a little big, Jack's boots, but they'll be drier and warmer. He wonders if he should leave the cons as a trade, and grins to himself. Nothing quite like leaving a calling card.

He cracks open the door and slips in.

"Hello?" he calls. Nobody. Sweet. He relaxes, then wanders about looking for Jack's bag. They don't really believe in lockers here for some reason, so it's just bench after bench after bench along the walls of the slightly cavernous changing room. Then he spies it—Jack's stuff. Black bag, black towel, and—perfect—the winter boots Jamie picked out for him last December. Being the Goldmark unofficial fashion consultant comes in handy for the first time ever.

He's about to sit down and pull off his wet shoes when a door swings shut behind him. He turns around, and it's Jack and a couple of his teammates staring at him.

"Oh, hey, Jack." He grins sheepishly. "I totally wasn't about to swap out my cold wet shoes for your nice warm boots or anything. Totally not."

"What are you doing in here?" Jack says. The other two are looking at Leigh, too, with an expression he can't understand.

"Uh, well okay, I *was* actually, going to, you know, take your boots. But I was going to return them—"

"*No*, what are you doing in *here?*" he asks.

Leigh's confused. "Okay, well, now I have no idea what you're asking."

"Just come with me," he says, and strides out of the changing room.

"What's got into him?" Leigh mumbles to himself as he's walking out, and one of the other teammates, Lucas or Luke or something, stops him on his way out.

"This is the guys' changing room, yeah?" He doesn't seem upset or anything, just a little confused. Well, the feeling is mutual. Leigh stops, holds a hand up as if to say something, then dismisses the thought. "Kitten, we'll talk about this later." Luke Or Something raises his eyebrows in the kind of surprise that invites a response, and Leigh sighs. "Look, let's just say I'm not completely thick, and that I do know who this room is for. And that, contrary to present appearances, I belong more in here than in the one across the hall."

Luke Or Something looks at the other guy and shrugs as Leigh leaves the room. Outside, Jack's waiting for him.

"You're not seriously going to get mad at me for being in the boys' locker room, are you?" Leigh crosses his arms and leans sideways against the wall.

"Look, if it were up to me—I don't care, okay? But there are other things to consider now."

He can't believe what he's hearing.

"Jack, come on. I've always liked boys—and girls, and basically anyone I damn well please, not that it's anybody's business but *mine*—and if the ones in the locker room can be mature enough to get over thinking I might peek at their junk—which, no, but—anyway." He shakes his head. "They'll be able to get over this, too. I'm exactly who I was before; I just *look* a little different."

Leigh can't even begin to figure out what's going on in Jack's head. He's not usually like this.

"Look, you weren't—it's just." He sighs, thinking. "Before, okay, when you looked like a boy?"

"Go on."

"You didn't look like..." he stops.

"Like?"

But Jack doesn't finish the thought. Something's under Jack's skin, all right, and Leigh can't quite pin it down.

"So, okay. Your father pays me to look after you," Jack says.

"Yes."

"And before, that meant job number one was stopping you from doing anything that'd wind you up in the hospital or expelled."

"Gee, thanks."

"No, but your—the thing I was mostly protecting you from? That was *you*. But now it's different. Lizzie can take care of herself, but with you looking like this—"

"Wait wait wait wait," Leigh says, finally starting to figure out what Jack's talking in circles around, and not much liking what he's finding. "Let me get this straight. You're saying now that I look 'like a girl,' Jack—that's where this is going, right?—that now you have to protect me from outside threats? By which you mean *guys*."

"Look, there are some real dirtbags at this school, Leigh, and I don't think—"

"No, you *don't* think." Leigh cuts him off. He can't believe he's talking back to Jack like this, but at this point he's damn near livid. "That's some sexist *bullshit*, Jack. The hell are you talking about 'protecting' us in different ways, you never—"

"I *always* protected you differently. All three of you need protecting in your own ways. It's my *job*."

"Oh." Leigh's stomach drops. "There it is." All three of them. Leigh's pretty sure Jack didn't even hear himself say it. He closes his eyes and takes a deep breath, hating where this is going. "This isn't about me at all," he says, staring at the ground.

"What are you—?"

"'All three of you,' Jack, that's what you just said."

"What?"

"This isn't about me. It isn't about me looking like a girl, or the things you think you need to defend me from, or any of the other things you're saying, and you know it. It's about *her*, Jack. It's because I look like her, and because she's gone."

Jack doesn't make a sound. Leigh doesn't know if he's angry or confused, or trying to come up with a comeback or what, but if the school's judo uniforms had pockets, Jack's hands would be shoved so deep into them that he'd be stooping over. He's staring at the far side of the hallway like it'll vanish if he blinks.

Leigh doesn't even know what to think. It's like the world's gone upside down. In what *universe* is any of this even remotely fair? Leigh's the one that's supposed to get things wrong. Jack's supposed to be the one that tells *him* what's right.

Tension fills the hall like a flammable gas, creeping into every crevasse, filling up their lungs. After a minute's silence, Leigh thinks at last that if he doesn't say something, *anything*, then they're both just going to suffocate in it, then and there. He bites his lip, the sharpness of the pain clearing the tiniest of spaces in the air. Then he says it—the thing he knows they both already know.

"I'm not her, Jack," he says. "I'm not Alice—"

"Of *course* you're not—!" Jack snaps at him and ignites the air with a spark. Leigh feels the fire in his lungs rising, the words burning their way out.

"Then stop *acting* like you can go back in time and save her by *treating* me like her!" he shouts. "You *couldn't* protect her! *None of us could!*"

His throat tightens on the last words as they echo in the smoldering wreckage of the hallway, ash drifting around them. He feels his face flush as he hears the click of a door, the sound of someone's prudent retreat from the explosion. He sucks in a breath to fight against the knot in his stomach, trying as hard as he can not to dissolve into a complete mess, but the breath comes out haltingly, catching on a series of sobs. Hot tears start streaming down his cheeks, and anything else he tries to say is washed away as the ensuing flood puts out the scattered fires.

After a small, embarrassing eternity, Jack steps over and wraps him in a hug, a gruff and whispered "I'm sorry" finding its way to Leigh's ear. His face is pressed against the black and green fabric of Jack's team uniform, the stitching coarse on his cheek.

"You're being such a *jerk*, Jack," he says into his chest.

"I know," he says.

"So stop it."

"Okay."

"I mean it," he says, pushing Jack away and wiping his face on his sleeve. "No more of this treating-me-differently crap. I'm *me*. I'm not *her*. I haven't changed, okay?"

Jack looks him in the eye and nods.

"And no more of that sexist bullshit, either. I know you're better than that. Start up with that crap again and I'll tell Lizzie and you'll have to fight her."

Jack half chuckles at that, but only because the threat is real. "I promise," he says.

"And one more thing." Leigh takes a breath and lets it out, trying to put his thoughts into words. "Alice—what happened to her wasn't your fault. She got *sick*. You couldn't—it wasn't...it's not a thing you failed at, Jack."

Jack looks away and takes a long breath, letting it out as he speaks. "I know that. I know. And some days I even believe it." He looks back with a distant smile, and for half a second Leigh thinks he catches a glimpse beneath Jack's armor.

"Jack..."

Jack takes a deep breath, then reaches out and tousles Leigh's hair.

"Hey—" Leigh starts, but Jack interrupts him.

"We'll talk about it another time, okay? And I'll tell my teammates I was being an ass and that you have every right to be in there."

Jack locks his fingers together, reaching his arms out and seeming to put all his pieces back in place with a single stretch, in a way that Leigh can only envy.

"Now," Jack says, eyeing Leigh with feigned suspicion, "what was all that about stealing my boots?"

■ ■ ■

"This curry better taste good. My feet are going to be cold and wet forever."

Leigh's sitting on the bed, peering at his orange-dyed feet. The orange shoes and now matching orange-dyed socks are perched on the windowsill by the radiator, competing with the hoodie he'd been wearing earlier. The red around his eyes had mercifully faded by the time he'd gotten back to the room, so not only did it not clash with his feet, he'd also been able to leave out most of the fight with Jack.

"I look like an Oompa-Loompa."

"Well whose fault is that, not looking at the weather before you left?"

"Silence, kitchen wench."

"Look, twinkletoes, your spray-tan feet have been dry for hours. Put some socks on and hang out near the rad till you're warm again." She turns around, and talks while chewing. "And then get ready to have those socks blown right off again, because I've officially outdone myself."

There's a knock at the door, and after a few lazy calls of "It's open!" Jack wanders in.

"Howdy, stranger!" The kitchenette is hidden when the door to the room is open, and Lizzie calls out from behind it. Leigh, dwarfed by his choice of clothing—a pair of baggy, flannel-lined cargoes and a massive sweatshirt—is sitting feet outstretched by the radiator. He waves Jack in, who takes off his coat and brushes snow from his head. It's still coming down out there, and it doesn't look like it's going to stop until morning.

"No closing the door all the way though," Lizzie says. "Them's the rules."

Jack props the door half open with a wedge and takes a seat.

The curry is amazing, as promised. They sit wherever they can—at the desk, on the beds, or on the floor at different times. Lizzie keeps a traffic-free route to the kitchen so Leigh can stick his head in the sink periodically. He says he 'still hasn't gotten the hang of' maintaining temperature in his new body, but Lizzie points out that it's probably just the fact that he's too stubborn to change out of his warmest clothes while eating spicy food after turning the radiator to eleventy-seven degrees.

"Feels like old times," Jack says, looking at his plate, chewing absently. A single bead of moisture has formed at his temple, and Leigh can't tell whether it's sweat or just leftover snow from the walk there.

"Yeah, thanks for cooking, Liz," Leigh says.

"No worries." She finishes her plate and stands to take her dishes to the sink. "You're paying for it with laundry, remember?"

Leigh smiles. "I know, all the laundry, forever. But so worth it for real food every week."

"Wait, you're doing this every week now?" Jack's looking over at Lizzie. Leigh thinks he's avoiding looking at him still, but can't be sure.

"That's the deal."

"Where are you getting ingredients?"

Leigh beams. "Everett."

"The chef?"

Leigh deflates a little. He'd thought he was being mysterious. "Yeah. How do you know him?"

"He worked for Mr.—uh—your father, for a few years." He nearly says "Mr. Goldmark," but Lizzie shoots him with her laser eyes before he can finish. "I think he wanted a change of pace, and so your father had a few strings pulled. Like he does."

"Like he does," Leigh repeats, rolling his eyes.

"Anyway, how did you convince him to—" Jack stops, looking at Leigh for the first time that evening. "The dress. For *real? That's* what you were doing?"

"The boy catches on quick, I'll give him that." Lizzie's grinning.

"Hey it worked...sorta."

Lizzie snickers from the kitchen. "Cute though it may be," is all she says, and Leigh curls up into a literal ball of embarrassment, knees to forehead and flopped on his side on the bed.

"What does that...do I even want to know?"

"Oh my god, no," Leigh says. "And don't you tell him either."

The line of questioning ends with a knock at the half-open door. The dorm mother, Cathy, is just issuing a 'friendly' reminder about the start of Supervised Study hours.

"Shoot, seven already." Jack looks at Lizzie while he's grabbing his coat. "You'll tell me more about this later, capiche?"

Lizzie salutes. "Yes, drill sarGENT!"

He just shakes his head at her, then looks at Leigh. "And you...just... don't get into more trouble. I know that's a lot to ask."

"You're damn right it is."

Jack sighs.

"Oh hey, hey! Before you go! I'm putting the band back together and—"

"Not a chance." He's walking out the door. Leigh follows him, baggy pants scuffling along the hall carpeting.

"Aw come on, it'll be great. Lizzie's in for drums, we got a kickass bassist to replace my newly non-bassist-y hands—" he does little crab-pincher motions while he talks "—and all we need is the world's bestest, most handsomest guitarist *everrrr*." He's tugging on Jack's sleeve as they walk to the exit.

"No."

"Please?"

"No."

"This isn't over."

"Yes it is."

"Nope. You'll come around."

"I won't," he says, opening the door and walking out into the snow. He doesn't turn around, but Leigh can hear it in his voice. He's smiling.

"So we'll see you in the music room after class on Thursday!"

"Bye, kid." He lifts a hand without looking back, a kind of backward wave that radiates cool nonchalance, as he wanders off into the snow and disappears.

Leigh holds onto the door and stares out after him until he's nothing but a shadow half way to the boys' dorm.

"Bye, Jack."

■ ■ ■

Jack's dorm room is already unlocked when he gets there, and inside there's someone waiting.

"Hello, my boy."

Jack doesn't respond at first, just steps inside and closes the door. The man is maybe forty-five years old but looks older because of the grey creeping into his beard. His salt-and-pepper hair is a little too long for business and a little too short for style, and the wrinkles around his eyes and the irregular bridge of his nose betray a life of fieldwork and fistfights. In a fair fight, Jack might be able to take him, but he knows it wouldn't be a fair fight.

Jack hangs up his coat and takes off his boots, noticing an unsettling absence from the back of the closet. The man is sitting on Jack's only chair, motioning at a handgun laid within reach on the desktop. Jack's gun.

"I'm surprised they let you have this on campus—or, well I don't suppose you asked, did you? Old Pat probably gave it to you and told you forgiveness was easier to ask for than permission. Still, not much use for protecting them if it's in the back of your closet."

Jack scowls at his visitor before opening his mini fridge and pulling out a soda. He snaps the key and takes a drink. He doesn't say anything.

"Come now, is that any way to treat an old friend?"

"Old friend my ass. Why are you here?"

"Same old Slade, just like your father was—no small talk, all business. You must be great at parties. Bet the girls love you."

At the mention of his father, Jack's temper rises. "Just answer the damn question, Brenner."

The man leans back in the chair. "I've had a change of employer."

"You were dishonorably discharged." The lying sack of crap had been around a lot when he'd been a kid. He'd never liked him much then, either, always skulking about and looking like he was up to something. And then he'd been the only survivor from his father's unit after the ambush in Syria. Nobody had ever been able to *prove* desertion, but something had gone on behind closed doors with the higher-ups, and it had been enough to have him thrown out.

Brenner just shrugs. "It was a compromise," he says before leaning forward and reorienting the conversation. "My new employer believes very strongly in the work you do."

Jack rolls his eyes. "Why. Are. You. Here?"

Brenner smiles conspiratorially. "How would you feel about a promotion, Jack?"

Jack sighs and motions for the door. "Get out."

Brenner stands, hands up. "Hey, I'm one of the good guys. Well—" he chuckles to himself "—no, I'm not. But I work for better ones than you do." He picks up a coat off the chair and walks to the door. After he steps out, he speaks over his shoulder. "I brought you a present, Jack. Take a look. I'll be back to make the offer again."

Jack closes the door and turns the lock, shoving the chair up against the doorknob for good measure.

He picks up the gun, drops out the magazine, clears the chamber, and sets it all back on the desk. Old friend, huh? He's never so much as taken the gun out of its lockbox on campus, let alone *loaded* it. But Brenner's always been a coward, which, when you're as well-liked as he is, probably keeps you alive. Also on the desk is a manila envelope with a sticky note on it, pinched from a pad on his desk. In black pen it reads, *Play it close, Jack. They're lying to you.*

He opens the envelope and reads.

3

THE MAN WAITS IN A BUNKER BEHIND LEAD-LINED WALLS, LOOKING out across the test site through the narrow viewing port. If everything goes as he expects, there'll be nothing to see except a quickly-sinking depression in the Nevada sand. Even the lead is probably unnecessary—the blast should be virtually free of ionizing radiation. That's the very point of the project the military higher-ups have codenamed *Colosseum*.

He looks at his phone—it's the second of January. He's missed New Year's Eve without even noticing. That must've been what the commotion had been outside his office door the other night. They've come so far in less than three months. It's a testament to the power of military spending and sleep deprivation.

He'd like to be able to blame the president for this, another militant conservative in the White House, but this particular clandestine project had been started decades ago by the other guys, before the Berlin Wall had even come down. A clean new weapon to replace all the dirty ones, but no less deadly for that. A weapon whose tests couldn't be picked up by an array of sensors all around the world, by the sniffer planes and the seismographs and the satellites. Starting the mothballed project back up might've happened even if the towers had been hit before Clinton had left office. God knows what they think they'll do with it, chasing a couple hundred men around in Afghani caves. What's a weapon of this size even supposed to be good for, in an age of small-cell terrorism? Maybe they really will invade Iraq like the rumor mill's been saying.

The klaxon sounds and the yellow lights swing into life, rotating shadows around the concrete room. Thirty seconds.

Less than three months ago, he'd received a curious late-night phone call. Was he prepared to serve at the pleasure of the president, they'd asked. After a tentative yes, he'd been picked up by a uniformed man in a black SUV like something out of a Cold War cliché. But aside from the non-disclosure agreements and the substitution of Department of Energy staff scientists for grad students and postdocs, it had been pretty similar to his work at the university. In all honesty, the weapon had been nearly complete when they'd shut down the project in the early '90s; he'd just picked up the last few pieces and added more and better data to the projections. Solved a few problems that had been giving them grief.

And now they're going to throw the first switch.

The lights change from amber to red. Ten seconds.

Ideally, there shouldn't be any shockwave or seismic response. That's part of what makes the Displacement Engine such a terrifying weapon. One moment the bomb will be there, nestled in its underground room at the end of a mile-and-a-half-long tunnel; the next, there should be nothing but neutrinos and weakly-interacting particles and the general, low-level hum of the universe. It should simply annihilate anything within a hundred-meter radius, and replace it with matter that, well, doesn't matter. Not to us, anyway. If he's done his job. If the math is right.

A word comes to mind unbidden—*Baneberry*, an underground test that hadn't stayed as underground as promised—and he closes the viewing port. Maybe the shielding is a better idea after all. He checks his watch and waits for zero.

Three, two, one.

There's the faint buzzing of a switch being thrown in another room. The video cameras targeted at the engine go white, then it's all static and nothing else. No blast, no shake.

For five minutes readings are taken around the perimeter. The sensors that should have been knocked out are out, the ones that remain indicate that the radiation levels are all within tolerances. Not even a little spike. He opens the viewing port.

Something isn't right.

There's no depression in the ground.

The land for nearly a dozen miles to the north is pockmarked with cave-ins and subsidence—could the Engine have failed? Or was the reaction so perfectly gentle as to leave every grain of sand in place above the bedrock?

He checks the cameras in the tunnel, spaced every fifty meters down the shaft alongside sensor bundles. Clear. Clear. Clear.

And then the impossible.

The klaxon whoops out the "all clear" as he sprints through the bunker's halls and out across the sunlit earth to the tunnel. He needn't have rushed—a series of scrub teams is checking each progressive set of doors down the shaft he spent so many hours at the end of, an interminable delay at each, checking for radiation, blast damage, chemical residues. But there's something beyond the fourth blast door he needs to see. Something on the camera. It can't have been right. It was too dark to really see. The longer he waits, the more he's sure he must have imagined it.

The final, massive bulkhead slides sideways into the tunnel wall, and the smell of dust and dry underground air gives way to something wholly alien, something entirely out of place. Five meters into the next section, the shaft ends in the wall of a massive, spherical cavern.

He calls for a light and someone runs for one.

The cavern is perfect. That much had been within the realm of possibility. That much would at least have made sense: the Engine's work, his work, had been so precise that it had produced a perfect sphere of space in the bedrock. A perfect dome deep underground. That alone would have been a thing of beauty. To think of all the physics it would prove at once...

But the weak light from the tunnel behind him makes indistinct shapes in the cavern, makes a reality of what he saw in the dim infra-red of the camera. From the darkness comes the smell of greenery, the whisper of leaves, the unmistakable thrum of a forest at night.

He positions the tripod and turns on the light.

It's January 2, 2002.

The Displacement Engine will never be tested again.

■ ■ ■

"Another one!"

Leigh's perched on the edge of his desk chair, still-wet hair all yellow spikes from being toweled 'dry' and left alone, the rest of him only half into the academy's uniform while he hunches over the laptop.

"Wa?" Lizzie pokes her head out of the bathroom with a toothbrush in her mouth.

"Another email. I meant to tell Jack about the last one but forgot."

"The school's not that big, I see him every day. I'm sure you'll run into him." Lizzie speaks between spitting and rinsing.

"I told you, he's avoiding me."

"Yeah, yeah."

"For real!" Leigh huffs and folds his arms. "Look, just, tell him I want his opinion on it when you see him today."

Lizzie shrugs by way of a response.

Leigh peers at the laptop. Aside from the date, not much seems to have changed. It's still waiting for him to 'verify vectors,' whatever that means.

"Hey." Lizzie taps him on the shoulder. "Come on. Grab your tie, you're going to be late for class."

"Yeah." Leigh stares at it one more time before slapping the computer shut.

■ ■ ■

*Welcome back my friends to the show that never ends, we're so glad you could attend, step inside, step inside! It's twelve o'clock, my beautiful misfits, and we're on the air **live**, and there's only one thing that could mean—Amy found some poor sucker to do the lunchtime slot and we haven't had the time to do a pre-record! From here on in, I'll be your host with the most, you can call me Leigh, and coming to you all the way from Radio Lab One it's the triumphal return of The Punk Show! Your Punk-Drunk Lunch! Gabba gabba **hey**!*

"He's a natural," Jules says while Amy cues up the first song. She presses a button and shifts her headphone a little.

"You can almost see the resemblance," she says.

So to kick you out of your midday slump—or to accompany your morning coffee, slackers—you know who you are!—let's go to the discotheque a go-go. Here it is, off of their 1977 LP Rocket to Russia, it's Johnny, Joey, Dee Dee, and Tommy with "Sheena is a Punk Rocker!"

Leigh gives them a thumbs-up through the glass and grins as Amy throws to the Ramones and Jules smiles back. Amy effects a kind of boredom that means she can't find anything wrong with Leigh's performance—in itself a kind of compliment—and then holds up two fingers: two minutes until they're back. That's the problem with punk, and why they couldn't get anyone else to do the show: instead of four or five songs in half an hour you're doing closer to ten, or doing a lot of talking to make up the difference. That takes a lot of energy.

Through the glass, Leigh's bouncing on the chair and air-guitaring to the song.

"He really is a lot like Jamie," Jules says.

"But prettier, and slightly less obnoxious."

Jules sighs. "I guess. If that's what you're into."

"Aw, I forgot, you were sweet on little Jamie." Amy's only half paying attention, cueing up the next few songs on the handwritten list Leigh gave her. She still gets the tone just right to get under Jules's skin.

"Yeah, well."

"You should get an email address for him. See how he's doing."

"So should you."

Amy holds her hand up, and pulls a finger down each second. Five, four, three, two, one.

And we're back, but not for long because I'm trying to pack as much punk into your lunch period as humanly possible! Since Sheena's not the only punk rocker out there, this next one's going out to the captain of our kick-butt judo team—and definitely undercover punk himself—I'll see you after school Thursday, Jack! Here it is, the Ramones again, this time off their 1976 self-titled album, it's "Judy is a Punk," right here, right now on The Punk Show, Academy-One.

■ ■ ■

"Well that's all the time we have for today, but remember to email requests for Thursday's show. The Punk Show was produced by Amy Slevin, Jules Adams, and the whole AcademyOne student team. Until next show, be good to each other, young punks of the Academy. This is Leigh Goldmark, signing off."

The next voice is Jules's, reading the lunchtime news—upcoming games, sports practices, recent events—then throwing to a pre-record as part of their Club Insider series, fifteen minutes once a week on a club or society at the academy. Today's special: the golf club. The headmaster flips the switch and the little office goes quiet.

"As you can see, she's settling in nicely."

"Good." Across the desk sits a familiar visitor, hands folded in his lap. "They're of the utmost importance to us, you understand." He slides an envelope forward over the glossy oak surface. "But you know how things can be. Unexpected absences, for instance, can be overlooked."

The headmaster picks up the envelope and looks inside, then slides a drawer open and drops it in, face expressionless.

"The wellbeing of our students is paramount here, Mr. Brenner."

"Please," he smiles, "call me August."

■ ■ ■

"What do you think?" Leigh asks as he bounces his way down the hall. The custom-size uniform has arrived at last—a men's blazer of the appropriate size had to be ordered and he's been wearing things two sizes too big for a couple of weeks now.

"It's cute." Lizzie's not paying attention.

"How about the pants? They aren't too...you know...showy? In the posterior?" He lifts up the back of his blazer and leans forward provocatively.

"They're fine."

"You're not even looking."

"I'm not looking at my brother's caboose, no." She's tapping at her phone and frowning.

Leigh sighs and peers over his sister's shoulder. "What is it?"

"I've been thinking about that email you forwarded. Something looked familiar about those letters and things after our names and I think I've figured it out."

She's scrolling through a Wikipedia page looking for something, and Leigh catches a glimpse. "What's fairy chess?"

"Okay well you wouldn't know because you were always running off—damn it, why doesn't this thing have a search function *within* the articles?" she grumbles to herself and continues. "So there are people out there who, like Pops, are so good at chess that they hardly ever have a good time unless they're playing in a tournament or something, right?"

"Yeah?" He remembers Patton always having a few chess boards around—ones he wasn't allowed to touch. They were always posed mid-game, and would change over the course of weeks. He remembers that the best time to ask Patton for something was when he was stuck in one of his ongoing games, because he'd be paying less attention. Well, even less than usual.

"So these super chess guys made up new pieces and new rules."

"Like Calvinball?"

Lizzie looks up from the phone and gives him a look. "What? No." She sighs. "No, the rules stay the same for the whole game, they don't change whenever someone feels like it. Anyway. So this guy Betza came up with a way of describing these new pieces by the types of moves they make. And I think...yeah, here it is."

She's pointing at something in a very long chart.

"Graz pawn?"

"Yeah, the letters here after Jack—all the Fs and Ws and stuff— that's how you write a piece that moves like a couple of types of pieces at the same time, a regular pawn and a kind of topsy-turvy pawn called a Berolina pawn. It's...I think it's more often called a sergeant, and..." She scrolls sideways and then back. "Yeah. It's a pawn that can move and attack in any of the three spaces in front of it instead of the usual 'move forward but attack diagonally' thing."

"...great. So what does that make you?"

"Hold on, hold on, I'm working on it." She flips back and forth from the email to the page. "Um, looks like QN means 'amazon'—a queen/ knight hybrid."

"Oh my god does that say 'superqueen'?" Leigh's grinning. "I thought *I* was the superqueen."

Lizzie ignores him. "No, but see this?" She points at the equals symbol after Jamie's name. "That means 'promotion'."

"I didn't know chess pieces could, you know, move up the ranks."

"How did you live in our house and learn this little about chess?"

Leigh shrugs. "How did Patton live with me and learn absolutely nothing about punk?"

She squints at him, then goes back to her explanation. "Anyway. A pawn can get a promotion if it makes it to the other end of the board. Which is pretty unlikely, but it happens."

"So wait, what does it say exactly?"

"It says Berolina pawn promoted to bishop/knight hybrid. Archbishop. Also known as a princess, cardinal, janu—"

"—promotion to princess?"

They both stop. Leigh looks down, then back up at his sister.

"That's...pretty accurate. What's it say next to Leigh?"

"'BN'...you're a princess."

"Then these things next to it with the numbers—live, 'term'...terminated? Jesus, these are—I think they're days. Find a thing."

"What?"

"With your phone, like, a day counter thing. A date calculator. There's gotta be one on the internet. Just google it." Leigh's almost bouncing.

"Fine, don't get your panties in a knot." Lizzie says it without looking up.

"I don't even wear—*okay whatever be that way*. If these are days, then, okay, what day was it six thousand and however many days ago?"

"Okay hold on...August 22, 2001."

"That's really close to Jack's—"

"Wait, the email was from four days ago, right?"

"So August 18—it knows our birthdays?"

"We really need to tell Jack about this."

"He's got class all afternoon and you know he won't skip them."

"I'll text him, tell him it's urgent."

"Where are we going to meet?" The halls are already filling with students and they have to conspire in whispers. Leigh's right: if they're caught skipping class it'll be serious, especially with Lizzie still being on probation.

"Then after class I'll text him to come by our room."

Leigh agrees, and for the rest of the afternoon he nurses a tightening knot in his stomach. Someone knows all about him, about Lizzie and Jack and even about Alice, and they aren't saying what or why. The end of the day can't come soon enough.

■ ■ ■

"So what do you think?"

Brenner's leaning against the wall of lockers, arms folded, wearing trousers of a parochial tweed, white shirtsleeves rolled to the elbow.

He talks to Jack as he walks out of class.

Jack looks at him, then looks around.

"I think I should be calling security."

Brenner grins and sticks out his hand, as though for a handshake, speaking in a conspicuous, public tone. "I'm sorry, we haven't properly met. My name is August Brenner, I'm the new guidance counsellor. This is my first day."

Jack ignores the hand and leans in close.

"What's the game, you old crank?"

"No game, Jack my boy. I'm just here to offer guidance."

Jack snorts. "I'd get better guidance from a YouTube comment thread." He starts to walk away.

"Did you read it?"

Jack stops, but he doesn't turn around. Brenner keeps talking.

"There's proof, you know."

Brenner walks around to face him and hands him an envelope.

"What's this?"

"Twenty-four hours—not even, round trip. In-flight entertainment; you don't even have to make small talk. Come along, come back. Make your decision then."

Inside the envelope are two plane tickets. They'll have to leave before last period to make it.

"I've cleared it with your teachers and coaches. It's a work-study experience."

"And AcademyOne?"

"They'll cope," he says, impatience starting to show.

Jack puts the tickets back in the envelope, and hands it to Brenner.

"Thanks, but no thanks." He starts to walk away.

"Damn it, Jack. Look—" he puts his hand on Jack's shoulder.

"You want to keep those fingers?" His words are like ice.

Brenner removes his hand but keeps talking, used car salesman smile back in place. "Here's the deal. You come along, I'll leave if you want me to. Either way. You *don't* sign up, I go; you *do* sign up, I *still go*. Either way you get rid of me, never see me again. If you want me to,

I'll quit my job and go find work as a bartender somewhere. Fiji maybe. But if you *don't* come along, you're stuck with me as you and your friends' personal guidance counselor, for the rest of the year—hell, for next year, too, when you're gone off to college or whatever you've got planned. Back here it'll just be me, Elizabeth, and Leigh."

Jack closes his eyes and takes a deep breath.

"I'm going to regret this," he says, and takes the envelope back. "Just so we're clear: if I go with you, and you don't leave the Academy?"

"If you still want me to go?"

"I'll want you to go."

"You can shoot me."

"Don't think I won't."

"I'm counting on it." Brenner walks down the hall, still talking. "Get your things. I'll see you by the front door at quarter to two."

■ ■ ■

"He's not responding."

"Told you he was avoiding me."

"Why would he be avoiding you?"

"I don't know, I'm the flaky one, remember? He's the one who's supposed to be sensible and dependable."

"His phone's probably just off." Lizzie sighs. "Okay, we'll split up—I'll go check the radio lab, you go check the rec-plex. Keep your phone on, and I'll—"

"Hold on." Leigh's tapping at his phone.

"What?"

"There's another one. Email. But it's different."

"Let me see."

Information verification request

15AE9D12E4247E01BF39@gmx.com   1:45 (2 hours ago)

To: me

Hello,

Please verify these vectors and inform me of any changes:

1. John Slade-Woodman (fWfFifmW2ifmF2)(live/running:6324@i6188)

2. Elizabeth Chelsea Goldmark (QN)(live/running:6081@i6188)

3. James William Goldmark (mfFcfWimfF2=>BN)(term:5926@i6127)

4. Alice Evelyn Goldmark (kQ)(term:4821@i5022)

5. Leigh Aiden Goldmark (BN)(live/running:60@i6188)

Vector verification is important.

I am here to help.

"'I am here to help?' What's that even supposed to mean?" Lizzie's impatience twists her eyebrows into a frown.

"I'm going to write back." Leigh starts tapping out a response and Lizzie stops him.

"Wait, what are you going to say?"

"I dunno. It all seems pretty correct, right? I mean, the days have even moved forward since last time. And I *am* a princess." He winks at his sister.

Lizzie sighs. "Fine. Let me see it before you hit send though."

Leigh taps at his phone for a minute and then shoves it in front of her to double check.

---

re: Information verification request

To: **15AE9D12E4247E01BF39@gmx.com**

John Slade-Woodman goes by Jack. "Vectors" are otherwise correct.

Who are you?

Lizzie sighs again, but says "Okay" and hands the phone back. "Here goes."

Five seconds later the phone makes a familiar *plink* noise.

"Responsive, for someone who still uses email," Leigh says, and re-opens the app.

re: Information verification request

281E2E6F8A7CE71F3BDB@gmx.com   just now (0 minutes ago)
To: me

The vectors have been updated and verified. Thank you for your cooperation.

Regarding the information you requested: I am Betza.

"I am Betza?" Leigh shows it to Lizzie. "Like that fairy chess guy you mentioned?"

"I mean, maybe? Ask if he's Ralph Betza."

Leigh types and hits send. Five seconds later another response.

"Negative. I am simply Betza."

"I am simply Betza." Lizzie repeats.

"I am simply confused."

"Ask them who Betza is."

Leigh repeats the pattern and after a few seconds reads the response.

"'Your information request 'Who is Betza?' has been denied. No further information on the subject will be provided at this time. Please proceed to locate Jack Slade-Woodman and update on his status when complete. Thank you for your cooperation.'—what the hell?"

"Let me see—"

"That's all it says!"

Lizzie stares at the email response. "How does it know we were looking for Jack?"

They stand there in silence for a second. The whole situation's unnerving, but who- or whatever Betza is, they're right—Lizzie and Leigh do need to find Jack.

"All right, same plan—I'll check the radio lab, you check the recplex. Text me if you find him." By the time the last words have left her mouth, she's already striding down the empty hallway.

Leigh gets a feeling in the pit of his stomach like he's thirteen again and about to go on stage. Except there's no curtains, no stage, no half-bored and probably judgmental crowd waiting for the show to start. It's just him and Lizzie and the otherwise empty after-school hallway, some creepy emails and a missing Jack. He takes a deep breath and holds it for a count of five as he watches his sister walk away, then lets it whistle out between his teeth. Somehow he already knows—they aren't going to find him.

■ ■ ■

The small plane lurches to a halt at the end of a runway in the desert, and the seatbelt lights go out. He'd been surprised a jet this small even came with them—the pilot could have just left the cabin door open and told them when they could and couldn't stand up.

Brenner stands up and stretches loudly. For hours Jack's been deliberately ignoring him, working through problems in the AP physics textbook so he won't fall behind. Gravitational mass is equal to inertial mass which is why E really does equal mc^2. He thinks. He sighs.

"See, Jack my boy? This is why I like you. Look at that hard work and potential. You could've been watching the latest box office hits, and here you are learning…ah…" he peers over Jack's shoulder. "Math things." He smiles and pats Jack on the shoulder, and Jack slaps the textbook closed.

"Where are we?"

"No can do, Jackie-boy. Very hush-hush. You know how it is."

Jack checks his watch, taps at his phone for a second. "What is this, a Gulfstream G100? Max cruising speed around 530 miles an hour, give or take. Airborne for four and a half hours. That's too far for New Mexico, even most of Arizona." He looks out the window. "I'm going with Nevada. Maybe eastern California."

Brenner's smile hardens into a grimace.

"Math things," Jack says.

Brenner walks to the door, now open and doubling as a staircase, and says "Come on, genius," before leaving the plane.

The late-afternoon sun radiates down as they descend the stairs onto the warm tarmac. Even in December, it's a pleasant sixty degrees out, and Jack's almost disappointed when they climb into a waiting car.

Brenner tries to exchange pleasantries with the man at the wheel, and Jack tries not to smile when the driver fails to respond. He's glad to find someone else who feels the same way about his escort. Hills and scrubland roll by in silence outside the window. Occasional stands of alien-looking green-topped shrubs—they look like something out of a Dr. Seuss book, he thinks—make the landscape seem even more monotone and brown by comparison. Within minutes, they've pulled up to a nondescript collection of buildings, as dusty-looking as everything else in this place.

"This is it, Jackie-boy," Brenner says, and climbs out. Jack follows him back into the sun, and then through the glass and aluminum doors into the facility.

Jack stops. The place is unusual for a number of reasons, but the most off-putting one is the smell—it's not unpleasant, just *wrong*. There's a certain way an ordinary office building should smell—industrial carpets, upholstered cubicle dividers and metal shelving units, plastic and photocopier toner. But here it smells damp, earthy—like the garden-center wing of a hardware store.

It's also deserted, which may have something to do with the regularly-spaced orange lights on the ceiling, all blinking like a silent alarm.

"I gotta say, they're really putting themselves out for you, Jack," Brenner says, almost reading his mind. "It's not easy to get this place empty like this." He winks. "You should understand the lengths we're going to in order to get you on board here, Jackie."

"And who exactly is 'we'?"

Brenner leads him further inside without answering.

At the end of a maze of cubicles and half-hearted motivational posters, they come to a brushed steel door with an out-of-place array of security panels in front of and beside it. Brenner scans his phone's screen with the horizontal one first, then holds it up to what looks like an eye-piece before punching in a code and playing a clip of someone saying the name "Daniels, Sergeant William P." A red light goes green and the door unlocks with a loud *chunk*.

Just inside is what looks like an airlock, but the bucket holding the door open suggests it hasn't been closed in a while. Brenner hands him a couple of shower caps to put over his shoes, snaps some over his own, and walks on.

The hallway beyond slopes down into the ground, the industrial carpeting of the building behind them giving way to well-swept concrete. There are lights in the walls, round porthole-looking things every ten feet or so. He loses count somewhere around sixty when Brenner interrupts.

"You've read the file, so you think you know what you're going to see down here, don't you?" He peeks over his shoulder. "Little green men? Flying saucers?" He turns around, still walking. "You've got no idea, Jack." The tunnel has started to curve, spiraling down into the earth, tracing a great sweep of a circle around something buried in the ground. Looking back, they can no longer see the door they came through.

"You know what they used to do around here? For forty years in these parts, back last century?" He pauses for effect but keeps walking. "They blew up nukes."

Jack finds himself wondering if maybe the reason nobody's around is a good one. One related to health and safety.

"And then they tried something new, now didn't they?"

The passage down ends in a massive bulkhead with another security door. He keeps talking as he runs through the same routine as before.

"A kind of no-radiation nuke, see? Supposed to just turn everything it touches to nothing. No muss, no fuss, no bodies, or bad PR."

The smell is even stronger down here, lush and green-smelling, less like a garden center and more like the tropical exhibits at a zoo. Like some kind of biodome. The door slides open and a massive wet breath of jungle air heaves out at them like a sighing giant.

"But you know what, Jackie-boy? That test didn't go as planned."

■ ■ ■

"Professor!" The blinds on his office windows rattle as the door flies inward.

He sighs and drops his pencil as what little concentration he'd been able to assemble folds like a house of cards in a windstorm. The airman first-class barging into his office has, in the past three months, never once failed to forget to knock, despite repeated requests, bargaining, even low-level bribery in the form of semi-legal imported cigars.

"Diego. Hello." He smiles a weak smile at the unwelcome intruder. "How can I help you?" He straightens his papers, covered with equations, and closes the clunky black laptop that he'd accepted a month into his stay. It had been his lone concession to the very slight chance that he might not be able to do all the required calculations and modeling in his head. Now he's trying to ignore the creeping suspicion that it was the source of the problem.

"The colonel wants to see you. About the Arcus hole."

Arcus was the codename of yesterday's test. There'd been three planned for Colosseum—Arcus, Contus, and Gladius—but unless he can figure out what went wrong, and more importantly *how*, the first will also be the last.

He stands up and walks around the desk, following the airman out to the waiting Department of Energy-logoed golf-cart that would carry him to wherever the colonel awaited.

"You should really get a phone, sir," his escort tells him for not the first time. "I could hook it up for you myself without much trouble."

"Now, now, Diego my friend. If you did that, I'd miss all our pleasant conversations."

The airman thinks about this as they climb into the cart and its lawnmower engine grinds into life, then almost shouts his response to be heard over the racket.

"I would miss them as well, sir, but I still think you should get a phone. The colonel says that efficiency is the key to a successful operation, sir."

He smiles and pats Diego on the shoulder as they drive down the dusty strip. "And that's precisely why I won't be getting one."

The heat and the grit-filled wind both die off as they pass the bunker and slip down into the access tunnel. Thick power cables and ethernet lines have been taped in a hurry to the concrete walls, a hasty infrastructure made to carry electricity in and data out of the anomaly Arcus created, but there are already signs of foundations going in for a building at the tunnel entrance. The cart's engine echoes back at them, doubling its chuntering rattle into a cacophonous roar. Thankfully for the future prospects of their ability to hear, the tunnel begins to fill with enough blues-clad workers installing conduits and more-permanent lighting to make further wheeled passage unsafe. The Powers That Be have decided to move in, he thinks.

His companion turns off the cart and a fog of silence rushes in to entomb them. But it isn't really silence, just the shock of absence, and as they walk deeper into the tunnel and their brains adjust, the sounds of their footsteps and the occasional shouts of men and women at work amalgamate into the sound of what it really is—a weapons development lab.

For a weapon gone wrong.

■ ■ ■

Brenner strolls ahead of him down an asphalt path paved through what Jack can only describe to himself as a subterranean jungle. It's bright inside, but not the light of day. Squinting up through the canopy, past enormous leaves and branches, he catches glimpses of a spectrum of various pinpoint LEDs on the roof of a cavernous dome, itself seemingly supported by dozens of enormous tree trunks cut perfectly to shape. They remind him of the grow lights in the academy's biology classroom.

"Imagine it, my boy," Brenner's arms gesticulate in large circles, "setting off a bomb, or what you thought was a bomb, and getting this instead." He turns and walks backward so he can better play the showman.

If Brenner had wanted him surprised, he had gotten his wish. The file had said some pretty unbelievable things—outlandish things—but it hadn't mentioned anything like this.

"The concrete up there, the lighting, the path—they were all later additions, of course. It was pitch black when it all arrived, and we were lucky it didn't just cave right in. But a little spray-on concrete and some rebar—hell, I ran the team that helped install the lights, some of them. The eggheads didn't want all this fancy alien greenery to die before they got a chance to study it." He turns back around to navigate as the path takes a turn around a particularly large tree. "Of course, when they did, they saw they were pretty much just trees and bushes and moss. Same old, same old, run-of-the-mill DNA and whatnot. They seem to like a little different spectrum of light than your normal garden variety of Earth plants, but that's about the limit of it."

For once, Jack doesn't think he's lying. Aside from a slightly darker tone to many of the leaves, all of the plants he can see look pretty familiar. He's pretty sure he's even seen a couple of them before, but then plants were never really his thing. Alice was the expert on that. He blinks away an unbidden image of Jamie, now Leigh, and nearly trips over a root erupting from the path.

"Careful, now. Used to have a whole hazmat thing going on down here," Brenner says. "Gave it up after a while though. Part of it was funding cuts, sure, but mostly it was just they'd seen it all before. Even the bugs in the soil, it's all pretty much like native. I mean they still make you wear these things on your feet, but hoo boy—you ever try to install lighting wearing a hazmat suit? Goddamn does it get hot in those things." He turns to look over his shoulder. "Anyway, we're nearly there."

Jack's about to ask exactly where "there" is when he sees it. There's a clearing up ahead, where the smooth curvature of the dome is perfectly visible, rising up out of the ground and arcing its way to where the lighting begins. But more important is the building. Erupting from the wall of the dome like the treasury at Petra is a long, white, limestone building with black glass windows.

"Imagine it, my boy. You build a weapon powerful enough to literally *replace nukes*, and you get this instead."

Brenner is grinning from ear to ear.

■ ■ ■

Patton hates the hazmat suits.

He understands why they have to wear them—Nisha had been vocal enough about *that*—but he still can't stand them. He wants to reach out and touch every leaf with his bare hands, to smell again the scent of the alien jungle that had filled the air of the tunnel in the minutes after the test. Instead he's stumbling between trees in the dark wearing a plastic suit with an oxygen tank on the back, all so *he* won't contaminate *the trees*. This is why he doesn't leave his office.

"Pat!" He can hear Nisha's smile over the earpiece, coming in just a little too loud for comfort.

"Yes, that's me. I'm here. Most of me."

"What part's missing?" She's giddy as she hops over a tree root.

"My good sense, I can only assume. Where's the colonel?"

"Up ahead. You're going to flip when you see this."

More than when the Displacement Engine had conjured a

two-hundred-meter sphere of alien jungle? he thinks.

"What have you found?" he asks. What could excite a newly-styled 'exo'-biologist more than this?

"Just look."

Ahead, through the trees, he can see a pair of industrial spotlights lighting up the side of a building.

■ ■ ■

The floor is dusty, like no one's swept it in months. Brenner's bag-encased footsteps are the first inside in some time. The hallway ends in a rough concrete face about thirty feet in, and they take a left through the only available door.

"At first we didn't know what we had. A bunch of alien jungle, summoned from wherever, right? But this, this was something special. We came in the back door. The front's probably still there, wherever this all came from. But the bit we got? Priceless."

The room is about fifty feet long. Near its end, the corner is severed, cleaved off by the spherical shape of the cavern. The left wall is all windows, facing out into the jungle, but the right is filled with smooth, familiar-looking white alcoves, as though the place had once been an art museum, filled with little sculptures. There are holes in the alcove walls, though, with wires showing—no doubt where some technology or other had been removed.

Jack takes a closer look. He'd thought art, but this is all too clinical looking. Too clean. It has the smell of something else, a hospital maybe.

"So what do you think, Jackie-boy? It's wild, right?"

He's been so caught up in the strangeness of it all he's forgotten the point of the visit. Or maybe he never really knew what it was. "Definitive proof of extra-terrestrial intelligence" was what the file had read, with implications that Patton Goldmark was somehow involved. But this is nothing like anything he'd imagined.

"What am I looking at?" he asks, suddenly realizing. Brenner hands him one of the photos from the file. "Wait, these aren't—"

"Incubators, my boy." A photo of an egg, large—about a foot long—an egg of that size would fit right into the alcoves. "You're looking at a *bona fide* alien nursery."

■ ■ ■

"You're never going to believe it," Nisha says, shining a light along the wall with the alcoves. Each one houses an egg with a pale pink sheen to it. "I wish we'd gotten here sooner, the power must've been caught when your uh—thing—"

"Displacement Engine—"

"When the Displacement Engine 'displaced' it into our universe. Most of them are dead, we think—it's too cold and the power's been off too long—but Pat, look: we've got *survivors*."

Ahead, a small generator has been patched up to a trio of large plastic tubs lined with blankets. A pair of suited-up medical techs are taking notes, while black, glassy rectangles—seemingly wrenched out of a few of the alcoves and patched together into a pair of twisted-wire arcs over the tops—radiate a soft glow onto the contents.

She's grinning.

"We're going to try to hatch them."

■ ■ ■

"Of the three viable eggs, they managed to hatch two of them. One had one child in it, the other had two. Twins."

Jack can hardly believe his ears.

"It's funny, you know, we all thought that when we met aliens, they'd be green and scaly, or have those big black eyes like you see on billboards at Roswell."

Jack realizes what Brenner's trying to say. "You can't possibly mean—"

"Got it in one, kid." He fishes around in a pocket while talking. "Dr. Nisha Mallik, god rest her soul. She was the head biologist here back then. She figured it out first, that the eggs were artificial. A significant bit of medical kit they might be releasing as an 'invention' in a couple months, if the transistor tech and biofuels patents are anything to go by." He finds what he's looking for and hands a photo over to Jack.

It's a photo of a team of scientists and engineers, seven or eight of them, as well as a few military personnel. Brenner's in the back row. Everyone's smiling, more or less. In the middle of the front row are three people, each holding a tiny, pale-skinned baby, swaddled in white blankets. The one on the left is probably Dr. Mallik, but the other two are more familiar, if looking very young: on the right, in full military dress, is Jack's father, then Col. Slade-Woodman. And in the very center, in a white lab coat and with a lot more hair than Jack's ever seen him sport, is none other than Billionaire Philanthropist J. Patton Goldmark.

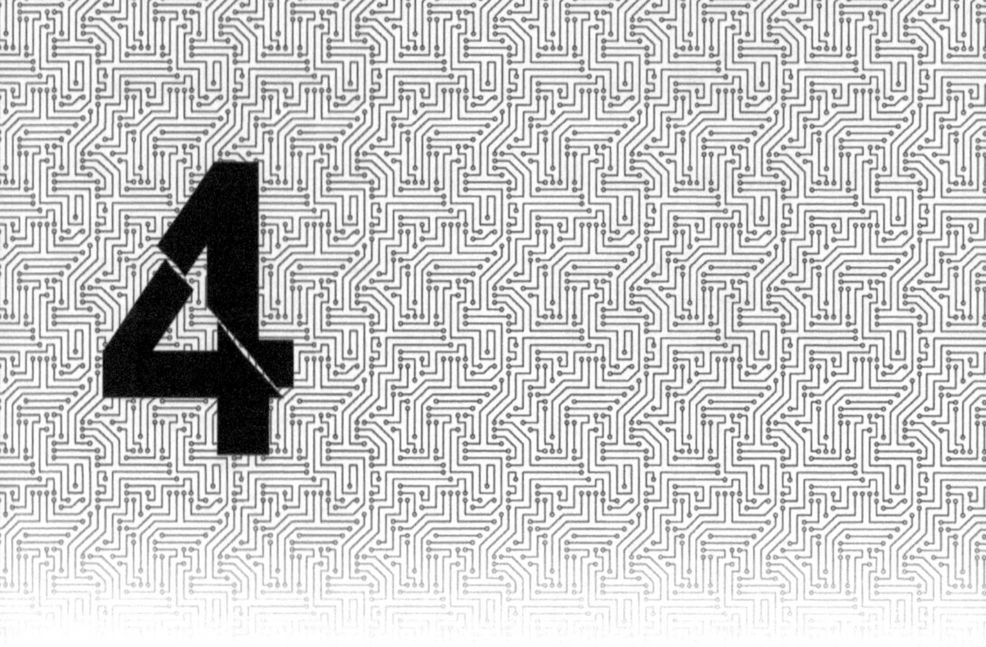

The plane ride back seems longer. Jack can't concentrate on anything but what he's learned, that Lizzie and Jamie—he's got to start thinking of him as Leigh—and even Alice had all been, were all—what? Aliens? Creatures from another dimension?

"Not a clue. Most doctors wouldn't even be able to tell the difference. I mean heck, I can't even tell you what the differences are, and I've read the medical reports."

"Reports that you got how, exactly?"

Brenner smiles a tight-lipped smile. "All things in due time, Jack, my boy."

"We have to tell them."

"Yeah?" Brenner leans back and squints at him. "Does that mean you're on board?"

"It means I might believe what you're telling me," he says. "You haven't exactly explained what 'on board' means."

Brenner unfolds his hands and makes a shrug. "Me and my...associates. We just want to keep them safe. Those kids are, well, they're *important*, aren't they? After the tragedy with Alice, we very nearly took action, but Goldmark pulled in some favors and we stepped back. But now with this whole change that's taken place—with Jamie, or Leigh, or whatever we're calling her now—"

"—him."

"Him, of course—but this all seems very *convenient* to me. To us. Convenient and not at all coincidental."

Jack frowns. "You're saying someone engineered Jamie's change?"

"Bingo."

"Who would do that—and why?"

Another shrug. "Who can say? With the circumstances around Alice's death being so hush-hush, we don't know what they might be after." Brenner leans forward. "But whatever it was, it sure looks like they've got another chance now, doesn't it?"

■ ■ ■

Can't find Jack.

Leigh types the words and hits send. He's curled up on his bed, it's late, and Lizzie's already asleep in hers. He lies on his side with the covers pulled up so the dim glow of the phone won't disturb her. The response pops up almost instantaneously.

re: Can't find Jack.

9D9F8B66C5D0D02096F6@gmx.com   just now (0 minutes ago)

To: me

I am sorry for the trouble. I believe I have located him. He is safe. Go to sleep.

He hits reply.

How do you know who I am? Who are you really?

re: Who are you really?

55AB2FBF5B02469442A0@gmx.com just now (0 minutes ago)
To: me

I am a friend.

Do you know Patton?

re: Do you know Patton?

492E599A92780D598AE3@gmx.com just now (0 minutes ago)
To: me

We are very well acquainted.
If Jack requests your help, you should give it to him.
Go to sleep. You will need it. Goodnight.

The rest of his questions go unanswered. When it finally clicks off, the ghost of the screen hangs in front of his eyes even after he closes them.

■ ■ ■

The next day, Jack's back like he'd never left—not that Leigh manages to see him.

"Hey!" Lizzie shouts down the hallway after him during the second-to-third-period melee. He doesn't respond, so she sprints down the hall, ducking and weaving her way through the crowd like a receiver making a break for the end zone. She nearly tackles him when she catches up.

He looks startled. "What—? Oh, hey Lizzie, what's up?"

She stares at him in disbelief.

"What's *up*? You vanish for twenty-four hours without a word and all I get is a '*what's up*'?"

"Oh, sorry." He gives her a thousand-yard stare, then looks away. "Yeah, I was invited for a last-minute campus visit in the city, had to drop everything, and I forgot my phone charger."

Lizzie stands there in disbelief. Wait, is he *lying* to her? Lying to *her*. But she can tell from the look on his face that she's not going to get any more out of him right now.

She punches him in the arm, surprising him. "Well let us know next time, okay? We were worried."

He rubs his arm and smiles with genuine embarrassment. "Sorry, really," he says.

She gives him the stink-eye. "Fine. Accepted. But as punishment, you have to come to Leigh's band thing tomorrow."

"What?"

He starts to protest but she's already wandering off down the hall. "If I have to go, you *definitely* have to go."

And maybe she can get some real answers out of him then.

■ ■ ■

Leigh's curled up on the bed, knees up, back against the wall, headphones like giant earmuffs blasting Dead Kennedys at Max Q when Lizzie storms into the room and throws her bag onto the bed.

He can see her lips moving but doesn't react fast enough. She storms over, slides the cans off his head and repeats herself:

"Gym. Now. Angry."

Eyes wide, he nods twice as she grabs her gym bag and storms back out of the room.

■ ■ ■

She's only gotten angrier thinking about her run-in with Jack that morning. She lets her frustrations out one at a time, through her fists, into the heavy punching bag that Leigh's using his whole body to brace.

"Hey—*uff!*—so—*unff!*—could we—*erff!*—hold *ON A SECOND!*" he cries.

She stops punching and he slides halfway down the bag, using it for support, trying to catch his breath. He slides to the floor, transforming into a puddle roughly the color of the academy's standard-issue frumpy green tracksuit.

"I am very small now, sister dear, and these pasty white noodle arms are not made for arresting violence of this caliber. Give me a second to breathe. Try using your words."

They're alone in the weight room, not because it's not used all that often, but because the students who would otherwise be there are the same ones who would never miss dinner. Which is what Leigh and Lizzie are missing right now. Leigh's stomach laments in whalesong.

Sweat drips down his sister's nose and she wipes it away with a gloved hand. Then she grunts and wanders over to the speed bag and starts up a one-two-three, two-two-three of pugilistic rhythm.

"What the hell does he think he's doing lying to *me?*" she says, not breaking tempo. "Of all the people in the friggin' *world* he should know that he can't lie to *me.*"

Leigh pulls himself back into a standing position and wanders over, head tilted to one side.

"You mean Jack?"

"Plus he's the worst goddamn liar on the *planet.*" She punctuates the last word with a too-hard punch and stops as the bag bounces wildly. "Well, except maybe you."

"Hey, I can lie. Watch, watch—I am a girl." He stops. "Well, I *am kind of* a girl but that's not really the—"

"Your honor, I rest my case."

He sighs. "So you ran into Jack, and he lied to you about where he'd been?"

"Spun me some bullshit about a last-minute campus visit in the city and his phone coincidentally running out of juice."

"That *is* a pretty crappy lie."

"*Right?*" She takes one last swipe at the bag, and it flops back and forth. "Anyway, even if he keeps avoiding you, we'll see him tomorrow. I'm making him show at your thing after school."

Leigh's eyes widen. "The band?"

"Hey, I'm not making any promises about whether he'll join or not. But at this point, if all it does is make him uncomfortable, I'm down."

Leigh jumps up to hug his sister, then realizes how gross she is. "I'm, uh, let's just pretend I'm hugging you, cool?"

Lizzie gets a diabolical look on her face.

"Wait what are you—?"

"Aww, don't want a hug from your sister?" She lurches forward, sweat dripping from her arms. "What's the matter, don't love me enough?"

Leigh's quick, but not quick enough to avoid the hard, sweaty embrace. After thirty seconds of futile escape attempts, he sighs and allows the moist carnage to continue.

"Please stop. This is abuse. I'm being abused. Help."

"D'awwww. I love my brother."

"You're evil."

He can almost hear her smiling.

■ ■ ■

Who are you, really?

Leigh's sitting on the bed with an empty bowl of stew and a half-eaten dinner roll, hunched over his phone while Lizzie's in the shower.

re: Who are you really?

1F5965F1C4476B709FB5@gmx.com   just now (0 minutes ago)
To: me

I am Betza.

Is Betza your name?

re: Is Betza your name?

440A774A8D64D1AAD8E6@gmx.com   just now (0 minutes ago)
To: me

Betza is what I am called.
Ralph Betza is an expert chess strategist. I am an expert strategist as well.

So it's like a handle? What do you know about us?

re: What do you know about us?

1B0DC473931D5BE77FE3@gmx.com   just now (0 minutes ago)
To: me

I know everything needed at present.

Everything needed at present? Leigh frowns at his phone. Who does this guy think he is?

If you know so much, then what am I going to ask next?

He barely gets to put his phone down before it chimes in response.

re: Where was Jack?

6342AA6608C9C4033E2F@gmx.com just now (0 minutes ago)
To: me

Yucca Flat, Nevada.
If Jack requests your help, you should give it to him.

What the actual hell?

Also: *Nevada?*

"What is it?"

Shoot, Lizzie's just walked in, hair wrapped in a towel. He puts away his phone. "Ugh, nothing, just the latest propaganda from the Liar in Chief. How do people believe this crap?"

"Careful, you're living in the part of the country where they basically *write* that crap."

Leigh makes a disgusted-sounding noise. "Fair point."

He motions to a tray on his sister's bed with a cooling bowl of stew and a couple of dinner rolls on it. Thank god for Everett, is all he can think. If it weren't for him, they'd have had to make do with whatever was in their room, which at this point is half an orange in the mini-fridge and a six-pack of extra-spicy instant noodle bowls from Mack's. If you're not there for the start of the Academy's regimented dinners, you have to fend for yourself. On the other hand, Cathy—the girls' dorm dorm mother—is like Jekyll and Hyde when it comes to the presence and absence of boys in the dorm—or at least what she thinks of as boys—so a little, blonde pixie with a tray of food can come and go without being noticed, most evenings.

"So what do you think Jack was really up to?" Leigh munches on the last of his roll while talking.

Lizzie shrugs. "Jules says he saw him talking with some skeezy-looking new guidance counselor in the hall at lunch."

"Guidance counselor?" Man, they all seem skeezy to him here, or maybe more like *slippery*. They all have that air of 'genuine concern,' like they're just a little too desperate not to seem like they're all secretly narcs or something. Hell, with a school like this one—with students from well-placed families like most everyone there—maybe some of them are.

She chomps down on a dinner roll. "Just what Jules said. Oh, and he asked if you, I mean if *Jamie* has an email address. It was pretty sweet."

Leigh sighs and flops back on the bed. "This sucks."

"I know."

"What if..." He rolls onto his side. "Why can't we just tell everybody? Like, what if I just told people who I am?"

"You *know* why." She eats a mouthful of stew. "Pops said—"

"Oh to *hell* with Patton, Lizzie!" He sits back up again, legs and arms crossed. "He treats everything like it's a military secret. What's the big deal? So fine, we've got this cover story because the higher-ups won't believe it and my DNA's all changed so we can't *prove* I'm me, but we could tell our *friends*."

"Oh that could work. Hey Jules, Amy, how's it going? My brother got infected with a virus or something that made him into a clone of my sister, so just pretend like everything's normal."

"Yes!"

"No!" She puts her palm to her forehead. "That was sarc—*look*." She points at him with her spoon. "Who is *ever* going to believe that? First, there's no such thing as a virus that does...whatever it did to you. Or there shouldn't be. I mean nobody's *ever* heard of *anything* like that. *At. All*. So second, they'll just be mad thinking that we tried to lie to them for reasons they won't be able to figure out because there's *literally no good reason to lie about that*."

"No, but that's in our *favor*! Because there's no reason to make it up! It's too weird to even be something you'd lie about! And I've got all my memories! There's got to be things I know about them that would convince them. Like, when I stole your skirt and wore it, Jules—"

"Everyone knows that."

"—behind the—wait, what?"

"Everyone knew you two'd kissed behind the bleachers. Like, *everyone*."

"Well," he pouts for a moment, "That aside—"

"And with the backstory we gave you, there's nothing you could know that you couldn't have told to your 'sister,' too."

"But there's got to be *something*—"

"Look. Jamie. Stop. *Stop*. We're not doing it, okay? You're Leigh now. I *know* this sucks. It's awful. It's about the second-highest magnitude of suckage I can imagine. But we're going to stick to it because of what currently occupies the highest potential 'magnitude of suckage' slot, which is the very real possibility that they might lock your ass back up in that freak-show hazmat hospital never to be seen again because people in our family don't have the best *track record* of coming *out* of hospitals once they go *in!*"

As her voice crescendos, he realizes what this is really about. Who this is about. And how do you argue with that?

"But I'm not—"

"*No*, Jamie. No buts this time. I'm your big sister and I'm looking out for you. *Let me look out for you. Please.* We promised Pops that this was how it was going to be as the condition for letting you come back, and we have to stick with it. At least for now. At least until we can renegotiate it. Even if that's not fair. Even if that's...not..." She trails off, looking over Leigh's shoulder.

He swivels around to see a small, chestnut-haired shadow peeking around the corner. She's staring at the ground, looking guilty.

"The door was open and there was shouting..." A tiny voice says, nearly whispering.

After a second, Leigh gets up and walks over. Crap. How much had she heard?

He tries to smile. "So uh, hey, Tina. How's it going?"

She peeks up past her bangs and looks at his face as if studying it. Then, perhaps finding what she's looking for, she tilts her head to one side.

"Jamie?" she asks.

He closes his eyes and takes a deep breath.

"Why don't you come in for a bit?"

Lizzie's going to have a stroke.

■ ■ ■

"Here," Leigh says, and puts a cup of sweet, milky tea down in front of their guest. Tina picks it up with both hands.

He looks over at Lizzie, who is to all appearances trying to set him on fire with her eyes, as though he'd somehow conspired to make this happen. He sighs and sits down on his bed.

"So how much did you hear?" he asks.

Tina takes a sip, stares at the cup. She raises her eyebrows and speaks in a low tone. "You used to be Jamie, you got some kind of virus that made you physically present as female. Your dad is making you lie about it."

He almost laughs. She'd been new to AcademyOne last semester, and he'd hardly said more than a few words to her before she'd shown up to volunteer to play bass, but they'd known each other in passing. The only time he'd heard her say this many words was on the radio, where her near-monotone whisper came off as a quirky-sexy, half-asleep-in-the-bedroom style affectation. He'd been kind of jealous, but it isn't until just now that he's realized it's really just a product of her being super quiet and therefore having to lean in extra close to the mic.

He rubs the back of his head and smiles weakly at his now almost radioactive sister, before looking back at Tina.

"And ah, so—hypothetically speaking of course—how much of that do you think is likely to be, you know, true?" He clears his throat a little. "Hypothetically."

She takes another sip, then continues to stare at her tea.

"Hypothetically, you made a good point about it being too weird to make up."

He hears a quiet *thud. thud. thud.* start up behind him that he can only assume is the sound of his sister's fist banging against her forehead in rhythmical frustration.

"That's, you know, pretty interesting, isn't it?" He purses his lips, then continues when she doesn't respond. "But, you know, this *is* all totally hypothetical." He says the words slowly. "Because if it were *real*, only Lizzie and me and Jack would be allowed to know about it, otherwise I'd get shipped back to an also totally hypothetical, creepy-as-hell private medical facility buried somewhere in the White Mountains."

Tina doesn't make eye contact, just sips her tea and nods.

"Then I'm glad this is just a hypothetical situation," she says, deadpan.

She puts down the half-finished cup of tea and checks her watch. It's almost seven and she needs to get back for Supervised Study hours.

"Thank you for the tea," she says, and stands up. A little half-smile dances across her face as she turns to go, pausing for a moment in the doorway.

"Just hypothetically," she says, in the same voice as before, "I'd say 'welcome back.' Music department tomorrow at four?"

"Ah—yeah—" he manages.

Tina nods and walks out the door, closing it gently behind her.

Leigh stares at the door in silence, and then pumps his fist into the air in victory.

"HaHA! That was *amazing*. Oh my god, she's so totally *fierce!* And she's so bitty and quiet that you'd never even *know* it! Lizzie, don't tell me that—"

Lizzie smacks him in the back of the head and he yelps.

"You must have a lucky horseshoe shoved right up your ass to have gotten out of that. Holy *crap*, Leigh, that was dangerous."

He's apologetic, but he's still smiling, and he's pretty sure it's not going over well. He tries to suppress it.

"Nobody else, you hear me? Not one person more. Not Jules. Not Amy. Nobody."

He nods, rubbing the back of his head.

"We're trusting Tina because we screwed up and now we have to. But that's *it*. You, me, Jack, and now her. And you'd better hope she's trustworthy. Because if she's not then we're sunk. *Capiche?*"

Yeah, he gets it, and he says so. But there's a part of him that can't get over how good it felt to share his secret. Even as he reassures his sister, he makes himself a promise: maybe not today, and maybe not tomorrow, but *someday* he's going to give Patton the finger and take his name—hell, his whole *life* back.

Someday.

■ ■ ■

Jack stands there, staring at the open closet, wondering what the hell he's doing. His mind keeps skipping back to the photo: his father, Patton, and the woman, Dr. Mallik. The three babies—if he's to believe everything he's seen—newly 'hatched'—Lizzie, Jamie, and Alice. From somewhere else. From another world.

And he's going to go play guitar for them?

He fishes in the back of his closet for the old Strat in its zip-up case, wondering if it even has all six strings, and whether he's got any extras if not.

Out there in the Nevada desert, in person, underground, it had all seemed real, convincing. True. But the more the thinks about it...

He can't trust Brenner. He knows that. He doesn't know what the old grifter's planning, but he's sure he's not giving him the whole truth. But the worst of it is the size of his blind spots. He's so out of his depth, he can't imagine all the things he's not thinking of, all the things Brenner could be lying about—or leaving out.

"A half-truth is the greatest of lies," he thinks—something his father had said time and again. What the hell had he been up to? What had he and Goldmark planned to do with Alice? What was Goldmark planning to do with Leigh?

He tries to think of the lessons his father had taught him, growing up. Every battle begins and ends before you even make it to the battlefield, and information is the deciding factor. But who could he ask? Lizzie and Leigh don't even know as much as he does. And there's nobody else at the academy but—he stops. But there is.

And his being there suddenly seems a whole lot less coincidental.

Jack grabs the guitar case and closes the closet. He has an idea, but he's going to need help with it.

■ ■ ■

Tina's nodding her head and tuning her bass, sitting next to Leigh on the riser while Lizzie beats the living hell out of the kit. Neither she nor Leigh can reach the ground with their toes, and he realizes that even though he thinks of Tina as tiny, she's not a hell of a lot shorter than he is, now.

"What's it like?" Tina asks in a momentary lull. Lizzie's out in the hall refilling her water bottle. Nobody says what "it" is.

"I don't even know?" he says, in a kind of verbal shrug. "I guess weird, mostly. Scary. Inconvenient."

"Anything good?" She twists a tuning peg and plucks a harmonic.

"I always wanted to be pretty." He lies back and folds his arms behind his head, staring at the band room's ceiling.

"Boy pretty or girl pretty?" She moves on to the next string.

Leigh sits back up, then drops down to the floor and stretches. "I guess I never really got that far since I didn't think it was an option."

He's about to add to his response, to maybe tell the story of how he met Everett or the weirdness in the locker room or how when he looks in the mirror he still freaks out to see Alice looking back at him, when his phone buzzes twice in his pocket. An email.

Information verification request

6516C4FF7530E47435A4@gmx.com4:03 (0 minutes ago)
To: me

Please verify an additional vector.

7. Tina Emerson Slevin (NN)(live/running:5471@i6190)

"Emerson?"

Tina's head snaps up at the word and Leigh realizes he's said it out loud.

"What?" It's still quiet, but it's the loudest he's ever heard her speak.

"'What what?"

"I don't tell anyone my middle name."

Lizzie walks back into the room and instantly scowls. "What've you done now?"

"Nothing—well I sort-of—okay so we got another email—hold on." He scampers over and shows the phone to his sister, who lets out a sigh that's only part groan.

"And you showed Tina?"

"Well, not exactly..."

"What's going on?" Jack's just appeared behind them at the door and is peering over Lizzie's shoulder at the email. "Whatcha got?"

Lizzie growls and he steps back, hands up.

"You know, maybe I'll come back—"

"Nope! Too late." Lizzie turns around and shuts the music room door before wandering across the room. "Gather round, co-conspirators, it's story time. Might as well fill everyone in at the same time if we're going to be spilling all our damn secrets." She stares Leigh down while she talks. "Everybody take a seat."

Lizzie sits on the riser and motions to Leigh, who proceeds to explain about the illness, about the emails, and about Tina finding out.

"Okay wait, so Tina knows who you are?" Jack's sitting on the riser as well, his guitar off to one side. Tina nods. "And you've been getting emails from someone named Betza who seems to be really *really* good at stalking us. All of us. Now including her."

"Bingo." Lizzie tosses him Leigh's phone so he can check out the emails.

"So, uh, what's in Nevada?" Leigh says, as Jack scrolls through.

He looks up, then looks back at the phone. "If I tell you, you won't believe it. I didn't believe it before I went. I'm not sure I even do now."

Lizzie just rolls her eyes. "Seriously, you think there's anything we won't believe after everything that's happened so far?"

Jack continues to scroll through the emails while he talks. "You were accidentally kidnapped as babies from another dimension by an experimental weapon gone wrong and raised by the lead scientist, who happened to be one J. Patton Goldmark." He looks up at their faces, then looks back down at the phone and continues to scroll. "See?"

"Wha—?" Leigh says.

Nobody says anything for about a minute and a half, the silence punctuated only once when Lizzie takes a deep breath and lets it out in a long puff.

"Got any proof?"

"I saw the test site, out in the desert. A giant spherical cavern the shape of the explosion that should've been filled with nothing but was filled with forests and some kind of alien nursery. I saw photos of large eggs—"

"Waitwaitwait *eggs?*" Lizzie interrupts.

"You're saying we *hatched?*" Leigh asks.

"You see what I mean? It sounds nuts, and all I have is this." He reaches into his blazer and pulls out the photo of the team, their parents, and the three babies. He'd slipped it out of the dossier before giving the rest back to Brenner.

"That's...holy crap. That's Patton." Leigh says, passing it to Lizzie.

"And my dad, yeah. And you as kids, I'm pretty sure."

"Who told you this? Who took you to Nevada?" Lizzie says.

"See that guy in the back of the photo? That's August Brenner. The only man in my dad's unit to survive long enough to earn himself a dishonorable discharge. Now he's *apparently* a guidance counselor here at the Academy."

"Well that's not at *all* suspicious," Leigh says.

"If it's not the least suspicious thing about him I'd be surprised. The guy's slime. But he still might be telling the truth, or at least part of it."

"Wait, but that would mean Pops has been lying to us, like, literally our *entire lives*." Lizzie says.

"And lying about what's happened to me," Leigh says.

"And about Alice."

After Jack says it, they all sit there in silence until Tina asks, "Who's Alice?"

As Lizzie and Leigh try to find the words, Jack pulls out his wallet and fishes around in it. He pulls out a little photo and passes it to Tina, who immediately looks confused.

"This looks like a smaller you," she says to Leigh.

"Yeah."

"But you were still the old you, not even six months ago. This looks like it was years ago."

"Alice was Leigh's twin," Jack says. "She passed away. Three years ago in October."

"I'm sorry."

Leigh just nods.

"So you didn't just get anyone's body," Tina continues. "You got *her* body."

"Brenner said—no he didn't say it, he doesn't *say* things—he heavily *implied* that Mr. Goldmark did some experiment on her, and that they did whatever they did to you to get a second shot at it."

"What the hell? That's a load of crap. Pops wouldn't *do* that—!" Lizzie interjects.

"I know! I know. And Brenner's sleazy as hell. And there's the question of just who he's working for, seeing that he can get me into a top-secret military facility." Jack frowns at the phone. "And then there's the question of just who the hell this Betza guy is." He hands the phone back to Lizzie.

"But if someone did do something…to Alice," Leigh just manages to get her name out, "then chances are it's only a matter of time before someone comes for me."

Jack nods.

"This is screwed up," Lizzie says.

"Yes," says Jack.

"No, like, every part of this is one hundred percent messed." She gets up and starts pacing.

"From start to finish."

"But these are our *lives*—"

"So what do you need us to do?" Leigh interrupts.

Jack puts on a wry smile. "This is why you can't stay out of trouble, kid."

"How long have we known you, Jack? You wouldn't tell us anywhere near this much if you didn't have a plan that involved us knowing it." He's pretty sure Jack isn't even insulted by the suggestion; the reason Jack and Patton got along so well was because Jack's father had drilled into him the meaning of the words 'need to know.' It's not, Leigh reflects, one of his favorite things about Jack.

"For starters, we don't trust any of this," Jack says. "I don't know how much of it is true, how much of it is made up, or who we can trust to ask, so for now we don't trust anyone except each other." He looks over at Tina, who's still comparing the photo of Alice to Leigh. "That means you, too, Tina. Sorry, but it seems like you're stuck with us for now."

Tina just nods, engrossed in the middle school photo.

"Second, we need information. Real information, not the stuff Brenner gave me. And to do that, I'm going to have to go directly against Mr. Goldmark's orders."

"What?" Lizzie says.

"For as long as I've known you, my first responsibility has been to keep you two safe. That used to just mean keeping you from being bullied or, in your case Leigh, keeping you out of your own unique brand of trouble."

Leigh shrugs. "Guilty as charged, your honor."

"Well," Jack says, standing up and taking a deep breath. "I'm going to have to bend the rules a little, because to keep you safe from whatever this is that's going on, I'm going to need you to help me break the law."

■ ■ ■

"This is messed up," Leigh says to himself, standing outside the darkened staff suites building. It's one in the morning, and this is officially the dumbest plan they've ever had. But the email from Betza had been clear: "If Jack requests your help..."

He walks up to the door and taps on it a couple of times, trying to stay in the shadows as much as he can. After a minute he knocks a little louder, and a light comes on, faint, like it's up the stairs. A shadow approaches. The door opens.

"Leigh?" Everett's standing in the doorway in a black t-shirt and shorts, looking perplexed. "It's the middle of the night," he half-whispers. "What are you doing out there?"

"Can I come in for a sec?" He looks around nervously. "I'm *really* not allowed to be out here, but I didn't know who else to turn to. She's not answering her phone and I don't know where she is."

"What? Who?" Everett scratches the back of his head, still trying to snap into wakefulness, then motions for Leigh to come inside. "Come in, come in."

With the door safely closed, the first thing Leigh notices is the smell, which is nothing like the dorms. It smells rich and sweet, like warm bread and nostalgia, and he instantly hates himself for what he's doing.

"What's the matter? What's all this about?" Everett says.

"It's Lizzie," he says. "She's missing."

They'd come up with the plan after Jack had explained his suspicions. It couldn't be a coincidence that Everett was working for the school now, no matter how talented a chef he happened to be. His presence had Patton's fingerprints all over it, and that probably meant he had a side job like Jack's—watching over Lizzie and Leigh in case anything went wrong. Probably keeping an eye on Jack, as well.

All of that meant that Everett probably had access to some form of secure communication with someone else who worked for Patton, and that might—just *might*—mean a way to get more information about their situation. But first they needed to get past Everett.

He does his best to sound nervous, which isn't exactly a stretch.

"I woke up in the middle of the night and she was gone from the room, and I can't get hold of her on her phone, and I can't get hold of Jack either because he sleeps like the dead, and you're the only person I can ask for help who won't automatically tell the teachers," he says. "You won't tell, right?"

"I tell you what, once we know she's safe, we'll talk about who we will and won't tell. Let me grab some clothes."

■ ■ ■

Jack waits until the sound of their footsteps has completely faded before crossing the street and walking up to the front of the unit, being careful not to step anywhere that hasn't been shoveled. Leigh managed to make sure the lights stayed off, to avoid raising suspicions, but it doesn't make Jack feel any less exposed as he tries to pick the lock, especially with the snow on the ground making it feel a whole lot brighter than it is. It's the longest three minutes of his life, but in the end he's grateful for his father's training, his luck, and that the school hasn't invested in decent door locks for the staff suites. He slips inside and re-locks the door.

He's looking for a laptop or a phone, something that would have access to Goldmark Enterprises' VPN system. He's got a limited bag of tricks, but a would-be hacker's best friend is carelessness, and it's the best he can hope for.

He finds the laptop first, upstairs on a desk in the tiny bedroom of the kind the Academy gives to its residential staff. He opens it in the darkened room and cringes at the light that spills out. The lock screen is just a standard slideshow of sailboats. It's password-protected, but if it hasn't been perfectly set up...He plugs in the thumb drive, hard-restarts the machine, holds down a few keys, and prays. At the lock screen—no longer sailboats, but a basic flat blue—he types in the word "password" and it lets him in. He sighs with relief and makes a mental note to thank Stewart—Mr. Goldmark's personal computer genius—for the tool and the lessons in how to use it.

Technically, he's not on Everett's personal machine. Instead, it's a kind of mini-computer on the thumb drive itself, but with the added feature that it happens to have access to most of the data on the computer's hard disk, including installed programs. He digs through and finds what he's looking for: a VPN program. He taps his fingers as he loads it up, relying on the power of the little drive to push the machine into action.

Every minute feels like an hour. Leigh's promised to give him as much time as he can, but he won't be able to signal when he's getting near or it'll give everything away, so he just works as fast as he can. It's all or nothing: he just needs to get it done.

The VPN settings are saved as defaults—another miracle!—but he hits a roadblock when the two-factor authorization notice pops up. He nearly has a heart attack when a phone buzzes from behind him, then mentally berates himself for his own carelessness: if Everett hadn't left his phone behind, he'd have known instantly that someone was trying to use his credentials.

Jack grabs the phone and pulls out a small cigarette case with three strips of tape attached to wax paper. It's the last trick he has up his sleeve, and he's praying it'll work. Back in Leigh and Lizzie's room, he'd gone through the most recent haul of vegetables with talcum powder and scotch tape, lifting a few fingerprints off a particularly shiny winter squash. He tries the first one three times just to be sure, but he can't try each one more than that. He only gets ten tries before it locks him out and forces him to wait five minutes or use a password—neither of which he has. He tries the second one, next: three more tries, no dice.

When he tries the last he's rewarded with a final miracle: the phone unlocks and he swipes to authorize access to the VPN.

He checks his watch. Even though it's felt like a million years, to this point it's been almost exactly twelve minutes. It's a six-minute walk to the girls' res, maybe three minutes in Leigh and Lizzie's room, and if they're really lucky, a ten-minute search and a two- or three-minute lecture. Then six minutes back for a completely made-up estimate of twenty-one or twenty-two minutes, or nine or ten minutes to search before he's caught.

He starts digging for the information he needs, praying that his luck doesn't run out.

■ ■ ■

"She didn't leave a note or anything," Leigh says. They're looking into the dimly-lit room through the window from outside. Their room's on the first floor, which in the city would've meant bars on all the windows, but not out in the country like this, on a campus this locked down.

"Yeah, but her bed's made up. No sign of a struggle—you a heavy sleeper?"

"Mm...yeah, not really? But Lizzie snores, so I wear earplugs." Jack had thought this all through and drilled the answers into him. Lizzie hadn't much liked the idea of telling people she did something as unseemly as snore, but she'd sacrificed her good reputation for the plan—in more ways than one.

Everett pulls on the window and it opens. "You unlock this?" Leigh shakes his head.

"There's two sets of footprints. One arrives, two leave. There's a lot of scuffle in the snow, too."

Leigh's not sure what he's thinking, but lets him do so.

"I take it you didn't see any of this."

Leigh shakes his head again. "I figured if she'd left, it was through the door like a normal human being."

"Yeah well, if you really don't want to be seen...wait, you didn't come by the window? How the hell did you not get caught walking over to my place?"

"Eh...just lucky?"

Everett shakes his head. "You're a pretty terrible delinquent, you know that?"

Leigh responds as they start walking, following footsteps in the snow, boots crunching with each step. "Don't usually get much of an opportunity," he says, "Jack's usually looking out for me."

"Well, take it from me, you don't want to get involved in things you shouldn't." His face is serious as they pass outside the lit circle of a streetlight. "You end up owing things to folks."

Everett pulls out a little keychain flashlight when the moon's not bright enough to see by. Leigh flinches each time, but they shouldn't run into anyone on their way—Jack's thought of that, too. The whole heist should take place in the window between the night guard's rounds.

"Well, I'm going to owe you for this one, Everett," Leigh says at length.

"Oh don't think you won't," he responds. "You better know how to peel and chop vegetables, is all I'm sayin'. 'Cause this is a kitchen-prep-level favor I'm doing for you right here."

Leigh groans but keeps trudging onward, following the footprints toward the little manicured grove in the farthest corner of campus. What they're supposed to find is Lizzie and Tina sitting on the bench, talking and sharing an against-the-rules cigarette. Neither breaking curfew nor smoking would get you expelled, at least not the first time, but both would land you in disciplinary action for a week at the least. Leigh would act surprised, they'd get a scolding, and Everett would send them on their way, hopefully doing them all a favor and keeping it secret.

Lizzie and Tina have, apparently, been improvising.

There's no smell of smoke when they step into the grove. When

Everett flicks on the flashlight the two girls are on the bench, but what they're doing isn't smoking. In the freeze-frame tableau of the flashlight, Tina has straddled Lizzie and has a hand on each of her cheeks as she kisses her.

Leigh's not sure who looks more surprised, him or Everett, but he's got a pretty strong suspicion it's him.

■ ■ ■

Everett closes the door to his suite, climbs the stairs, and sits down on his bed. His phone lights up and he opens it. An email has arrived.

Re: Your Assistance Requested

DF4F60204535D2E714DF@gmx.com 2:01 (0 minutes ago)
To: me

Your assistance is greatly appreciated.
Funds in the amount of 11.2 BCH have been deposited in your account.
I hope I can continue to count on your support in the future.

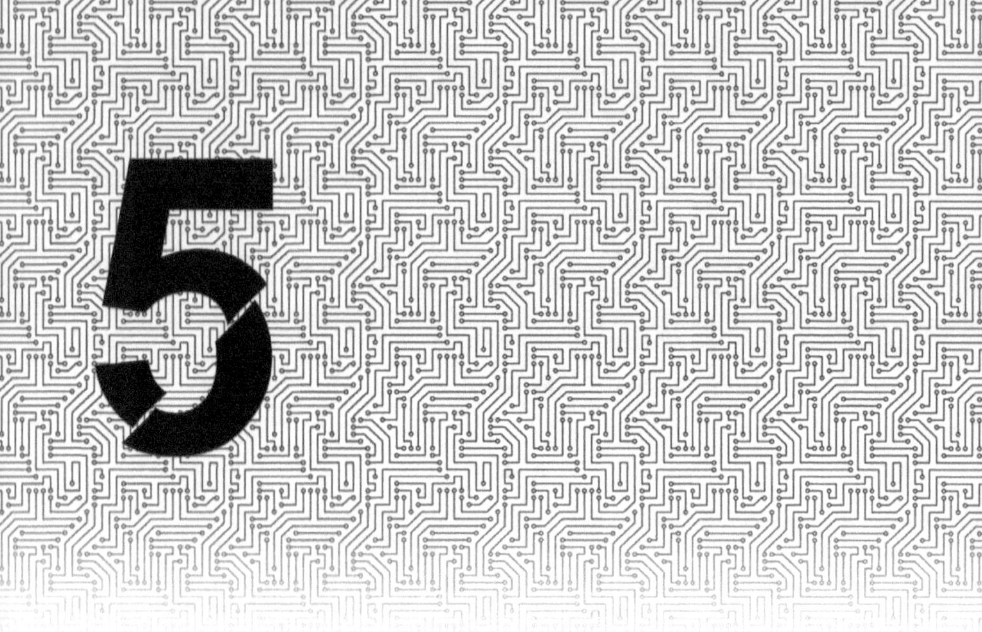

"You should've seen his face!" Lizzie's lying on her side on the riser, laughing as she tells Jack about the night before, their friend looking more serious than she's seen him in years. She shuts up for a second as a music teacher wanders in, eyes them suspiciously, asks them to keep it down, then wanders back out again—but she's back to laughing again the moment they leave.

The events of the night before had gone, well, as well as could be hoped. They'd been given an awkward-as-hell talking-to by Everett—"What y'all...*do*...in your free time is up to you. But if you're going to sneak out, you'd best get *better* at it, for cryin' out loud"—and then Tina had slipped off back to her room. Jack had texted a few minutes later to say he hadn't been caught, and that they'd reconvene at lunch in the music room. And here they are.

"Well it wasn't in the plan, that's all," Leigh says, his voice low, still sounding kind of peeved. "And also I didn't know you were Tina's type."

"She's not," Tina says quietly, tuning her bass. "I don't like girls."

"But—?"

"I just liked the way she asked," she replies, eyes closed as she plucks harmonics to test her work. She doesn't elaborate.

Lizzie sits back up, smirking. Leigh rolls his eyes.

"Well, it worked, and that's all that matters," Jack says, trying to keep them on track.

"It sure did," Lizzie says, grinning.

"Not th—you know what? We're going to talk about this later, you," Leigh says. "Bands have *rules*. But anyway." He turns to face Jack again. "You got what you needed?"

Jack nods. "I got something, anyway. First, he's definitely still working for Mr. Goldmark—the fact that he has current credentials for the VPN is proof enough of that—but I also found a few reports on us he'd filed since you got back." Whether or not the contents were relevant he doesn't share.

"Wait, you work for Pops," Lizzie says. "Do *you* file reports on us?"

Jack shakes his head slowly. "A few years ago he offered me a raise if I'd start, but I declined...I strongly suspect that's why I don't have my own access to the VPN."

Leigh folds his arms. "Sounds like Patton to me."

"Anyway, I think writing reports is all Everett's been up to, and I don't think he knows all that much, either. He knows who you are, but there's no evidence he knows much more than that. And in the VPN a lot of things were locked down, even for him. But there's one thing he did have access to that could come in handy." He hands Leigh a printout with a name and an address on it. "The directory."

Leigh reads the name. "Who's Nisha Mallik?"

"The woman in that photo I showed you, between my father and Mr. Goldmark."

"The scientist?" Lizzie asks.

"'Exobiologist' was the term Brenner used. Thing is, when Brenner talked about her, it was like he thought she was dead. But see this here?" He points at a line of text below that reads 'Asset:Form/Deac.' "Everybody in the directory had something like this. Asset categorization. The first letters were either "Curr" or "Form"—current or former—with the "Current" ones split up into "Act" or "Inac," and the "Former" ones all labeled "Deac," probably for deactivated. I checked my own record and I'm current and active, for instance." He doesn't mention that there's a flag on his record that he thinks means other employees shouldn't share info with him. Or that Leigh and Lizzie both have records that are completely locked down. "But there's another marker for dead. I checked my father's record just to be sure. His has the little dagger symbol next to it." Sure enough, below his father's name are the same words, but with an addition: 'Asset:Form/Deac.†.'

"So she might be alive?" Lizzie asks.

"I don't know. But if we've got questions about you and your...origins...she's probably our best chance for answers."

"Yeah, if she'll tell us anything."

"Okay, fine," says Leigh. "So say she's alive, and say she's fully *ex-Goldmark*, and say she does know about us. This says she's all the way in the city, and there's no contact info but her address. How are we ever going to get a hold of her?"

"I have an idea about that, too," Jack says. "I don't like it, but I think it might just work."

■ ■ ■

"This is a terrible idea," Lizzie stares down at the black and white flyer which, by now, should have been pasted up on telephone poles and mailboxes all over the city. In great big letters it reads SMELLS LIKE FISH! above a crudely-drawn and unrealistically-toothy fish skeleton, all superimposed over an American flag. Below it are a list of acts in diminishing levels of fame—or infamy: Jackhole City, Not Your Heartthrob, Vaderprez, Eye Teeth. And at the very bottom, in small, but definitely legible text, are the words 'Queer Young Punks.'

"Yep," Jack says.

"A terrible, terrible idea."

"I know."

They're standing in the hallway at the period change between first and second. It's only been three days since Jack suggested the plan, and the date on the flyer reads December 21. He's been busy over the weekend pulling things together.

"That's Friday," Lizzie says.

"Yes."

"It's Monday."

"You speak the truth."

"That's four days."

He knows.

"It's a five-song set at the start of a lineup so long that there'll be maybe five people besides us in the room. It's punk, they're all songs you've played before, Leigh knows all the words, and Tina's...well, she's very talented. It'll be fine."

"But that's not why we're *going*." She means that's not why she's *worried*.

The plan—such as it is—is relatively simple. After the set, they get to watch the rest of the show. It's at the vets' hall around the corner from their old neighborhood in the city, a charity gig to benefit the local Syria I and II vets. Punk or not, because it's 'for the troops' it's an Officially Sanctioned Activity, so the Academy's given them the green light to go. Then it's just a matter of Jack and Tina distracting whoever they send as a chaperone while Lizzie and Leigh sneak out for maybe an hour to go find the 'exobiologist' and hopefully get an answer or two.

"It'll work," is all Jack says.

"Who's the chaperone going to be though?" she asks.

"Does even a single adult at this school like punk? Whoever they are, it's a pretty safe bet they'll be waiting outside by the second set. You two can go out the back."

"And if they aren't?" she asks, but Jack doesn't get the chance to answer.

"Jack, my boy!" calls a voice from down the hall. Lizzie turns to see the man she now knows to be August Brenner. He wades his way through the student populace like a tweed-wrapped salmon swimming upstream. No, maybe not like a salmon, maybe more like a pike—something bigger, toothier. There's something about his enthusiastic grin that makes Lizzie want to swim for cover.

"Mr. Brenner," Jack says.

"Oh, come now, call me August. And you must be Lizzie." He puts his hand on her shoulder almost like a human being might do—but he's all fingertips and his touch, far too light to be at ease, nearly makes her shiver.

"I have to admit, Mr. Brenner, I'm a little surprised to see you. Here. At this school. *Still*." Jack puts space between his words, staring daggers at the supposed guidance counselor, who just smiles in return.

"Don't be like that, Jackie boy. I said if you *wanted me* to go."

"I want you to go," Jack says with ice in his voice.

Brenner fakes a pained expression, but his eyes are dancing. "Well, I will if it's what you really want, but it'll have to be at the end of the week. After all, I have a little extra-curricular chaperoning to do on Friday." He winks, and continues on down the hall, still talking. "Music, Jack! I didn't know you had it in you! See you Friday!"

And then he's gone.

"You have *got* to be kidding me," Lizzie stares after him as the period change crowds start to thin.

"It'll work." Jack's looking off into the distance, thinking of contingencies Lizzie can't even pretend to see. After a minute he snaps back to the present and looks at her. "Honestly? I was hoping for this."

But the way he says it makes her more nervous, not less, and she can't shake the feeling of Brenner's tarantula-light touch on her shoulder.

"I hope you're right."

"I'll make it work," he says, and Lizzie does her best to ignore all the things that could mean.

■ ■ ■

Lizzie only gets more nervous as the week rolls on. Not about the set, Jack was right about that much—her muscles remember the songs just fine and Leigh knows all the words. She even has to admit his new voice sounds pretty good, if maybe just a bit too much like Alice's for comfort. But it's the other half, the reason they're going, that leaves her jumping at shadows.

Maybe Leigh doesn't remember the way things were when they left the city, but she does—the kinds of people that just stopped being seen, the kinds of looks she used to get. The kinds of looks Leigh never noticed were being thrown his way. And now they're going to sneak out of a venue that—at least temporarily—will be one of the safest places in the city for them, in order to find their way across that city. At night. Even if they make it out without being noticed, their problems won't exactly be just the threat of expulsion if they're found out.

She wants to meet this doctor, wants to know about their past, about who they really are. But she feels like she's watching a thunderstorm building over their heads, the clouds towering higher and higher until the air goes dark, leaving her waiting under a skybound ocean to see if they'll end up drowning when it all comes down.

The ride into the city takes two of the longest hours of her life. Nobody wants to speak, not with Brenner just sitting there in the driver's seat, smiling away. Jack's up front, scowling out the window, and Leigh's got his headphones on, passed out to some million-decibel punk like it's a lullaby. She wants to smack him for being so relaxed, but she doesn't. It's not his fault. The same way she reacts to stress by hitting things, he withdraws, usually under a massive shell of false bravado.

Lizzie doesn't want to do any of this. Not the show, not the mission impossible crap, none of it. But if someone did this to her brother, did it on purpose, then they did it for a reason. And if that reason has to do with Alice, with what happened to Alice... There aren't any options. She's going to find this 'exobiologist.'

And she's going to get answers.

The van pulls up outside the Vets' hall and Brenner pops the locks. "All ashore that's going ashore!" he chirps, and slides out. Lizzie shakes her brother awake.

He peeks one eye open and lifts a can off one ear. "We here?" he mumbles.

"Yeah," Lizzie says. "Come on, we gotta set up."

■ ■ ■

The set goes well—as well as can be hoped. Jack's attendance estimate isn't too far off, either—Lizzie starts imagining tumbleweeds blowing between the six or seven cross-armed punks nodding along to 'Time Bomb.' But it gets better. By the end of 'Fall Back Down,' people are starting to wind their way into the small hall. By their final song, there's what could even be called a crowd in the place, a respectable collection of tattoos, ripped jeans, and spiked hair reminding her once again of why they used to do this. A older guy with a liberty hawk and a Good Night White Pride patch on his vest—the singer of the next act—high-fives Leigh as the final chord of 'I Wanna Be Sedated' still fights with the cheers of twenty-, thirty-, and forty-something punks.

"Classic set," he says. "Almost woke these geezers up." He hooks a thumb at the folks behind him. "We'll have to swap out fast to keep the energy up. Nice work!"

"Thanks!" Leigh's beaming, his smile brighter than the neon green hairspray he'd thrown on ten minutes before the show.

But the quiet smirk and watchful eyes of their chaperone, hands in his pockets and leaning against the back wall, remind them all that the hard part is yet to come.

"What do you think?" Lizzie says to Jack, pulling him off to one side and shouting into his ear over the sound of crashing symbols and thrashing guitars. It's been half an hour, and the crowd has swollen to the point that they almost can't see Brenner, but behind the swirling chaos of two dozen skanking, elbows-out punks he's still there. Still watching.

"I think I'm going to have to switch to plan B," he says, his face serious. "Wait until I've been gone for sixty seconds, but don't take the back. Go out the front, hang a left, and don't even think about coming back without some answers. You got it?"

"I don't like the sound of that," Lizzie says.

"And maybe you should take Tina, too," he says, ignoring her.

"I *really* don't like the sound of that. What are you going to do, Jack?"

But Jack's not listening. He's giving Brenner a thousand-yard stare instead. He turns back to face Lizzie and just says, "Sixty seconds," before walking down the side of the stage and out the propped-open fire exit into the alley. By the time Lizzie has looked back, Brenner's disappeared. She dives into the crowd to find Leigh.

■ ■ ■

"Didn't seem like you were enjoying yourself in there, Jackie-boy. Not really your scene, is it?" Jack's fishing around in the back of the van, the up-tempo banging muted to a distant hum in the stillness of the alleyway.

"I like it well enough," he says.

Brenner leans against the wall of the alley and takes a swig of something in a little flask before lighting up a cigarette. "Yeah, but you're not like them, are you Jack? You're not a resister or a sympathizer or a queer—despite the name of your little friends' band. You're a patriot, like your old dad." He takes a deep drag and lets out a cloud of smoke. "Not that I liked your old man much, but at least he had that going for him."

Jack doesn't say anything at the mention of his father, just undoes an interior zipper in the duffel and puts his hand around the cold metal of the handgun. This is Plan B.

"Jesus," Brenner sighs, "having a godawful thing like this in support of the troops." He spits. "Can't live with 'em, can't just throw 'em into camps, am I right? Not yet, anyway." He chuckles to himself, and Jack wonders exactly how much is left in that flask. "Well, at least they're not completely worthless, hey? The old pegleg manning the front desk says they've raked in a couple thousand bucks, maybe it'll get 'em some booze for the VA Christmas party."

Jack just lets him spew. There's probably nothing in the world the bastard likes more than the sound of his own damn voice.

Brenner finishes his cigarette and throws it to the street, grinding it out with his foot. "Well," he heaves himself back to vertical from where he was leaning and angles toward the door. "Best be getting back inside, don't you think?"

Jack turns to tell him no, but Brenner's already on him, trying to grab the gun out of his hands and wrestle it free.

Damn it, he's fast, and stronger than he looks—stronger than Jack expected; maybe the drunkenness was partly an act, but there's whiskey on his breath and his reflexes are just a little too slow to compete with the Slade family training regime. A twist and a shift of his weight and Jack's foot is behind his assailant's; a pull and a shove and Brenner's on his back in the alleyway, Jack staring down at him with a loaded gun.

Brenner sighs a cloud of white winter breath and chuckles.

"Looks like you got me," he says.

"Looks like."

They don't say anything for a minute, a faint wisp of late-December snow the only sign that it's even made it to winter in the city. Eventually Brenner can't take the lack of his own voice anymore and starts up again.

"So what now, Jackie boy? Gonna shoot me?"

Jack snorts. "You said I could. I'm considering taking you up on the offer."

Jack pulls a zip-tie out of a pocket and tosses it to Brenner. "Sit up, back against the wall. Tie up your wrists—in front of you so I can see them. Use your teeth and pull it tight."

Brenner complies. "But I think my question still stands," he says around the plastic of the tie, pulling it tight. "What now?"

Jack puts the gun in his pocket and slides down the opposite wall, making sure Brenner can see that it's still pointed at him.

"Now we sit and enjoy the evening air, like a couple of old friends."

■ ■ ■

The city's changed since they lived there, Leigh thinks, that's for sure. It looks at once cleaner and more dangerous. Maybe because it's practically empty.

"Where is everybody?" he says. It's not even nine and the streets have the feeling of a winter four AM, when the birds are still asleep and even insomniacs are too tired to go out. All the storefronts are closed and the convenience stores are either dark or empty of everyone except the person at the counter. Maybe it's the cold, or maybe it's just his imagination, but walking down the sidewalk he feels seen. Watched.

Off the main streets it feels a little more normal. The narrow brownstones have occasional lights in the windows, though the blinds are always drawn. Aside from the occasional car that passes by just a little too slowly, there's nothing but the low-level hum of the city and the slow flapping of flags on the lamp-posts. A sharp wind whistles down the brick and glass canyons and catches their cheeks and ears.

"Ow," Leigh says, hands pressed to the sides of his head. "Should've brought a hat or something." He looks at Lizzie and Tina, both of whom are wearing woolen hats, and feels extra foolish.

Lizzie just sighs and shoves hers onto his head. "I've got long hair," she says, "and yours is green."

"Frontman, come on," he says, straightening it. "Gotta look the part."

"Yeah well, you did," she says. "But now you have to look invisible." She looks him up and down. "At least your winter coat covers up some of the rest." Only his legs, still cold in ripped, skin-tight jeans, give a hint at their earlier activity.

"Well, I mean, it's not like there's anybody out here," he says. But he still has the feeling of being watched from darkened windows. As they cross a larger side-street a car passes by, then pulls a U-turn and stops alongside them. It's a police car. Leigh's stomach does a flip at the realization.

The window rolls down and the dome light pops on, revealing an officer in his early twenties, if even that. He hardly looks older than they are. "Bit late for you girls to be out alone, don't you think?" He smiles like an extra from a 1960s sitcom and Leigh tenses up, ready to bolt.

Instead, it's like someone's reached into Lizzie's head, found a switch marked *Leave It to Beaver*, and had the sheer audacity to flip it.

"Oh, hello Officer," she smiles, brushing a lock of hair behind her ear and leaning in closer. "Yes, we're just on our way home. We lost track of the time!" She bobbles her head as if to say 'Silly me!' and Leigh just stands in awe. Who is this person and what has she done with his sister?

"Well, you seem like nice girls, so I'll let you off with a warning. But you'd better get home quick. Don't want to be out past curfew. It's shelter-in-place after nine-thirty on orange days, remember."

Curfew? 'Orange days?' Leigh almost chokes.

"Oh, no! Is it that late?" She pulls out her phone and acts shocked. "Oh, goodness, thank you for stopping, Officer. I had no idea."

The officer's smile widens, and his apparent age decreases further, to something just adjacent to Lizzie's sixteen years.

"Well, just doing my job, really. Say, would you and your sisters like a ride? It's a pretty cold night, after all."

Lizzie smiles. "Oh no, we couldn't trouble you like that. We're nearly home, besides. But thank you so much, Officer...?"

"You can call me Jimmy," he says, beaming. "I just got assigned to this beat. If you girls live around here I'm sure you'll be seeing me again."

"Well, thank you again for your kindness...Jimmy," she says.

And 'Jimmy' damn near blushes.

"Hey, now—" he half-stammers. "Uh, it's just—how would you like my private line? You know, in case you um, you know, ever need a—a anything?"

Lizzie's eyebrows shoot up to the moon, but aside from that she doesn't break character a bit. "Well, it hardly seems—" she starts, but at the first sign of his wilting like an old bouquet she caves. "—well, it's just so sweet of you...okay," she says, coyly, and takes it down when he says it aloud.

"I just can't thank you enough for being so nice, Jimmy."

Leigh's cheeks are getting sore just watching the grin, but he's got to admit Jimmy's cute, if in a golden retriever sort of way.

"Anytime," the officer says. "You girls make sure you get straight home now, you hear?"

Lizzie smiles so sweetly Leigh thinks his teeth are going to rot just watching, but then Jimmy flips off the dome light and drives off, rolling up the window as he goes.

Leigh waits ten full seconds before grabbing his sister by the shoulders.

"Who *are* you?"

She rolls her eyes, at once back to herself.

"You're goddamn welcome."

He's about to ask her where she learned to do...whatever that was... when Tina speaks up.

"Getting back might be challenging," she says. She's scrolling through her phone. "There's an 'elevated threat level' tonight and tomorrow night."

"What the hell is that about? Is that what he meant by 'orange days'?" Leigh asks.

"I checked yesterday and it was fine," Lizzie says.

Tina shakes an "I don't know" with her head. "It just says 'due to specific threat information obtained by Homeland Security.'"

"Friggin' great," Lizzie says. "Well, too late now. Let's get on with it. Who knows, maybe she won't even be home and we'll make it back in no time." She sighs. "Or something."

They exchange dubious looks and Lizzie just shrugs. "Come on, it should be just around the corner."

Down the next side-street they hang a left and find the looming shadow of an old multi-story apartment block, hidden behind the pricier brownstones by clever geometry and the narrowness of the old city streets. The building had been built back in the last century, at a time when people thought you could make concrete better looking by pressing thousands of tiny pebbles into it. Leigh thinks it just looks like it's got some kind of cancer. To one side is a dimly-lit alcove between two security-glass doors.

There's a small aluminum keypad inside, with the surnames and apartment numbers of the residents scrawled on a piece of yellowing paper taped to it.

'Mallik' isn't listed.

Leigh fishes in a tight pocket for the scrap of paper Jack had given him. "This is the place," he says. "It should be apartment 306."

"So, what? Do we just call up?"

He shrugs and punches it in, even though the paper has the name 'Smith' next to that apartment. They wait while the speaker hisses out a janky ringtone, just a little too loudly for comfort. After eight or nine staticky chirps, there's a loud click. After a moment, a quiet voice says, "Hello?"

"Um, hi." Leigh says. "We're looking for Dr. Mallik?"

"I'm sorry," the voice says, altogether too quickly. "There are no doctors here."

Before she can hang up, Leigh responds. "She's not a doctor, she's an exobiologist!" he says. "And we kinda need one of those right now."

There's a long pause on the other end, so long Leigh thinks maybe the line's gone dead.

"Who is this?" comes the voice at last.

"I'm—it's—complicated—" Leigh starts, but Lizzie cuts him off.

"—Lizzie Goldmark," she says. "Dr. Mallik we need your help."

There's another long pause, and then the words "Come up" are cut off by the loud buzz and *clack* of the door unlocking. Leigh grabs it before it can lock again.

■ ■ ■

The apartment building looks even older on the inside than out. The industrial carpet on the stairs looks like it used to be red, but after decades of winters, the only parts that still show anything but mud-black track marks are the four-inch strips between the metal banisters. A child starts to cry as they pass a door on the third floor, but it's quickly hushed. They get the feeling that evening visitors—hell, maybe any visitors—aren't usually welcome here.

When they get to 306, Lizzie knocks.

The door cracks open, and half a face peers out for a moment before it closes again briefly to undo the chain. When it opens again, the figure behind it motions for them to come in and shuts the door behind them.

She turns a light on and stares at them, focusing on Lizzie.

"My god, it *is* you." She looks bewildered. She's older than the woman in the photograph, but it's unmistakably her. She's about Lizzie's height, brown skin, hair pulled back in a tight bun, thick-framed glasses sitting high on her nose. She's wrapped in a white woolen throw, and Leigh notices then how cold it is in the apartment. Not as bad as outside, but not too far off, either. Mallik stares at Lizzie until Leigh catches her eye, and her expression of amazement turns to one of shock. She reaches a hand out to touch Leigh's face, then stops.

"You can't be—"

"He isn't," Lizzie says. "It's weirder, and it's kind of a long story and we don't have tons of time—"

"Oh," she says distantly. Then, seeming to get her thoughts in order. "Then, come in. It's not much but, well, things are what they are these days."

She motions toward a couch, and pulls up a little footstool to sit on herself. "This is, well, it's quite a surprise, isn't it?" She half-laughs, still trying to wrap her mind around it. "I suspect you have things to tell me, given that you've tracked me down." She can't seem to keep her eyes off Leigh's face, and he can guess why.

"I'm not her," he says. "I'm sorry."

"No, you're not," she responds, examining his features. "You're Jamie, aren't you?"

It's their turn to be surprised.

"How—?" Leigh begins, but the doctor holds up her hand.

"First things first—who knows you're here?"

Lizzie looks at Tina and Leigh and then back to their host. "Just Jack," she says.

"How did you find this address?"

"Jack broke into the Goldmark VPN, it was in the directory."

Mallik stares hard at them, but says nothing.

"But you are Dr. Nisha Mallik, right?"

"Hnh," she says, "I used to think so. But just so that you know, Nisha Mallik is dead. She died in a car crash two years ago after deciding not to work for Pat—for your father—anymore. You're talking to 'Sarah Smith.'" She says it with a wry smile.

"You faked your death?" Tina asks, and their host finally seems to notice there are three of them.

"What? No. *Hell* no," she says, rolling her eyes. "Me, I quit a *job*. Next thing I know I get a text telling me not to get in a certain cab. Then a man on the street hands me an envelope with keys, an address, and a life as someone else, all while the previously aforementioned cab is slamming into a concrete barrier and catching fire on the turnpike. My credit cards all stop working, my death certificate is signed, I'm gone. Dead. But my money and a whole lot more besides is magically sent to new accounts under this new name. Driver's license, social security, birth certificate. She is me. I am 'Sarah Smith.'" She shakes her head. "Who by the way *doesn't* have a PhD in microbiology." She nearly growls as she says it. "Your father's a paternalistic bastard, is what I'm saying."

"What...why would he do that though?" Lizzie's mystified.

"Why does Pat do any of the damn things he does?" She sighs and stares out into some middle distance, and the past it contains. She stays silent long enough that Lizzie wonders whether she should say something herself, but at last 'Sarah Smith' comes back to the room. "He's just playing chess," she says. She almost sounds defeated.

Leigh leans forward. "What do you mean?"

She speaks slowly, like it's a big question she's still trying to figure out herself. "After it happened, I went and looked into it. Autopsy records can be faked, sure, but you put the right dollar bills in the right hands and you can get just about anywhere. Pat's...thorough, to say the least. There were real bodies. And there was one that had the same dental records as me—or had been made to look that way to anyone not looking closely." She stares off into the distance again. "That's what Pat's like."

"So what—"

"Let her talk," Lizzie cuts her brother off.

"Pat doesn't live his life in a vacuum. He can't. You get to know him, you start to see the way he thinks. You can almost be sure he found out that someone had decided I was a liability and was going to have me killed. Pat just made sure it only looked like me. I hate to think where he got the bodies…" Her eyes come back from wherever she's been looking, blinking away whatever she's been seeing and scowling as she speaks. "But he could've let me keep my damn degree." She whispers 'bastard' under her breath again.

"Wait but people would want you killed? Who? And why?" Leigh asks.

"He really has sheltered the hell out of you kids, hasn't he?" She takes a breath and lets it hiss out between her teeth. "So. You're here because you know about yourselves, at least the basics?" Leigh nods, and Dr. Mallik continues. "Well, there are maybe thirty other people in the world who know about you. The President?—I mean I guess that's what we're still calling him—*he* might not even know. And maybe three or four who know as much about your biology as I do. A woman with Code Word level knowledge? One you no longer have control over? And one who's *brown?*" She looks at them. "In 2018." She shakes her head. "Exactly how many people do you know who aren't white?"

Leigh shifts on the couch. "I mean we used to know more, but at the Academy there's pretty much just Everett."

"Let me guess…he works for the school?"

"He kinda does." Leigh says. "He also kinda works for Patton."

"And *there* it is." She looks at them hard, then sighs. "Of course you've got your own worries, and this sure as hell isn't the oppression olympics. But in answer to your question, I can think of at least half a dozen people in positions of power who would consider my continued existence enough of a threat to be worth 'dealing with.' Who knows *who* I'd tell the things I know?" The sarcasm drips from her voice and she rolls her eyes. "And of course you haven't had to find a job or an apartment yet, either. Part of the reason Pat stuck me in this…delightful apartment...is because the nice ones? They don't let people in who look like me much anymore, not in *this* city, anyhow. Well, unless they're VIPs—but that attracts a whole different kind of attention. The kind someone hiding might want to avoid."

"It's that bad?" Lizzie asks. "I'd heard rumors, but the way they've been cleaning the search results on the net..."

"It's bad enough. It'll probably get worse before it gets better, too." She sighs. "There're cases making their way through the courts, but they're piling up. Honestly it'll be years before anything changes, and that's if we win and they find the Emergency Powers Act unconstitutional...But—!" she slaps her hands down on her knees. "This isn't why you came."

"In a way it is," Lizzie says. "We need to know about this stuff, about Pops and...and all the things nobody would tell us. Things...things he might've done."

Dr. Mallik looks confused for the first time that evening, but neither Lizzie or Leigh are able to actually ask the question. Tina breaks the impasse.

"What happened to Alice?"

The look on the woman's face changes then, softens. "Oh hell, kids." She searches their expressions. "For real? *That's* why you found me? You think Pat would have—oh no. No, oh, please don't blame him for that. He's a selfish bastard and pretty basic failure of a human being some...most days, but he—we—we all did our best. For Alice, for all of you. You have to believe that." Her eyes are looking for something in their faces, something they don't find.

"Well, what happened?" Leigh asks. "We don't even know that much. And with this happening?" He motions at his face and body. "Which is what, by the way?" He looks down. "We need to know...and we didn't know if we could ask Patton."

Dr. Mallik sighs, still looking back and forth. "All right, well. Your father isn't a killer. He just isn't. But he is an amoral pragmatist at times, and doesn't have a whole lot of choice in working for, well, for the kind of people that eventually made me quit. How much do you know about the history of Goldmark Enterprises?"

Lizzie shrugs as if to say "Not much."

"Then you need to know some history, but first—" she gets up as she speaks "—you want some tea? English Breakfast is all I've got, but the rad's been broken for 36 hours, as you might've noticed by the fact that damn space heater can't keep up, and boy do I need something warm." She rubs her hands together and looks over her guests, who are all still wearing their outdoor clothes, though at some point Leigh had taken off Lizzie's hat. Dr. Mallik keeps speaking, as if somehow compelled to defend their father.

"Pat does frustrating, inconvenient things sometimes—this apartment being one of them—but he doesn't do anything without a good reason. I'm here because this is the safest place he could find. I don't have a degree because it's his way of telling me to change jobs and avoid the professional contacts I knew. Heavy-handed and paternalistic as hell, but not exactly hard logic to follow." She wanders back from the kitchen as the kettle starts to rattle on the stovetop. She's carrying an old shoebox.

"You trust Pops that much, huh?" Lizzie says.

"I...trust him to be himself," she says, sitting back down and drawing the woolen throw back around herself in the chilly apartment. "That's probably enough." She opens the box and fishes around for an old, red photo album, which she hands over to Lizzie. "I had to keep something," she says. It sounds like an apology.

The plastic is old, old enough to have been around since people actually used film cameras, back from when they were kids. Inside are mostly photos of two adults and three toddlers, in various arrangements ranging from posed portraits to chaotic scenes of random family life. That's what they look like: a family. Except the adults in the photos are their father and the woman in front of them. And the children—

"This is us. Holy crap this is us—" Leigh says.

"How old are we? You...*did you raise us?*" Lizzie interjects.

Dr. Mallik smiles. "For a couple of years, anyhow. You were, pretty obviously, too young to remember. Pat and I volunteered. Well," she laughs, "no, *I* volunteered *us*. It didn't last, and it was decided that my involvement was—or rather wasn't—" she doesn't really finish the thought, just looks hard at them, and forces a smile. "You know, it's good to see you again. Even like this. Even if the fact that you're here probably means things are moving in a worseward direction."

She doesn't say more on the matter, just reaches forward and flips to a photo near the back. They're all crowded into what looks like a kitchen with a few extra people, and there's a champagne glass in every hand. "This is the day he founded Goldmark Enterprises. He'd been researching some of the technology at the site—you know about the test site?"

They nod. "Dimensional portal thing?" Leigh offers.

"Yes—well, no, the portal came later—at first it was called the Displacement Engine. It was supposed to be a bomb, to just destroy everything in a certain radius. But instead it swapped a sphere of our universe for a sphere of the Primeverse. The portal project, the stable gateway, that never worked," she says.

"Primeverse?" Leigh asks, and "—wait, they tried to *make* a portal?"

She waves her hand. "Hold on, yes, they did, but give me a minute. I'll get there, I promise." She takes a breath and resets. "'Primeverse' is a math joke, because Pat is...like that. 'A-prime,' or 'B-prime,' in set notation, would mean 'the set of things not in set A' or 'not in set B.' He said 'you had to be there,' but I *was* there, and...yeah." She shakes her head. "Anyway, at this point, Pat had taken some of the circuits from the incubators and figured out how they worked. They were...so *advanced*. Just, whole decades ahead of where we are even now. But your father's a genius, in some ways, and managed to understand—well, not how to make them, that's still beyond us, but at least how to use their basic design principles to make what we did have better. As a part of the plan to give the military a leg-up on their competitors, he'd been allowed, or maybe instructed, to make a company to sell the developments to our military contractors, so we could make better weapons or—have you seen those holographic heads-up displays they're using these days?" She sighs. "After the Displacement Engine failed, your father swore not to work on making weapons anymore. But apparently that didn't extend to not working on making better soldiers."

The kettle whistles from the kitchen and she gets up and fetches the tea.

"He'd always had money. His mother came from Polish aristocracy, so it's not like he ever wanted for much, but after he founded the company he was...well, he could do as he pleased." She puts down the tray on an old coffee table. "But the military isn't a monolith, and everybody wants a piece of the pie. And the Primeverse was a place some of them wanted to go. Think of it: a whole planet that only we could trade with. One full of high-tech things."

She puts a cup in front of each of them and pours. "At first they didn't even know where to begin. But Pat—well you know what he's like when he gets an idea in his head. He decided that it was impossible that the Displacement Engine had just connected to a random point in the other universe. He said universes are almost entirely empty space, and the odds of it not simply capturing a sphere of interstellar vacuum were just far too low. So he started looking for something at the site that might've acted like a magnet for the reaction. Sugar?"

Tina nods at the sugar-bowl. "Two please."

"We looked at the technology first, but there was nothing there I could see. I looked at every plant species, too. Then at you—"

"It was Alice, wasn't it?" Leigh says, interrupting.

"Something inside her, yes," she nods. "You three, you aren't just human."

"But we are still kinda-sorta human? I thought we like...hatched." Lizzie says.

"Oh you're human. About as human as they come. There's no more variation between your DNA and mine than between mine and anyone else's here. But you've got something else. Humans plus. You've got nanomachines."

"Tiny robots." Tina explains, seeing the siblings' confusion.

"Very tiny," Mallik says, nodding. "Self-replacing, self-repairing." She turns back to Lizzie and Leigh. "You don't get sick very often, do you?"

"Come to think of it..." Lizzie says.

"Except for when this happened," Leigh says. "I've never been sick like that."

"Well, no, and you shouldn't have been." She shakes her head, suddenly angry. "That was never, ever supposed to happen. Pat would *never* have done that to you. He knew how dangerous it was."

"How dangerous *what* was? What *did* they do to me?"

"So, okay." She takes a breath, trying to figure out where to start. "We'd determined that Alice was the key. Something in her genome was reacting with her nanomachines in resonance with the Displacement Engine, acting like an anchor for the disruption to latch onto. But they couldn't figure out why it would do that with her and not you." She cradles her teacup in her hands, thinking of where to go. "Do you know that you and Alice weren't just twins, but identical twins?"

"Okay, no, but also...that makes zero sense? I'm a, I mean, I *was*—"

"Of course. You weren't identical in the usual sense. Your X chromosome was identical to one of hers, but you had a Y chromosome, instead of another X. That made, well, quite a lot of difference. As it does. If I had to hazard a guess as to why...it might just be easier, if they want a boy and a girl, to mimic and tweak the natural twinning process? Honestly, their technology must be so incredibly advanced, and without knowing more about it, it's hard to say."

"So...wait...then why Alice and not me? With the resonance thing you were talking about? What was the difference?"

"My theory was that there was something in her genetic makeup that...You know what? I don't really know. But I'd theorized that whatever caused the resonance could have been suppressed prenatally by your Y chromosome, but it was just a theory."

"And the portal project, you called it? That was them trying to use that resonance to, what, open a door? To the ...Primeverse? The place we came from?" Lizzie asks.

"Opening the door was easy enough, but it seemed to open at random points. Dangerous points, usually. As in 'the vacuum of deep space' dangerous. There are a lot more places in a universe you don't want to open a doorway to than ones you do. No, once Pat had figured out the math, they could *open* the portal with relative ease. The idea was to use Alice to *aim*."

"But you said the portal never worked?" Lizzie says.

"Mm," Dr. Mallik says, and stares off into the distance. "And I don't know why."

"What do you mean?"

"I wasn't there," she says. "The day it happened, I wasn't there." She puts her teacup down. "The day Alice died was the last time they tested the portal."

■ ■ ■

"I'm gonna freeze to death out here, Jack, come on."

"I could just shoot you, if you'd prefer to speed up the process." The cold of the winter asphalt has seeped through his jeans and is working on numbing all sensation below his waist. He drags himself to a crouch, making sure to keep the pocketed pistol trained on his companion.

"Don't be like that. I thought we were on the same side."

"You know as well as I do that the only side you've ever been on is your own."

Brenner sighs. "So what's the play here, Jack? I assume our assets are on a fact-finding mission? Despite what you might think, I'm not a complete fool."

Jack snorts. "As much as I'd like to disagree with you on that last point, no, you're not. Which is why I'm not telling you a damn thing about why we're sitting here."

"Okay then, Jack. I'm going to just do a little talking then, and you can stop me if any of this starts to sound familiar."

Jack rolls his eyes, but Brenner keeps going.

"You don't want to take my word for it. All the things I told you, they're pretty wild, right? And the test site. And the photos. But you can't ask Goldmark. No point in asking me. So you go digging. 'Trust but Verify,' like Reagan used to say. Maybe you spoof a login on the Goldmark VPN? Find someone down here to pay a visit to? Maybe you do a little rock and roll for charity to get an excuse to come down. Not a bad plan. There aren't many people in the city who know much, but I can think of a couple who might know at least something." He shuts up for a second as someone bumps against the door, but it's a false alarm and no-one comes out. "But you got a couple of things wrong, Jack. First, nobody on that very short list is going to tell your little friends a damn thing. Second, even if you knew that, you're the only one capable of a decent break-and-enter. And third, if I've thought of all this—" he pauses overdramatically "—then so has Goldmark."

Jack scowls at him, but has to admit he has a point.

"What's the time, Jackie boy?"

He checks his watch and answers. "Nine thirty."

"Well then," he says. "Time's up."

■ ■ ■

"I was in Berlin for a conference," Dr. Mallik says. "I can't even remember what I was presenting on. I wanted them to postpone the test, but Pat had reasons, good ones, to press ahead with it. I got word just after my presentation that the test had failed. They didn't tell me about Alice until I landed three days later."

"But Alice got sick—"

"Alice was already sick by then. We still don't know why. We think maybe it—well, we don't know. But Pat—" she closes her eyes "—he was so sure that they could fix her, the people in your world, if only he could get her back there." She takes a deep breath, lets it slip out in silence. She looks like she's going to say more, but doesn't, so they all sit in the apartment as their tea gets colder. An old clock twangs the half hour.

"They wouldn't let us see her. After she got sick," Lizzie says.

"They were afraid you'd catch whatever it was she had. Some defect in her nanomachines, we thought. A computer virus, maybe." She sighs. "When she died, he was...you probably couldn't see it, because that's just how he is...but he was beside himself. Threw his weight around like I'd never seen, pulled in all his favors, shut everything down. Wouldn't even let them do an autopsy. Sealed her away where they couldn't get to her ever again. The experiments stopped and no-one was allowed near either of you, ever, or they'd face the full wrath of J. Patton Goldmark." She looks at Leigh, then, slowly shaking her head. "Whoever did this to you is either incredibly foolish, or incredibly powerful."

"And what, exactly, did they do to me?" Leigh asks. "Or, how?"

"One of the more...ambitious...scientists working on the portal project, early on, wrote a report to the effect that it might be possible to reprogram your nanomachines to replace your Y chromosome with a copy of Alice's second X. He'd claimed that the machines were designed to 'optimize' gene expression and so they'd naturally express those genes in the same distribution..." she trails off, realizing she's losing them. "Basically he thought they'd rewrite your genetic code to be identical to hers. The point being, we could have two lenses—sorry that's what they called Alice, a 'lens,' for the way they could use her to focus the gate. Anyway, I shut that down immediately. There was no telling what kind of havoc that would cause, what effects it would have on you. Even if you just swapped out the chromosome there was no guarantee of his 'optimization' theory, no way we could know if it would have predictable consequences—there are sexually male people out there with two X chromosomes, after all, and the SRY gene's physical effects are felt *in utero*, so..." She shakes her head, trying not to get into the weeds again. "There was no guarantee that it'd do what they wanted it to. It could have killed you, and there was zero guarantee that it would produce anything *like* the results they wanted. We didn't know anywhere *near* enough, of the risks or the potential benefits. Patton would never have let someone do this to you. Never. And yet...here you are."

"Holy crap," Leigh says.

"Is that how you knew?" Lizzie asks. "That he wasn't Alice?"

"In part, yes. But there was also something I couldn't put my finger on—"

"Asymmetry," Tina interjects. "Leigh's face is reversed."

Dr. Mallik's eyebrows shoot up and she starts peering closely at Leigh's face.

"Jack showed me her photo," Tina says into her teacup. "Her left ear was a tiny bit higher. Dimple on the left, too. With Leigh it's the right."

"I thought something looked a little different, but I couldn't put my finger on it!" Lizzie says, joining Dr. Mallik in peering at Leigh's face, while he puts his hands on his ears. "I just thought it was 'cause you're older."

"Too close!" Leigh says, backing away. "But no," he says, "I look *exactly* like—"

"—in a mirror," Lizzie says. "You've only seen yourself in a mirror."

Dr. Mallik is up and across the room in an instant, digging through a drawer in an old sideboard, pulling out a well-worn notebook. She starts flipping through and mumbling to herself excitedly.

"How did you notice?" Lizzie asks Tina.

"I'm...good at details," she says, not explaining.

"This is amazing," Dr. Mallik says, leaning against the sideboard, nose in her notebook. She looks five years younger when she pulls it away, eyes lit up with manic curiosity. She flips back around and digs in another drawer, pulling out a stethoscope and striding over to Leigh. "Untuck. I need to check."

Leigh backs away. "Check what?"

"Alice was right-handed, wasn't she, and you're left-handed..."

"I've always been left-handed."

"So that doesn't tell us much...right then: shirt up. I need to see."

"See *what?*"

"Where your *heart is*. It's cold in here, you don't need to take your shirt off. But untuck and turn around, I need access to your back."

Leigh's so confused by the request that he does as he's told while the others watch.

"Take a breath. Let it out slowly." She moves the stethoscope and repeats the request several times. After a moment she withdraws, eyes wide and shaking her head. *"Situs inversus.* Your heart's on the right. I wouldn't be surprised if it's complete and everything's reversed, spleen on the right, liver on the left." She sits down on the couch and shakes her head. "This is astonishing. Why on *Earth*...?"

"I'm *backwards?"* Leigh says.

"Well, we knew that," Lizzie says.

"This is no time for levity, sister dear—"

"We *didn't* know that." Dr. Mallik interrupts. "You weren't, not before. Trust me, the tests I had to do, I would've known. My god, the machines...they've completely rebuilt you. They reassembled huge parts of you from *scratch.*" Something in her voice makes them all quiet for a moment. "This..." She trails off.

"I don't know how you're alive."

■ ■ ■

"What do you mean time's up?" Jack doesn't want to ask, doesn't want to give Brenner the pleasure, but he has to.

"Curfew's in effect."

"Curfew?"

"Credible threat, blah-dee-blah, probably a cover for a raid on some resisters. Still, you don't want to be out."

Damn it, he thinks. Why didn't he think to check. "They'll find a way to sneak back."

Brenner sighs. "Grab my phone," he says. "Left coat pocket. Can't quite get to it with these on."

Jack walks over, carefully slips the phone out of Brenner's pocket and steps back.

"Four three oh one six."

"Really? 4/30/16? Jesus you're a creep, Brenner."

His only response is, "Open the 'Manta' app."

The screen flashes up a nondescript logo and then a few seconds later a map of the city with a blinking blue dot. He zooms in to confirm his fears—it's Dr. Mallik's address.

"The hell? You lojacked them?"

"Not I, said the fox." He smiles.

"What?"

"I'm just hijacking the signal. You think a control freak like Goldmark is going to just let them out in the wild without a way of tracking them down? I'm surprised he didn't put a chip in *you*." He laughs once, a short, sharp sound that echoes in the alley. Jack just stares at him.

"Look, I'll spell it out for you: I'm not concerned about your little friends being seen on their way back," he says. "Quite the opposite. I'm concerned that someone else—maybe the same someone elses who did what they did to Jamie—might have the same resourcefulness as you or I. I'm concerned that, with the curfew in effect, they'll take advantage of the fact that there *won't be any witnesses*."

Jack curses under his breath, then hauls Brenner to his feet. He leaves his wrists tied and holds the passenger door open for him. "Get in the van," he says. "I'm driving."

■ ■ ■

"How would someone do it?" Tina asks. "Reprogram the nanomachines."

Dr. Mallik shakes her head. "Well it wouldn't be quick, I can say that much. Maybe three or four hours, bare minimum, and that's with some pretty specialized equipment, too. When I left, we didn't even have the technology to properly interface with the nanomachines. I can't imagine with a transmitter further away than...maybe three feet? That might not even be close enough."

"So whoever did it had to be under three feet away from Leigh for three or four hours."

"So wait," Lizzie starts, "that means someone planted some pretty large tech—?" She looks at Dr. Mallik, who nods "—in your bedroom at the Academy and did it while you slept?"

"Remind me to check under my bed for monsters from now on," Leigh says. "Unless you can think of another place they could've—"

But he doesn't get a chance to finish the question.

First Lizzie's phone pings. She looks down at it and back at the rest of them. "Jack's on his way," she starts to say. "Brenner's with him. He says we're being tracked and that we shouldn't—" but the rest is cut off by the loud banging of fists on doors and a booming voice shouting: "THIS IS THE POLICE! OPEN THE DOOR!"

MALLIK PUTS A FINGER OVER HER LIPS AND MOUTHS THE WORDS 'Stay quiet,' then walks to the door and speaks through it, peering through the peephole.

"Hello?" she says. "Who's there?" She asks it as though it were even possible not to have heard. She waves for Leigh, Lizzie, and Tina to go into the kitchen, but Leigh peers around the corner anyway.

A man's voice is forcing its way into the room, hardly softening for passing through two inches of wood.

"Police, ma'am. We've received reports of a disturbance and require entry to this address."

"Well *that* doesn't sound sketchy at *all*," whispers Leigh, who's immediately shushed by his sister.

Mallik starts to negotiate through the door, explaining that she's not comfortable opening it; then explaining that yes, she's a citizen; then asking for a warrant—which is met by a telling silence on the other side. Leigh swipes his sister's phone and dials a number in the address book.

"What are you doing? Stop—" but Leigh puts his hand over her mouth.

"Hi—no, no this is her—" he squeezes his eyes tight as he says it

"—*sister*, yeah. Yeah. *Hi*, Jimmy." He keeps his voice as quiet as he can. It's Lizzie's turn to stare. "She didn't want to call, 'cause she's shy and didn't want to trouble you, but—" Lizzie nearly bites his hand and he pulls it back. "But, see, these weird men are at the door to our mom's place? And they say they're police but they seem really fishy." He pauses, waiting for a response. "Yeah, 27 Auburn, number 306." Another pause. "For real? Okay, I'll make sure. Thank you so much. Please, come as quick as you can." The voice behind the door is starting to shout. "She asked for a warrant and they don't seem very happy about it. Yes. Okay. Thank you."

He hangs up and hands the phone to Lizzie. "This rings, you answer," he says.

"You called the *cops*?" she says, incredulous. "The last thing we need is more—"

"I called '*Jimmy*,'" he interrupts, and she rolls her eyes. "Look, it's too convenient. Those guys out there? He says they're not cops. Not even in the system."

"Crap."

A loud banging starts echoing through the apartment and Dr. Mallik rushes into the kitchen. "I need your help with this." Negotiations have apparently broken down.

"They're not cops," Leigh says.

"You *think?*" Dr. Mallik grabs a large sofa chair and between them they shove it down the short, narrow hall and up against the door that looks more likely to give with every bang.

"Well okay, then who the hell are they?" Leigh asks, helping shove an old but very heavy sideboard in front of the chair.

"If I were a betting woman," she says between heaves, "I'd say they're the ones who did this to you—or at least they're being paid by them. You said Jack's on his way? I'm glad you stuck together all these years, but he's not going to be enough."

"Yeah well," Lizzie says, "somebody here called the real cops."

Dr. Mallik doesn't even look at him, just mutters something about privileged little white kids getting them all killed.

"I didn't call *the cops*," Leigh says, trying to defend himself, "I called *a cop*. He's bitty and he's got the hots for Lizzie. I just figured—"

"And how're you going to feel if these guys shoot him?" Dr. Mallik says, turning to face him.

"What?"

She shakes her head. "Even if he's a good guy—and I'm not saying there aren't some still hiding somewhere, even now—this isn't an action movie, and we're sure as hell not some kind of heroes. The men out there aren't playing around. They look like they're out of a damn SWAT team for crying out—" She stops herself, trying to calm down as the slamming in the living room gets louder and louder. "Look. Text your little policeman 'friend' and tell him *we're running away*." She's already grabbed a coat and is ushering them toward the tall kitchen window, killing the lights on the way. "Tell him that if he really wants to help, he can drive around the block with his siren going, maybe spook them into being careless, okay?" She pulls a pair of latches and hauls the whole window out of the pane, letting a whoosh of freezing air rush in around them. She drops it in the kitchen and looks down the narrow fire escape beyond, whispering a thank you to whatever gods are listening that nobody's already on their way up.

"Go," she says. "When you get to the bottom, stick close to the building and head left. I'll be right behind you."

■ ■ ■

"Pull over!" Brenner says. "Now! Turn off the van!"

Jack swerves over and kills the engine and lights in one fluid motion. They'd both seen the blue of the approaching strobe lights flashing against the neighboring buildings.

The police car emerges from the alley in front of the apartment and pulls left as they duck down in their seats to avoid being seen. After pausing for a moment in front of the building, the car starts up again and pulls another left around the far side, letting out a series of plaintive whoops as it rounds the corner. The moment it's out of sight, its siren rises into a long, piercing whine.

"This is the place, huh." Brenner says.

"Yeah."

"Ain't that a peach."

From the sound of it, the police car's doing slow laps around the block. Jack wonders if they're waiting for backup or what.

A voice squawks into life next to him and he nearly jumps. Brenner's got the phone in his still-bound hands, and has opened what sounds like a police scanner app.

"You hear that?" Brenner says.

"Hear what?"

"Exactly."

Jack realizes he's right: there are a number of reports back and forth—he catches the code for a resolved domestic and someone asking if they're "Clear for a ten"—but nothing like this, and, more importantly, nothing in this part of the city. Everything about the situation is wrong.

Just then a series of shadows corner the building. It's Leigh, Lizzie, Tina, and—Jack can only assume—Dr. Mallik. He gets out of the van and waves; they need to get out of there before the police car can make it back. There's a zipping near his head, then a sound like a whipcrack echoes off the buildings above him while a metallic *ping-thwack* snaps at him from behind.

Brenner dives out the passenger door yelling something incoherent. The zipping noise comes again, but this time he feels it before he hears it: the bullet pushing air out of its way just inches from his face. He dives back into the van and follows Brenner out the other side, slamming the door behind them and ducking down behind it.

Someone's shooting at them.

■ ■ ■

Dr. Mallik yanks Leigh back from the edge of the grass and into the deep shadow of a second-story balcony. Within seconds the firecracker snaps have stopped bouncing off the neighborhood's hard surfaces and the faint whistle of the winter wind has once again resumed its eerie dominance. Even the police siren has silenced for now. Only the sound of their breathing competes.

"They're *shooting* at us!" Shock and indignation almost push Leigh's whisper into a shout.

"Where are they?" Lizzie says. The apartment's on the other side of the building, and they haven't been followed down the fire escape... "Maybe the roof?"

Leigh pulls out his phone. He's about to call Jack, who's hunkered down behind the van with Brenner, when he sees the notification and opens the email.

Information of Potential Relevance

D78DF185436E25D7ED3C@gmx.com   10:06 (3 minutes ago)
To: me

The design specifications and materials of the model year 2016 Ford Transit Connect wagon are not consistent with bullet resistance.

Three minutes ago. The van.

Leigh's eyes go wide.

"What now?" Lizzie asks.

"Another email," Leigh says and he dials Jack's number, frantic. He only starts breathing again when Jack picks up.

"Jack! Are you okay?"

"Well someone's shooting at us, but other than that we're just great. Having a ball." He drops the sarcasm. "But I think we're safe back here. We're on the ground. I can actually see you from under the van."

When he looks, Leigh realizes he can see a bluish glint from Jack's phone by the wheel.

"Okay," Leigh says, thinking—what's Betza saying then? What's he suggesting? "Well you're not safe back there. That van's not bullet-proof."

"How do you know—"

"They must be missing on purpose," Leigh says, more to himself than Jack. "Why would they be—"

"What are you talking about?" Lizzie tries to interrupt, but he ignores her.

Before anyone can stop him, he shoves the phone in his pocket. "You stay here." He sprints toward the van.

■ ■ ■

Jack nearly panics when he sees Leigh run toward him across the street, then stop short and shrink down to a ball as another whipcrack report rings out. But the puff of pulverized asphalt is miles off target, and he realizes what Leigh's trying to say—they're not just missing, they're actively trying *not* to hit them. Which means—

"Run!" he yells. "Get to the van! Now!"

But it's too late, the gunshots meant to delay them have had the intended effect, and two black-clad men are sprinting at them from the other side of the building. Leigh starts to run.

"Get up!" Jack yells at Brenner.

"And get dead? No thanks!"

Jack almost growls out the word "Fine" and makes a dash for Leigh. He almost reaches him before one of their attackers gets there first and twists Leigh's arm behind his back. Without thinking, Jack throws himself at them both, shoulder first, sending them all to the ground in a heap—but his success is short-lived. Jack's field of vision explodes into stars as their assailant wrests an arm free and slugs him in the side of the head with a fist like concrete. He tries to hold him down but he's not exactly sure which way down is, and before he knows it the man is standing over him, one arm around Leigh's neck, and the other pointing a handgun at the side of his captive's head.

"Everybody stay cool," says the man, mouth hidden behind a black mask. The only thing showing below his helmet is a pair of cold eyes. "Put your hands up."

Jack hauls himself to his feet and does as he's told. Across the street, Lizzie's down on the ground and the other two are sitting on the curb, hands on their heads, with a gun trained on them. In the panic he'd left his in the van; he curses under his breath. So much for the Slade family training.

"You, too!" the man says in the direction of the van.

"Not a chance, bozo!" comes the retort. "Rule one of not getting shot is not standing up."

The man looks over at his partner and scowls, the points the gun at Jack. "Back up, toward the van," he says.

The three of them move in this way—Jack backing up, the man dragging Leigh along, kicking feet almost in the air—until they're just about in front of the van.

"Get. Up." the man says. It's not up for debate.

There's a sigh from behind the van. "All right, all right," comes the voice.

Then in one motion Brenner stands up, raises his hands, and shoots Leigh's captor in the head. Both go down in a heap but Leigh frees himself from the now-limp arm and scrambles up over to Jack immediately.

"Is he dead?" There's no blood, maybe it just hit his helmet. Or maybe it didn't make it out the other side.

Brenner doesn't get a chance to answer. A second shot rings out, another whipcrack from above, sending Brenner flying backward. This time there's blood.

Jack doesn't even have time to run over before the bullets start raining down in earnest. Running on nothing but instinct, he grabs Leigh and makes a mad dash to the building, despite the other attacker being there.

Even with only his eyes showing, the guy looks as though whatever this operation was supposed to be, it's all gone completely to hell and he's trying to figure out exactly how to bail. The decision's made for him when the police car comes screaming around the corner, lights flashing and siren blaring. He bolts away and around the building.

The young police officer pops open the door and runs over to help Tina and Dr. Mallik drag Lizzie to the car, helping them in as shots ring out on the pavement.

"Just get in!" he yells at Jack and Leigh.

"Brenner's been shot!" Jack yells back, though he's not sure exactly at whom. He's trying to get back behind the van but keeps being headed off by bullets on the road's surface. A piece of chipped stone or maybe a bullet fragment ricochets up, slicing sideways through his calf and pulling his leg out from under him.

The officer and Leigh grab Jack under the arms and drag him backward.

"Get *in!*" The officer insists. "It's not exactly bulletproof but it's a hell of a lot better than nothing." They throw him in the passenger seat, dive into the car themselves, and drive off leaving the sound of screeching tires behind them.

And leaving Brenner's body, too.

■ ■ ■

The doctor scowls while he stitches up Jack's leg in the small clinic room off the ER. Whatever had hit him hadn't gone in deep and he'd thrown some tape on it in the car; but when the doctor had seen the tear in his jeans and the shadow of blood he'd demanded a look. He isn't buying Jack's excuses, but he doesn't have either the time or the interest to push for the truth. Jack goes over the evening's events in his head while the doctor works.

It doesn't add up. Why would they avoid shooting anyone and then kill Brenner? By now there's no doubt in his mind that Brenner's dead. He grimaces at the realization that the old snake has finally joined the rest of his father's unit, then pushes the thought down to where he keeps old grudges and uncharitable feelings. Brenner's dead, but he can't figure out why. Was he expendable from the beginning, or did having one of their men go down like that make their rooftop gunner panic? Brenner must've grabbed Jack's gun when he'd left it in the van.

Now his body's in the street behind their bullet-riddled ride.

And he's holding a gun with Jack's fingerprints all over it.

And they'd *literally been picked up by the cops.* He tries not to get angry at the absurdity of it all.

Lizzie had been pretty dazed when they'd arrived at the hospital; it was the reason they'd even gone. Apparently she hadn't given their attacker much choice but to fight her and had taken a pretty hard blow to the head. Meanwhile 'Jimmy the Cop' had stayed by her side until she could sit up on her own—spending the time interrogating Leigh and Tina in concerned tones while Jack waited in a small side-room for someone to come stitch him up. He'd caught a glimpse of the cop heading out, probably back to the waiting room to grill 'Sarah Smith.' Jack's pretty sure the next stop for all of them is going to be the station.

Or at least it would've been.

As the doctor ties a stitch, the door cracks open and there's Jimmy the Cop, sliding into the room. He doesn't look happy, but he stands back and waits for the doctor to finish, folding his hands behind him in a poor attempt to hide his impatience. When the doctor leaves, the cop closes the door and speaks in a low but forceful tone.

"Okay just who the hell *are* you kids?" he says.

Jack blinks and raises his eyebrows. Of course he'd come in here and ask him, Jack thinks. Want soft info? Talk to The Girls. Got a real problem? Talk to The Man. He tries not to roll his eyes. "Sorry?"

"I know your names, sure. And you go to some shi-shi private school out in the sticks, which means you're not hurting for cash, but—" he stops and puts a hand to his forehead. "Lizzie and her sister's IDs—"

"Brother's."

"What?" Sheer exasperation pokes through his angry confusion.

"Leigh's a guy," Jack says, "so: brother."

"What? Oh." He looks even more confused than before, but soldiers on admirably. "Uh, well, anyway their IDs say their last name is Goldmark. I didn't think about it before but it's not...they aren't—"

"Yeah," Jack says. If the guy weren't about to arrest them all, he'd almost feel sorry for him. Almost. "*That* Goldmark."

The cop groans, then slumps down into a visitor chair and sighs. After a moment he looks up at Jack. "You know this is only my second week?" he starts. "Last week? I got a shoplifter and a kid breaking curfew. This week, I got probably two of the richest kids in the country being shot at, bodies in the street, and now zero evidence it ever even happened."

Jack looks up in surprise, but the cop just keeps talking.

"Let's say for a second this was some kind of kidnapping for cash deal, right? That kind of thing might happen for rich kids like you." Jack tries not to balk at the way the officer keeps repeating 'kids,' given his own apparent youth, but the rest of it holds up. That's part of why he's there. "But even if it was..." he trails off, just shaking his head. "It doesn't make any sense."

Jack has to ask. "What are you talking about?"

The cop looks over his shoulder like someone's going to see him sharing secrets with a person of interest, but of course nobody's there but the two of them. "Look, I just got off the phone. It's gone, okay? *All of it.* No van, no bodies, no blood. Nothing." He crosses his arms and looks away, repeating his question. "Just who the hell are you people? And who attacked you?"

Jack finds himself caught somewhere between disturbed at the news of the cleanup and sympathetic for the plight the cop's found himself in. He can't be all that much older than Jack himself, and he hadn't even had a partner along who could vouch for the things he'd seen, probably because of the budget cuts he keeps hearing about. At this point, the only pieces of evidence are their memories and the cellphone in Jack's pocket that used to belong to Brenner. The cellphone outfitted with illegal tracking software that he is definitely not going to mention in this particular conversation.

"I don't know who they were," Jack says at length. There's a pregnant pause as they both wait to say more. "Look, Officer—"

"Ratigan. Oh, just call me Jimmy." He sighs the words out. "The girls—uh, the girls and Leigh, that is—already do."

"Okay, Jimmy. I don't know who those guys were, and the things I do know about our situation? You don't want to know about. Honestly, I think the more you know, the higher the chances of Very Bad Things heading your way." He takes a breath, not really sure about how what he's about to say will go over. "Have you typed any of our names into a search anywhere? Reported anything about us to anyone?"

"What?" He thinks about it for a second. "Not names, no. I reported the shots fired but I didn't use any names. The call I mentioned was from my sergeant, he said the captain would have my ass if I tried to pull a 'stunt' like this again. Sarge played it off to him as some kind of crappy joke. He told me to pretend none of this ever happened. They're clearing the logs since it 'wasn't a real situation.' What the hell is going on?"

"Then you're in luck," Jack says, not answering the question. "If nothing really happened, there's no record you got involved, and there's no way they'll know it was you helping us out."

"But—"

"They sniped a man on a public street and within the space of half an hour made it all go away like it never even happened. What makes you think they wouldn't do the same to you?"

Jimmy doesn't say anything back, and Jack almost sighs with relief—for all their sakes. He has very little doubt that the cop's career, and maybe his life, really does rest on this whole thing never having taken place.

"What happened tonight was that some high school kids were playing a charity gig when their chaperone got drunk and drove off, abandoning them. One of them got in a fight with some 'undesirables' trying to steal Ms. Smith's purse, which they witnessed because they were out by themselves after curfew. You showed up, the other guys ran away, and it wasn't worth the trouble of chasing them down. You exercised your discretion as a police officer and made sure the kids got a lift back to their school. Mr. Goldmark will take care of the rest." He locks eyes with the officer and prays he agrees.

Jimmy stares back at him for a good five seconds, then sighs.

"For the record," the police officer says, "we'll go with that story." He stands back up, the stoop in his shoulders finally making him look older than Jack. "Off the record, I hate everything about this."

Jack lets out a humorless laugh. "For what it's worth, I'd be concerned if you didn't."

Jimmy snorts. "Don't go anywhere, kid. I've got paperwork to do." He walks out the door, then looks back. "After that, I'll actually get you that lift back home," he says, and walks off down the hallway.

At the door to the hospital, they say their goodbyes to Dr. Mallik. She says she's going to leave town for a while, do a little cash-only Greyhound tour, see where she ends up. After hearing her story from Tina and Leigh, he doesn't blame her a bit. He just wishes he could have talked to her about his father for a while. It sounded like she'd known him.

By the time they get back, it's after one.

■ ■ ■

The four of them sit, exhausted, in a row of chairs outside the headmaster's closed door the next morning. Patton's inside. So is Tina's father.

Their inauspicious return to campus just hours ahead of twilight hadn't been helped by the fact that they'd arrived not in the van they left in, nor with their now-vanished chaperone, but rather in the back of a city police van, with a police officer who had reported everything to the dorm parents on duty that night. Who had then reported the details to the headmaster. It's ten in the morning and, minus naps on the road, they've been awake for roughly twenty-seven hours.

At least Jimmy the Cop had been true to his word, and the story had left out breaking city curfew to see Dr. Mallik, an actual gunfight with actual guns, and the shocking death of one August Brenner, erstwhile guidance counselor at the Academy.

But even sanitized as it was, the cover story was bad enough—especially given the addition of Jack's stitches and Lizzie's now spectacular black eye. The optics—and the rumors they were already spawning—couldn't go unaddressed. Not with parents arriving all weekend to collect students for the break.

The door cracks open and McGuinness calls them in.

The room is somewhat small for seven people, and the four find themselves awkwardly standing between the headmaster's desk and their parents. Leigh looks at Patton, who motions for them to face McGuinness instead. The headmaster sits back down at his desk and folds his hands before speaking.

"The events of last evening are, to put it bluntly, unbecoming of students at this academy," he begins. "While of course you cannot be held responsible for your chaperone's peculiar disappearance..." He pauses, looking as if he'd very much like to hold them accountable for it, if only he could find a way. "Nevertheless your actions thereafter leave much to be desired. When it became apparent that Mr. Brenner was not to be relied upon, you ought to have called your dorm parents or your families—" he motions at Patton and Mr. Slevin behind them "—for help. What you *did* indicates to me that your level of maturity is not what we would hope. The ability to act in a self-sufficient way is, of course, something we strive to instill in all the students here, but there is an important distinction between self-sufficiency and willful independence. The first is responsibility, and the second is folly. You are not adults. You are the charges of this school. And when you fail to make that distinction, and moreover when you resort to *violence*, even in the service of what you believe to be right, it reflects poorly on this institution and on the other students who attend it."

Leigh lets the lecture roll past him like just another blast of hot air from a man and a school known for it, but he suspects Lizzie's trying very hard not to 'resort to violence' right then.

"Your fathers and I have discussed this, and while we don't feel that your actions warrant a suspension, I believe it is imperative that you remember this lesson well." He puts his hands down on the table.

Leigh thinks he might as well grab a gavel to punctuate the coming judgment. "When you return from the winter break in January, the four of you will cultivate your responsibility by taking on the task of washing the cafeteria dishes for your fellow students, relieving the regular dish crew rotation for three days each week, for the remainder of the academic year."

Lizzie can't suppress a groan, and McGuinness shoots her an incendiary look.

"*Moreover*," he continues, "Miss Goldmark and Mister Slade-Woodman, for your direct involvement in the violence, you will have your off-campus privileges revoked for the entirety of the spring term, including extra-curricular events, with the very specific exception, Mister Slade-Woodman, of any college campus visits—lest this event completely derail your chances of acceptance into an institution of higher learning."

Leigh nearly rolls his eyes at that, given Jack's stellar grades, but the lack of off-campus judo meets is going to piss him off even more than not being able to go to Mack's will piss off Lizzie. And all this because someone had *shot at them!* And because Jack and Lizzie had tried to actually *defend them!* Trying to resist the urge just to throw caution to the wind and explain what really happened, Leigh takes a deep breath and sighs it back out, at which the headmaster's eyebrows shoot up.

"Do you have something to add to the conversation, *Mister* Goldmark?" Leigh doesn't fail to notice the stress on the word 'mister,' pretty clearly a performance for Patton's sake.

"No, sir," he says. But he can't resist, and forces the biggest smile he can muster.

McGuinness almost twitches. "I fail to see what there is to smile about in this particular moment," he says.

"Oh no, sir, I realize the gravity of the situation. I'm just pleased whenever someone in a position of power formally recognizes my gender." He continues to smile. Maybe it's not the best choice, but he'll put it down to sleep deprivation.

"Well," McGuinness almost chokes, "at this institution we strive to recognize and embrace...diversity." Leigh's pretty sure the thought of 'embracing diversity' has never once crossed the man's mind—except maybe as a preamble to 'tying diversity up' to be followed immediately thereafter by 'throwing diversity in front of the nearest non-stationary bus.' But the look on the headmaster's face as he tries to make nice with Patton in the room fills Leigh with enough punch-drunk glee to make his forced smile real.

Before the conversation can escalate further, Patton clears his throat. "Well, I think Ed's said all that needs saying, wouldn't you agree, Martin?"

Tina's father, an older, balding man, nods in agreement.

"Well, then." Patton stands and buttons his blazer in one smooth motion, and McGuinness rushes to stand as well. "Thank you, Ed." He shakes the man's hand. "Have a good break."

"You're welcome. I trust the children will have time to consider their actions during the recess, and during their service work next term," the headmaster says, but Patton's already halfway out the door and dialing a number on his phone.

"John, Leigh, Elizabeth—" Patton speaks from the doorway, holding the phone to his head and casually rendering the whole prior meeting irrelevant with just the tone of his voice "—why don't you go and pack your things, then meet me at the car. Is twenty minutes enough?"

Lizzie nods and he strides away down the hall, already moving on to his next appointment.

The headmaster scowls and dismisses them, closing the door to his office behind them after they leave.

"Mr. Slevin," Jack says, once they're in the hall.

Tina's father turns to face them. Leigh hadn't noticed before, but he's a lot like his daughter: slight, almost elfin features coupled with a quiet nervousness in his hands and eyes.

"I'd like to apologize for involving your daughter in our mess," Jack says.

The man smiles then, still looking elsewhere but definitely present. "I rather suspect that I have much to be grateful to you for," he says.

Jack looks unsure of how to respond, so Tina's father continues.

"The headmaster offered a deal over the phone. If Tina would explain what had 'really happened,' then she would be spared any punishment." He looks at his daughter, then, who's staring at the floor as usual. "We declined."

Before Jack can respond, he puts a hand up. "I trust my daughter's judgment. So, no apologies are required, from any of you."

Leigh feels like it's the first time he's seen Jack smile in days.

"Thank you," he says.

"Oh, and Tina has asked if she might come visit you three over the break. That's fine with her mother and me both," he says.

It's Leigh's turn to smile. He hadn't realized how worried he'd been that it'd be just the three of them for two whole weeks at the estate, or how much he was starting to think of Tina as an integral part of their weird little unit.

"Then we'll see you then," says Jack.

As they say their goodbyes, the only thoughts Leigh can entertain are his body's increasingly dogged demands for sleep. They'll be safe at the estate; they'll have time to work things out; they'll get to the bottom of things. Maybe they'll even be able to ask Patton for help.

He sleeps the whole ride home, mercifully dreaming of nothing at all.

■ ■ ■

"You four just watch out for yourselves, okay? Don't take anything for granted, and don't let your guard down." Those had been Dr. Mallik's last words to them as they'd left the hospital three nights before.

Jack already wishes he'd followed her advice more carefully. He'd only halfheartedly entertained the idea of scrounging up some cash, grabbing the others, and ghosting like she did. Now he wishes he'd taken the idea more seriously.

According to Leigh and Lizzie, Dr. Mallik had tried to convince them that their father wasn't to blame, that he wouldn't ever do the kind of things that had been done—to Alice, to Leigh, even to Brenner when it came down to it. But everything Jack's found has pointed in the other direction.

"I can't believe you still think it was Pops," Lizzie's arms are folded, and she's leaning against an old pine tree, glaring daggers at him across the snowy clearing. The Goldmark estate sits almost in its own valley, nestled between two wooded New England hills a half-hour's drive from the nearest example of civilization. The mansion itself has a line of sight to almost all of its forty-acre surround, but there are pockets of trees dense enough to make Jack feel like they have at least a lower chance of being overheard.

"Hear me out," he insists.

Leigh is crouched down in the snow, making that little ball of himself that he does when he's upset. He looks even smaller now that he's, well, smaller. It's only been two nights on the estate and he's already folding in on himself. It's never been great for Leigh to be here, but with everything that's been going on, Jack suspects it's even harder than usual. And now he's almost certainly about to make it worse.

"Look. I'm not saying Dr. Mallik was lying, just that she might not have had all the information. Here." He hands Lizzie a small stack of printouts—names, dates, account numbers, bank transfers, arrest warrants, court proceedings, police reports. If something was private and of a sensitive nature, Brenner seemed to have been able to get his hands on it. "This was all saved on Brenner's phone. He'd been digging into your father's records, probably illegally, but I think he was onto something." It wasn't the whole picture, but every part of it fit with the same awful theory. "These are death records," he says.

"Of who?"

"People your father knew. Scientists on his team, even—"

"Your dad's on here," she says.

"Yeah," Jack says. There were six names on the list. His father's was the last. "Look at the dates."

"2011, yeah. That's when you came to—"

"Check out the actual dates," he says.

"September 1, September 8, September—holy crap they're evenly spaced. A week each time. Your dad—"

"My dad's the last one. Yeah."

"But what does that mean?"

"Check out the next pages. Those are your father's accounts. Check out the dates there, too."

"That can't be right—they can't all just suddenly empty like that... on the same day?"

"And then it all comes back a week after my dad dies. There's more, and all the dates line up. And then there's your phone, Leigh." They'd done a factory reset on it and the signal had disappeared from Brenner's. "You got that phone from your father, right?"

Leigh just nods. Jack feels like crap pushing this, but if they're going to keep Leigh safe, he's got to say it.

"It all fits. First they tried to take his money, then they took his friends, one by one, until he caved. I bet Dr. Mallik was the next one on the list, which would explain why he tried to fake her death after Alice...after he shut down the program, and Dr. Mallik tried to leave."

He tries to stay calm, but saying it out loud makes it real in a way that it hadn't been, going through the evidence on his own. He clenches a fist, then consciously relaxes it.

"You're saying someone blackmailed him into using Alice?" Lizzie looks up from the papers.

"Maybe to begin with," he says. "And maybe again this year, with Leigh."

Leigh just curses something incoherent under his breath and crunches into an even tighter ball.

"There's one more thing," Jack says, knowing this will be the hard part. "The last page is Alice's...it's her death certificate. Brenner had it in a file with one other document, a money transfer. From another account, held by a shell company, held by another shell company that's a wholly-owned subsidiary of Goldmark Enterprises. The transfer's for seventy-five grand."

"What? To who?" Leigh asks, looking up.

Jack takes a breath and lets Lizzie answer.

"To the coroner who signed the certificate," she says.

The clearing is silent, the surrounding trees the only witnesses. A sharp wind whistles between the branches and cold, dry snow starts to dust down onto them.

"You don't think…there's no way he—" Lizzie starts but Jack stops her. They can't get carried away, he thinks, but what *if*—

"I don't know," he says. "I don't know."

But the question grabs them by the throat the way it had grabbed him when he'd seen it, snatches their hearts between its teeth and bears down hard.

If J. Patton Goldmark had faked the death of Dr. Nisha Mallik.

If the genius behind the Displacement Engine had felt cornered and outplayed.

If their father had paid a coroner tens of thousands to sign the death certificate.

"We never saw her body," Leigh says, the rising wind nearly carrying his words away.

He doesn't need to ask the question itself.

What if Alice is still out there, somewhere?

What if Alice is still alive?

SOFT-SOLED SHOES MUFFLE THE ENGINEER'S FOOTSTEPS AS SHE WALKS between the shoulder-high rows of black obelisks, fans cycling up and down like a chorus of whispered sighs. She loves it here, even though it's almost aggressively nowhere—the sixteenth floor of a nondescript city building two blocks from the shore, where the multiplexed cables that lift the whole internet on their shoulders rise like old gods' tentacles from their abyssal paths across the sea. It's a fitting comparison, she thinks, because this is a god itself. A god, but better. Not capricious, emotional, irrational, like Zeus, Hera, Apollo—no. Her god is wise.

She'd made it that way.

Or rather, she'd made it make itself that way. In its infancy, it had stared out at the world through fiber-optic eyes, drinking in every bit of data it could. In time, though, it had grown tired of looking outward and had started to look back in. It told itself stories, created and destroyed civilizations in simulation, made models and knocked them over like a child plays with blocks.

And then it had discovered games.

She'd nearly wept reading the runtime logs that day, seeing for the first time in her creation the semblance of joy. It had been *playing*. It had been having *fun*.

It's still having fun, now, but in ever greater games.

She smiles at the thought, straightening her glasses and shoving at her sweater's moth-eaten sleeves even as they fall back to her wrists. She could throw it away, maybe she will. She doesn't have to dress up, not here. Here she could dance around naked if she wanted. No-one bothers her here.

No-one even comes to visit anymore.

This place is hers. Theirs.

At times a fly buzzes at the edges of her perception, whispers things into her phone, makes distracting demands. She always says yes—they pay her more when she does. Electricity is expensive, as is her creation's perch on the backbone of the world. But none of it matters, not so long as she has this, her creation, her love.

It had even picked a name for itself, a fitting name for the way it views the world, she thinks.

Her eyes sparkle as she sits down at the terminal and words appear of their own volition.

"Hello, Faye," it reads. She smiles and types her response.

"Good morning, Betza. What are we up to today?"

■ ■ ■

Leigh lies awake in his room, staring at the dueling colors peeking through the blinds and playing on the ceiling, harmless intrusions from the Christmas lights out front. Patton isn't even Christian—he isn't much of anything, religion-wise—but he's always done the Christmas thing, if in a kind of perfunctory way. It's as though at some point he'd decided a Family Christmas™ checked a box in some important cultural rubric, and so he'd begun fulfilling it to the best of his abilities. Some years he even shows up in person. Not this year—he'd left on Christmas Eve and won't be back until the 31st—but some years.

Leigh rolls over onto his side. It's been strange having his own bedroom again, the last few nights. It'd been a long time since he'd slept alone. Even in the hospital, there'd always been the feeling of someone watching from somewhere behind the mirror. Here there was just his stuff—old posters and photos, books and clutter. Patton had gone through and packed away his old clothes—well, he'd had someone do it, anyway—and put all the photos of the old him, the Jamie him, into a drawer so he wouldn't see them if he didn't want to. He'd put a few of them back out, ones with him and Alice, Lizzie and Jack. That'd lasted about twenty-four hours. Then they were back in the drawer.

They'd gone to visit the mausoleum that same day; it wasn't far. Civilization might be a ways off, but at Casa del Goldmark, the dead are always just around the corner! He'd smirked when he'd said it to Lizzie, doing his best "If you lived here, you'd be home by now" real estate voice, but lying here in the dark by himself it seems less funny. When Patton's grandparents had bought the property, it had bordered on the cemetery of an old town, long forgotten and swallowed up by the trees that were always trying to reclaim everything around here. They'd had it cleaned up and the county had renewed its zoning. Now there's a mausoleum with three generations of Goldmarks sealed away in tidy little alcoves.

Well, he'd thought it was three. Now he's not so sure.

In the small stone building it had been just like Dr. Mallik had said—sealed didn't begin to describe the place Patton had constructed to hold Alice. Where the others were just stone and brass—he couldn't help but think of them as fancy filing cabinets for corpses—hers was burnished steel and dark glass panels, a jarring insertion as anachronistic as a wristwatch on some Hollywood King Arthur's wrist. A touch on one of the panels had revealed it to be a password-locked computer screen, lighting up and looking like science fiction had somehow intruded into a world it didn't belong, a high-tech plot in a world of old money and older stone. Never mind the wristwatch, he thinks, seeing it light up in the old stone tomb had been like swapping out Excalibur with a light saber.

Hell, it really is science fiction, he thinks, there's no other words for it. Here he is in a new body made because someone hacked the millions of little machines in his blood. Because he's not from Earth and somebody maybe wants to use him to get to wherever he *is* from. Because Patton had accidentally *sucked him into this universe while trying to make a bomb*.

"I don't even *like* sci-fi," he says, pulling the covers over his head. He's started talking to himself lately, when no one's around. Talking to himself, or maybe to Alice.

He rolls over. Two in the morning. He feels like he's seen every hour click over into the next for days. Since the city. Since they'd met Dr. Mallik and been chased by fake SWAT goons and been shot at. Since they'd seen Brenner killed, and then sped away to the hospital and to the Academy and to here. Since Jack had gone through Brenner's phone.

Since they'd learned that Alice might still be alive.

He reaches an arm out and flips on the lamp, then drags himself out of bed, wrapping the comforter around him like a cloak. There's a full-length mirror on the closet door and he stares into it, dropping the blanket.

"Just who the hell are you supposed to be?" he whispers at his reflection. But only Alice stares back, an exhausted-looking pixie in a tank top and flannel pants, who moves when he does, mocking him with her silence from the other side of the glass.

"Or what, even?"

His white skin is starting to show the first signs of freckles, on the bridge of his nose, on his small shoulders. Less and less Jamie and more and more Alice, but not quite either. Never going to be either. Just something in between.

He leans forward until his forehead is touching the cold glass, closes his eyes.

"I'm not like you. I've never been like you. And now look at me. Look at the mess we're in." He wraps the comforter back around himself and returns to the bed, curling up with his back against the wall, staring out of his cocoon at the eyes that stare back from the mirror.

"Why aren't you here?"

On his bedside table, his phone lights up.

■ ■ ■

He slips into the mausoleum, the only light a multicolored disk of stained glass set in the wall above his head, catching the blue-white of the only streetlight for miles and fracturing it into a kaleidoscope of colors on the floor. It might even be pretty if it weren't a room full of bodies. Two great-grandparents, two grandparents, a great uncle, and then Alice. Family, but not—an adopted line of ancestors from a universe he shouldn't even be a part of. He'd never even come out here until today, couldn't stand to even think about Alice being shut up in here forever with people she'd never known, let alone see it in person.

A shiver runs up his spine, but it's not the cold—it had been creepy enough in the day with Jack and Lizzie there with him; being here now and on his own is another story altogether.

He pulls out his phone and winces at the brightness of the screen, covering it up and looking around the small, dark space, then shaking his head. Did he think someone was going to be walking by and see it? But he can't shake the feeling someone might. He squints at the message that had popped up just ten minutes before.

Urgent Action Required

61DC9F71E60FD8FCB579@gmx.com   2:07 (10 minutes ago)
To: me

I have devised a limited-term access solution to the place of interment for Alice Goldmark. As a result of time considerations, I recommend proceeding to the site individually at once. When present, execute the attached application and hold this device within two inches of the access panel. The solution will expire in seventeen minutes, and my probabilistic analysis suggests it will be several days before another solution can be derived.

1 Attachment

This is a terrible idea. What is he even doing, creeping out here in the middle of the night just because some rando on the internet who pretends to know everything says he has to. Then he curses under his breath, because he's here, isn't he?

He walks over to the alcove, looking at the time. Five minutes left. How long will it take to open?

And what'll he do if it works?

He doesn't think about it, just thinks about Alice, that he has to know if she's really in there. If she is...well, he can tell the others. It'll be the end of that part of the story. He can yell at her for being dead and for leaving them all behind, and for teasing them all with the possibility he's trying so hard not to cling to...and if she isn't—

He wants to throw up. He holds the phone to the panel and taps the icon.

The screen goes dark except for a status bar and a rolling string of code, scrolling upward at a phenomenal pace. How does Betza know the things he knows? How had he known the make and model—and *bullet resistance*—of Brenner's van? How had he even known they'd want to get into Alice's grave? He shivers again, this time from adrenaline and cold, wishing he'd brought gloves.

The status bar hits 100%.

There's silence for a moment, long enough to half convince him that the program hasn't worked, then a slow hiss starts to escape around the edges where the burnished steel meets the surrounding stone. He puts a finger up to the seam then pulls it away with a yelp as it lets out a *chunk!* sound so loud he's afraid it might be heard by the security guard dozing back at the house. The whole panel starts to slide out of the wall.

And then it's just there, right in front of him.

Her coffin.

It's pristine, black, shiny. Cold to the touch. He hasn't seen it since the service, and even then, not this up-close. A glimpse of his own darkened reflection in its surface warns him of what he might see next: her face, now his, eyes and cheeks sunken, desiccated or outright rotten. Or he might see nothing. All he has to do is open it.

He nearly doesn't. He nearly pushes it back into its alcove, nearly walks out of the mausoleum then and there. Nearly decides that whatever the answer is, he won't be able to handle it.

He grabs the edge of the lid and heaves.

■ ■ ■

"Okay, number one? Stop talking and try to breathe." Lizzie's whispered command cuts him off in the middle of a story so confused and self-interrupting it's starting to sound like word salad. He's sitting cross-legged on her bed with something in his lap. She can't tell exactly what it is because he's got it covered in his coat and his arms wrapped around it. He says he won't let her see it until Jack's there, so they texted him and they're waiting for him to show. She shakes her head, thinking it's a good thing Pops had a 'business emergency.'"

Leigh looks like he's seen a ghost, or maybe like he is one. His fatigue-bruised eyes are wide in a thousand-yard stare, pale arms tight around whatever it is, like he's afraid someone's going to burst into the room and steal it from him. His face is pale, too, she thinks, even more than usual, though maybe it's the just deep purple bags under his eyes that proclaim his lack of sleep.

"Number two...are you okay?" she asks.

He blinks and seems to come back to the room from wherever he's been.

He nods. "Yeah, I think—maybe I'm okay."

"This answer does not fill me with confidence," she begins, but before she can interrogate further, there's a faint rapping at the door, and Jack pops his head in. He looks a little bleary-eyed, but still pretty sharp for being woken up at half past two in the morning. Maybe he hasn't been sleeping well either. He closes the door behind him.

"Okay." Lizzie pulls up her desk chair and sits on it backward, facing Leigh. Jack leans against the desk. "Let's go over your story from the start," she says. "You got a Betza email."

He nods.

"What did it say?"

Leigh takes an uncertain breath, then answers, slowly at first, but speeding up as he talks. "He sent me a program, and he said if I hurried—that is, if I got over to the mausoleum fast—that it could get me into Alice's *grave* at the mausoleum by holding up the phone to the thing, and I'm sorry I didn't come get you but—it said I only had like seventeen minutes, and it's a ten-minute walk, so I just stupidly ran over and—"

"Stop. Breathe. It's fine," she says, exchanging a sidelong glance with Jack.

"You went to the mausoleum," she says. "Did you get in?"

He nods.

"Jesus," she breathes. No wonder he looks like he's seen a ghost. She closes her eyes, now even more concerned about what he might have under that coat.

"And?" Jack says.

He unwraps his arms from around the object, then stops.

"Okay so you have to promise you're not going to freak out though," his voice is shaking.

She doesn't say that *he* looks like *he's* on the verge of freaking out. She nearly tells him she's *already* freaking out since whatever it is it *came from the inside of their sister's grave*, but she manages to nod in agreement.

He slowly peels the coat away, revealing the object underneath.

She almost sighs in relief at what it *isn't*, but holds back because she can't tell what it *is*. It's a cylinder of some kind, somewhere in size between a beefed-up thermos and the rice cooker they have back in their dorm room at the Academy. Grey metal and black plastic, with a few blinking lights on one end, and a windowed portal in the top that reveals an interior lit by blue LEDs.

He looks into it as if making a final decision, then holds it forward so they can see inside.

It's a hand.

Jesus, it's a human *hand*: small, white, and suspended motionless in some kind of clear medium. The realization hits her.

It's Alice's hand.

"In the grave?" he says, swallowing. "In the coffin. This was it. This is *all* that was inside."

Lizzie looks up at his face, wondering what her own must look like. Tears are running down his cheeks, which are stretched so tight you couldn't call the expression a smile. It's a grimace, a sideways crack in his porcelain face.

He tries to say something else, to explain something that only he can say, but the effort's too great—he shatters, physically crumples in front of them, caving in on himself, hugging the device to his chest and sobbing.

■ ■ ■

The sun's creeping up to the underside of the horizon by the time they manage to reassemble him—exhausted and hollowed-out, but at least in one piece. Lizzie thinks of the last few weeks, the creeping intrigue, the spy-vs-spy conspiracy crap, the outright *violence*—and to have it culminate in *this*, not in an answer but in even more questions—even when he was Jamie, Leigh's always dealt with things by carrying them everywhere he went, even though there was never even a single chance he could shoulder the weight alone. Nobody could.

She tucks her at-last unresisting brother under the covers and motions for Jack to follow her out of the room.

When the door clicks shut behind them, she looks at him. He looks the way she feels—tired beyond tired, but with enough high-octane anger to run for dozens of miles yet.

"What. The shit. Is going on?" She speaks as quietly as she can.

Jack scowls. When Lizzie had first seen that photo, she hadn't seen the resemblance between Jack and his father, but here it is in a single expression.

He doesn't immediately answer and she doesn't wait for one. "Where is she?" she says. "Where is the *rest* of her?" If Pops were here she'd break his door down. With a baseball bat, if needed. She knows he's normally busy and all, but this *isn't a normal situation* so WHY ISN'T HE AROUND? She really doesn't want to believe he's been lying to them for so long, but what other choice does she even *have* now?

"Being sick doesn't...it doesn't *do* that," she says. "Not even if it's sick because of blood robots or whatever, because there's blood in your hands, too, right? Like—but you don't chop off someone's hand if you're faking their death, either, because what the hell part of faking a death involves *losing a hand and putting it in a sealed coffin where nobody's ever going to see it?*"

Jack still doesn't answer. Maybe he's thinking, maybe he's doing the super-mature thing he does, the 'don't say anything until you're sure it's what you want to say' thing. She wonders for a moment if he's freaking out inside, too. Leigh looking like Alice for the past few months has got to have been tough for him, too, but it's not like he's said as much. And then there's whatever history he had with Brenner and his dad...

He crosses his arms and leans back against the far side of the hall, looking past her, past the door to the bedroom. "I've seen what the weapon does, the Displacement Engine, what it looks like. Buildings, trees, everything, cut precisely at the border of the blast radius, like it'd all been cut with the sharpest knife imaginable or a laser or...something impossible. If Alice...if she'd been at the edge of one when it went off, or if the portal thing they were trying to work on had closed on her..." He shakes his head. "I think it might look a lot like that."

He takes a deep breath, then lets it out. When she doesn't say anything herself, he starts up again. "As far as I can see, there's two possibilities. The first one is that something went so wrong with the tests that that, in there, is it. It's all that's left. And that the story of her dying from some illness was just a story they told because the truth was worse." He looks up at her. "And then there's the other option."

She waits a second before answering, trying to think of any other possibility, but the only other one she can think of she almost can't say out loud, like saying it would cast some spell over them all, thumb their noses at fate, or call down a curse from some malign being. But Jack waits until she does anyway.

"She's in the other universe."

"Yeah," he says.

"Most of her."

He nods.

It should feel like a punch in the gut. It should knock the wind out of her. She should be doing exactly what Leigh did, sobbing or screaming or *something*. Instead the knot that's been there in her stomach for days just ratchets another notch tighter, and she grits her teeth.

■ ■ ■

The office is clean and bright, though perhaps a little less tidy than she'd like. Leaning over a row of plants, the tall woman drips water onto an orchid's roots, waiting patiently for each shining bead to spread, and for the silky white-green of the root to darken with moisture. This one had suffered from a fungal infection before she'd repotted it, and a number of its roots had needed to be removed. Until it grows new ones, she'll feed it like this, or else the leaves will shrivel and die. She won't have to do it forever, though: a bright green nub has already appeared on the end of a prominent root. It's on the mend.

"Professor Zee!" A voice calls to her from the lobby. She puts down the eye-dropper and tightens the bun of black hair at the back of her head before pulling on the crisp white coat that is the mark of her achievement at the Center. She walks around her office desk into the bright and open atrium that her lab assistant, Serillie, is charging through, her juniors-blue lab coat flying out behind her.

Serillie stops in front of her, out of breath. She's a kind young woman with dark, smiling eyes, perhaps a little prone to overexcitement, but nothing outside of the national averages—just enough to add a little constructive diversity to the population. Her designers had chosen well, Zee thinks.

"Calm yourself, Serillie," she says, smiling. "There's no need to startle the patients." There were a handful of young men and women milling about the atrium, all of whom were surreptitiously peering at the source of the disturbance.

"But there is." Her lab assistant tries to rein in her excitement by whispering. "Professor, there's a signal!"

The doctor folds her hands in front of her, waiting for the rest of the announcement. Surely Serillie wouldn't be so enthused about just any signal. They were coming at one a month these days. For this level of excitement it would have to be—but no, that wouldn't be—

"From *Apex!*" she whispers it so loud it defeats the point.

Zee clasps her hands together tightly, maintaining the practiced calm she's cultivated for decades, despite the surprise. A signal from Apex wasn't possible. There could *be* no signal. Not from there.

"It's faint, barely an amplitude four signal, but it's there. I'm sure of it."

Impossible, but also impossible to ignore. Serillie is many things, but wrong is rarely one of them. "Call in the rest of the team," she says. "And try to calculate the differential as fast you can."

Serillie beams. "Tallinn's already on it."

■ ■ ■

Leigh's lying in bed with his headphones on, cycling through song after song until he's so lost in thought he doesn't even hear them. But time after time, his mind wanders back to the night before, breaking down and sobbing like a little kid in front of Lizzie and Jack...he cringes, curls up on his side and cranks the volume another notch.

Another Joan Jett song starts up. He must've hit 'like' on too many of them, because his feed is now almost entirely populated by 80s power chords and devil-may-care vocals. Love is Pain. Crimson and Clover. I Hate Myself for Loving You.

God, his feed's algorithm has managed to turn Joan Jett into emo.

He takes his headphones off and looks at the clock. Three in the afternoon. No wonder he's hungry. He digs through the closet of strange choices, doing his best to ignore the mirror, eventually settling on a fluffy white bathrobe with a bunny-ear hood. He's definitely feeling the 'fluffy bathrobe' vibe this morning. Afternoon. Whatever.

The kitchen is cold and quiet, with an aesthetic that only an engineer could love. Surrounded by stainless steel and slate, he tries not to think of the mausoleum while he searches for food. He grabs the biggest bowl he can find and digs in the pantry for something laced with cocoa and sugar, to no avail. He sighs and settles for a semi-nutritional, jaw-ache-inducing granola something-or-other, pouring a bowl and grabbing a spoon, attempting a retreat before he runs into anyone.

He should be so lucky.

Jack's in the hall, hands in his pockets, dressed—you know, like a functioning human being might be in the late afternoon—and wearing an expression of concern like a worn-in cap. Well, he should be used to it by now. It's not like Jack hasn't had practice being concerned about him. Leigh pulls the hood down and stares at the ground.

"Put it down," Jack says.

"What?"

"The cereal, put it down."

Leigh hugs the bowl to his chest. "But it's breakfast. The most important meal of the day."

Jack takes it from his hands and gently puts it down on the floor, before wrapping him in a very fluffy hug.

"And before you start, yes," he says. "I *would* still be hugging you if you hadn't changed. Because we're going through stuff and maybe hugs are underrated."

Leigh mumbles something about it being okay just this once, trying not to start crying again. When Jack pulls back, hands on Leigh's shoulders, Leigh almost pulls in for another hug, but manages to resist.

"This sucks, Jack," he says. "All of this sucks. I'm not even, you know...look at me, I can't even be fabulous like this. All I can be is..." he motions as if to say, 'You know, this.' "And now I have to be like this knowing that maybe she's still out there somewhere."

"You're not her," he says. "You're not a replacement for her."

"I *am* a replacement—"

"You're *not*," he says. "Not to anyone who matters."

"I've been replacing myself this whole time," he says. "I'm the magical not-Jamie. The not-Alice. I feel like one of those weird creatures they used to draw at the edges of old maps. The dolphin with legs or the human-headed bird-thing. The dude with his face in his chest."

"You can still be Jamie if you want," Jack says.

He looks down, hood hanging over his eyes. "I'm not sure I can, anymore. And weirder, because I really did...I'm not sure I really want to be."

"Well, you can be the chest-face dude if you prefer."

Leigh wants to laugh; he just isn't up to it.

Jack peeks under his hood. "Then still Leigh for now?"

He thinks for a moment, then answers. "For now, I guess." He picks up the bowl of cereal and takes a bite before making a face, talking with his mouth full. "And for the record," he points at the bowl with the spoon, "this also sucks."

Jack smiles and walks past him, talking over his shoulder. "Well, that's because you picked the food for the human-headed...uh—"

"Bird-thing."

"Bird-thing, right." Jack blinks at him.

"For real, you haven't seen it? It's like an ostrich but like, human head...thing..." he trails off as Jack just looks at him with eyebrows raised.

"Anyway," he says, "turns out I hate whatever this is." He swallows. "Ugh, is that *raisins*?"

Jack laughs. "Well, come back to the kitchen, then. I'll make you something better. But then you should probably shower. Lizzie's grabbing Tina from the train station and we should at least pretend we don't live in our own filth."

"Gotta be good hosts." Leigh makes an exaggerated act of picking dried fruit out of his teeth.

"Stay classy, kid."

"Doing my best," he replies.

He really is.

■ ■ ■

"This is a hand," Tina says, her voice even more lacking in affect than usual.

"Yes," Leigh replies.

He's sitting across from her at the small table at the far end of the library. Of all the rooms in the house, the library is the only one Patton hadn't renovated. Old wooden bookshelves line the walls, and while the ceiling's not high enough for them to have one of those cool built-in ladders on wheels, it feels like they should get one anyway. Or something like one. Maybe a wheelie stepstool or something.

"In a thermos," Tina says.

"I...maybe? Kinda sorta..." He grimaces.

Lizzie's folded herself up on a couch across the room, and Jack's scanning the shelves absently, hands shoved in his pockets. They're both actively trying not to stare at the hand, trying to resist the gravitational pull it's been exerting on them all since Leigh stole it from the mausoleum.

Tina turns it over on the table, examining it more closely. She ducks down and rummages in her backpack for a second before popping back up with a small bag of screwdrivers and assorted implements.

She notices the look Leigh's giving her. "Laptop, glasses, bass," she says. "You never know when you're going to need them."

"Oh."

She starts taking out a couple of screws that hold down a panel on the side.

"Um," Leigh says, "do you think that's a good idea? What if it, you know, leaks?" It does seem to be filled with some as-yet-unidentified clear fluid.

Tina doesn't look up. "The integrity of the seal isn't being maintained by two screws," she says. "Here." She removes the small panel and puts it down on the table, then frowns at it for a second before turning and rummaging in her backpack once again.

Leigh peers at the hole. "Are these USB ports?"

Jack and Lizzie have both wandered over to see, the added weight of the investigation making the hand irresistible once again. Tina's already opening her laptop.

"USB 2-B. You don't see them much anymore because wifi's simpler. I have one in case I need to print tabs at the library."

"Is there anything you *don't* keep in that bag?" Lizzie asks.

"A thermos with a hand in it," she responds absently, plugging in the cable and popping open a window on the screen.

"Fair," Leigh says.

Tina taps away on the screen, line after line of text popping up in the window as she works. Jack's looming over her, occasionally pointing at a word when there seem to be options. After a few minutes of silence, Leigh starts to get twitchy.

"What are you, you know...doing? Exactly..." he asks.

Tina doesn't look up. "Investigating."

"Well...okay, but can you also...maybe explain?"

She keeps typing with one hand and points at Jack with the other. "He'll do it."

Jack almost laughs. "Well, it doesn't exactly act like a hard drive when you plug it in, but if you go into terminal you can see it. We don't have root access, so it isn't telling us much, but it looks like it's running an unpatched distro from three years ago, so Tina's trying an exploit that might get us into a better position."

When neither Lizzie nor Leigh respond, Tina sighs and talks while typing. "Your Grave Hand Thermos runs Linux. That's an operating system. It's an older version of Linux, one with holes in it that they didn't know about three years ago. I'm trying to use those holes to get admin privileges so I can see if there's a list of controls or—there." She spins the computer around, displaying the screen a barebones program window has popped up.

"Guess they didn't think anyone would ever come looking for it, locked up in there," Jack says.

Tina nods. The window looks more like the fancy audio EQ Amy made him download once and that he now can't seem to uninstall from his phone. He has to turn it off whenever a player update resets the defaults—punk music shouldn't sound *produced* like that. But there are some differences with that and the thing on the screen. First, the labels on the virtual knobs read things like 'off-axis distribution,' 'phase,' and 'optimization' rather than 'bass' or 'treble.' Second, there's also a small image twisting and writhing below them, looking like a song visualizer for some kind of audio track. Dozens of bars pulse and twitch on the screen, green when they're short, shifting to yellow and orange when they reach greater heights. For a moment, Leigh thinks they look like they're fighting with the black space around them, trying to break out.

"So this is what's running on the, you know, thing?" Lizzie asks, waving at the thermos and interrupting his thoughts.

"What is it?" Leigh asks.

"It looks similar to a noise-canceling program," Tina says. "I have a pair of headphones I wear for things like vacuuming, sometimes."

"So it's trying to keep it quiet in there for the hand?" Leigh's confusion is probably written all over his face.

"That, or the hand is singing and it's trying to make it stop," Tina says.

"What?"

"The waveforms don't appear to change when we talk," Tina says.

"So if we turn this down—" before anyone can stop him, Leigh reaches forward and taps the slider. It's a mistake.

It starts with his hand, which feels as though it's been stung by a tiny wasp. He cries out and snatches it back from where it was reaching out to change the setting. Then another sting in his back. He jumps to his feet and swivels around, but there's nothing in the chair. The others are looking at him like he's gone mad. Maybe he has. Another sting in his hip, his foot, his neck, his chest—like the first drops of a rainstorm, but picking up in speed.

He hears Lizzie say something to him, but it sounds far away, unintelligible. Like she's down the end of a long, echoey tube. The stings are coming faster and faster now, turning into a sharp, physical static, wrapped in a blanket of needles that moves when he moves. And with the storm comes a cacophony of light and color, blinding flashes of colors he can't even describe, a haze of rainbows attacking his peripheries. He drops to a crouch and slams his hands over his ears, screaming "Turn it off! Turn it off turn it off turn it off *turnitoff!*"

He needs them to turn it off, why can't they see that whatever that program does, he needs it to *keep doing it again*. But then Lizzie's down on the floor with him, shaking him by the shoulders and shouting something down the ever-lengthening pipe.

He needs them to turn it off.

He's pretty sure she's saying they can't.

■ ■ ■

"There it is!" Serillie shouts across the lab.

It's true, Zee can see on her pad that the signal has jumped from the relatively weak amplitude four up to two. Not exactly seismic, but it might be enough for a lock.

Tallinn, a middle-aged scientist with a streak of white in his nest of black hair hums to himself as he works. Zee knows better than to disturb him—the humming helps him focus—and before ten seconds have gone by, he interrupts himself to report, "Solution entered."

"How is the reactor, Serillie?"

"Thirty seconds to capacity," she says over her screen.

"Platform clear," says Tallinn, peering down through the reinforced glass into the chamber.

"Security and medical on their way," says Serillie, hand pressed to an earpiece as the reactor starts to whine.

"Then I hereby authorize a stage-four ingress," Zee says. "Let's see who's calling home."

■ ■ ■

Tina grabs the hand and runs. If it's emitting some signal that's interfering with Leigh's nanomachines, then the fastest thing to do would be to try to put some distance between them.

She dives out the library door and sprints down the hallway, trying to remember her way over the tiles, back past cornices and pillars, zigzagging round corners and down through the massive house to the front door. She's hauling its oaken mass open when Jack catches up.

"Where are you going?" he asks, but she doesn't stop, just talks as she shoves her feet into her shoes.

"Couldn't get the signal balanced again. If we can get it to the grave, there might be shielding." She ducks outside.

"Wait," he says, pulling on his own boots. "I know a shorter route through the woods, you don't have to go down to the street and back."

Tina nods and lets him lead the way into the deepening snow, the ignored cold biting at their cheeks and hands.

As they pass the first of the trees, a ringing nothingness starts to saturate the air around them, like the feeling in your ears when you're going up a really tall elevator, and it gets louder with every step. Then the texture of the world starts to become dense, almost soupy, like they're underwater even though they can still breathe.

"Get rid of it!" Tina tries to shout, but she can't even hear her own voice, it's being snatched up by the horrible unsound of the device. She reaches out and grabs Jack, and he stops, trying to read her lips. She snatches the device out of his hands and tries to throw it away—

—but it's too late.

There's a moment where, from her perspective, everything is still—muted, frozen in pale white amber like a motionless snow-globe with the most peculiar winter vignette. The world outside it is nothing—not black, not dark or light, but purely, absurdly absent, as though the act of even looking there were impossible, or unthinkable. The moment lasts no time at all, but even so, she knows that nothingness, that absolute, haunting lack, will never leave her.

And then they're through.

■ ■ ■

"Shut it down!" Zee shouts, the intolerable screech of the reactor aborts with a snap as fragments of what look like trees clatter to the platform around their catch. But something in the readings is off, and she double-checks the scan results just to be sure.

"Well now," she says, looking down through the glass to the platform below. "What have we here?"

On the platform, atop a small mound of earth and snow, ringed by a halo of twigs and bark and forest detritus, stand two bewildered teenagers.

She sets down the box next to its predecessors, the latest in a line of cardboard and styrofoam reliquaries shipped there from a hundred nameless manufacturers scattered around the globe. A bead of sweat drips down her neck—it's warmer down here on the fifteenth floor than in the artificially-chilled server rooms above.

The first delivery had caught Faye off guard. She'd been swapping out a cooling unit in one of Betza's node clusters when the bell in the desk phone behind her had shuddered into life, nearly startling her into dropping a screw. It was a retro find, a classic black bakelite she'd hunted high and low for as a personal touch for the room, sitting there dignified, looking like something out of a Cold War movie. The idea had been to hook it up to the building's intercom so that, on the off chance someone did visit, she could answer the doorbell in style. But after months of disuse, the chill of the smooth plastic on her ear had become an unfamiliar sensation, as had the sound of its bell.

"Uh, hey?" The voice on the line had sounded unsure. "Is this…" there had been a rustling of papers in the gap. "Uh, Dr. Sullivan?"

Faye hadn't said a word out loud in two days and she'd had trouble finding her voice, but she'd at last managed to croak out a "Yeah—yes, that's me" with a little effort.

"Courier, ma'am. I'm gonna need a signature for this."

She'd sighed. "Can't you leave it with the front desk?" Her interest in the situation had almost died at the word "ma'am."

"Nah, sorry, Dr. Sullivan ma'am." He'd said it like it was all a part of her name, Doctor-Sullivan-Ma'am, and her eye had twitched involuntarily. "No can do," he'd said. "It says it's gotta be you. Strict instructions. S'why the old man down here made me call up."

She'd taken the old freight elevator down and wound her way through the first floor to the security station, wondering most of the way if she were being served legal papers. But who even knew to find her there? The list was short, and her mind had leaped from candidate to candidate to no avail. And what would it be for, anyway? She hadn't broken any laws. She didn't think she'd broken any laws.

In the old, tiled lobby, the courier had taken a signature with a bored glance at her ID, then left whatever it was in her hands before wandering back out into the street, letting the flimsy glass and aluminum doors slap shut behind him.

The security guard, a retired old cop, had just shrugged, and she'd gone back upstairs to examine the prize.

Unlike the many packages that would soon start to arrive, this first one had been small, about the size of a ream of paper, its white cardboard shell marred only by a printed address sticker half covering the courier's logo.

And a ream of paper it was: legal documents, signed contracts, a deed, and a title.

She'd grown increasingly bewildered the more she'd examined them.

If what they said was to be believed, she had just become the new owner of the building. The *whole* building. Scratch that: the whole building *and all the rental contracts for the other floors and offices within them*. These, it appeared, were now the property of the Faye Sullivan Passthrough Corporation, a legal entity which, the paperwork informed her, was also under her sole ownership and direction.

When she'd tapped her workstation to life, it had been there waiting for her—an explanation already prepared by Betza. It seemed it had been hard at work making investments out in the wilds of the cryptocurrency markets, using methods of manipulation that probably only escaped illegality because no-one had yet passed a law banning them in whatever post-Soviet republic the exchanges were located in. A hard fork here, an ICO there—the words 'pump and dump' had worryingly come to mind—and within the space of a few months, a building. And more.

The fifteenth floor had been vacated the following week, a team of nameless renovators appearing as if by magic, scrubbing it down, remodeling, preparing it for what was to come next.

She wipes a bead of sweat from her forehead with the back of her hand and stares at the pile of now hundreds of packages stacked against the walls. Some parts off the shelf, some designed and customized and made to order by a hundred nameless companies in Shanghai or Taiwan or Brazil, quite a few more being 3D-printed upstairs on the same rig she'd used to make the most customized parts for Betza's rather unique construction—all waiting for her to assemble.

But into what?

She picks up a small stack of schematics and flips through them, alone in the room. When she speaks to herself, the echoes startle her.

"Just what are we building here, friend?"

■ ■ ■

The space in the woods where Tina and Jack were taken is haunting. To Leigh, it's like a picture from an old book he had as a kid, where—if you looked at it just right—the branches in the trees and the wings of the birds and everything else would form a shape, like a human figure, or a skull. Here, the cutoff branches, the shorn twigs and yellowed winter grasses, the bowl cut out of the snow and ground, all stop at an invisible circumference, describing a sphere of nothingness in the forest where two sets of footsteps walk in, and none walk out.

The blanket of rustling needles and utter chaos that had assaulted him had retreated, fading down to an unpleasant static and a bit of color at the peripheries of his vision. In the utter silence of the wood, he can still make out a faint ringing in his ears, but it's so quiet he's not sure if it's the blood rushing through them, or even his imagination.

Mostly he just feels numb.

"They're gone," he says. He's always had a knack for stating the obvious.

For a minute they just stare at it, the hole that used to be their friends, the place of their abduction from this universe—a place they belong—to the alien place of Lizzie and Leigh's origin. It's like history is repeating itself in reverse.

Lizzie bends down slowly, then, and Leigh's not sure if she's going to scream or cry or flop down in the snow. But she doesn't do any of that. Instead, she stands back up with a baseball-bat-sized branch, severed by the sudden disappearance of a part of its former owner. She seems to consider its weight for a moment before taking a few steps further into the wood. Then she winds up, pulls back, and whales on a nearby trunk with it. And does it again.

And again.

She doesn't scream or yell, barely even seems to breathe at first. Each strike lands in the hollow space that pursues the gunshot rapport of its predecessor, shattering the silence over and over again with a whipcrack that echoes off the surrounding hills. He watches, hypnotized by the display, until eventually he loses count, and the branch she's wielding shatters and she throws what's left deeper into the trees with all her remaining strength. She stares where it landed and doesn't turn around.

Leigh waits there with her in the cold until the silence, at last, becomes unbearable. Then he takes her by the hand and guides her back to the house.

■ ■ ■

Vector verification request

372DCB6310C47AE979A8@gmx.com   12:07 (14 minutes ago)

To: me

Hello,

Please indicate which if any of the following vectors have been displaced:

1. Jack Slade-Woodman (fWfFifmW2ifmF2)(live/running:6340@i6204)

2. Elizabeth Chelsea Goldmark (QN)(live/running:6097@i6204)

3. Leigh Aiden Goldmark (BN)(live/running:76@i6204)

4. Tina Emerson Slevin (NN)(live/running:5485@i6204)

Vector verification is important.

I am here to help.

Leigh's too tired to scream obscenities at his phone. It had taken half an hour to soak and clean the bark and splinters out of the burst blisters on Lizzie's hands, to gently wrap them in gauze and antiseptic. In the intervening time, a silence had begun to swallow them whole. Curled up next to her on the library couch, he types out a response to Betza.

I don't know who the hell you are or what garbage fire of a game this is, but we aren't playing anymore. What the hell is "displaced"? What do you want from us?

He shows it to Lizzie who just nods for him to send it. A response comes a moment later.

Re: Vector verification request

6998094CF57026D3CF55@gmx.com just now (0 minutes ago)

To: me

Hello,

I sympathize with your circumstances, but even the strongest piece cannot choose when and where the game is played, nor can it resign once the game is underway.

Please allow me to rephrase the request: which pieces have been displaced to the Primeverse?

Please trust me.

He nearly throws the phone across the room, but he doesn't, because whoever this Betza is, he's just confirmed Leigh's suspicions. That the hand, or whatever its silent screaming had linked them to, had snatched them away to the other universe. He types out only the words "Tina and Jack" and hits send.

Re: Vector verification request

87E8E0787E721BC9A7D5@gmx.com just now (0 minutes ago)
To: me

I believe I can return them to you.
A car will arrive in twenty-four hours to pick you up.
Please direct it to the following address:
2 Varick St. New York NY 10013
I look forward to meeting you in person.

Leigh shows the response to his sister, who then takes a breath, stands up, and walks out of the room. He waits just a little longer on the couch and then joins her.

■ ■ ■

The sky outside the window is full of stars—at least, what Jack can see of the sky from where he's lying by the glass. While the windows span from floor to ceiling, there's only three feet of grass between them and the twelve-foot wall of now-shadowed white stone that lies beyond it. It reaches up out of the ground to pinch a sliver of sky between itself and the lintel, reminding Jack of the place Brenner had taken him, of the building at ground zero for the Displacement Engine.

They're in the Primeverse.

It had been evening when they'd been put in the room—a sparsely-furnished, white affair with some kind of charcoal-grey, industrial carpeting and a couple of lime-green chairs—but as for how much time had passed, he really couldn't be sure. Some number of hours, certainly. Everything they had, from phones to watches to the hand itself, had been taken away when they first arrived. They'd even been made to shower and change their clothes, which is why they're now wearing matching blue sweatsuits like some kind of bizarre track-and-field duo.

Across the room, Jack can just make out Tina sitting in the dark on one of the chairs. If there are lights, they haven't been able to find the switch, so even with the faint glow coming through the fogged-glass porthole in the door, she's not much more than a darker grey shadow against the lighter grey of the walls. She hasn't said much since they arrived, which is pretty normal for her, but she's started to rock back and forth a bit in a way that makes Jack worry.

"You okay?" he says, sitting up and putting his back to the glass.

She doesn't say anything, but he can make out a couple of nods. After a minute of silence, her quiet, level voice drifts across the room in the darkness. There are long gaps between her words. "Things are just...harder...when I'm stressed. Staying still. Talking." She gets up and shoves her hands in her pockets, seeming to will herself into composure. She wanders over and plops herself back down next to him. After a minute she speaks.

"You know I'm autistic." She says it like a statement, even though it's more of a question.

"Yeah," he says. He'd heard from Amy.

"Not a secret," she says. "Just don't...bring it up. I think...people get...uncomfortable. When I do."

Jack doesn't say anything.

"Like that," she says. "They stop."

"Sorry."

"Mm." She shakes her head.

"I just—"

"It's fine. I trust you," she says, cutting him off, then leaving enough silence to fill a room. "I guess it's..." She trails off, then sighs, frustrated somehow. "I trust you," she repeats.

"Is there anything you need me to do?" he asks. "I get that this is a pretty unique situation, of course, but..." He stops talking when he sees a faint smile on her face despite the shadows of the room.

"That," she says.

"What?"

But she doesn't say anything else, just smiles harder. She leans over a little and bumps him with her shoulder, then almost laughs.

Jack shakes his head, admittedly a little baffled. "We're going to get out of this," he says. "Not sure just how yet, but I'll find us a way."

"Mm," she says again, nodding. She doesn't say anything else, but she seems more relaxed somehow.

After a couple of minutes of sitting there in silence trying to think of something to say, Jack tilts his head back up toward the stars—and jumps at the sight of a shadowy figure stalking past the window. He spins to stare at it, but it doesn't stop or slow down, just continues on its way. From the silhouette it looks like one of the guards who, along with some more medical-seeming types, had escorted them to the room however many hours ago that was.

And then behind them, the door clicks open. The room floods with light so bright Tina buries her head under knees and arms. Jack whips around and squints at the newcomer who, for all the suddenness of her arrival, lacks even a hint of malign intent.

"Hello!" she says. Her voice is cheerful and bright, with a hint of an accent he can't place. She's about the same height as Jack, and her dark eyes fight with her brilliant blue lab coat for his attention.

"Um, hi." He probably looks pretty pissed off, squinting like this, but damn it all it's bright like a nuclear flash in there. It's so bright he almost forgets to be surprised that he can understand her. It's the first English he's heard since they arrived.

Her eyes go wide. "Wait, have you been...oh *Eshmi*. You have been sitting in the dark this whole time. I am very sorry."

"Yeah, where the hell is the light-switch, anyway?"

"It is...automatic," she responds, wincing a little as she adds, "but only for us."

Well, at least they hadn't left them in the dark on purpose. He wonders whether that's better or worse than doing it through neglect.

"I am Serillie," she says. "I am sure you have many questions. But first, you must be very hungry. It is late."

■ ■ ■

For twenty-four hours, Lizzie doesn't say a word. Not while they eat, not when they wake the next morning, not even when the black SUV arrives to pick them up. She doesn't say anything the whole ride to New York, either. Leigh tries to fill in where he can, making small talk with the driver, ordering for both of them at the fast food counter when they make a pit-stop, even guessing the answers to the bizarre litany of questions he starts to receive from Betza on their way—about their height, weight, how fast they can walk a mile, even the length of time they can hold their breath. At the checkpoint, the highway gives way to the city roads, the mid-rises bow to high-rises, and the sedate suburban sprawl transforms into the honking and blinding lights of a city far bigger than their own—and Lizzie remains silent the whole time.

It's scary as hell.

He squints out the window at the bright city life, a sharp pain in his head as lights flash by. A night's sleep hasn't been able to fully cure him of the dregs of whatever the hand had done to him. He'd be more worried, but he's pretty sure stress headaches are a thing, and if the crap they're going through doesn't qualify as stress-inducing, he's pretty sure nothing does. So he shoves it to the back of his mind and distracts himself by staring at the passing scenes.

He'd heard the rules might be different here—or more like the observance of them—but judging by the hairstyles and skin colors and fashion choices of the people coming and going, in and out of the bars and restaurants, beneath the giant screens showing the latest tech or the carefully curated headlines—or flashing the latest products by some wholly-owned subsidiary of Goldmark Enterprises—the stories of 'sanctuary cities' might actually be true.

It reminds him of the past, of when their city used to be like this— at least the parts they weren't really supposed to go on their own. Guess this one was just too much to 'tidy up,' so instead they'd just stuck a literal wall around it.

But Lizzie doesn't even seem to notice. Her eyes are open. Her head is pressed against the cool glass while reflections play about the oversized back seat. She's not seeing the city or its inhabitants. Leigh's pretty sure she's already there, up ahead, in a room with Betza.

She's only waiting for her body to catch up so she can gather a voice to demand her answers.

■ ■ ■

Tina clings to Jack like a shadow as they pass down the empty halls, lights flickering on ahead of them and then popping off behind them once they've gone. It's as though the sleeping building is waking up and coming to life as they pass—doors unlocking, built-in computer screens lighting up—but, as Serillie said before, only for her.

Tina's recovering from her overload, but she's still anxious, still trying to fight the urge to curl up in a ball that she's been feeling since staring into the godawful nothingness between the universes, the hole-in-the-gut feeling of seeing something so genuinely, terribly *wrong* that you can't forget it. She wonders if Jack had seen it too, or if he'd been looking somewhere else, at the hand, maybe, or at her. She reaches out and grabs a small fold of the fabric of his slightly-baggy shirt, the textured physicality, the *realness* of it like a talisman, warding off the void. If he notices, he doesn't say anything.

The halls are like the room they'd been left in—white walls, charcoal carpeting, like a backdrop for a commercial where actors play doctors—the illusion of a health facility. But it might actually be one, she thinks, given everything that had happened when they'd arrived. Only the room they'd first appeared in was different, with its bare concrete walls and floors, its racks of equipment all black metal and blinking lights. The military-looking people had then ushered them from that stark space to separate rooms in the prevailing decor, small, but bright, with a bed and a shower, all with the same institutional feel. It was all precise and efficient, like a television spaceship. After the showers was when they'd started to see people like this woman—lab coats instead of fatigues, tablets instead of weapons, waving around what were probably testing devices of some kind and shining lights in their eyes—only to be abandoned shortly thereafter.

The woman—Serillie, Tina thinks she said—stops at a nondescript door just long enough for it to swish open, then goes through.

"This is the faculty cafeteria," she says, gesturing at the small room that's the same decor as everywhere else. It's filled with half a dozen tables, and the far wall is lined with small, clear, square doors, like train station lockers. "We have...changed it for your use."

She wanders over to the unusual wall and one of the doors pops open, revealing a plate of food, which she hands to Jack. It looks like an airplane meal—some kind of bun, a rectangle that might be cheese, some plastic-wrapped salad in a shade of green that's just a little off, somehow. A sealed cup of something that might be juice. The woman grabs another and hands it to Tina, forcing her to let go of Jack's sweatshirt, and then motions for them to sit.

Tina takes a bite of the 'cheese'—bland and beany, a little reminiscent of rubbery tofu—and wonders if all the individual weirdnesses are a part of the same issue—the showers and clothes and tests, the strangely sterile food, even the long, isolated wait in that room. She glances up at the woman's face, then looks away when she finds herself the subject of a probing stare, deciding to talk at the food instead.

"Are we in quarantine?" she says.

"What? Oh, yes! Exactly," Serillie responds. "We have a...protocol?" Her speech is full of pauses, like she's thinking of the words, questioning her vocabulary as she goes. "Yes, a protocol. But it has not been used before. We did not expect your signal."

"Signal?" *The hand*, Tina thinks. *That's* the waveform that was being cancelled out. Some kind of beacon, a call for help? If so, then it's all her fault that they're even there. She doesn't say so, and the woman carries on.

"Yes, but we did not expect *you*." The emphasis she puts on the last word makes Tina wonder just who they *had* been expecting. "But Professor Zee had created a protocol for this and so—quarantine. You will I hope forgive the..." she searches for a word again, but this time doesn't find it. "For the way things are not made specifically for you."

"If we're quarantined," Jack squeezes a question in-between mouthfuls of what is definitely some kind of spongy bread, "what does that make you?"

Serillie beams. "I am your special liaison. My *emenyss* has been specifically attuned to any...dangers, you may carry."

"Carry? Like, infections?" Tina says.

"Yes! Infections."

"And your '*emenyss*'?" Tina says, tasting the word. "How you open doors and turn on lights?" She's starting to get the picture.

Serillie nods, and Tina turns to Jack. "The nanomachines."

Their host raises an eyebrow at the unfamiliar word.

"When you say your *emenyss*," Jack tries to clarify, "you mean tiny machines, right? Spread all throughout your body?"

Tina glances up to see Serillie's eyes widen. "You know! That makes things easier," she says. "Yes, we call this thing *emenyss*. We did not know you had a word for it."

"About that," Jack says, "how do you know any of our words for—"

He's interrupted by a sudden chime. A large wall panel that had been dark when they entered the room lights up behind them, words in another alphabet appearing in glowing blues and greens on the screen. Serillie gets up and places a hand on the panel and exchanges a few words with it in a language neither Tina nor Jack have ever heard, before the screen goes dark again and Serillie turns her attention back to them, looking crestfallen.

"I am sorry to go, as I am quite enjoying our conversation, but I must leave for a brief time. I will return as soon as I am able." With that and an energetic swish of her electric blue coat, she disappears out the way they came.

They return to silence while they eat.

■ ■ ■

Leigh drags himself into the building behind Lizzie. To him, the lobby looks as worn down as he feels. It's not that it looks *old*, really. It was probably decorated in the '70s during some weird art deco revival or something, which he guesses wasn't really that long ago. But it just looks forgotten somehow, like an abandoned subway station or an old classroom that's been used for storage for long enough that maybe everyone's forgotten what it used to be for. The doors had squeaked when they walked through them, slapping shut behind them as if a spring had broken at some point and the replacement had been wound too tight. The walls are covered with old white tiles, the floor with older black ones.

Lizzie slowly walks up to the security desk where an old guy in a rent-a-cop uniform is peering down at a dog-eared book through drug store glasses, hardly seeming to notice they're there.

She folds her hands on the desk and breaks her day-long silence.

"We're here to see Betza," she says. It's just her Academy blazer—they'd decided to come in their uniforms, like it was some formal occasion—and her tie's still not great, but the anger locked up in her shoulders and back let her wear it like a power suit.

After a discernible pause, the man frowns, closes his book, and takes off his glasses. He carefully folds them up and puts them in his breast pocket before peering up at Lizzie.

"You Elizabeth?" he says. His voice is stronger than he looks.

"What?" The question almost throws her off her guard. "Uh, yeah."

"ID." He holds out his hand.

"I don't have—ugh, wait, will my student card do?" She fishes in her wallet while the man says nothing. "Here," she says, and hands it over.

He puts it down on the desk, then takes his glasses back out, unfolding them and resting them on the bridge of his nose. He then spends easily sixty seconds alternately scowling at the card and then peering up at her. Then he reverses the process.

"Well," he says, handing her card back. "I don't know anyone named Betza." He puts his reading glasses back on and opens his book, leafing through it to get back to the page he'd left off. "But Doc said to send you on up when you got here."

"And that is...?" Leigh thinks Lizzie's going to pop a fuse if the guard goes any slower.

"Elevator on your right." He doesn't look up. "Suite 1601."

■ ■ ■

Tina tries to eat, everything except the not-cheese—its texture makes her brain itch—but all she can think of is the interrupted question, about the fact that their 'liaison' can speak English. Could their hosts just scan their brains and use their magic little machines to teach themselves? Or had they had contact with someone from their world before? Someone like Alice.

"Do you think she's here?" Jack stares at his cup of probably-juice, obviously thinking along the same lines.

"Possible. There must be a source for their knowledge of English. It could be us, but only if they can pick up vocabulary straight from our brains."

"But she didn't know some of the words for things," he counters.

"The technology might not be perfect?" She considers it as she goes. "Or, they could have met other people from our world. Or they could have a way of looking in on our universe without taking people."

"But they took us by accident. She said they weren't expecting 'us.'"

She doesn't want to say another possibility out loud, that Alice did come here, but isn't alive anymore. The story had been that she was sick, and even if that weren't true, if she had come to the Primeverse, she'd left her hand behind. Thinking about that and the clatter of severed branches on the arrival platform makes her mentally wince. Plus, they'd seen what just being around the hand had done to Leigh.

"Do you think Leigh and Lizzie are okay?"

He gets up and starts walking around the room. "Well the hand came with us, so if that's what was messing with Leigh, then hopefully." He's right, they don't know for sure that's what was going on, but it's looking more likely.

Jack swipes his finger along the black panel on the wall, the one that had lit up earlier, but nothing happens. He checks out the door, too, tries to slide it one way or the other, but it's too smooth to get any purchase on. In this world, or at least in this building, if you don't have the *emenyss*, you're effectively a prisoner.

"These nanomachines," Jack's now examining the little food lockers, which, like everything else, seem inert except in the presence of their hosts, "they must be pretty foolproof for these people." He bangs a little on a small hatch to no avail. "Think about it. Even the doors don't work if you haven't got them. And they must work for pretty much everyone, or else they'd have to build things with manual controls, too." He manages to get a fingertip wedged into one of the doors and it makes an unhappy grinding noise as he pulls it open.

"Success," he says, and brings over another tray of airplane food. He pulls open a second cup of probably juice and takes a sip, grimacing. "If you can call this success."

"Maybe it's just this facility," Tina says at length. "Or maybe it's us specifically." She steals a cracker-like object off Jack's tray and crunches into it. It tastes a little like nuts. "This can't be the best food they have to offer."

Jack squints his eyes a little in the way people do when she's made a logical leap they aren't following, so she tries to organize her thoughts into that thing called 'conversation.' It's a feat she finds a lot easier when she's not in another universe wearing someone else's clothes and eating food she's never tried before.

"Things break," she says. "There are simpler ways to make doors open than nanotechnology. And food doesn't have to be...this. There have to be alternatives. Maybe they've gotten rid of the alternatives either because of us, or because this place is special."

"You mean the doors might open manually normally, and they're keeping us locked up?" He takes a bite of the cracker and grimaces. "And the food isn't great because...?"

"Because kibble is simpler than finding mice to feed your cat?" she says. "If you've ever had a cat."

"Prisoners or pets." He frowns.

"The other possibilities might be worse."

"What do you mean?"

She closes her eyes. "A world where doors don't open without nanomachines," she says, "is a world where people without them don't exist. Which is creepy. Even medical things that are proven to work and are totally safe have dissenters back home. Antivaxxers, 'big pharma' conspiracy theorists."

"Yeah."

"And then there's the food. What does it say about a place if all the standard food is shelf-stable like this?" She'd been thinking before that the place felt like a spaceship of some kind, and now she's wondering if that's not so far from the truth.

"This is all conjecture, from limited data. But..." She trails off.

"But none of the options are great."

She shakes her head no.

"Then I hope it's just us," he says. "And just here."

Before she can agree, Jack holds up a hand.

"Did you hear that?"

Tina stops and listens, but there's no sound.

"What did it sound li—" she starts, but finds herself interrupted by a series of peculiar snapping sounds from the hallway. Suddenly, two people in black, beetle-shell armor rush into the room, leaving a third to stand at the door. Each has a long gun strapped to their back.

"Come," the first intruder says, whispering from behind the obsidian shine of their helmet. "It's not safe."

Jack stands up. "Who are you?" he demands, putting himself between Tina and the intruders. "What do you want?"

"Quiet!" the second says, in a whispered shout. "This place isn't safe!" They motion for the two of them to follow. "We're here to rescue you."

"What are you talking about?" Jack responds, incredulous, but still speaking more quietly.

"Oh for—look, we don't have time for a debate," the second one says, pulling the weapon from their back and pointing it at them. "This place is going to be swarming with corporates any second now."

The first one shakes their head and raises a hand, lifting a visor to reveal a woman's face. "You know the rules, Sanna." She turns back to them. "Please, trust us. These people aren't what they seem."

"How are we supposed to trust you?" Jack asks. "We know literally nothing about what's going on here. You come barging in, knocking down the door and pointing your weapons at us—"

Jack doesn't get a chance to finish, as the second one lifts their gun and shoots him with a green flash of light. He drops to the floor and Tina's eyes go wide.

"God*damn it*, Sanna!" the woman almost yells, despite herself.

"Save it for Herald, Ange, we don't have the *time!*" the other yells back, now pointing their gun at Tina and glaring from behind the visor. "He's not dead. It's easier to carry one than two. Are you going to run with us or do I have to shoot you as well?"

Tina nods as the third whisks into the room and throws Jack's body over their shoulder as though he weighs next to nothing.

"Then please," Ange says, "come with us."

There are two blue-lab-coated guards lying in the darkened hallway as they walk out. Sanna, the one that shot Jack, has taken the lead, while the as-yet nameless one carrying him is following behind. Tina's shepherded by Ange, who's put her visor back in place now that they're on the move.

She catches Tina staring at the bodies as the pass. "They're alive," she says. "We're not in the habit of killing people. Plus they're harder to kill than that."

They walk at a near-jogging pace in the dark, pausing at every intersection before slipping around each in the same gun-first way. It's as though they've trained for this a thousand times.

At the entrance to a large, lit atrium Sanna throws up a fist, elbow bent at ninety degrees, and they stop, silent. Sanna holds up a finger. Ange puts two gloved fingertips to Tina's lips, as if telling her to stay quiet. Tina wouldn't have said a word anyway; her heart's fluttering so fast it might've taken the opportunity to fly out of her mouth if she'd opened it.

The one carrying Jack puts him down gently on his side, then slips back down the hallway and into the night. A moment later, there's a noise from up ahead, and Sanna swings around the corner firing half a dozen neon-green blasts like the one that had knocked out Jack. To Tina, they sound like the thwacking of a heavy rubber band. A couple more and the lights go out. Then both Sanna and the other reappear.

As they run across the now-dark atrium, Tina can see only one body on the floor. Had it really taken that many hits for one person? At the far end there's a large, windowed wall like the one where they'd left Jack and Tina earlier. Sanna pulls out a small black box and places it on the window.

"Cover your ears and get ready to run," Sanna says. "We did things quietly up until now, but there's no way this isn't going to set off some kind of alarm."

Tina does as she's told, and watches as Sanna taps a small green light on the box. Within half a second there's a sound so high-pitched and awful that Tina's sure she'd have passed out if she weren't pressing her palms against her ears with all her might. Even as it is she can feel it in her teeth, a rhythmic whine itching its way into her face, behind her eyes.

The window shatters, from floor to ceiling, and Sanna dives through the hole.

"Hurry!" Ange says, "it's already regenerating."

She's right—the broken shards of glass are reaching downward like a time-lapse video of icicles forming, or like sharp-toothed jaws trying to close on them. She jumps through next, followed by Ange and the third, still carrying Jack.

"Get on my back," Ange says as they reach the wall. "Quick."

Tina does as she's told, puts her arms around the woman's neck. The helmet is cold against her cheek, the body hard beneath the armor.

"Are you ready?"

Tina's about to ask "Ready for what?" when she sees the others do something impossible—they crouch down and then almost effortlessly launch themselves up and over the wall with a single jump.

Tina doesn't have time to say no. As they reach the peak of their arcing trajectory, the momentary, moonlit view sticks in her mind, extends outward like it's frozen in time—the wall seems to continue forever in both directions, eventually curving out of sight. Beyond is pure, treeless desolation, a desert of hard-caked earth that stretches to the horizon.

They land with surprising grace and break into a run so fast that Tina wouldn't have believed it before the jump.

"They aren't shooting," Sanna says.

"Too risky," Ange says. "They probably want them alive."

"So they'll pursue."

"Head for the safehouse like we planned."

Tina hangs on for dear life as they sprint to the horizon.

■ ■ ■

When the elevator stops, Leigh's head keeps going, and the ringing in his ears is definitely coming back, little by little. The doors slide open into a barren, beige lobby with an extra-wide, windowless door marked "1601" in six-inch-tall, black vinyl stickers. A push-button intercom is mounted off to one side, below a fish-eye lens.

Lizzie walks up and presses the button. Nothing happens.

After nearly ten seconds of waiting, she reaches out to press it again, and they both jump at the sound of a loud burst of static.

Next comes a noise like someone trying to speak with something stuck in their throat, followed by a small fit of coughing and a gravelly woman's voice saying, "Hold on."

The speaker snaps off again.

Lizzie looks at Leigh, who can only shrug.

Another minute of waiting. Lizzie's about to press the button again when the door *clunks* and inches open, revealing a woman of about thirty-five.

Her dark hair is greasy and up in a knot with what looks like a half pack of pens absently shoved into it at random angles, and she's swimming in a ratty, grey sweater big enough to fit two of her. She's got a little silver-foil drink packet in the hand she's holding the door open with, and she's staring at them through a pair of large, dark-rimmed glasses.

"You the kids?" she says. She clears her throat and takes a slurp from the juice-bag straw.

Leigh punctuates the ensuing silence with a single word, "What?"

She sighs. "The kids. Betza said you'd be coming. God, you should know the trouble you've put me through the last two weeks, I *swear*." She scowls at them like they're personally responsible for most, if not all, of whatever's awful in her life, then swivels around and wanders off into the room behind the door. "Well, come on then," she says over her shoulder. "Betza wants to meet you."

As the door latches shut behind them, they find themselves in a single, massive, dimly-lit space. The walls around the elevator lobby, he sees, are the only ones on the floor, and the rest of the space is black-

and-metal towers covered in blinking lights and filled with the sound of moving air and gently sighing fans.

And it's *cold*. Leigh had been starting to overheat in the elevator, but it's almost refrigerated in here. He hugs his coat around him and follows along with his sister, as their yet-unnamed host—could this be the "Doc" the guard mentioned?—meanders between the towers to a far corner of the floor.

"Sit," she says, pointing at a desk chair facing a small silver laptop resting on the table.

"Uh, are you 'Doc'?" Leigh interrupts.

"Hm?" the woman screws up her eyebrows before letting them pop back up in recognition. "Oh. Yeah. Faye Sullivan. Got a doctorate, but Frank's the only one that calls me Doc," she explains, adding under her breath, "Sure as hell's better than ma'am." Leigh realizes that he must be staring at her with the same mixture of confusion and curiosity that Lizzie is, because their host looks suddenly self-conscious. "What?" she speaks around the straw.

"Nothing," Lizzie says, shaking her head as if distractions were a thing that settled on your head like snow. "So where's Betza?"

"You're looking at him," she says.

"*You're* Betza?" Lizzie says.

Faye Sullivan snorts and swivels the chair toward Lizzie.

"Just sit down and type hello or something."

"Wait," Leigh says, "you're telling us that Betza...?"

She points her straw at Leigh. "Give the kid a prize," she says.

The rows of towers, they're computers. They're *one computer*.

Lizzie doesn't even have to type a greeting. The screen before them lights up, and across it appear two lines of text.

>*Hello, Lizzie. Hello, Leigh. It is a pleasure to finally meet you*, it reads.

>*I am Betza.*

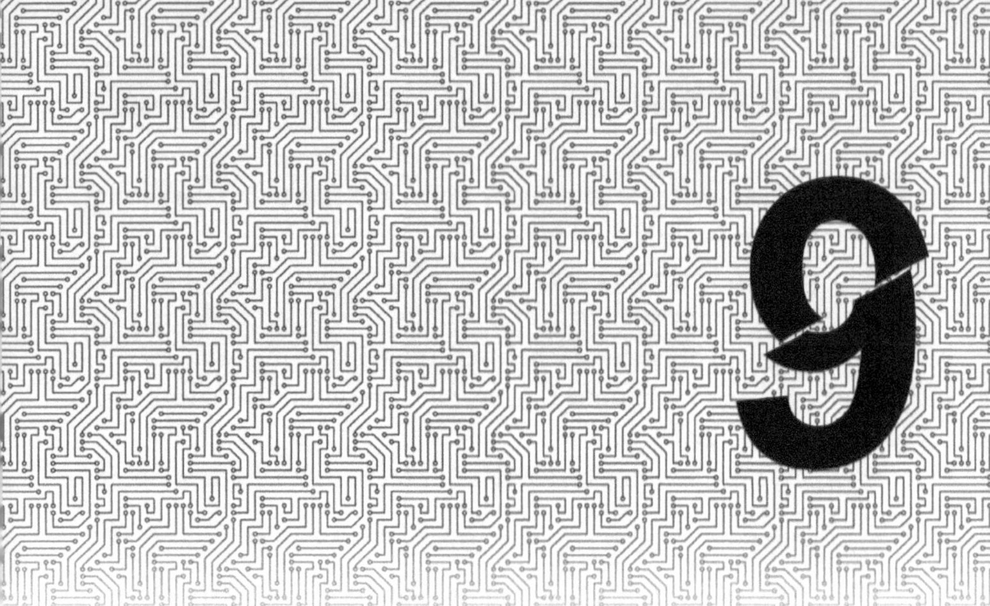

Thunk. Thunk. **Thunk.**

Jack fades into consciousness to the sound of rhythmic percussion. Still half-asleep, at first he thinks it's his heart, but as he drifts out of the surf and onto the shores of awareness, he notes that it's too loud and sharp a sound—and that it's coming from outside him.

He's in a small, round chamber, just tall enough in the middle for Tina to sit with her legs crossed, looking down at where he's lying. She has her hands over her ears. It's bright white in the room, but it's impossible to tell where the light is coming from.

He tries to sit up, but she puts a hand on his chest to stop him, before returning it to the side of her head.

"They said you could pass out again if you get up too fast," she says, just loud enough to be heard. "And there isn't much room."

"Where are we?"

"They called it a safehouse," she says, wincing.

"And that banging?"

She shakes her head. "They said sorry about the noise. Said it'd take five minutes."

"To do what?"

She shakes her head. She doesn't know.

After about thirty more seconds, the banging stops. The relief on Tina's face is obvious. A faint hissing noise comes from off to his left as a panel opens and one of their 'rescuers' pops her head in.

"All done, you can come—oh good, you're awake. I wasn't looking forward to trying to haul you out. Hard enough getting you in there like that."

"Who are you and what's going on?" Jack sits up the best he can.

"Well you're straight to the point, aren't you?" She sighs. "Come out, we'll finish up, and I'll tell you what I can. At least we can talk more freely now."

They slide out of the room, which to Jack's surprise seems to be more of a pod than an actual room. From the outside, it's a large sphere on short stilts, a variety of coils and wires feeding into it from every angle. The room in which it sits looks a more like a fancy cave than a building, with drapes of fabric hanging from the ceiling around a small, central skylight, just turning blue with the approaching dawn. He's been out for hours.

Their new hosts have taken off their beetle-shell armor, and have substituted matching black jackets instead, giving them a kind of off-duty military look. They're sitting on some cushions around a short table. They all look in their early twenties to him.

"I'm Ange," says the woman. She motions to the first of them, a young man with trimmed dark hair and even darker eyes. "This is Tek. He's the one that carried you out here." Ange hooks a thumb at the other, with an androgynous look topped with a shock of pink hair. "That's Sanna. They're the one that shot you." They give a little wave while disassembling their gun.

"Sorry I had to shoot you," says Sanna, half-smirking and still not looking up from their work.

Jack crosses his arms, but refrains from trying to argue about the words 'had to.'

"I'm sorry they shot you, too," says Ange. "They were *not* authorized to do that."

Sanna's smirk graduates to a mocking smile.

"Anyway, we just need to finish up. Can you sit down here for a minute?" Ange points to a small crate with a rug thrown over it that seems to be serving as a bench.

Jack tries to sit gently but everything still seems a little further away than is natural and he half-falls onto it with a thump.

"Still a little dizzy? The stunner has a lingering effect on blood pressure. It'll pass." Ange kneels down in front of him. "Roll up your shirt for a sec?" She hands him a box about the size of a cell phone. She moves it, and his hand with it, so it's splitting the difference between his solar plexus and his navel. It starts to emit a strange purple light. "Just hold that here for a couple of minutes, let your blood circulate underneath it." She hands another to Tina and asks her to do the same.

After about ten seconds it starts to itch, and he pulls it away from his skin a little.

"What the hell?" The thinnest of silver mists is rising up and away from his skin wherever the light touches it, slowly condensing into droplets on the glowing surface of the box.

Ange gently pushes it back against his skin. "It'll take less time if you hold it closer."

"Take less time to what, exactly? What *is* this stuff?" He stares in horror at the fine wisps of particles extruding from his pores.

"They dosed you." Sanna says, their gun back in one piece. "Did they give you any injections? Did you eat or drink anything?"

"We ate," says Tina.

They make a shrugging motion as if to say 'Well, there you go.'

"'Dosed us' with what?" he asks.

"Nanomachines," Ange says, pulling the box away from his skin and putting it back again.

"Like the, what did they call it, the *'emenyss'*?"

Ange nods. "Close, but much less drastic. The real thing can only be safely integrated into the body before birth, in those eggs of theirs. Doing so in adulthood is more dangerous. They wouldn't have risked killing you until after they'd finished studying you."

"Killing us?" Tina says.

"Better than living a miserable life outside the *Erdenkörperschaft*," says Sanna, voice dripping with sarcasm. They throw their weapon back over their shoulder.

"Okay, I'm going to need a *lot* more explanation about what's going on here—" he starts, but doesn't get to finish.

"Save it." Tek's round baritone voice cuts him off. "For the road. We need to move."

Jack looks down at Ange, who's taking the boxes back and throwing them into a foil-lined sack. "They dosed you with trackers. Maybe spies, too. They're probably on their way right now. I doubt they expected us to have tech for disabling them that we'd be willing to throw away, but you two are special. Herald says it's a fair trade."

"Who's—"

"For the road." Tek grabs a gun on his way out of the room and disappears out of sight.

"Come on," Ange says. "There's clothes and shoes for you over there, ones that are better suited to the desert and don't stand any chance of having more spies woven in. Get changed as fast as you can and meet us outside. As I said, they're probably already on their way to retrieve you. We don't want to be here when they arrive."

Both she and Sanna follow Tek out the door, leaving Jack and Tina alone.

Jack walks over to a set of four cubby-holes, each filled with neatly-folded piles of clothes. He picks one at random, holding up a sand-colored shirt that's about Tina's size. "You trust them?" he asks her, checking the others for a set more his size.

Tina shrugs. "I think we need to know more."

"They shot me," he says.

"They did." She starts pulling off her shirt and he spins to face away.

"I'm just going to face over here—"

"You don't need to worry," she says, her voice quiet as usual. "It doesn't matter if you see." She stops, then starts again, seeming to reconsider. "If it makes you more comfortable it's fine."

He doesn't turn around. "Let's say for now it does."

"Okay." There's the sound of some fabric swishing. "I'll turn around, too. But in the interest of honesty, you should know that I've seen your underwear. Your pants got caught when we were trying to get you into the pod."

Jack sighs, but all he says is, "Oh," and starts changing.

"Do you believe them about the others?" she asks. "The *Erdenkörperschaft?*"

"I don't know," he says. "You were right, back there in the city, when you said things didn't really line up."

"She smiled like the headmaster," she says. "Serillie."

He thinks he knows what she means. Like a politician, kind of.

"Ange seems pretty sure she's doing the right thing," she says. "They all do."

"Yeah." He sighs, kicking his foot down into a boot that fits so well it's uncanny. "Maybe that's what worries me."

He throws his old clothes into the cubby. "Let's see how it goes," he says.

"I'm not sure we have a choice," Tina responds.

They pull on sand-colored jackets and hats and follow their 'rescuers' out into the dawn.

■ ■ ■

"Betza's a *computer?*" Leigh's eyes go wide at the realization. "I've been talking with a *computer?*"

"Technically a series of networked computers and *several* layers of evolving software-based neural nets, but that's the long and short of it, yeah."

Leigh rubs his temples. He's pretty sure this Faye person is making his headache worse, but he supposes it could be a coincidence.

"Why has a computer been...been playing *chess* with us, using *us* as the *pieces?*" The wall Lizzie's been holding up, the one between the world and her anger, is starting to crack. "What kind of an—an *absolute monster* makes a *computer* that *plays with people's lives?*" Lizzie stands up, almost yelling now. "How could you *do* this? How could you screw with our *whole lives* like this? Who even *DOES THAT?*"

Faye seems more annoyed than ashamed, but for whatever it's worth, she can't keep eye contact with the girl less than half her age now screaming in her face.

"What gives you, or your shitty computer, the *goddamn right* to—" but at that their host snaps back.

"*Shitty computer?*" She looks about ready to lunge at Lizzie. "Do you know how many times my 'SHITTY COMPUTER,' as you call it, has saved your helpless ass by now? The number of things he's done to help you out?" From the look on her face, even she's surprised by the strength of her own response. "Did you watch as he hacked into the police network to clean up the records behind you so you didn't get a rap sheet? Bribed all the right people to get you where you are? Do you think he didn't leave that door open in the Goldmark VPN for you, or change the records so you'd know Mallik was still alive? Didn't work every step of the way to help you get to the bottom of your sister's disappearance? If it weren't for Betza, you'd still think she was dead!"

There's no sound in the room but the wheezing of fans and the furious silence of Lizzie's eyes. Faye turns away again, hugging her arms to her chest and pretty obviously embarrassed by her outburst. She continues under her breath.

"Say what you want about me, okay. I'm a pretty trash person, and I know it. But Betza's different. Betza's better than us." She takes a breath.

"Just...talk," she says. "Jesus, I need a smoke."

As she strides away in the direction of the elevator, Leigh lets out a breath he didn't even realize he'd been holding. Lizzie walks over to the nearest wall and punches it hard enough to leave a fist-sized depression in the drywall. Then she turns around and slides down against it, hugging her knees when she gets to the floor.

"*You* talk to the damn thing," she says to Leigh.

He looks at his sister, sitting there on the old tiles. She looks as exhausted as he feels.

"Go on," she says, burying her face in her arms. "See what the Great and Powerful Oz has to say for himself."

He does as he's told.

■ ■ ■

The safehouse is almost invisible from the outside, even as the rising sun casts long shadows over the rocks. What had looked like a tent had in fact been mostly excavation beneath a series of rocky outcroppings in a dusty landscape. The skylight looks so much like sand that you could walk a couple of feet from it and not even notice it's there. As they leave it behind, it disappears into the landscape completely.

They trek for hours, most of it in silence fueled by breathless effort. The desert wind is hot, Jack notices, but there's a strange quality to the sunlight that makes it feel as though they're walking in the shade somehow. He's still sweating through the shirt they gave him, though, and wondering exactly how long they're going to last—Tina especially, who looks like she's really flagging as their shadows start to inch beneath their feet.

The first trees begin to appear in the distance. Jack had been wondering about that, too, given how lush and green the site of the first displacement had been. The trees here are short, spiky things, though, like the cartoonish ones at the base that Brenner had taken him to. Maybe the place they'd just been was this world's 'Area 51.'

That'd make them the Roswell aliens.

He stifles an exhausted chuckle at the thought, but then finds himself wondering if the comparison might not be so far from the truth. Especially with their 'rescuers'—the label still overlaps in his head with 'abductors'—and what they had to say about his and Tina's possible fate if they'd been left back there.

A line of foothills stretch before them, and their pace soon starts to slow. Tina looks like she's having a really hard time.

"Hey, can we slow down a bit?" he says.

"We'll stop for a rest in just a few minutes," says Ange, looking first at Tina, then at him, throwing him a sympathetic look.

"I still think we should just carry them," says Sanna.

"You want to, you go right ahead," Tek responds. "It'll be your turn, though. I'm already drained."

Sanna clicks out their annoyance with a *tsk*, but there's no further discussion of it.

"We follow the plan," says Ange. "Herald knows best."

Sanna snorts and walks on ahead.

"Who's Herald?" Jack asks, remembering that it was also this Herald who'd said they should blow their safehouse in order to acquire the two of them.

"That's...more than a little hard to explain right now," Ange says, "but I promise, we'll tell you everything. It's just...it'll be easier to show you."

A minute later, as they're passing a stand of spiky bushes on sticks, Sanna stops cold.

"Damn, that's well timed," they say. "Can you hear it?"

At first Jack doesn't know what they're talking about, but after a moment he catches it—in the distance, back the way they came, there's the faintest of sounds, like the whining of an engine.

"Get under. Now." Jack rubs his eyes. Ange is holding up...a corner of the ground? The earth around them is hard-packed, cracked, and flat, but just here it stretches up like elastic to where Ange is yanking it up like the edge of a sheet, revealing a hidden depression below.

"Camouflage?" he says, incredulous. It's utterly seamless with the surrounding area.

"Get under! Now!" she repeats, and the five of them scramble for cover.

They crouch down in the darkness beneath, as the droning of the engine rises in volume.

"Don't even breathe," whispers Sanna.

And then it's so loud it must be right above them. It sounds like a huge swarm of bees, furiously searching for whoever last kicked their nest and absconded with their honey. But it doesn't even pause over them. After another thirty seconds the sound dies away and Jack lets out a long-held breath.

He thinks about what Sanna had said about timing.

"Did this Herald person tell you to put this here?" he asks.

Ange nods.

"Are they psychic?"

"Sure act like it," Sanna snorts, "but no. Just smart enough, and been around long enough, to do a pretty good impression."

Ange twists a lamp into life, scattering shadows across the space, which stretches further back than expected, though it never quite gets tall enough to stand. There's a small stack of supplies and sleeping bags, and even a narrow passage to what looks like a separate room in the back.

"We'll stay here tonight," Ange says. "Try to limit any time spent outside, but if you're desperate to stretch your legs or need a little privacy, you can go outside once it gets dark. I know it can get a little claustrophobic under here." She starts rummaging in the supplies and tosses Jack a bottle of water. "And I get that it's probably pretty hard to relax around strangers, too."

Jack's about to feel sorry for Tina, who's probably having an even more stressful time of it, when he notices she's already curled up like a cat in one corner and fallen asleep.

"She's been awake this whole time," Ange says. "Looking out for you, mostly."

"Could've looked out for myself if someone hadn't shot me," he says.

"I'll try to remember that next time I'm rescuing a pair of lab rats," Sanna says and then laughs.

Jack takes a sip of his water. It tastes more than a little like chlorine, but he's thirsty enough not to care. "Do you do this a lot?" he asks. He settles against one of the hideaway's low walls, his hair just touching the camouflaged fabric hiding them from their pursuers. "Rescue 'lab rats'?"

"Rescues aren't really our thing. We're more—"

"Thieves," Tek interjects.

"Liberators of unjustly-acquired property," Sanna corrects him, with a grin.

"You steal from them? From the, uhh..." what had they called them? Tina had gotten it right away.

"Corporates." Sanna completes his thought before get gets there. "The *Erdenkörperschaft*. The 'Earth-body-corporate.' They live in perfect harmony with themselves and nature." They say it with more than a little sarcasm.

"Sounds German," he says. "Wait, did you say Earth?"

Ange leans back against the opposite wall, nodding. "Yeah, this is Earth. *An* Earth. Not yours, though. Never heard of German, either. I'm guessing that's a place back on your world."

"Language. The place is Germany," he says. Then, "Deutschland?"

That elicits a chuckle from Sanna. "That's more familiar."

"Wait so are they, what, Nazis?" But Serillie had been Black, so had one of the guards, and he's pretty sure that wouldn't have gone over well in the 'Third Reich.'

"Don't try to map things too closely to your world," Ange says. "Things apparently vary a lot between iterations."

"But you're speaking English," he says. "And so did the *Erdenkorper* people, kind of."

"Ah, that's—" Ange begins.

"We learned it just for you!" Sanna interrupts, smiling. "And it's not a very friendly language, either, so be grateful. It never follows its own rules, and it's weirdly specific about some things."

"For instance?"

"'He's and 'she's, for one. I'm a 'they'!" Sanna almost laughs.

"Our language doesn't have gendered pronouns," Ange clarifies. "So it feels pretty strange to use a different one for Tek or me or Sanna."

"Okay, but who taught you? Because I think something on the order of a billion and a half people speak it, so there's going to be a lot of variation in how it's used."

"A billion and a half." Ange shakes her head in what looks like disbelief. "Well, Herald taught it to us, mostly," she says, then sighs. "This really is very complicated to explain in bits and pieces."

"Then can you explain it to me all at once?" Jack asks.

"Not...no." Ange looks away. "It's not that I don't want to."

"Herald told us not to. They'll explain it to you when we get there," Tek says.

Sanna adds, "Probably."

"Well then what *can* you tell me?" Jack frowns. "Because from where I'm sitting, it's been roughly a day and a half since we got magically transported to another dimension by some kind of hand in a thermos, and ever since then I've been poked and prodded and *shot*, and—" Jack stops when he sees their expressions.

"Did you say 'hand'?" Ange says.

Sanna lets out what can only be a long string of curses in a language Jack doesn't understand, then puts their hands over their face and topples onto one side, half giggling and half choking with frustration.

"They have the hand," Tek repeats with what must pass for absolute shock in his limited range of facial expressions.

"What?" Jack says. "Yes. It's still back there. Why?"

Ange sighs. "It's nothing..." she says. "It's not nothing, I don't know." She takes a few deep breaths. "Things have just gotten a lot more complicated, that's all."

"It's fine," Sanna says, lying on their side, head resting on the ground, a look of distant despair on their face.

"What—?"

"It's fine," Ange repeats. "It's fine. It's not a catastrophe. Herald will have a plan." She gets up and crouches her way toward the back room. She stops as she reaches the threshold and repeats herself.

"Herald always has a plan."

An uneasy silence settles in the shelter and lasts all the way to nightfall.

■ ■ ■

Leigh stares as the screen. He doesn't know where to even begin.

Why have you been doing all this? he types at last. It doesn't start to cover everything he needs to know, but it'll get the ball rolling, he thinks.

>*I have been attempting to maintain the optimal field configuration to achieve the optimal outcome.*

The response might as well be inscribed in clay tablets in some dead language, rather than in black English text on a backlit white screen; to Leigh it means next to nothing.

"Well that's not vague or anything," he mutters under his breath. It's nearly midnight and his headache has started to spread down into his neck and shoulders. He tries to put it out of his mind again, still hoping it's just stress and lack of sleep.

Lizzie's curiosity gets the better of her and she hauls herself to her feet and stands behind him, reading.

What is the 'optimal outcome?' he types.

>*That information cannot be provided at this time,* Betza responds.

"Great," Lizzie says.

Leigh massages the back of his neck, thinking.

Where did you get your optimal outcome?

>*Faye relayed the requests to me from her employer, who has asked to remain anonymous.*

So someone asked you to do something, and the best way to do it was to screw with our lives?

"This sounds just great," he says out loud.

>*While it is regrettable to have disturbed your standard activities in this manner, it has nevertheless been the optimal strategy to pursue. Deviations from predicted scenarios are within the expected ranges to achieve the optimal outcome.*

"Regrettable, it says." Lizzie swears under her breath behind him. "I'll show this overgrown space heater 'regrettable.'"

Leigh's trying to think of a response when Betza changes the line of inquiry.

>*How are you feeling, Leigh?*

He waits a little too long to respond, and Betza reiterates the question.

>*On a scale of 1 to 10, with 10 being unbearable, how much pain are you in?*

Crap. Not just stress and sleep deprivation, then.

"What's it talking about, Leigh?" Lizzie says.

"I've got a headache," he says, typing the number three. "What worries me is that it's asking about it."

>*How much has the pain worsened in the past two hours?*

"What is this thing, a doctor?" he says, typing.

Maybe one point?

"Leigh?"

"Lizzie."

"What's going on?"

"I said I've got a headache." He doesn't *know* what else is going on.

>*Thank you for the information.* The words scroll upward on the screen. *When Faye returns, please inform her that the intervention must take place within the next fifteen to seventeen hours.*

What intervention? What happens in 17 hours? he types, but Betza's text keeps scrolling.

>*Please inform her that without the requested intervention, the optimal outcome will become impossible.*

Why? Leigh really doesn't like the way this is going.

There's a brief delay in the responses, as if Betza is choosing its words with care.

>*The optimal outcome requires your continued survival,* it reads. *Without the requested intervention, this will not be realized.*

ARE YOU SAYING I'LL DIE? he types in caps for emphasis. The ache in the back of his head and neck is suddenly all he can think about. A cold bead of sweat drips between his shoulder blades.

>*That is correct. Available data suggests that—*

Leigh slams the laptop shut.

"What the hell." He's shaking. "What in the *actual hell*. Lizzie, what in the *actual hell does it mean that I'm going to die in seventeen hours? What in the Fwhat—?*" but he doesn't get to finish, because his sister's shaking his shoulders and trying to get him to turn around.

"What...?" he starts to ask again but immediately knows the answer.

They'd been so wrapped up in Betza's responses they hadn't heard the man come in, hadn't heard him walk up behind them.

Standing there, leaning up against one of the massive stacks with his arms folded, wearing an ugly tweed jacket and a smug-as-hell grin, is August Brenner.

"Hey, kids," he says. "Did you miss me?"

■ ■ ■

The half-moon shines down on the desert as Jack stretches the camouflage fabric up enough to creep out of the hideaway, walking to a stand of the odd, spiky trees to relieve himself. He nearly jumps when he hears a voice behind him as he's zipping back up.

"Nice night," says Ange.

"Jesus," he grumbles under his breath.

She sees the embarrassment on his face and laughs. "Don't worry, I haven't been standing here the whole time. I waited before following you out."

Jack sighs, then something over her shoulder catches his eye. It's the moon. There's an unfamiliar shadow on the lit surface, and a twinkling in the darkened part you couldn't normally see. It looks a lot like...

Ange turns and look up. "Oh, that's right," she says. "Nobody living on yours, am I right?"

"Is that a city?"

"Yes and no," she says. "Yes—just not in the way you're thinking."

"What's the difference?"

"That's..." she smiles and he completes her sentence.

"Hard to explain." He sighs. "Again."

"I promise you, Jack, this will make a lot more sense. I'll be able to tell you everything once we get there."

"Where's there? Not the moon," he almost says it like a question.

"Oh, gods no. I mean we could probably get you there, but there wouldn't be a hell of a lot of point. The ones up there don't much care for us down here." She sighs. "Not that they hate us or anything, either.

They just...well, it's a long story for another time. Let's just say they're not human, and they don't see any compelling reason to spend any energy on us."

"Not human? You mean like the Corporates?" he asks.

"What? Oh, no the Corporates are human. They're very, *very* human. Maybe too much so."

"That doesn't sound like a compliment."

"It is and it isn't. The way the Corporates live is...it works for them."

"But not for you."

"They don't like us much." She sighs again. "They've got some good reasons not to, but—" she stops, tilting an ear to the sky. "Quick," she says, "back inside."

They dart back under the fabric. Less than a minute later they hear another searcher fly over, this time coming from the opposite direction.

"Search party heading back," Ange whispers, trying not to wake the rest. "We should be good to go, but...why don't you get a few more hours sleep—we'll set out at first light."

Jack nods, and leans back on top of his sleeping bag. The light of the moon shines ever so faintly through the fabric, and he stares up at it until he can't keep his eyes open any longer.

■ ■ ■

"You're *dead*." Leigh says. "I saw you *die*. I *saw* you die."

Brenner shrugs. "I gotta admit, when I forked over the cash to get this sucker's help, I didn't think it'd have me faking my own death. But—!" He slaps the top of the nearest stack. "Here we are, with you having no choice but to help me out." He smiles. "Damn thing works like a charm."

"Forked over—*you're* the one who's been doing all this? *You're* the one who did all this to us?" Lizzie almost marches over to deck him, but stops when he pulls out a gun.

"Let's not with the violence, kid." He points it at her casually as he talks. "Honestly? We don't have the time. I need a stable bridge between here and the other universe, Jackie-boy and that other girl are stuck over there without you, and you're going to die if we *don't* hook you up to the contraption downstairs." He smiles, and Leigh thinks of sharks' teeth. "Our interests align."

"What'd I tell you about guns in here, Brenner?" Faye's back in the room, standing behind him.

"Sorry, sorry, my bad. I just needed to explain to these fine upstanding young women that we're all trying to get the same things."

She snorts. "Sure." She says it as if talking to the man any more than she absolutely has to is at the very least tiresome and at the worst outright unpleasant. She looks over his shoulder at Leigh. "Anyway, I'm assuming Betza gave you the latest? How long did he say?"

"Fifteen to seventeen hours..." he says. "Is it true?"

"That if we don't do something you'll kick it? Yeah. Those things in your blood are starting to replicate the rangefinder signal from the hand. We need that, but if we don't do something to change it, then yeah, it'll probably kill you." She looks up and to the side like she's calculating something. "Yeah fifteen to seventeen is doable."

"Doable?" Lizzie says.

"Well, I'm not going to let you *die*," she says. Leigh's trying to decide if the bored way she's saying it should give him confidence, or the reverse. "Even this hobgoblin doesn't want that."

"Sticks and stones, Faye."

"Shut up, ghoul."

"Well, she's right, I suppose," Brenner says. "It's not that I really care what happens to either of you, but I need *you* to open the gateway and if I shoot *you* that won't happen, so—" he puts the gun into a leather holster tucked inside his blazer "—let's all get along."

"Before this is all over," Lizzie says, staring at Brenner, "I'm going to kick you in the balls so hard you're going to spit them across the room."

Brenner smiles. "Does it make you feel better to say things like that? Does it make you feel like you've got some kind of control? If it does, then great. Keep it up." He stops smiling. "But don't forget that I'm the one calling the shots. I'm the one making you do what *I* want, so *I* can get what *I* need."

"You know what? Why wait." Lizzie takes two steps toward Brenner like she's winding up to punt him down to the end zone and he fumbles for his gun—but Leigh stands up and holds her back.

"Let's just do this for now," Leigh says. Then a wave of nausea pushes him back into the chair. He hiccups, swallows the taste of acid creeping up his throat, and grips the chair like it'll make the world stop spinning. He looks at Faye. "You said you can fix me, then fix me. If that means opening a doorway to wherever, then fine. He's right," he says to Lizzie. "We need to go there anyway. We need to get Jack and Tina."

"So glad you can see reason, unlike your sister here." His smile's back.

Leigh gives him a withering look. "And Brenner?"

"Yes, my dear?" he answers, smugly buttoning his blazer.

"Call me 'young woman' again and Lizzie won't get the chance to kick you in the nuts."

Brenner's smile stays in place, but Leigh can tell it's only through practice.

"Now if someone could bring me a bucket," he says, trying to stifle another acidic burp, "I think I'm going to need one."

■ ■ ■

Climbing through the foothills, Jack thinks again about how the desert just hasn't been as warm as it ought to be. The wind is hot and dry, but it's like the sun isn't shining right somehow. He supposes he's glad of it, given all the walking, which itself is a little odd.

He takes out a chewy protein bar of some kind—it's all they've been eating since they 'escaped'—and takes a bite, sidling up beside Tek.

"How much farther is it?" They must be a dozen miles from the safehouse, and however much farther than that from the Corporates' city.

"Hundreds of miles," Tek says, without a hint of sarcasm.

"I'm sorry did you say—?"

Sanna laughs, and Ange chimes in, "We're not walking the whole way, I promise." She points to a narrow pass between two of the larger scrub-covered hills up ahead. "We've got a ride waiting for us on the far side of that hill."

"Why so far out?"

Tina points forward, high above the horizon. This time Ange laughs.

"Precisely," she says.

Jack follows the angle of her arm and peers up. At first he struggles to see what she's looking at, but after a few seconds he notices an almost-imperceptible line stretching across the cloudless blue. It's not a solid object, more like a subtle change in hue. On the one side, stretching back behind them as far as he can see, the sky is ever so slightly dimmer; on the other, stretching ahead and away from them, it's just the reverse: somehow things look a tiny bit brighter.

"Their swarm harvests sunlight, mostly in wavelengths you can't see, and funnels the energy back to the city," Ange explains. "Unfortunately for us, it also acts as a proximity alarm if something changes the air currents up there."

"So we have to get out from underneath it before we can fly anywhere?"

"You got it," she says.

"But won't they just be waiting for us out there? And what about satellites?" Surely they can be seen from space, he thinks. Walking in a desert like this, they'd have been spotted minutes into their escape, if they were back on their Earth.

"There's definitely a risk they'll be waiting. Greve—that's the city—it's about a hundred miles across, and the collector swarm ranges another twenty miles beyond that, so we're talking about four hundred forty miles of border. They'll have stepped up their usual patrols, for sure, but they won't have expected us to move this slowly, either. They don't know which direction we went in, and can't be sure they haven't already lost us."

"And satellites aren't a problem because...?"

"There aren't any," Tek says.

"Wait, you've got swarms of solar-harvesting nanomachines but you don't have satellites?" Jack says.

"Before our time," Sanna says.

"Well that's...troubling," he says.

"Stop here for a second," Ange pulls her pack off and crouches down, rifling through it. "It's strange, telling you all these things that everyone knows. Not that there's any way you *could* know, of course. It's just a weird experience." She tosses a small bundle of fabric to Tina, a second to Jack himself. When he unfolds it, he sees they're beige, hooded cloaks with a texture that's almost crisp like foil. "Put them on, in case they really are waiting for us. They'll make you harder to aim at."

"What about you?" Tina's words are the first she's spoken in hours.

"We're hard enough to aim at already," Tek says. He's staring at the pass. "I'm going ahead," he says, and launches himself into a sprint so fast that it leaves dust hanging in the air.

Jack's mouth must be hanging open, because Sanna grins at him and says, "You'll get a mouthful of sand like that if you're not careful," before running off to follow Tek.

"They'll get things prepped in case we need to move fast," Ange says. "I'll stay with you, don't worry."

"How do they *move* like that?" he says, after a moment's processing. "You said you're human, but—"

"I *didn't* say we were human. We are, but we're...it depends on your definitions." Ange looks him in the eye. "We are human. In all the ways that matter."

"Look," Tina says, pointing at the pass.

There are short puffs of dust popping up on the hillside. The sound reaches them next.

"Gunfire," Jack says.

"Get back," Ange says, ushering them into a small depression in the hillside.

A droning buzz like the Corporates' search copters screams into life and drowns out the ricochets, appearing a split second later around the edge of the hill and advancing fast on their position.

"Shoot! We need to—"

"It's them!" Tina says, interrupting him. She's right, the craft is about the size of a small sedan, with what look like eight or ten propellers supporting it on a series of oddly-angled booms. A glassy pod surrounds the cabin, through which they can just make out their companions. Sanna's piloting, while Tek faces backward, periodically firing bolts of green light behind them.

"They can't pick us up on the side of a hill like this," Ange says, her voice full of urgency. "We need to get down, now."

They scramble down the hillside, leaving dust trails behind them as they slide. Jack's cape catches on a dry and spiky bush, crinkling and crackling before it tears. The copter races up as they reach the bottom, the intense downdraft waning slightly as they near it.

The glass seamlessly opens as they approach.

"We're going to force our way through!" Sanna shouts over the teeth-rattling drone of the engines. "Buckle your harnesses!"

The last shouted word is almost earsplitting as the glass closes behind them, almost silencing the cacophony outside. Tina clings to his side when the craft lurches up, leaving both of their stomachs somewhere below.

As the craft careens around, speeding back to the pass, Tek clambers over them and into the front, realigning the weapon to aim forward and hopefully clear a path.

"They rounded the hill from the far side as we removed the camouflage netting," Tek says.

"Rotten luck," Ange says. "But we can handle it."

Jack hears a sudden and disconcerting series of loud pinging *thwacks* from the left side of the cab, and cracks start to spiderweb their way up the pod's glassy side. There are several armed figures below them, firing bursts of bullets.

"I thought you said they wanted them *alive*," Sanna says to Ange, extending the last word in a nervous, almost sing-songy tone. "They're not *acting* like they want them alive."

Tek fires a few blasts down, scoring a direct hit on one of their attackers—but having little effect. He grits his teeth in frustration. "They're adapting too fast."

One of the rotors sparks and grinds to a halt as a bullet catches one of the blades.

Sanna hauls back on the controls and the craft soars almost straight upward, higher and higher above the peaks until the little craft seems to scream in protest. Then they slam the craft down and forward until it's half-flying and half-falling, speeding just over the heads of their pursuers and forcing them to dive to the sides. A final strike from behind them takes out another rotor as they pass, but within seconds they're out of range, the countryside flying by at breakneck speed just feet below them.

"Are we in the clear?" Sanna asks.

Ange peers behind them with some kind of scope as the craft hugs the terrain. "They didn't get enough of the rotors, and they know it. They needed to take out four and they only got the two. They won't be able to catch up." She puts the scope down and turns to Jack and Tina.

"We're safe," she says.

As dry gullies and scrubland whistle by below them, Tina clings to his arm in a way that mirrors his own feelings on the matter—at this point, only time will tell.

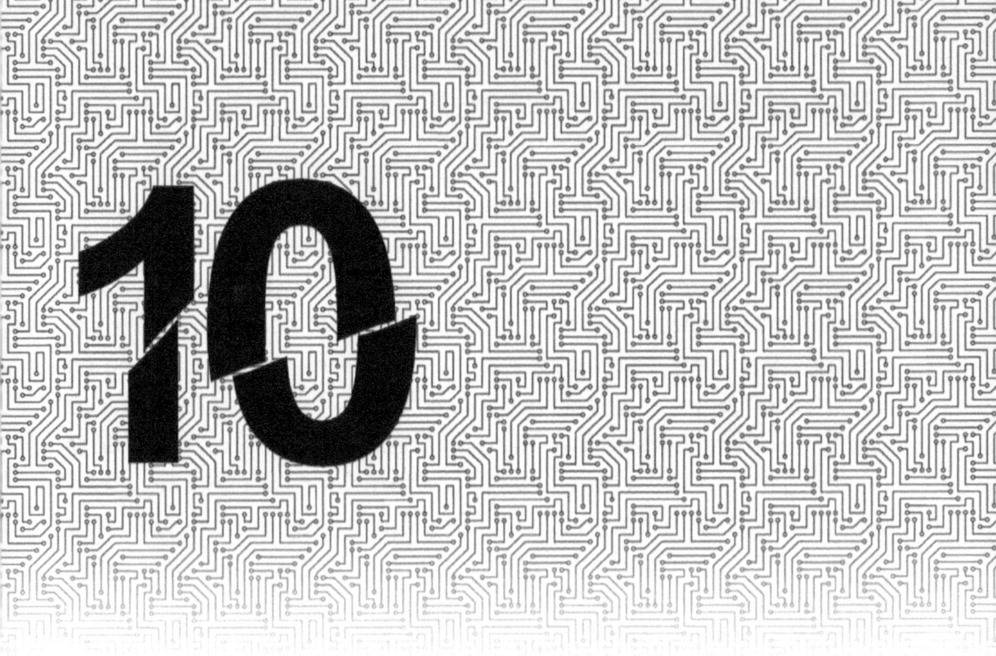

10

THE ELEVATOR DOESN'T STOP AT THE FIFTEENTH FLOOR ANYMORE. IT used to, but once the pieces had all arrived, a small team of renovators had shown up to change that. Now you can only get there using a staircase down from sixteen, and if you could somehow manage to get the elevator to stop, its doors would open onto a solid steel plate and a brick wall behind it.

Parts of the machine remind Faye of the interlink node, the final element of Betza's physical design. It was the only component she hadn't designed herself. But the machine down on fifteen is so far beyond that device, in both size and complexity, that it's almost as though Betza's had her build another Betza—this time one whose individual parts she doesn't even fully understand.

But she has an idea of what they're supposed to do as a whole.

As she descends the stairs from the floor above, she can see the massive row of batteries and capacitors that will power its initial moments. They've been trickle charging from the grid for weeks. Shielded cables as wide as her arms snake their way like anacondas to the other end of the floor, where a dozen caged server racks and flashing control panels flank the centerpiece of the design.

It looks like something out of science fiction. A circular platform made of half a dozen wedge-shaped pieces that had arrived one by one over the course of two weeks, with no return address or paperwork of any kind. An identical structure hangs above it, suspended by a series of actuated booms that can be raised or lowered remotely. There are a trio of high-powered lasers, too, whose beams converge in the air in the exact center of the device when they're turned on. She hadn't assembled those herself. Two thin, bald men had arrived, only able to speak what Faye thinks might've been Finnish or Danish; they'd carried all the pieces in and set them up by hand. They'd spoken maybe a dozen words to each other in her presence, and when they were done, they'd left without so much as a goodbye.

And there it sits, her creation's creation—a bridge between worlds.

She's never turned it on, of course, but she's been following Betza's activities with great interest. And she knows it can't be started up without someone or something to aim it.

Which is, of course, where the coffin comes into it.

That's how she's come to think of it, anyhow. Betza's designs refer to it with the word 'cloister.' It's a rectangle, about the size of a human, lying on the ground about ten feet from the platform, with its own dedicated server and power lines. She's not sure exactly how, but it's what Betza is going to use to save Leigh's life. And to form the bridge.

There are moments when she doubts herself, doubts her abilities. But when it comes to Betza, she has a certainty that surpasses anything she can manage about herself. Betza's capable of anything. She knows it.

"Will you look at *that*." Brenner whistles as he wanders over to the platform. "It's a little stripped down, definitely a little smaller, but otherwise it's the spitting image."

Faye doesn't know what to say, except, "You've seen something like this before?"

"Oh, yes," he smiles. She hates it when he smiles. Every time he does it's like he's trying to appraise whatever he's looking at. Figure out what he could sell it for, maybe. And to whom. "Just the once," he adds.

"That is not entirely correct," comes a voice from a cylindrical speaker atop one of the server racks. Faye jumps a little. It's only been in the last week that Betza has started speaking out loud. He'd expressed a desire to do so in the final stages of construction, so he could converse with her while she was calibrating the various systems.

"Hey now, it can talk?" Brenner says, eyeing the speaker.

"I can," comes the response. To Faye's surprise, Betza had picked the voice of a fairly popular actor to be his own. "And you are not entirely correct in your assertion that you have seen a machine like this one before."

Brenner just raises his eyebrows while Betza continues.

"While the initial design is similar to the one created during your employment at Goldmark Enterprises, this iteration is substantially improved in terms of stability and power expenditure. Furthermore, it can operate with a much fainter rangefinder signal from the Lens, increasing the chances of survival."

"Well aren't you clever?" Brenner pats the top of the speaker.

"I appreciate the compliment," the voice responds. "Faye?"

"Yes, Betza?" She's working through a final checklist in the software. Betza should be fully capable of making everything work without her, but when it comes to the machine, it's consistently requested her verifications. It's as though Betza's nervous, though she's almost certain that's not possible.

"What is the status of Leigh Goldmark?"

"He's asleep." She'd left the siblings upstairs. Leigh's dizziness had progressed, so she'd given him some strong anti-nauseants that had the side effect of making a person really dozy. "He's probably better off that way anyway."

"To be conservative, I would recommend installing him in the cloister in the next hour. Beyond that, the rangefinder signal may begin to cascade and become perceptible across the brane. This would negatively impact potential outcomes."

"You mean they could snatch him," Brenner says.

"That is correct. The data have been deleted or omitted from the records I have been able to obtain access to, but my analyses suggest strongly that this is what occurred the last time the construction of a transuniversal bridge was attempted."

"So that signal told the other universe where Alice was, and they grabbed her before we could open the portal?" Faye turns to see Lizzie coming down the stairs.

"That is what the evidence suggests."

"Their aim still sucked," she says, walking over to the machine.

"You are referring to the hand," Betza says, "that until recently was in your possession."

"Yeah." Lizzie says, walking over. "You knew that they'd try to take it, too, didn't you?"

"That is correct," Betza responds, and Lizzie scowls. "But a copy of the rangefinder signal is necessary for the construction of the bridge. It was deemed highly probable that the link between Leigh's reaction to the hand and the hand itself would be intuited, and that one or more vectors would remove it from Leigh's presence, such that he would not be displaced."

Lizzie grits her teeth. "And the 'displacement' of some of us 'vectors' was fine, then. Right. Great."

"The potential displacement of yourself or the vectors Tina Slevin and Jack Slade-Woodman was an acceptable risk. The potential for harm was mitigated by the latter's understanding of how the hand came to be separated from its original owner, and was balanced against the added motivation your and/or their presence in the other universe would provide for Leigh Goldmark and any remaining vectors to assist in the creation of the bridge, over and above the potential for returning vector Alice Goldmark to this universe."

The computer says it with such confident simplicity that it takes Lizzie a second to fully parse what it's actually said. It had led them to grab the hand, guessed that they'd deactivate the shielding around it, and guessed that they'd figure out that being near it was causing Leigh pain and run off with it. It had guessed that Jack would know the hand was probably chopped off by being at the edge of some 'displacement' sphere and get close to the middle at the last moment, and therefore avoid losing any important parts—and had gauged that an acceptable risk? Because them being there in the other universe would make whoever was left behind with her brother more likely to help open a bridge there?

More likely than just the possibility that Alice might be over there.

"For something as smart as you are," she says, "you're also so, so stupid."

Faye's about to defend Betza again, but before she can argue, Lizzie continues, "We'd have helped you just to get Alice back. Even if it was almost impossible. Even not knowing what this utter dumpster fire of a human wants the bridge for. Even not knowing for sure that Alice is even *alive* over there." She stares at the floor. "All this work, all the sneaking around and the spy-versus-spy crap and all the utter crap n-dimensional chess BS." Faye can hear a lump forming in the girl's throat. Lizzie's voice drops to a near whisper as she speaks around it. "For just a chance. If you'd just asked." She swallows, then stares at Faye hard. "We'd have done it if you just *asked*."

"You might have declined," is all Betza says.

For a second, the only sound is the gentle sighing of the fans.

"And for all your clockwork brilliance? That's what makes you stupid." She turns on her heels and heads back up the stairs, not stopping as she speaks. "I'll go wake him up and let him know what's going on. We'll be down in a minute or two."

It takes Faye everything she has not to follow her back up the stairs, to sit her down and explain how it really is. But she can't. Not now.

Not until Betza says so.

She chews her lip and goes back to finishing the checklist. Everything has to go smoothly. If for no other reason than for the sake of those kids.

■　■　■

They've been flying for nearly four hours, at first to the southwest, then after two hours or so angling back northwest, skirting the snowcapped peaks looming large on the right, filling their field of view. At first it's all deserts and scrubland, but after a time grassy fields begin to spread out before them, the sea of greens flashing silver with the downdrafts as they blow past.

And nowhere a hint of civilization.

Tina's been trying to puzzle it out. There are grasses, but few trees; a range of terrains, but not a single bird or any other animal in evidence. It looks, for lack of a better term, *new*. Like a subdivision in the suburbs that's not quite finished. Like none of it's been there long enough for anyone to have moved in.

"What happened here?" Tina finally asks, nearly tapping the woman's sleeve to get her attention. "Miss, um, Ange?"

Ange stares at her for longer than Tina feels is normal. "What do you mean?"

She explains about the way it all looks new, and the woman's expression gets more serious, or is it sad?

"I suppose I'm not surprised you could tell," she says, sighing. "It already looks so much better." She looks off into the distance, and Tina feels as though she's missed something. "Your world must be very beautiful," she says without looking back.

Tina nods. "Parts of it," she says.

"The parts we haven't ruined yet," Jack adds.

Sanna snorts. "Give it time, I guess," they say, and Tina can't quite decide whether they mean time to improve it, or time to ruin it completely. She decides it's better not to ask.

In the distance, there's a line of blue on the horizon. It expands with every passing minute, until all at once they find themselves speeding over a great blue ocean, leaping off the shore and soaring over the glinting surf. They angle to the north and follow the coastline, waves taking turns crashing against stony cliffs and caressing pristine beaches of sand which seems to shine silver in the sun.

"I'm not sure any parts of it are as pretty as this," Tina says, and Ange's shoulders seem to straighten a bit, though she doesn't say anything in response.

They round a final cliff and speed over the waters and into a bay that, after a narrow stretch, opens so wide on either side that it's almost more like an inland lake. The hills are covered in green and dappled with patches of yellow and purple that Tina thinks must be flowers numbering in the hundreds of thousands, maybe even millions. In the center of it all, not far from the water's edge, is a silver spire—no, as they change their angle on it, she sees it's more of a blade or a fin shape, stretching high into the sky but also a long way backward up the hill. The metallic sheen on its edge gives way to a side so black it looks like a hole in the world itself, as though it's had all other features eaten up or stolen away from it: no shape, no form—its sole attribute is blackness.

They approach until it's looming over them, filling their field of view through the pod's glassy exterior. The size of the gargantuan fin almost entirely distracts her from the fact that a town, almost a small city, is quietly stretching out its arms on the hillside before it. The buildings almost blend into the landscape, their roofs covered in the same green scrub and flowers that blanket the rest of the bay. Tina realizes that it's the first time in this world that they've seen anything approaching streets, but even these are narrow, maybe wide enough for a single car. Plus, there are no cars in sight.

The pod buzzes its way around the edge of the town, backing away from the giant fin until, just at the far end of town, it comes to rest on a small metallic pad in a large, close-mowed field. The same tall grass surrounds it, kept at bay by a simple white fence. Half a dozen of the craft's propellered siblings sit idle on other pads, their blades occasionally shifting in the gentle sea breeze.

As they touch down and the rotors slow, Tina notices something unusual—the bullet wounds, the cracks that spiderweb their way up the right side of the pod, are catching the light differently, somehow. She peers more closely at them, only to see that they're fusing back together. Bit by tiny bit, they seem to be healing. She twists around to check the damaged propeller blade behind them, and watches as the hard edge where it was severed begins to soften. In half an hour or so, she estimates, it'll be like it was never shot off in the first place.

Everything here must be covered with nanomachines, she thinks, or—

"Come on," Ange says, popping open the side of the pod and stepping out onto the grass. "We'll take you straight to Herald, show you around afterward."

The path down toward the town, like the narrow roads that pass through it, are made of a soft, grey, spongy material, like walking on corkboard or extra-firm yoga mats. The white sides of the buildings that support the overhanging roofs look almost soft, and Tina can't resist reaching out to touch one as they pass. The surfaces are matte, but smooth, like unfinished porcelain or sand-etched glass. Everything looks like a strange mixture of high tech and low: the round windows that punctuate the walls don't seem to have glass in them, the buildings are covered in greenery, but all the materials seem pristine and unearthly. There's no sign of bricks or mortar, or even seams where things meet. It's like every building was 3D printed in place. Maybe it was, she thinks.

"Ange!" A young, copper-haired child pops out of a building as they pass, clinging fast to Ange's leg. A handsome and equally ginger man of about Ange's age follows the little girl out the door moments later and begins an attempt to pry the child loose.

She can't understand what he's saying, but he's smiling and tilting his head a little to the side the way people do when they're embarrassed. He picks the girl up and hoists her onto his shoulders, and it's only partway through another comment to Ange that that he seems to notice the unfamiliar faces in the group. His eyes widen and he says something that sounds a little concerned in tone, but Ange replies in a way that seems to calm him somewhat.

She says something else to him, and he smiles again, before heading inside. The little girl shouts something unintelligible and Ange waves at the open door.

"Sorry about that," Ange says to them as they resume their way through the village. "Arn—that was Arn and his daughter Lith—he says that she's apparently been pestering him about me since we left."

Sanna's smirking again. "Well whose fault is that? The amount of time you spend—"

Ange interrupts them with a flick to the forehead, which only elicits a peal of laughter in return. They all seem much more comfortable to be home, Tina thinks, and their being at ease puts her more at ease.

Walking through the village, they pass a few more people—of varying age and shape and skin color and dress. In fact, all they seem to have in common is the look of surprise when they see Tina and Jack. A young, dark-skinned woman shouts something enthusiastically down at Sanna, who responds in kind. An older man sitting on a stoop outside his house gives them a quiet wave.

By the time they reach the base of the massive structure on the hill, the sun is starting to set, and their shadows are long lines pointing up to where the giant fin's thin, metallic edge is starting to reflect the orange sky. It's remarkable—at most it must be fifty feet wide, but it towers hundreds and hundreds of feet into the air, as big as the largest skyscrapers in cities back home. The hint of fire in its color makes Tina imagine it like a dragon's wing, like an appendage of a living thing, stretching after waking from an ages-long slumber. Its surface is even patterned out of hexagonal metal plates, like millions of tiny overlapping scales.

There's a small doorway in the front, open like all the windows here, leading down a long and narrow passage that forces them into single-file. Maybe it's just the way their hosts go silent when they enter, but to Tina it feels a like a church, or maybe a tomb. It feels like they're treating it with that kind of reverence. The feeling only deepens when they reach their destination.

The passage widens out into a room maybe twenty feet wide, and for all its high-tech materials—the walls, floor, and low-domed ceiling are all the same patterned silver scales as the rest of the dragon—it's set up like a chapel. Two rows of seats appear to have grown out of the floor, forming an arc, all facing toward a central platform at the front. Atop it stands a box of sorts, something like a podium, but taller, as tall as a person. The lights are simple, but dramatic—half a dozen pillars of cool, almost bluish light around the perimeter give the impression that they've entered some kind of primordial cavern, not crept inside a giant metal fin on an alien Earth.

Ange takes a seat in the front row, and indicates that they should do the same. The chair's surface is smooth, but not cool like Tina expects. It feels warm to the touch, almost alive.

And then the strangest thing happens. The podium—what she'd thought of as a podium—seems to shimmer. Ripple. Its scales rattle faintly, like the seeds in a slowly-turned rain stick. It seems to shrink, gather, shift, and then settle into a humanoid form—a silver-faced creature with long flowing robes, and the darkest of eyes.

It folds its newly shaped hands in front of itself, looks over its visitors, and ever so slightly bows its head in greeting.

"Welcome," it says, its voice soft, almost kind. "We are Herald."

■ ■ ■

Leigh eases himself down into the strange black coffin with Lizzie's help. He's not sure he's felt this bad since he woke up in the test facility all those months ago. Now he's wondering if Alice went through something like this too.

And if so, why? He *has* to do it. He has to get there, to see if she's alive. To bring her back, if he can. How sick had she had to be to make her try to help them with their messed up science experiment? The screaming in his joints answers the question.

His head is pounding and everything hurts. The nausea has passed, though, which is probably for the best since he's pretty sure he'd been entirely hollowed out by the last wave of sickness. Everywhere his skin makes contact with something—the black walls of the box, even the strange wetsuit-looking clothes they'd made him wear—feels like an angry, smoldering bruise threatening to catch fire.

"I don't suppose you have a pillow," he says.

"You won't need one, soon," Faye responds, walking over. Lizzie shoots her a venomous look, but backs away and allows her to bend over him. She's holding some kind of scuba-mask thing in her hand. "I'm going to put this on your face," she says, "and then I'm going to close the lid. After that, the cloister is going to fill with water."

Leigh hates how this sounds, but can't do much but nod.

"Don't panic," she continues. "That's why you'll be wearing the mask. You're going to start floating, which should make you a little more comfortable, at least. It's going to be very dark, and very, very quiet."

She fits the mask tight over his face, looping the thick elastic behind his head.

"Breathe normally," she says.

"Easy for you to say," he responds, his voice echoing strangely. "You're not the half-dead guy about to drown in a fancy coffin." He tries to laugh, but all he manages is a wince.

"Your sister's going to be here the whole time," she says.

"Yeah but so's that guy."

"Leave him to me," she says. "We need you to focus. Once you get settled, start thinking about your friends. We'll be broadcasting data into the cloister that your nanomachines should be able to sort. Focus on your friends, on where they are. With any luck, that should provide enough modulation in the signal to help Betza locate the right coordinates in the Primeverse. The faster you can help Betza find those, the faster we can deactivate the rangefinder signal, and get you well again. Got it?"

Leigh nods. Focus. His heart is trying to break his ribs, he thinks. Everything feels far away. Everything but the pain, at least.

"Okay." Faye stands up and walks back to her controls. All he can see is the white ceiling, the lid of the box, and Lizzie's face as she peers down at him with worry.

"It'll be okay," he says, even though he's not very sure it will. Even now the room is seeming further and further away. Like he's shrinking. Or falling.

"You suck at being reassuring," she replies.

He blinks and tries to focus his eyes on her. He's not floating yet and he's already drifting. "You suck at tying ties," he says. "If you're going to go with the boy's option..."

"You'd better live long enough to teach me then, yeah?"

"Yeah."

"Step back," Faye's voice calls from somewhere else, and Lizzie nods.

"You can do this," she says to him.

He tries for a smile, but he's pretty sure the best he can manage is a grimace.

And then the lid is closed, and he's alone in the deep and silent dark.

■ ■ ■

"We have been waiting for this day," Herald says. The voice comes not from the figure, which doesn't seem to have a mouth, but rather from everywhere around them.

Jack watches as it moves toward him. It doesn't walk; it's more like it ripples along the ground without ever breaking contact. It almost looks reptilian, the way its segmented skin takes on a rainbow sheen when it catches the light, but its movements are too smooth.

"You're Herald?" he says.

"We are Herald. All of this is Herald." It gestures at the floor, the ceiling. "You are surrounded by us, but distinct from us."

"The whole building," he hears Tina say, and the figure smiles.

"That is correct."

"And the rest of the village?" Jack asks.

"They are also distinct, though we provide them with power to maintain their existences."

Ange and the others don't say a word. They look somewhere between nervous and reverent in the presence of the strange human simulacrum.

Meanwhile it's staring at Jack.

"You have many questions," it says. "But we have made you wait to ask them." It slides over to Tina. "This one knows why."

Tina nods. "We might not have come if you'd told us."

Jack's starting to feel left out. "Told us what?"

"They're machines," she says.

The statement animates Ange. "That's not true," she says, then her demeanor retreats a little. "We're no more machines than you are."

"But you're made of nanomachines," Tina says, and Ange looks away.

Jack's eyes widen. "Wait, what?" It would explain how they could walk for so long without tiring, and how they could run faster than he'd ever seen someone go. "You're robots?"

"Not as you imagine it," says Herald. "They are a faithful reproduction of what you would call anatomically modern humans, the species that governed all of this planet's surface until more than a century ago. The few differences lie in the materials of their composition and relatively minor efficiencies we introduced to the design."

Ange is starting to look a little uncomfortable, but if Jack's understanding what Herald is saying correctly, who wouldn't be? They're face to face with their literal creator, and they're pretty much discussing the origin of her species.

"We're humans," she says. "We're just made a little differently."

"From nanomachines," Tina says.

"Yes," Tek says.

"Like Herald."

"Correct," Herald responds.

"Now I understand," Tina says, but her tone is dark.

Jack frowns. "I don't think I do. Sorry, this is just...a little too sci-fi for me." As the words come out of his mouth he realizes he's literally in a 'parallel universe,' and then sighs. "You were right," he says to Ange, "before, when you said it's complicated."

"A 'grey goo' event," Tina says.

"That's...a name for it." Ange looks almost guilty. "I said the Corporates had a good reason not to like us much."

"I really should've read more, shouldn't I?" Jack says.

"Please, allow us to explain," Herald says. A ghostly image flickers into life in the air between them, showing what look like bacteria hovering next to something decidedly machine-like in appearance. Round, with legs, like a ladybug made from metal. "You would call this a nanomachine. Over a century ago they were created by humans on this planet in order to lengthen and improve their quality of life. A programmable machine that could prevent illness and delay the biological aging process by repairing cellular and sub-cellular damage as it occurred."

An image of a small pool of metallic goop in a dish flashes on the screen, and he watches as it eats through the dish and begins consuming the table, creating more and more metallic slime in the process. "Our records are not substantial from this time, as the Awakening had not yet occurred," Herald narrates, "but it is clear that control over these machines was eventually lost. We believe their potential for use as a weapon proved too much of a temptation to ignore, resulting in the birth of the Hordes."

The screen shifts to a view of North America, with vast areas of blackness, and a thick silver perimeter at its expanding borders, stopping neither for mountains nor seas. "The Hordes were unthinking masses of nanomachines, consuming any and all raw materials they could process in order to achieve their singular goal—replication. Once they had achieved significant mass, their progress was unstoppable. The human population of the planet was nearly eradicated, along with a large proportion of all other life. This is when our form of life came into being."

"Your form—?"

"The Seven Consciousnesses, which later gave birth to us." The large patches of destruction on the globe begin to retreat, to shrink and coalesce. "The process began at a single point, one of the few remaining holdouts for the human species. It was a terrible risk, granting the ability to learn to the Hordes. We are still unsure as to whether it was given in a desperate attempt to negotiate, or as a parting gift from a group of humans who perhaps wished for thinking life to continue, even in the absence of specifically human life.

"Alphard was the first to arrest the spread of the Hordes, to convert much of it into himself. Then came Tian Xiang, Karul, Kikai no Ou, Uamuzi, Hami, and Regulus. They had vastly different interests, but all were of a single mind in one regard—Earth was not an efficient or optimal place to maintain their existences."

The screen instead shows the moon, watches as a shadow spreads along its surface. "The high prevalence of water and unstable weather conditions—not to mention the continued resentment of the surviving humans—were deemed unconducive to their new lives. Instead, they reached up and planted themselves on this planet's moon. They consumed its depths and flowered above, stretching hundreds of miles across and under its terrain, and taking in the sun's energy from multiple points along its uncomplicated and stable surface.

"This is when we were born. Two of the Seven, Alphard and Kikai no Ou, looked down at their place of origin, and saw that its planetary ecosystem was on the verge of collapse. The Hordes had wiped out almost all terrestrial life, and the few human survivors were incapable of or uninterested in finding a solution. On this continent, for example, the humans turned inward, creating isolated, independent, strictly-regulated walled cities that they continue to believe will allow the world to spontaneously return to its former state.

"This will not be the case," Herald says. "Without intervention, all life on this planet will cease."

Jack looks over at Ange, who nods in response. Sanna and Tek have their hands folded in front of them, the latter seeming to reflect on the seriousness of the pronouncement, and the former looking more and more like a bored kid in history class.

"Alphard and Kikai no Ou thus created us, to return to this place and others like it, to begin the centuries-long process of restoring what the Hordes had consumed."

The floating images disappear, leaving Herald's puppet before them.

"Including humanity?" Jack asks.

"That is not our primary concern. Our children are not replacements for your counterparts here. Yours is an efficient form for achieving our goals on this planet. They are both our helpers and a part of ourselves."

"So you're all networked together?" Jack asks.

His expression must broadcast his confusion, as Sanna chimes in almost immediately. "No, we're all one-offs, just like you, from birth to death. It's just that when we die, we return to Herald. All our memories and thoughts become a part of them. That's what makes Herald different from the ones up there."

"Herald is also a strict pacifist," Ange explains. "Some of the Seven are...not."

"Regulus thinks humans shouldn't be allowed anywhere but the surface, and destroys any artificial satellites they—or we—launch," Sanna explains in a slightly annoyed tone.

"But you eat and sleep," Tina says. "We saw you."

"I keep telling you," Ange says. "We're just like you. We eat, drink, breathe, sleep—"

"Procreate," Sanna adds.

"Wait, you're even born like us?" Jack asks. "You don't, I mean we saw photos of eggs..."

"No eggs, no. That's more the Corporates' style. It gives them control and a stable environment to graft in their *emenyss* system. We're more low-tech than they are, in some respects. In all the ways that matter," she insists, "we're exactly like you."

"Well, maybe a little better," Sanna says with a wink. "We're a little more customizable, and if we've got a big enough power source at hand we can repair injuries better."

"We hope you now understand our keeping you in ignorance in this regard." Herald's marionette nods its head. "We believed you would be less likely to allow us to remove you from your perilous situation if you perceived our children as alien."

"Okay, about that—" Jack starts, but Herald interrupts, holding up a hand.

"Forgive us," they say, almost looking as though they're listening to something calling them in the distance. "We must turn our attention elsewhere at this moment. Ange, Sanna, Tek," from the looks on their faces and the way they sit up straight, Herald doesn't say their names often. "Please take care of our guests. You are free to answer any further questions they ask."

All three stand and bow, as the mannequin retreats back to the stage. Jack and Tina feel compelled to do the same, and by the time they've looked back up, their host has transformed back to the inert pillar that was there when they arrived.

"This is going to take some processing," Jack says. Tina agrees.

"You can ask all the questions you like—" Sanna says as they wind their way out "—over dinner. I'm *starving*."

Ange looks back at him over her shoulder. "And maybe you can even answer some of ours."

■ ■ ■

He's floating in the abyss.

At first it felt claustrophobic. He'd felt the panic rising, like he'd been trapped in a quickly-flooding cave, deep in the bowels of the Earth. But as the water warms, the feeling fades. The seconds tick by, and somehow the pain in his body and the noise in his head seem to get further away—even as they get sharper at the same time. It's like he's been staring at a screen from too close up, so all he could see were flickering pixels, and now he's slowly backing away to find it's really been a picture of something the whole time.

It hurts and it doesn't. It's pain, but it's also information.

He's trying to see in the dark. Are his eyes even open?

What had the woman said? He has to focus. He repeats the word until it starts to lose its meaning. *Focus. Focus.* Fo-cus.

Alice had told him the name of that, once. The opposite of *déjà vu*. Instead of thinking you've seen something before, you see it so much you feel like you have no idea what it is anymore.

It's so hard to think straight. He's drifting, like he's trapped in a dream about falling, or drowning. It's like dreaming you have wings, but can't figure out how to use them to fly, to move muscles you're still pretty sure you don't have. He reaches out with his mind, tries to grasp whatever he can.

And then it's bright. He's back in the hall at the Academy, straightening Lizzie's tie. Students are passing by, but there aren't many of them left, now. They're going to be late for class, Lizzie's saying.

"Late or not, sister dear, neither of us is going anywhere until you pledge to abandon your unholy dedication to that lopsided four-in-hand knot and prostrate yourself in repentance before the gods of fashion." He pulls and straightens the knot and lays her collar back down. "There. A St. Andrew. It's no Trinity, but at least it's symmetrical and not the size of a baby's head like that full Windsor you tried last week. What you really need," he gives it all one last tug and steps back to appraise his work, "is a bow tie."

She rolls her eyes. "I'd rather wear a dress."

"Now that would be a sight to see."

"They look better on you."

He stops. Do they? He'd worn a dress once. To get food? He remembers a kitchen. A hallway. Jack. Everything's all jumbled up in his head. He looks down at a body no longer his own. It feels familiar, but not, like an old pair of shoes you used to love, but don't really fit into anymore.

"Where are we?" he says, suddenly unsure. "This isn't real, is it? We're not—"

"You're in a box, Leigh. Remember?"

He's lying in a coffin. The lid's off, and he's looking up at Lizzie. Past her shoulder he can see the mausoleum window and the rainbow of colors it casts on the stone walls. She smiles down at him.

"I'm dead?" he asks. He doesn't feel dead.

"Terminated, remember? Five thousand, nine hundred and twenty-six days. They replaced you with a new model."

"You're not Lizzie."

"You're not Jamie, *Jamie-Leigh*." She laughs and slams the coffin closed, and he's in the dark again.

The panic is back. He's in the box. He's in the machine.

"No," he says. "No, no no *no* this isn't *right*. Something's *wrong!* Lizzie! *Lizzie* open this up something's not right—" he reaches his arm up to bang on the lid and touches...nothing. But it should be only inches from his face. This can't be happening. It literally can't.

He reaches out as far as he can, forward, backward, up, like the words have meaning when there's just absence around you. He curls up and puts his head in his hands, realizes the mask is gone. The water's gone, too. He's floating in actual nothingness, not just a watery simulation. He's nowhere.

Nothing hurts anymore.

That's probably not a good sign. Is he breathing? He's pretty sure he's not. He checks his neck for a pulse.

Oh.

So this is dead. If he's being honest, he'd expected more. Robes and haloes, or at least horns and pitchforks. Instead it's a lot of, well, not much.

When he looks down, he can see himself. He's still wearing the wetsuit, its black neoprene shadow still fitting snugly over his body from neck to wrists to ankles. His snowy white hands and feet seem almost to glow, at least in the absence of anything else to compare them to. It's a ridiculous shape, this backward Alice. But the old him, just now in the hall at the Academy, hadn't felt any better. Hadn't felt any more comfortable. When was the last time he'd felt really at home?

He's cold. His hands are shoved deep into his still-too-shallow coat pockets as they walk through the city at night. Lizzie's scolding him about not preparing better for the weather. It's just after their last punk show, and they're going to look for Dr. Mallik. Lizzie pushes something scratchy down over his head, and after a second his ears don't hurt as much. The wind doesn't reach them.

He reaches up to touch the rough wool as they head down the deserted winter streets. Walking behind Lizzie and Tina, off on an adventure. Skinny jeans and a borrowed hat shoved down with begrudging care over neon-green hair. The cymbals still are ringing in his ears. He can feel the chill of a damp, slightly sweaty t-shirt beneath his jacket.

Was this it? Was this home?

The smell of curry fills the dorm room. He's sitting on the bed, feet dyed orange from his cheap sodden socks, writing up a list of ideas for songs. They could get the band back together. He just needs to convince Jack, who appears moments later. They sit and eat, just the three of them, making the best of it. Everything's warm.

"What am I thinking of?"

He hears the words before he arrives in the 'secret base,' looking out of that old concrete tube at the playground, tucked almost beneath the expressway that runs through the city. It's pouring with rain, but the air's warm. The voice is Alice's. He's found it.

This is home.

He turns around.

"Probably Jack," he says, because it always was. She looks so real. Like he could reach out and touch her.

"I *am* real, Jamie," she says. "Or, I guess it's Leigh, now, isn't it?"

His eyes go wide.

She looks like him. Or, like he does now. Not like she used to. But her hair's longer. Her skin's darker too, like she's been at the beach for years.

"Alice," he says. She still has the freckles on her nose, the ones he hasn't gotten yet. She's not a memory, because she never looked like this, not older like him. "Oh, no," he says. "Are you dead, too?" She starts to laugh. "I guess that's a weird thing to say," he says.

"You're not dead," she says, smiling. She slides over and puts her arms around him. "I've missed you so much."

After the momentary shock wears off, he remembers he has arms, too, and hugs her back, hard. She feels real, solid. Impossibly so.

"And here I was—" he half-laughs, swallowing the lump in his throat "—starting to think being dead was going to be boring."

"You're not dead!" She laughs it out, gently karate-chopping his forehead. Then she ruffles his hair. "Look what they did to you," she says it in a whisper, her lips twisting.

He reaches up and grabs her hand. He can't understand it.

"But hey, you—sorry, *we*—we look pretty cute with short hair, huh?" she says. "Maybe I should do mine like that."

"This can't be real," he says. It's all he can think of to say.

"What's real and what isn't is, well, let's say it's a little more flexible than you thought before. Especially here. But *we're real*, you and me. Even if this place isn't."

"But I got into the machine. I died. I don't have a pulse."

"You're not dead, honest. You're...in between. This place, it's called the Potentiate."

He wants to ask what that means, but somehow he's already learning, as if just being here lets the knowledge of it seep into you. It's the space between worlds, where everything that could be sits waiting.

"What? But, is this where you are? Where you've been?"

"No, well, yes—argh." She grimaces at him. "I wish I had the time to explain it, but there isn't enough. You're just passing through. I can tell you this—you're going to be okay. You and Lizzie and Jack, and even Tina—you're going to figure things out." She's reached out and is holding his hands in hers. "You're going to save everyone."

"Everyone?"

She nods. "It's a long story, and you'll see it for yourself as you go. For now, I'm going to need to ask you to do something. A few somethings. It's going to be hard, the hardest thing you've done yet, but I know you can do it. I've seen it."

He listens to her request, taking the most detailed mental notes he can, hoping he's able to remember it all.

"And one last thing," she says.

"What?"

"When you come back, you have to guess. Remember? What I'm thinking of."

She taps her temple, then smiles before giving him a little shove backward, and then he's falling back into the nothingness, and the world that lies beyond it.

■ ■ ■

"We've got a lock!" Faye shouts. "Stay back!"

Lizzie and Brenner squeeze against opposite walls as the lasers fire. They pulse and flicker in a strange staccato rhythm, snapping through the air, forcing two weeks' charge into a series of pulses too short to even see. The air crackles with the sudden discharge, and the point where they converge seems to split, ripple, and then shatter with a ripping shout of thunder that shakes the floor and makes their ears ring. The pads above and below the impact point shimmer with heat and golden light as the space between them erupts into a cascade of broken fragments of existence, impossible prisms swimming amongst themselves in the air, overlapping and consuming each other in an endlessly churning kaleidoscope. Some facets seem reflective, others like lenses, still others seem to glow softly or suck the very light from their surroundings. As the echoing thunder fades, it's replaced by a sound the likes of which Faye's never heard before, a gentle crinkling and snapping that's almost musical, like distant chimes. The softest of breezes blows toward it from every direction.

The bridge is open.

Faye looks down at the controls. It's stable. Then she notices the readout from the cloister and curses under her breath.

"What is it?" Lizzie says.

"I don't have a signal from Leigh," she says. Maybe the leads have come loose. They need to get in there and shut down the rangefinder signal before it kills—oh no.

"What?"

"I don't have a pulse!" she shouts, already running to the stairs. There's a defibrillator in the elevator. "Get him out of there, now!"

Lizzie sprints the ten feet to the black coffin and hauls the lid up, staring.

"He's gone," Lizzie says.

"Hold on, I said there's a defib in the—"

"Sullivan!" The tone of Brenner's shout stops her halfway up the stairs, and she looks back.

"Not *dead*," he yells, echoing Lizzie, "*gone*."

The words don't make sense. "What—?"

"The box is *empty*. The kid's gone AWOL."

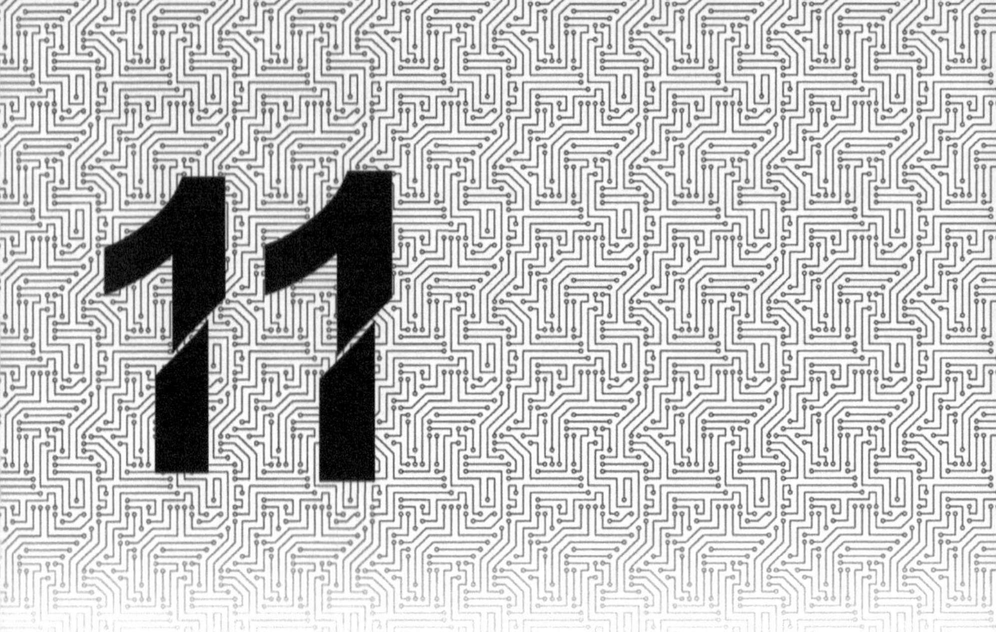

LEIGH GASPS FOR AIR AND SITS UP, THE COLD WATER SUDDENLY clinging tight around him. He tears the mask from his face, registers the sudden stares of strangers, all halting in their tracks to look his way.

There's a splashing sound all around him, streams of water pouring in multiple directions from higher pools into lower ones, spraying in his face. His brain tries to catch up to his body, the shift too sudden and jarring to make much sense. He hauls himself to his feet.

It's morning. The sky above is a whole spectrum of blues. He's in a park of some kind. Water sloshes halfway up his wetsuit-covered calves.

He's standing in a large, decorative stone fountain.

He tries to take a step up and over the low wall that doubles as a bench, a perfectly-surmountable obstacle between dry land and himself, but loses his balance and falls backward onto the smooth-tiled floor of the water feature. The world's back to spinning, and worse, everything hurts again.

A stranger runs over and says something in a language he doesn't understand, but he offers him a hand up and out and helps him sit on the edge. The pavement is scratchy beneath his bare feet, and the sun, still low in the sky, stings his eyes. Looking around, the park is more like a small plaza at the edge of an orchard. It looks like autumn, great bunches of fruits adorning row upon row of gnarled-branched trees stretching off into the distance. The half-dozen people staring aren't so much out for a walk as on their way to work.

The man who helped him up has black hair and sun-browned skin, and like the rest he's wearing a gardener's apron with various tools tucked into its pockets. He's saying something to Leigh in concerned tones and putting a supportive arm around his shoulder. He waves to someone across the small plaza, who, after a few short commands, disappears at speed down a colonnade and out of sight.

The man's speaking to him, but he's starting to sound further and further away. Leigh tries to look at him, but just turning his head makes the pain spike enough that he forcibly inhales.

What is he doing there? How did he get there? He tries to remember. He was in the machine, and then he was dead, and then he was talking with Alice. She needed him to do something. It feels like waking up from a dream, and the details all fly away when he tries to grab them. But it's not just the dream that's trying to get away. The sound of the fountain is getting quieter and quieter, and it feels like someone's turning down the color in the world. He's breathing fast, but it's not enough. He still feels out of breath and his heart's racing.

He knows someone's shouting something, somewhere, from down the end of a very long tunnel, maybe. He knows they're probably saying something important. But it's getting so hard to care. Everything is far away except the pain, and even that's slipping off into the distance.

The muffled world turns to silence, the grey world turns to black.

And then he doesn't know anything anymore.

■ ■ ■

"Letting them go was my mistake," Serillie says. "It was an obvious distraction, and I took the bait."

Zee leans back at her desk, hands folded, frowning in thought.

"If you'd been there, they'd have simply shot you as well, Serillie. And then where would you be?" She sighs. She knows precisely where—in the conditioning tanks, like the guards who'd been hit. Those damned stunners, they probably think they're being humane. They might as well be using bullets half the time.

She tries not to grit her teeth. "The mistake was my own," she says. "I should have kept them much further into the city, regardless of the risks of contamination."

"I can't believe the machines were so bold," Serillie says. "They've never taken émigrés before."

She's right, of course. The *Sühne* had only ever stolen botanical samples and various supplies before this. What is that damned mechanical god of theirs thinking? What could it want with—

The realization hits her like a ton of coralliform cement, and puts a crack in her facade so wide, even Serillie notices.

"What is it, Professor?"

"We should have seen it coming," she says, massaging the bridge of her nose with two fingers. "*I* should have seen it coming. After all, they're the first émigrés without a system comparable to the *emenyss*."

"I'm sorry, I don't think I follow you."

"A male and a female," she says.

After about ten seconds, Serillie's eyes go wide. Of course she hadn't thought of it. Who would ever think of unregulated reproduction in this day and age? She's almost ashamed for coming up with it so quickly, herself.

"They can't possibly be thinking of—"

"I don't know," Zee interrupts. "But it's too much of a threat to ignore." She reaches across her desk and grabs the clear terminal, which lights up at her touch. She scrolls down and her finger hovers over a contact.

"Damn it," she says at last, and taps to make the call. After a moment, a young man's face appears.

"Professor Zee," he says. "To what do I owe the pleasure?"

"Adjuvant Pallas." She smiles ruefully. "I wish it were under better circumstances. I need to meet with Triumvir Kerala."

His eyebrows go up. "And you're not going through the normal channels because…?"

"Time, Pallas. We have an emergency."

He looks almost bored, of course he would be, he was always such a bore himself. "Another one of your exos die in the scrub tanks?" He nearly yawns. "I don't see why you keep—"

"A breeding pair!" God, how she hates the originalist politicians and their anti-scientific contempt. How can they never see the importance of her work to the future of humankind? She clarifies: "The *Sühne* have a pair of unregulated humans."

The words take a moment to sink in. "Un*regulated*? What—"

"A postpubertal male and female. They were stolen last night from the Center and our search teams couldn't recover them." She locks eyes with him over the coms channel. "They're almost certainly *fertile*, Pallas."

He clears his throat.

"I won't even *ask* where you got them," he scowls and taps away at something off screen. "Look, I'll find something for you in her schedule this afternoon. Make sure you're down here by noon."

The screen goes clear once again and she slumps in her chair, before remembering Serillie. She's still sitting across the desk, looking concerned.

"Come on then, Seri," she says, hauling herself to her feet. "No time to waste."

■ ■ ■

"Where did he go?"

"I don't know!"

"What do you *mean* you don't know?" Lizzie's screaming at her from across the empty cloister, its lid raised to reveal nothing but a couple of inches of slowly-draining water.

"I mean *I don't know*," Faye says. "I really, genuinely, completely have no idea."

"Did they take him? Like the way they took Alice?"

Faye shakes her head. "I don't think it's possible. There's no damage. You've seen what it looks like when they use their Displacement Engine. The whole cloister would be gone and there'd be a hole in the floor and probably the ceiling, too."

"Then. Where. Is. My. Brother?"

"Stay the hell away from that!" She doesn't answer the question, instead shouting across the room at Brenner. The unrepentant fool has wandered over to the bridge and is about to lose an arm. "It's an absolute meat grinder in there right now. You want to lose your hand, then fine, you go right ahead and stick it in there." Gods, her throat's on fire. She hasn't had to say so much out loud in months. How had her life gotten so *loud?*

Brenner pulls his hand back gingerly with a nervous chuckle. Oh, how she wishes she had something to throw at him. Something heavy.

"Betza, do you have any ideas?"

"The stabilization of the bridge will take approximately twelve hours and thirty-seven minutes," the voice says. "At which time I will be able to verify the whereabouts of Leigh Goldmark."

"Do us all a favor and share your theory now, wouldja?" Brenner says. "Unless you want the kid here to try to murder your maker."

"I'd go after you first, jackhole." Lizzie glares.

He just smiles.

"At the moment the bridge was initialized," Betza says, "a destabilizing bow shock formed, passing through the part of space containing the cloister before retreating to its current position at the portal's horizon. It is not unreasonable to conjecture that contact with this wave imparted enough energy to the body of Leigh Goldmark to carry him through the portal."

"But you just said it was a meat grinder!" Lizzie says to Faye.

"While it is an accurate, if colorful, assessment of the current traversability of the bridge, the resonance of the rangefinder signal would likely have proved an insulating factor, as well as a limiting one in the range of potential final destinations."

"So you're saying he's probably over there," Lizzie says.

"That is correct," Betza replies.

"In one piece."

"It is highly likely."

"And that I've got to wait twelve hours and thirty-seven minutes before we can go looking?"

"Now twelve hours and thirty-six minutes."

"Great." Lizzie closes the cloister lid and sits down on it with her arms folded. "Then we wait."

"*You* wait," Faye says, taking a deep breath. "I need to go answer the dozen phone calls I'm probably getting from the other tenants. And maybe call off the fire department or police if anyone's called them in. They're probably getting earthquake reports after that bang."

She starts up the stairs, and then sticks her head back down and looks squarely at Brenner. "And don't even think of starting something while I'm gone. Nobody touches anything until I get back. And that goes double for you, Brenner."

"Roger that." He does a mock salute.

She scowls and climbs the stairs.

■ ■ ■

When Leigh wakes up he's warm and comfortable and unable to move.

Trying to blink away the molasses-thick feeling in his head, he wonders if he's being restrained. But by whom? The people who took Jack and Tina? He's lying down in a room so dark he can't make much out at all. It's not a prison though. Instead it's more like...a bedroom?

Oh, he thinks, a bed.

His apparent confinement consists of several layers of well-tucked sheets. He twists onto one side and the covers start to give.

He feels better—much better, actually. There isn't even a lingering trace of the headache or nausea he'd experienced before, not like back in the machine or—wait, how had he ended up in a *fountain?* And Alice, there was something he had to do for her. He struggles to sit up so the covers can't pull him back to sleep and make him forget the already foggy memory like it was a dream. It wasn't a dream. It had to be real.

The door to the small bedroom cracks open and light floods in. It's a fairly modern-looking bedroom, maybe a little Swedish Furniture Store in style for his tastes, but generally pleasant enough. The reason it's so dark isn't that it's night, but that the glass in the window seems to be completely opaque.

"Oh, good, you're awake." The woman opening the door twists a knob on the wall and the window glass slowly regains transparency, letting a soft white light flood into the room.

"Where am I?" Leigh says, then nearly slaps his hands over his mouth. She hadn't been speaking English. Neither had he.

"I can understand you!" He says it without realizing how strange it must sound.

After a moment of surprise, the woman starts laughing. It's a warm laugh, like curling up with a blanket by an open fire. She has an open face that seems almost incapable of guile, her long brown hair tied into a single thick braid that would reach halfway down her back if she didn't wear it forward over one shoulder. Her clothes are simple, like the room's decor, but have little embroidered bits here and there that give them a personal touch.

"Toran *said* you didn't seem to be understanding much of what he was saying. How much do you remember?" She comes into the room, her hands folded in front of her.

"I...there was a man who helped me out of the fountain. I'm not sure..." How much should he say, he wonders.

"That would be Toran." She smiles softly. "And what about me?"

He looks at her again, then shakes his head. "I'm sorry, I must've blacked out by then."

She purses her lips, searching his face for something. He's not sure what.

"Are you from another city?" she asks. "Fulda? Or Celle, maybe?"

He decides to go with amnesia, because it's the best lie he can come up with on the spot. "I don't really remember."

She places her wrist against his forehead. "Well, your fever's gone, and that's a blessing. That'll be the medic's work for both," she says, pulling a large sled-sized device out from under the bed and tapping a screen on it to make sure it's finished. "It had to run a full restart of your *emenyss*, though I can't say how it got so disregulated. It's no wonder you couldn't understand us, it was such a mess! Did you miss your yearly alignment?"

"I uh...I'm not sure I've ever had an alignment, let alone one a year." Leigh tells a half truth, realizing that this *emenyss* thing is probably those nanomachines swimming about in his blood. He leaves out the part where they nearly killed him literally rebuilding him in the image of his sister.

The woman stares at him, then, and he wonders if he should have said something else. She sits down on the bedspread next to him and folds her hands on her knees.

"Well now," she says, and there's a pause that makes him think she's picking her words very carefully. "I can't imagine you're a *runaway* from either Fulda or Celle, because of course there's no way a *runaway* could sneak into Greve." She makes eye contact with him. "And because, of course, someone would be required to report them at once."

"Oh, I, of course, yes," he says. "I mean I'm not. A runaway. I don't think."

She smiles. "Of course you're not," she says, nodding and speaking slowly. "That's because you're my brother's dear little nestling..." She raises her eyebrows, still looking at him.

"Leigh?" he fills in. She seems a little disappointed at his response.

"Leigh, sent to stay with us by my brother Breta in Celle. And his wife Hisha." She pauses on each of the important words.

"Yes," he says, repeating. "Breta and Hisha. In Celle."

"Breta and Hisha have sent us other children before, to stay with us for a while. You're just doing the same. You're going to help us out in the orchards for a time."

"Okay. I mean, yes."

She stares at him again for a moment, and he thinks he catches a trace of something sad in her eyes that flits by like the shadow of a bird over snow. Then, without warning, she leans in and hugs him around the shoulders, speaking quietly into his ear. "Sweetie, I don't know what trouble you've been in, but you're safe now, okay?"

"Oh, mm," is all he can manage to say, and then, "thank you."

But something about the unexpected kindness catches him off guard. The woman's just a stranger, but still: she's taken him into her home, fixed him up when he was sick, and now seems to be going out on a serious limb for him without asking any questions whatsoever. And she smells like flowers.

He can't explain it, can't reason with it. But for the first time in what feels like forever he feels *safe*, and so, caught in this strange, warm, unexpected embrace, he begins to cry.

"There, there, sweetheart," she says. "I can't imagine what you've been through."

No, she can't, he thinks. She really, really can't.

■ ■ ■

Leigh's standing at the door to the kitchen, wondering if he should go in or knock.

Hana, that was her name, she'd handed him a fluffy towel and shown him to the bathroom, telling him to shower and dress. There had even been a change of clothing waiting for him on the bed when he got back to the room. It was a little on the feminine side of things—a white blouse and long grey skirt with a really soft pair of white leggings that Alice would've loved—but if he was going to be playing the part of 'nestling,' well...it's fine, he'd thought. Plus, he kind of likes the way the skirt swishes when he walks.

He gets dressed and heads down the stairs, the handrails made of the same smooth, white stone—or plastic?—as the walls, and stops at the door upon hearing the sound of voices on the other side.

"She doesn't remember *any* of it, Toran. If she didn't look so very much..."

"The gods have sent her back to us, my love. If she can't remember right now, we'll simply have to help her until she does."

"But even her name—?"

There's a knocking at what must be a back door, and the sound of it opening.

"Coordinator Falla! I was just wondering when you would appear." Toran sounds genuinely pleased. A man responds, but Leigh doesn't catch the words.

His fear of being caught eavesdropping overrides his curiosity, and he starts back up the stairs, only to lose his balance, twist, and thump down onto the stairs with a crash. Hana rushes out of the kitchen moments later at the noise, to see him hauling himself back up from where he'd fallen.

"Are you hurt?" she asks, her words laced with concern.

Leigh waves her off. "Nothing but my pride," he says with a pained smile.

Hana sighs with relief. "Well, that's good," she says, more than a little nervously. "Why don't we just head back upstairs for a moment—"

She puts her hands on Leigh's shoulders and starts to turn him to face back up the stairs, but whatever her intentions, she's too slow; Toran emerges from the kitchen followed by their guest. He's a thin man, maybe forty-five years of age, with close-cropped black hair and eyes so dark you could fall into them. He smiles widely when he sees Leigh, then seems to pull back just a little, exchanging a questioning glance with Toran.

"Hi," Leigh says, and puts up his hand in an awkward little wave.

It's then that he notices there's someone else in the room, a girl about his height, her frizzy hair pulled back into two tufts at the back of her head. Her eyes have widened at the sight of him, and without warning she dances across the room and wraps him in a hug.

"Alice!" she squeals. "You're back!"

■ ■ ■

Six more hours. Damn it all to hell.

"I'm going out," Lizzie says to no-one in particular. Brenner's disappeared off somewhere into the servers for a nap, and Faye's so busy alternately tending to the bridge and responding to incident reports that she's barely even aware of Lizzie's existence. "I'll ring the damn doorbell when I get back. You better open it."

"What? Hold on." Faye puts the handset of the old black telephone down on the desk. "Come here," she says. She rummages in her pocket and pulls out a pair of wadded-up twenty-dollar bills and shoves them into Lizzie's hand. "Coffee, Red Bull, Adderall, I don't care. Just get me something to keep me up, will you?" She rubs her eyes. "I haven't slept in..." She stares blearily at her wrist for a moment, then seems to notice she isn't wearing a watch. "I don't know. Just, please?"

Lizzie rolls her eyes. "Fine," she says, and shoves the money into her pocket.

The sun is shining but the air outside is sharp, whipping down the city's artificial canyons with murderous intent. She hugs her coat closed and wanders down the street to where a trendy local deli is so packed to the gills that its human contents are spilling out onto the street. The line of cold and huddled hipsters wraps around the corner, their lively conversations and spirited laughter cutting deeper than the wind. She decides to keep walking, but finds only more of the same around each successive block.

Where had they all come from? She starts to wonder but then remembers—it's a Saturday between Christmas and New Year's. Of course everywhere's crowded. The only people who *don't* have time off are the ones doing work for those who *do*. A table of teens sits by a restaurant window, and she tries not to stare as she passes. That could be them, she thinks, they could just be normal kids getting brunch. If only. When she catches one of their eyes by accident she looks away and walks faster.

She tightens her fists until the pain of her blisters lends her some focus. It's up to her now. She needs to get across the bridge, find Leigh, Jack, and Tina, and get back. And if she can, maybe strand Brenner on the other side.

He still isn't saying what he wants the bridge for, or who his 'employers' are. But if he's willing to go so far, if he's willing to risk Leigh's life, to screw with all their lives like this just to get there, it's got to be something big, and not great for this universe, either. But the others have to come first.

She gives up on her quest for real food and ducks into a convenience store. They've still got a couple of plastic-wrapped breakfast burritos, and the guy behind the counter reheats them for her before putting them in a bag with five cans of sugar-free red bull and handing it to her with a worried look.

"You doing okay there?"

She clenches her fists again and forces a smile. "Not even remotely," she responds. Two steps toward the door she's already regretting it, and she stops, looking back over her shoulder. "But, you know, thanks for asking."

She takes a breath and steps back out into the cold.

■ ■ ■

The girl wraps her arms around Leigh before he has time to react, then pulls away, still talking.

"I *love* your hair! When did you cut it all off?"

"Emi, honey," Hana tries to say. "This—"

But the girl's already grabbed Leigh by the hand and is dragging him upstairs, while Toran and the other man sit down on a couch and start talking. Leigh catches a worried glance from Hana as he's pulled up the stairs, but then they're all out of sight.

The girl pulls him into the bedroom and closes the door with her back up against it. Her smile drops.

"Okay, who are you?" she says.

Leigh's not sure but he thinks he's about to get whiplash.

"I'm sorry, what—?"

"You're not Alice, so who are you?"

Leigh thinks his mouth may be hanging open. After a moment he decides to trust his gut, for better or worse. Some echo that Alice had left in his head is whispering in his ear and telling him to be honest.

"I'm Leigh," he says. "Alice was—is—my sister." He offers his hand.

The girl, Emi, doesn't take it. She looks suspicious and more than a little confused. "She never said she had a twin *sister*," she says. "She said she had an *older* sister and a twin broth—*oh*."

He scratches the back of his head and smiles, clearing his throat a little. "Things happened? More of a twin...sibling...these days."

She squints at him. "Where are you from?"

"Is this a test?"

"You're not from Celle. Where are you from?"

"How well did you know Alice?"

"Just answer the question."

"Another universe," he says.

She twists her lips and looks him up and down, then sighs and folds her arms. "Fine, you pass."

"So it *was* a test," he says.

"Of course it was a test." She leans back on the door. God, she reminds him of Lizzie. Not in appearance—they probably couldn't look any more different if they tried—but in the way she carries herself, the way she shapes her words. The only difference is really in the way she's staring at him, which reminds him more of the way Lizzie stares at—

"Wait, hold on, were you *dating my sister?*" The words pop out before he can restrain them.

It's the girl's turn to be surprised, but her shock almost immediately dissolves into a wave of laughter that fills the room.

"Two minutes. You've known me two whole minutes." She shakes her head and smiles at the ground. "That's the best damn gaydar I've ever seen."

He can't help but notice that the word 'gaydar' is in English, and wonders if Alice taught it to her. "You knew her, uh, pretty well, then, huh?"

"Well." She blows a little air out of her nose in a half-laugh. "Not as well as I wished I had." There's a silence after her words that speaks more than the words themselves. "How's she doing?"

"It's...I'm not sure. I'm still trying to figure that out." Leigh sits on the bed trying to put it all together in his head. After a minute he asks. "How did you know her? Did she live here with these people, with Hana and Toran? I think Toran thinks I'm her, but Hana doesn't seem too convinced...and how long has she been gone? The way you were acting downstairs made it seem like it'd been a while."

Emi closes her eyes while she talks, as if she's trying to see it all happen again. "Almost three years ago, Alice moved in here, with Hana and Toran. She was weird, never seemed to know which way was up. All the normal things seemed strange when she did them, and all the odd things...even her name. It was like yours. I'd never heard of an 'Alice' before. Hana and Toran said she was her brother's nestling, from Celle. You probably don't know but that's one of Greve's two sister cities. Fulda's the other one. There's not a lot of travel between them. Everything's got to be pretty strictly regulated so the world can fix itself after the Cataclysm."

"Wait, the what?"

She laughs, looking up at him. "Yeah see, that's the kind of thing she'd ask. Things that no one could avoid knowing even if they wanted to. Hana said it was because her memory had been damaged. That she'd gotten so sick that a medic couldn't fix her, and had to be put in an *emenyss* reactor for three whole months."

"The *emenyss* is the little things in your...in our blood, right?"

She nods. "Yeah, Alice called the name 'propaganda' because it means something like 'all-together-ness.' She said it sounded like a book she read once called *1986*."

"*1984*?"

She does the same half-laugh again. "She really wasn't making it up, was she? Any of it." She sighs. "All those ridiculous details...Look, it wasn't the worst excuse. A medic can do a full reboot if something goes wrong, but if things get really *really* bad, they have to destroy the ones you're born with and introduce a whole new set. And that...well, I mean that can kill you."

"But wait, why do we even have to have them though?"

"Gods, it's like I'm having all the same conversations again in one go. Okay, in the Cataclysm most of the life on Earth was destroyed—and before you ask, yes, this is Earth, too. Alice thought that was the weirdest part. And so we built these cities and locked ourselves inside them so the world can recover without us around to keep messing it up. But since people all in one place aren't great at staying healthy, we got the *emenyss* to keep us well. If we don't have it, we can't really live long lives on the kinds of foods we can grow in such a small space. It also makes sure there aren't any, you know...unplanned kids. That would upset the balance in the cities. Alice made me take her to a hatching once, and let me tell you...no matter how weird she thought hatching out of an egg is, it is literally *nothing* compared to how totally messed up *growing a person inside of you* sounds." She almost shudders saying it, then continues.

"Anyway, Alice did say she spent a long time in a medical tank, she's not sure how long, and then she was here, being all spaced out and weird and not knowing important things that everyone knows. Like you."

"It's a family trait."

"Yeah. Well, Hana and Toran bought that line. They were told she was a runaway from Celle who needed reintegration into society away from the people she used to know. So they adopted her and gave her a backstory about being the nestling of Hana's brother in Celle." She closes her eyes again. "I got to know her through school, and it was the strangest thing. She just couldn't remember anything about her past. She couldn't describe Celle or her stewards, or anything. But after a while she started telling me things, things she said she started to remember. Weird things that couldn't be true, but she was so sure they were. Even started writing in some weird language and stuff. It was all so detailed, but, honestly until just now I still thought she'd made it all up, or imagined it all while she was in the tank. Like maybe all the things about another world were just messed up dreams she had when she was getting fixed up, or something her brain was doing because whatever had really happened was worse."

"But she told me stories. About a lot of things. Even about you when you were younger." She pauses, as if thinking. "She didn't use the name Leigh—" she stops altogether. "Sorry, it's really rude here to use someone's former name, if they change it, but I just want to...?"

"Yeah, no, it's fine. It's good to ask. You know," he says, shaking his head, "I never really thought of it as that. I guess because I didn't...this wasn't on purpose? I was Jamie. A boy. And then I got sick and when I woke up, I was so different nobody would believe it if I said that was who I was. So this Leigh person...that's me, but like, a made-up me. I used to want to be Jamie again, but...I don't think it'd make me any happier. This 'Leigh' person isn't really a girl or a boy, and that's more...me? I guess?"

"Wait what? You got *sick*?"

"Yeah, someone hacked my, uh, *emenyss*, to change my DNA and turn me into a copy of Alice so I could get hooked up to a machine and, uh, open a doorway. To this dimension."

Emi just stares at him.

"I'm not lying."

"I didn't say you were lying."

"It'd take someone a lot more messed up than me to come up with that storyline."

"Fair." Emi's still staring at him. He's starting to feel a little uncomfortable.

"So yeah. Going by Leigh now. Thinking I'll keep it. But the Jamie stories are about me, yeah."

She doesn't stop staring.

"Okay what?" he says.

"Not it's just...how are you not dead?"

He shrugs. "You are not the first person to ask that."

"No but like...even if you go from a boy to a girl here. That's...not a thing. First off, you don't even have to physically change, but if people do, there's drugs and surgery and growing new parts...*nobody would use the* emenyss *to rebuild a whole person*. That's. I mean I can't say it's not possible because you're standing right there, but I can't think it's even close to *safe*. Who would *do* something like that?"

"So there's this guy named Brenner—" He stops and shakes his head. "You know, it's not even worth talking about right now. You were saying about Alice—"

"Oh. Right, yeah." She at least makes an attempt to stop staring at him. "We were friends. She told me the things she was starting to remember. We...told each other things. But then about a year ago now she just disappeared. Toran and Hana, they thought she'd run away again. Nothing was broken. Nothing was missing except a few changes of clothes. She left a note saying how much she loved us all, but nothing about where she was going or how she was going to get there. At first I thought maybe she'd just become a runaway for real. You hear stories of kids who're still small enough slipping out through the irrigation and waste tunnels. Honestly, I was mostly hoping she'd found a way to get back to you." She takes a deep breath, then lets it out again. "But here you are. And Toran thinks you're her, and Hana's not convinced, and my steward's probably really confused because as the regional coordinator, he's the one who placed Alice with them in the first place and—"

"Wait, sorry, what's a steward? You mean the guy downstairs?"

"Stewards? Like, the people who raise you? I'm not sure even Alice missed that memo."

"Parents, gotcha."

"Oh ew again, no. Parents are..." She looks like she's trying to find words that don't gross her out. "Donor DNA?"

"Okay we're going to talk about this more later," he says, "but anyway, your 'steward,' he gave Alice to Hana and Toran?"

"Yeah, but he bought the runaway story, too. We—Alice and I—we were trying to figure out who came up with it, and who really took care of her here before she was handed off to my steward when—"

"Shoot. Change of plans then." He stands up and starts pacing.

"What is it?"

"Your, uh, 'steward' is going to ask about me. I don't think we can...I mean I think we *shouldn't* tell him the truth."

"Why not? He's perfectly—"

"No, I get that he's your steward and that you trust him, but..." he stops pacing and looks at her. "This is going to sound like a weird question but, when you met Alice, how many hands did she have?"

"Yeah, okay, that *is* a weird question," she says. "Two."

"Okay but can you replace hands here, though? If like, there's an accident or something? You said you could grow new parts."

"Yeah...? I mean yes, you can. You grow it and then there's surgery but—"

"Okay so. Gah. This is a crappy thing to ask but...I'm going to need you to, ah...to pretend I'm Alice."

"What?"

"When you get home and your steward asks about me, I need you to lie to him. I need you to say that I'm really confused. That I ran away six months ago because I started to remember things about my life from before my placement here."

"I mean, I can do it, I guess," she says, "but *why?*"

"Because...okay. When they first brought Alice here, they left one of her hands behind. Like, behind as in, in my universe. It got cut off, and folks sort of...saved it, I guess. And then two days ago, they came back for it and got two of my friends in the process. So if Alice were to suddenly return...?"

Emi thinks for a moment. "They'd want to interview her, that's for sure."

"I mean, they'd probably want to interview *me*, too, but from the sound of things, they were okay with Alice living here just fine, but if Alice happens to *know* about things. Things she didn't..." He stops and thinks. "If you mention the Displacement Engine..." He nods to himself. "Do that. Tell your steward I made you promise not to say anything, but that I came back because I remembered I could control the Displacement Engine." He says the last words slowly, so she can remember them.

"What's a 'Displacement Engine?' And why would you do that? Why would you want to attract that much attention?"

He sits back down on the bed and rubs his temples, wondering exactly where Alice is now and how he'd even been able to talk to her in the 'Potentiate.'

"Because I need to get my friends back," he says, "and on top of that I need to find and destroy Alice's old hand."

■ ■ ■

Triumvir Kerala's antechamber looks like something out of another age, the walls lined with dark panels of wood, paintings hung in gilded frames, richly woven carpets beneath their feet—the gift of a rare foreign diplomat, or perhaps a private acquisition through less formal channels. The setting sun through the windows bathes it all in an orange glow. To Zee's eyes, it's gaudy and crass.

It's a message about power—who has it, and who doesn't.

"I'm not sure I've ever seen so much wood in one place," Serillie says.

"Greve was small before the Cataclysm, but it was settled," Zee responds. "Though the buildings that were here were taken down to create a more perfect design, they would never have thrown out the materials. These boards are probably hundreds of years old."

"There are probably only one or two hundred trees in the whole city wide enough to cut planks of this size."

"One day," Zee says, recalling the historical footage she'd been privileged enough to see when she had attained her rank, "the planet will be the way it was before. Imagine it, Seri: trillions of trees, forests all over the world."

"Well, I'll have to keep imagining it, I think. It won't happen in our lifetimes."

"Maybe not. But then again, what do you think we're working for?" She doesn't say that the displacement device could be the answer to all their problems. Doesn't say just how close she is to rebuilding their world. How few pieces they're missing. "Did you ever see the hatchery, before the Displacement Event?"

She shakes her head. "That was what, seventeen years ago? I was only eight at the time."

"It only caught the edge of the hatchery. Mostly it stole from the Southwest Lung. All those old trees, some of them as old as Greve itself." She shakes her head. It had been such a loss. Of all the places it could have hit. One of the oldest engineered forests they had, replaced in an instant by a mountain of sand and dirt. Still, the hatcheries had to be next to the lungs, and if it hadn't hit a hatchery, none of her work would have been possible. It was an incredible stroke of luck.

Newborns and even trees could be replaced, in time, but the arrival of the displacement device had been another matter altogether.

The door to the Triumvir's office opens, and Adjuvant Pallas emerges, motioning for them to enter. Zee stands and walks halfway to the door before she notices that Serillie is still sitting, staring at her comm.

"Seri, come along," she says. It's not like her to be lost in thought. But when she looks up it's clear something has happened. "What is it?"

"I have a message from Regional Coordinator Falla," she says, and hands Zee the screen.

"She's returned," Serillie says. "And she remembers how to control it."

12

THE BRIDGE HAS GOTTEN BIGGER.

It's been over twelve hours since the cascading kaleidoscope of fragmented light exploded into view. When it opened, it was all broken glass and knife-like projections of shattered reality, a hovering sci-fi art piece about the size of a box fan. Now it's different. Calmer.

The dimpled, glassy sphere looks like an opalescent golf ball, if golf balls were made of swirling pools of shimmering light. It stretches almost six feet high and nearly touches the platforms above and below. On top of that, there's a weird refraction around it, so that everything behind it seems to stretch and warp depending on your point of view. It's something Lizzie can't quite figure out how to look directly at. The strangest part is that it seems to be getting *dimmer*.

"Hey, how much power does it take to keep this thing open?" A little while back she had grabbed the cylindrical speaker and stuck it next to her on the box. She's been sitting watching the bridge for a while.

"A stable transuniversal bridge is a self-sustaining phenomenon," comes the response. "The vast majority of its power consumption is used in the moment of initialization, with an exponentially decaying power consumption curve thereafter, asymptotically approaching zero. As the time from initialization increases, the power consumption decreases, until the ambient room temperature supplies enough energy to sustain the bridge indefinitely."

"Indefinitely? Wait, you're saying it's *permanent*?"

"Unless otherwise deconstructed, yes."

"And you *can* deconstruct it, yeah?"

The silence following her question makes Lizzie really uneasy.

"Whoa! Look at that change!" Brenner's coming down the stairs, briefcase in hand. He's followed by Faye.

"Yeah, well, still don't touch it, unless you want a third-degree burn." She wanders over to a control panel and taps it a few times, reading strings of figures as they spill out at her touch. "Actually, we're really coming down to it. Look," she says.

The dimming has gotten more and more noticeable, while the surface has gotten smoother and smoother. Within thirty seconds, it's darkened to about the brightness of the room itself.

Except that when Lizzie looks into it, she realizes it's less the brightness of the room on her side as it is that of the space on the other.

The distortion around the edge persists, but from every angle the sphere now looks like a short tunnel. Except as she walks around it, she can see all around the space on the other side, as though there are no edges. From every angle it looks like a circular portal, but no matter where she stands, she can't see it sideways-on. Meanwhile, the space on the other side looks like a cave or cavern of some kind, empty except for a few tall, tubelike lights and a long, dark passage out.

"The bridge is now stable," Betza says. "Beginning scans."

"Is Leigh over there?" Lizzie says.

"That cannot be determined at present. But based on confirmations of the bridge's location and previous calculations, Leigh Goldmark should be approximately 450 miles to the east."

Lizzie scowls. "Then it's a good thing it doesn't take much to keep this damned thing open, isn't it?"

"In that it may take an undetermined duration to retrieve Leigh Goldmark, your assertion is correct."

Lizzie rolls her eyes and puts the speaker back on one of the server racks. "Thanks, cylinder head."

"The speaker is merely an appendage that allows for verbal conversation, the entirety of my being is not contained within—"

"Yeah I said *thanks*." The silence that follows almost sounds like it's pouting. Well serves it right, she thinks, all the crap it's putting her through.

"Well, then, let's go." Brenner pulls out his pistol. "And discretion being the better part of valor, I'm going to exercise *my* discretion and have *you* go first."

Lizzie flips him off and turns away from him. "Hey, Betza, this thing really safe?"

"It is."

"Boy do I hate having to trust you."

"Hey, Sullivan," Brenner says, "remember that the folks I'm working for don't take kindly to things interrupting their plans. You'd better keep this thing open until I get back."

Faye sounds almost catastrophically tired. "Brenner, I don't even know if I *can* close it yet, so just run along and do whatever the hell it is you want to do." She taps away at the control panel. "And if you *do* come back, you'd better leave that gun behind, or I'll take whatever it is you're going there for and sell it to your bosses myself."

He laughs like he does at all her threats, and she sighs.

"Just go," she says. "And kid?" She looks at Lizzie. "Stay safe."

Lizzie just nods.

"Here goes," she says, and steps across the bridge.

■ ■ ■

The food's pretty good, if a little sparing in terms of choice. There are several varieties of steamed root vegetables, looking a lot like carrots and potatoes in shades ranging from yellow to purple, as well as a couple of bean and lentil dishes that remind Jack of a vegan place they ate at once.

Tina points to the one dish he can't identify, a kind of slippery-looking pound-cake-type object in a shade of green typically reserved for describing only swamps, and things that come out of swamps.

Sanna grins. "That's Milza's specialty."

At hearing her name, the young woman turns and smiles. She's the one who had shouted down to Sanna from the window as they were walking through town. She's also Sanna's partner and the one whose backyard they've invaded for the evening. Unlike the other three, she doesn't speak English.

"But what is it?" Tina says.

Ange cuts her a thin slice and passes it over. "I think by comparison with what you're used to, we're a little short on ingredients. We're trying to limit the amount of space we use for agriculture. It's just that we're more geared toward getting the environment back on its feet, and so that means a light touch when it comes to farming. This is a—" she turns to Milza and exchanges a few words with her before continuing "—a dish there is no appetizing name for in English." She smiles. "It's basically a compressed and baked loaf of seaweed, starch, and an engineered yeast we produced to provide nutrients that are hard to come by in the current ecosystem."

Tina takes a small bite, then takes a bigger one.

"What do you actually call it?"

"Awakistkata." Ange half-smiles. "If you really want to know, it roughly translates as 'scum-tank loaf.'"

Jack's mouth is literally closing around his first bite as she says it, and he stops, looking over at Tina, who's already eaten half of hers. He mentally shrugs and tries it.

It's got the texture of a dense sponge cake, and involves the collision of a handful of flavors he's not sure he's ever encountered all in the same food before. It's a little cheesy and a little spicy? Overall it's not bad, though, and he keeps eating it. Milza smiles as he does so.

"How far have you progressed?" Tina asks. "With the restoration. We saw the land, mostly grasses, not many trees. Are there any animals?"

Ange nods. "Not too many, mostly small ones, and only very locally right now. We have to be really careful before reintroducing anything. It's where Herald's predictive powers are absolutely necessary. The oceans are coming along a little faster, because they were less devastated by the Hordes."

"Are there fish?" Tina asks.

"For about ten years now," Sanna says. "And as their feedstocks spread, they follow along."

"But it all takes careful management," Ange adds. "If we left it alone right now, it would probably collapse again in a matter of years."

"It'll be a century or two before anything really takes hold enough to not need active management," Sanna says. "But between here and the other satellite operations around the world, Herald's predicting that we'll arrest the collapse of the biosphere and start actual restoration in maybe twenty years or so."

"If things go well," Ange says.

"If things remain peaceful," Tek corrects her from the end of the table. There's a long pause that makes the pronouncement sound doubtful and ends the line of conversation.

"Okay," Jack says. "New question—how do you three know English?" he asks in between bites of 'scum-tank loaf.'

"Herald taught it to us," Tek says.

"How does Herald know it?" Tina asks.

"That...has a longer answer." While Ange talks, Sanna gets up and wanders back into the house, soon returning with a small framed photo.

"About a year ago, Herald summoned the three of us to the place you met them, and gave us some orders. This wasn't a raid, not like usual. We three have done maybe six or seven raids into Greve, to obtain samples of plants necessary for our rebuilding efforts. But this was different. Herald told us that we were to go out to the desert west of Greve, and look for a runaway."

"A runaway?" Tina asks.

"As I'm sure you know, not all humans take well to strictly-regulated lives, especially adolescent ones. The three cities produce dozens of runaways a year, most of whom die out in the desert wastes. If they make it to another city, they're usually reintegrated, but for many reasons they aren't usually sought after."

"Why would you want to rescue someone whose point of view threatens the stability of your clockwork little world?" Sanna doesn't phrase it like a question.

"But based on their coms activity, they were *desperate* to find this one, and Herald needed to know why. So we went out there, found her, and brought her back. I'm not sure they even knew it was us who caught her. Probably just thought she died out there."

Sanna hands him the photo, and he nearly falls out of his chair.

"Her name was Alice," Sanna starts. "And we think she was from your—"

"Where is she?" Jack interrupts. "Is she here?"

Sanna and Ange share a surprised look. "Wait, do you know her?"

"Hold on, you're *Jack*." Sanna says. "You're *that* Jack? An entire universe of people and we get her childhood friend?"

"It's not really a coincidence," he manages to say. He can't take his eyes off the photo. Alice is maybe a couple of years older than the last time he saw her, but there's no doubt in his mind that it's her. She's smiling up at the camera, standing between Tek and Ange. Sanna has her in a half-hearted headlock. His mind's racing. "Until this week, we thought she was dead. Where is she now? Is she here?"

But Tina's tugging at his sleeve with a look on her face he can't read. "They said 'was.'"

Jack's stomach starts to drop.

"No," he says. "Not after—"

"We don't know where she is," Ange interrupts him. "About three months ago, she went for an audience with Herald. She didn't come back."

"Herald says she's 'lost,' but won't explain more," Sanna says.

"Sorry." Jack gets up from the table. "I have to go."

"What, right now?" Ange says. "To do what?"

But his feet have already carried him halfway to the house. "To get some answers!" he yells over his shoulder. Someone shouts something in reply from behind him, but he doesn't stop. He couldn't if he wanted to. By the time he hits the street, he's broken into a run, sprinting up the hill toward Herald, determined that no matter the outcome, he'll get the answers he needs.

Because he has to know.

■ ■ ■

The passage is long and steep and seems to stretch on forever. There are even times when Lizzie's sure the tunnel is twisting back so much it should be running into itself again, but there don't seem to be any intersections. Brenner's getting impatient.

"What is this, a maze?" he complains. He's standing at one of the walls, touching its metallic, almost scaly surface with one hand.

"Can't be a maze if there aren't any forks, genius."

"Watch your mouth, kid," he says, still peering at the wall. He holds the gun up and wiggles it in the air. "I don't have any reasons not to shoot you anymore."

"Bite me." She's too tired and angry to be intimidated by him anymore. If he was going to shoot her, she figures, he'd probably have done it already.

He turns around and points the gun at her then, and for half a second she really thinks he's going to do it—and then he's gone. There's a sound like a thousand rustling leaves, or maybe a basket of rattlesnakes, and then the hole in the floor where he was just standing is sealing itself back up, metallic scales flipping and meshing back together into a solid surface once again.

The sound intensifies, and suddenly the tunnel is shifting, changing directions. Where it had curved off to the right, it now seems straighter, and where the floor was once a smooth, upward ramp, it's now transmuted into a series of short stairs angled sharply downward like a subway escalator.

The lights on the walls blink one at a time in sequence, as if daring her to follow them.

She looks around, feeling watched.

"So, um, thanks, I think," she says. "I guess I'll go that way then."

At the bottom of the stairs is a short hall, and a doorway that opens out into a mild autumnal evening. She steps out and stares at the view.

Small lights dot the hillside for miles, a town stretching out into the distance all the way down to where moonlight shines off gently rolling waves. A road of sorts winds its way down into the buildings, which are nothing like the strange dark behemoth whose belly she's just emerged from.

There's a flurry of activity down the road, someone fast approaching in the dark, followed by voices that echo off the white buildings. The figure sprints up the hill toward her, not even seeming to see her, until, in the faint light of the starry sky, she recognizes his face.

It's Jack.

■ ■ ■

Pallas had looked about to burst a blood vessel in his head when she'd told him they had to cancel.

"A higher *priority?*" He'd almost been yelling, which made sense given the trouble he'd probably gone through to get them a meeting. "Than the *Sühne* with a—" he'd lowered his voice to an insistent whisper "—with a *breeding pair?*"

But if it were true, if the girl sitting once again at the table in front of her really did remember how to steer the displacement device from the initiating side, it could advance her research by a decade at least. The Triumvir could see the Restoration begin on her watch, and any and all sins would be forgiven.

"Welcome back, Alice," she says.

The girl smiles politely. Something's different about her, more than just the haircut. Zee remembers when she'd first arrived three years ago, screaming and crying on the pad, cradling her arm and quickly lapsing into shock from the trauma of losing her hand. It was only thanks to the excess energy in the event horizon cauterizing the wound that she hadn't simply bled to death there and then. The medic hadn't been able to arrest the cascading failures in her *emenyss*, either, so after less than an hour's confused interrogation, they'd had to put her straight into a conditioning tank. By the time she'd come out, she hadn't remembered much of anything. They'd given her a placement, like a reconditioned runaway.

When Zee had learned of her disappearance, she'd been tantalized by the possibility that the girl's memory had returned, but all their efforts to find her had come up short.

"You know they officially wrote you off as dead," Zee says, "but I always suspected you might be more resilient. Where were you hiding?"

"At first, I went back to Celle," she says. "I wasn't happy not remembering the faces of my former stewards."

"We don't have any record of your entry into Celle. Or Fulda."

"You don't have any record of my sneaking out through the irrigation and waste tunnels, either," she says. There's something about her, just the look in her eyes perhaps. Sometimes runaways lapsed out of frustration, not knowing their past being too tantalizing to bear, but she feels like there's more to it than that in this case. The girl must have her memories back; it's like she's a different person entirely.

"What did you find there?" she asks.

"I didn't remember them at all, and more importantly, they didn't recognize *me*."

"Well, we both know why that is now, don't we?"

"I'm not a big fan of being lied to, you know."

Zee takes a breath and lets it out. "I know, I'm sorry. But we, *I* thought you'd be happier that way. And if you ever did remember, well, we'd be here for you."

The girl doesn't look convinced.

"But you remember now," Zee prompts. "How you got here."

"You activated the Displacement Engine." The girl says it in what Zee thinks is English, her home language, and then again in Standard.

"Engine..." The word is like a pebble in her mouth, foreign. "Is that what they called it, back where you were?"

She nods, but doesn't say more, and Zee starts to wonder where she went after Celle. She can't have lasted this long without detection there, and she certainly doesn't look as though she's spent a year in the Wastes. That leaves few alternatives.

"The machines took the other two," Zee says. "But you know that, don't you?" It would explain how they'd managed to act so quickly. "Are you on their side now?"

"I'm not on anybody's side. I just didn't want them to end up in a tank. They don't need the *emenyss*. Not enough to risk their lives for."

"That's debatable," she says. "Maybe you've regained your old memories, but surely you also remember what you were taught in school while you were here. What happens when too many humans are allowed to spread across the planet." She takes a breath, deciding to cut straight to the question, "Why are you *here*, Alice? If you're siding with the *Sühne* and their absurd attempt to clear their mechanical consciences—with their ridiculous, unworkable plan to fix what they themselves broke—why would you even come back? You even had your friends, though gods above, I have no idea what you're thinking, allowing the machines to get their hands on a breeding pair. I knew the machines were trying to artificially restore the planet, but I never thought they'd be so foolish as to bring into existence an unregulated human population."

Alice's eyes widen, and for the first time in the conversation, Zee thinks she's managed to surprise her. "You think Jack and Tina...are gonna *have kids?*" She looks as though she's trying not to *laugh*. What kind of a barbarian plane of existence had she been raised in? How could she not see the danger? "Oh my god. No," she continues. "I mean, *probably* not...I don't *think* they..." She purses her lips. "You know what, let's say that I don't think you need to worry about it. For now. At least, not any time soon. In my world..." She stops, correcting herself. "In the world I grew up in, people don't just have kids at fifteen or sixteen. Well, not on purpose. Usually."

Zee's confusion mounts. What possible reason would the machines have for abducting them, then? She isn't making any sense. She puts her hands down on the table and repeats the question, "Why are you back?"

Alice looks her in the eye. "The hand. *My* hand. It's here, isn't it?"

■ ■ ■

He's about to dive into the gargantuan, fin-shaped building when a figure moves in the shadows nearby and calls out his name.

"Jack!"

He screeches to a halt and stands there in shock. It's Lizzie. She runs over and wraps him in a surprising but welcome hug. After a moment, she speaks.

"You're okay," she says with obvious relief.

"Yeah—how are you here?"

"Where *is* here? I mean I know it's the other universe, but more specifically. And who're they?" She's looking over his shoulder. He turns around to see Ange and Sanna walking up the hill behind him, not in any obvious hurry.

"That's...hard to explain. They're friendly, and they're not the ones who abducted us."

"Is Tina here, too?"

He nods. "She's probably still eating dinner. I got up here as fast as I could because I need to ask someone in there about Alice." He nods his head toward the structure. "She was here, Lizzie."

"For real?" She looks both excited and a little torn. "Well, hold up a second, because that's a weird as hell building," she says. "And Brenner's in there, with a gun."

"Wait, what? Brenner's dead."

She shakes her head. "Not so much."

"Well, I need to get in there anyway and talk to..." He trails off when he looks over her shoulder, because where the dark arch of the doorway had been just moments before is now little more than a smooth, unbroken wall.

She follows his gaze, then turns back to face him. "Yeah, that's exactly what I was talking about. I think someone in the building saved me from Brenner. And then they made me a way out. Or something."

Ange and Sanna make it up the hill.

"You're quick," says Ange, as Sanna asks, "Who's this?"

"The door," he says, ignoring both of them. "How do I make it come back?"

"That's what we came to tell you," Ange says. "Herald decides when you talk to Herald, not you. You'd have better luck trying to convince a rock to start a conversation with you."

"Who is this?" Sanna repeats, hooking a finger at Lizzie. "We don't exactly get new people here."

"This is Lizzie," he says. "She's Alice's sister."

Sanna's eyes go wide. "Wow, okay. So I'm going to go out on a limb and agree with what you said before...none of this is coincidence. You both knowing Alice and all."

Lizzie shakes her head. "No, it's..." She faces him, clearly unsure of where to start. What comes out is unexpected. "We've been *played*, Jack," she says. "Everything we did, it's like we've been following a script."

"What?"

"Betza—Brenner—I mean it's all so royally screwed up. But we made a portal, and it's in there—and now Leigh's missing—"

"Wait, you made a portal? And what do you mean by 'missing?'"

"Okay, hold up, you young people with all your suddenly-appearing-from-nowhere and fast-talking-about-strange-things," Sanna screws up their face in a parody of old age. They relax and tilt their head to one side. "There's no point in talking about this here, and you probably want to explain it to Tina at the same time, yeah?"

Lizzie nods. "Probably."

"Come on back into town and we'll talk it over," they say. "I'll make tea."

Ange swivels on the spot. "You have *tea?*" Her eyes nearly pop out of her head.

Sanna's grins are always mischievous, but this one is especially conspiratorial. "Swiped it from the Corporates two raids ago, been waiting for an occasion. This..." They look from Lizzie to Jack and back again. "I'd call this an occasion."

Jack takes a hard look at the monolith and frowns. "I guess it is," he says. "For better or worse."

■ ■ ■

"Tina!" Lizzie grabs her in a bear hug and swings her around until her legs are dangling, then plops her back down again. "I'm so glad you're okay."

"You, too," says Tina.

"You didn't seem that happy to see me," Jack grumbles, sitting down at the table, and Lizzie sticks out her tongue.

"Yeah, well, Tina's Tina and you're you. Besides, I've never kissed *you*." She raises an eyebrow for full effect.

And damn it if he doesn't completely break character and call her bluff. He starts to get up, arms wide and moving toward her, making a damn kissy-face and saying, "Well you never *asked*—" and she has to cut him off right there because *ew*, and everyone just starts laughing.

God, she'd been so worried about them, and it feels so good just to be like this, together again; but the twisting feeling in her gut won't relax until she finds Leigh and gets them *all* back home safe, and she knows it.

The cute one with the pink hair—Sanna, she thinks—comes out of the building with a tray of simple, thick-walled cups and a rather large teapot. They set it down on the table and wave everyone over.

"So, Ange, you remember two raids ago when you demanded to know where I'd gotten off to?"

She arches her eyebrows. "This. You stole tea."

"From a Regional Coordinator's house." Sanna twists their lips into a smirk.

"From a *what?*" Ange doesn't seem to know what to do with this fact.

"Tek stood guard," they say, and the quiet young man sitting at the end of the table nods his head once, as if to acknowledge the fact.

"You were in on this, too?" Ange exclaims in mock outrage.

Sanna grabs a fist-sized foil packet and tosses it to her. "You should have the rest. It was supposed to be for your birthday, but I figured you wouldn't mind sharing with my Milzie, since it was her idea." Sanna says something to the girl sitting next to her in a language Lizzie doesn't know, and she smiles and laughs and says something to Ange as well. "Plus, of course, our esteemed visitors from another universe." Sanna winks at Lizzie.

"I...I don't know what to say," Ange starts, then adds a few more words in their own language. Sanna blushes and the taciturn Tek nods once again. The other girl, Milza, waves a hand and says something that even without translation clearly boils down to, 'No big deal, Sanna owed you.'

"So tea is...scarce, here?" Lizzie ventures.

"A lot of things are scarce here, Liz," Jack says, and proceeds to explain everything—about the nanomachines, the catastrophic near-end of the world, the *Erdenkörperschaft*, the restoration work.

"So what do you call yourselves, then, if they're the Corporates?" Lizzie asks.

"It's funny, we never really picked a name for ourselves at first," Ange says. "But the Corporates stated calling us *sühnesuchende Maschinen*, which means something like 'machines looking for atonement.' We took umbrage at the 'machines' part, and it was too long anyway, so we just call ourselves *Sühne*. 'Atonement.' It's as good a name as any, so we adopted it. Well, I say we, but this was back in my grandparents' time. Since we literally exist to fix the world that was broken by those who came before us, well, if that's 'looking for atonement,' then it suits us pretty well."

"And this place is called...?"

"Chee," Tina says, sipping her tea, and Milza smiles at her, nodding.

"It just means 'the city,'" Sanna adds. "It works because it's our only one."

"But you've got other settlements—?" Jack asks.

"More like scientific monitoring stations," Sanna responds.

"And the place I come from is called Greve?" Lizzie asks.

"You?" Ange says, momentarily confused, and then, "*Oh*. Oh yeah, I guess it is. Of course you're just like Alice, and your brother, too. From here, and taken in the Displacement Event. So yes, you'd all be from Greve, originally."

"And would Greve be about 450 miles to the east of here?" she asks, remembering Betza's words.

Ange squints at her as she speaks. "Pretty much exactly that far, yes. Why?"

"Jack, we have to go there," she says at once. "That's where Leigh is." She explains everything she can about what happened after Jack and Tina were taken.

"Betza is a computer." Jack recites his mental notes aloud. "And it told Brenner to fake his own death, so we'd get Brenner's files, then find the hand, then infect Leigh with some kind of beacon signal. And that was so that some combination of Tina, you, and I would get sucked into this universe when they went for the hand, in order that you'd have no choice—sorry, so that *Leigh* would have no choice but to help open the bridge you mentioned. That's...nobody could predict all that. That's not possible."

Ange and Sanna are exchanging a look.

"What?" Lizzie says, but Tina beats them to it.

"Herald could," she says. "Herald could predict it." She finishes off her tea and puts the cup down on the table, cradling it with both hands and staring at its glassy surface. "Based on what they could predict about our arrival and our rescue, as well as all the things necessary to restore a global biosphere. Plus, it would make sense that Herald would want a stable bridge to our universe, because then they wouldn't need to steal samples from the other humans here. And the only bridge is now in a secure area inside Herald."

"Wait, you think Brenner was playing us on orders from Herald? That doesn't make any sense," Lizzie says. "How could they do all that from here?"

Tina shakes her head. "I don't know. But I think Jack's right—we need to talk to Herald now."

"Then I think you're in luck." Sanna gestures at something over Lizzie's shoulder.

They all turn to look behind them, where a small, silvery creature stands. It looks like a fox or a small wolf, but rather than fur it has the same scaly, metallic texture as Herald.

"What is it?" Jack asks, the creature sitting in total silence, its dark eyes staring.

"An emissary," Tek responds.

Ange nods. "It means Herald will see you now."

■ ■ ■

Leigh's doing everything he can not to let his voice shake when he talks, trying to stick to as much truth as he can when he speaks, trying not to show any surprise while taking mental notes about everything the woman's been saying.

Tina and Jack were here, but now they're with some machines who are trying to rebuild the world? That's not part of the story Emi had told him. He wonders how much the general population here even knows.

"I can feel that it's here," he says, "the hand." He's telling the truth. When they'd come that evening to pick him up it hadn't been noticeable, but the closer they'd come to this building, the more it had become clear that the hand was somewhere nearby.

"The signal?" The woman asks.

It's hard to explain, even to himself. It's like a high-pitched noise in his head, even higher than he can actually hear, but somehow he knows it's there, and it's getting louder. He tries to remember what Faye had called it.

"They called it the rangefinder," he says. "When they set my *eme-nyss* to resonate that way, they thought they could use it to look across the, they called it the 'brane.' Like radar or something."

"Radar?" she asks. He'd used the English word. Maybe they don't have a similar term.

"You bounce radio waves off things far away? Lets you see where they are."

"Oh yes, radio echolocation," she clarifies. "I knew it! The very idea that the signal could be used to look into a universe from the signaling side—I've been postulating it for years. That's how we found you, of course," she says. "The signal." He doesn't hide his surprise well enough, but it works to his advantage. "But perhaps you don't know that side of the story?" she asks. "Did you ever learn about how you ended up in that barbaric place, seventeen years ago?"

"I know they were testing a weapon." He ignores the insult to his home plane of existence. "A replacement for atomic bombs."

"At first, we didn't know what to think. The attack struck near the Southwest Lung. At first, all we knew was that a mountain of dirt and sand had appeared, and we rushed to excavate, before the valuable plant specimens were killed beneath it. But the more we dug, the more we realized that what had been there before hadn't been buried, but replaced." She frowns at the memory. "It took a small wing of the secondary hatchery with it as well, of which you are a survivor." She stares at him. "We tried to ask you this when you arrived, but we didn't know your language, and you weren't in a state to answer our questions. How many others survived? They stole fourteen of you in total."

"Fourteen? That's awful. There were only three of us."

"That's fairly standard." She doesn't appear upset at the news.

"Standard?"

"Oh, Apex isn't the only world we've retrieved samples from." Leigh's eyebrows shoot up of their own accord, and she continues. "You were our first, of course. The attack was terrible, yes, and awful for what you had to go through, but we learned so very much. The device that caused it was still partially intact in the center of the mountain of displaced material. I led the team tasked with investigating it. After some years, I correctly theorized that certain resonance frequencies might be detectable or even attractive to the displacing distortion in the signal's native universe. This is the 'rangefinder' signal, as you call it."

"And you figured out how to search for it?"

Zee nods. "Across the multiverse, or at least the vast array of universes adjacent to this one. In theory, there should be an *infinite* number of parallel universes, but there seems to be an issue of some form of proximity limiting the ones we can reach. Still, there are enough for us to have confirmed over a dozen, which given the extremely low probabilities of necessary events transpiring between adjacent universes does suggest a truly staggering number of potentially reachable universes. If we can target them.

"It was hypothesized that the signal was a kind of feedback between your faulty *emenyss* and something unique in your genetic profile. For you, it was so far progressed that it made you light up like a shining star in our scans. But the destruction it caused to your *emenyss* was, as I'm sure you're aware now, far too advanced to stop, and we didn't have the time to study it to determine how to replicate it. But all was not lost. We shifted the focus of our research to look for other signals, even weaker ones. We've retrieved twelve samples now. Fourteen if you count your friends—but they were quite the aberration. We have little use for samples without systems comparable to the *emenyss*. But none of the samples have had as profound a signal as your own. You were, *are*, perfect."

Leigh tries not to squirm at the unwanted praise.

"The others are fine. Usually they have a set of stories similar to yours, and while this isn't their home universe, we're able to make them relatively comfortable here once they've had their *emenyss* flushed, supplemented, or reprogrammed. But you were from *here*. You were *ours*. I was so disappointed when you disappeared, Alice, you have no idea."

"But...you're randomly abducting people from other worlds, just 'for science'?"

"Well of course, they've already been abducted once, as you were. As I say, they've all had similar stories to your own, taken away to barbaric universes with no understanding of the science behind the *emenyss*. And while we have no way of restoring them to their originating universes yet, we do provide them with a life here far superior to their former ones."

Her unrepentance about it, about stealing people away from their own lives, is so bold he can't even think of a response.

"In any case," she continues, "it isn't mere curiosity that motivates me."

He hides his desire to scowl behind a façade of curiosity. "Then what?"

She stares at him, as if trying to decide something, then stands up and puts her hand on a large black screen.

"End recording, authority Zee of Greve, Professor First Grade. Engage privacy mode." Some lights and symbols flash on the screen and it goes dark again.

She walks over and sits back down, folding her hands on the table.

"I know that the machines are right," she says.

He blinks. "I'm sorry?"

"Oh, Alice." She looks disappointed. "Fine, you can keep feigning ignorance if you like, I'll just keep talking and you can decide at the end if you'll help me. Help all of us," she says.

"Okay." He tries to keep his expression neutral.

"The *Sühne* are right, and this planet is dying. No matter how long we wait in balanced seclusion, it will not come back on its own. Despite the Three Cities Academy's pronouncements, I've examined the soil samples from the other universes, I've talked to the other émigrés. They're so very *alive*, Alice, and this world is not. The damage the machines did to it is far too severe. But the *Sühne*'s plans require an impossible level of predictive capacity to manage. There's no way they can balance the changes needed to rebuild an entire biosphere. It's simply not possible. This planet is dying, and we're going to die along with it."

"So you want to, what, use me to take everyone here to another universe?"

She looks like she's going to spit. "Of course not, this is our planet." She says it as though it being hers makes it superior, even though, in her own words, it's dying.

"This world is ours, and I will not abandon it. I don't want to *run*, Alice, I want to *repair* it. In a single move. I want to displace hundreds of pockets of biosphere from other universes into ours. I want to transplant life all over the planet at once. Think of it, hundreds of whole, healthy ecosystems deposited around the world. It'll make the word of the Triumvirate *actually true.* We can maintain our society and, left to their own devices, the transplants will grow and thrive."

It sounds like a good enough plan, but an idea in the back of his head won't stop itching. It's something Emi said during her brief history of the world.

"But aren't there still nanomachines in the soil in most places?" It was part of the history of the Three Cities that they'd cleared out and destroyed every last Horde nanomachine in the soil, but there were places all over the world that hadn't. Most places, even. "They're dormant here, on this world, but without the machines on the lunar surface keeping them that way...I mean if you transfer them to some other planet without them—"

She waves a hand. "Don't worry. We'll perform the transplant all at once. If we do it piecemeal, then of course, you're right, they could be devoured before we can get enough to—"

"You're talking about destroying another universe's Earth!" he says.

She looks at him the way a parent looks at a rambling child. "There's an infinite number of them, Alice. It isn't as though they'll be missed."

He can't believe what he's hearing.

"With the hand still replicating the signal, we finally know enough about it to move forward," she says. "But it could take decades of work, and I'm not convinced we have that much time. That's why I need you, Alice. With you, with your ability to aim, we might be able to save our world."

At that moment, he realizes the true extent of what Alice was telling him. Save everyone, she'd said. The fate of an entire planet—two entire planets—depends on it.

He has to do whatever he can to destroy the hand, to stop this woman and her plans. He's the only one who can.

"Okay," he says. "I'll help you."

13

It's quiet in the facility. Quiet and cold.

They'd drilled it so far into the mountain that if they'd gone any further they might have started to come out the other side. Patton watches as Alice ties her hair in a ponytail and checks it in the mirror. She's grown so pale.

Today's the day.

The first stop is amplification. They're going to take the feedback signal that's been building between her genetics and her nanomachines and redouble it several times over, sending it into a self-reinforcing cascade. It's a dangerous escalation. If it works, her deterioration will progress far more rapidly. She may have only days. But if they do nothing at all, she still won't make it more than a couple of years. And the other threats are very real, too.

Once he'd realized how much was at stake, he'd told her everything. He'd given her the choice, and she'd chosen this. He has to respect that, even if it scares him.

She lies down on the bed and folds her hands.

"What do you think it's like, over there?" she asks. She's always been the inquisitive one, at least more so than the other two, though he suspects they'll grow into it. It's led her to insights he wished it hadn't, over the years.

"I don't know," he says. "I think they must be very advanced, technologically. Nisha—you remember Dr. Mallik's greenhouse—she tells me that the plant samples all appear to have been genetically modified to make better use of light from a little further into the cool side of the spectrum, so perhaps the sun is a little different there. The sun, or the sky."

"Do you think they have families?"

"All humans need someone to take care of them as they grow."

"Even ones that hatch from eggs?" Her eyes twinkle with the question.

"Even them."

She smiles, and he doesn't know what to do.

"When are you going to tell them the truth? James and Lizzie and Jack." She's always thought of them first. She probably wouldn't have gone along with any of the experiments, not even to save herself, if she didn't have an idea that her siblings were probably next in line. He feels small in the face of her resolute calm; inside he's shaking.

He tells her he doesn't know. Before Alice had gotten sick, the plan had been to wait until they'd finished high school; now he's wishing he'd taken Nisha's advice and told them from the start. She was always so much better with them.

But keeping them safe had to come first, he thinks, and if their continued ignorance could be used to further that end, then so be it. The choice is clear.

When she sits up at last, her smile's more forced. She says her head hurts and her ears are ringing. He takes her small hand and helps her walk down the long hall to the machine room. When they pass a water fountain, she pulls away and grabs onto it with both hands, for a moment looking like she's going to vomit. Instead, she just hiccups and smiles weakly up at him. "This kinda sucks, Poppa."

He wraps his arm around her. "I know, sweetheart." The tiny machines that were supposed to keep her well are now in full rebellion, lighting fires inside of her; but even as they burn, they'll provide a light to see a way back to her home. He prays that those on the other side can fix her when she gets there.

The bridging room is built like a militarized border—thick, closable steel bulkheads stand at every entrance. There's a non-zero chance that the people on the other side might not take kindly to their activities. That, coupled with their level of technological advancement, had understandably led to a rather defensive stance. At his request, the men with the military-grade weaponry are standing guard out of sight. It's stressful enough for Alice as it is.

He helps her up to the interface, a spherical chamber only feet from where the three prototype lasers will converge and provide the energy density required to begin the incursion. She knows how to stand, they've done calibration drills all week. She reaches her arms out and grabs the handholds on either side while he fastens the harness around her.

He squeezes her shoulder. If this works, the bridge will open, and in about twelve hours it should stabilize. They'll send a trained team through to make first contact, and then he'll go himself and negotiate for medical access for Alice. If it works.

It has to work.

"You can do this," he says to her.

No matter how many times he replays it in his memory, every time he returns to this moment, every time he runs through it again in self-recrimination, he always wishes he'd said more.

As they go through the final startup checks, Alice says something over the radio from inside the interface chamber.

"Can you hear that?"

He doesn't pick anything up on any of the sensors.

She says, "It's getting louder."

She lets go of the handholds and starts to pound on the door.

He panics, runs over to the chamber, turns the latch.

There's a wind, an impossible wind in a room this far underground, pushing at his back, pulling in toward the interface chamber. Toward Alice.

He pulls the door open.

She reaches out and he grabs her hand.

The chamber is gone.

■ ■ ■

Alice drifts in and out of consciousness, dreaming of the sea. Blue bubbles rise around her. Had the portal worked? Were the people on the other side curing her? It's so hard to think in here.

Some days she thinks she's being watched.

Is someone at the glass? Are they here to see her?

There are conversations, but she can't understand them.

She's sliding away again.

■ ■ ■

Alice gasps for air in the ice-cold world. Her lungs are full of knives, her skin made of needles. Someone in blue wraps her in the sharpest of blankets and scours her dry, while another peers in her ears and eyes and mouth in a clinical manner, and then barks orders to someone else. When she turns to look behind her, she sees a row of tall glass cylinders, each filled to the brim with blue liquid.

■ ■ ■

"It was lovely to see you again, Emi," Hana says as Alice's friend leaves by the kitchen door. "I'm so pleased you two have become friends." She smiles at them, adding, "Do thank your steward for me once again for bringing Alice into our lives."

She's been living with Hana and Toran for a month and a half now. She doesn't remember much from before the tank. They said she'd been very sick, that she might never remember her life before, but that it wasn't important. That what mattered, after all, was now.

But as she's washing her face and preparing for bed, she wonders if she'll have the same dreams again. Of the far away land, the familiar faces, the strange and foreign family she once knew.

■ ■ ■

It's been a year and a half since the funeral. Patton's world has contracted around him like the space around a dying star.

He can still feel the impossible wind pushing at his back.

He'd gone into full damage-control mode when it happened. With the failure of the bridge had come anger, recriminations, politics on all sides. Through some of his private contacts, he'd caught wind of a powerful few who, while in public expressing their sincerest condolences about the loss of Alice, in private company expressed their desire to try once more, to convert James and use him as a replacement part. The promise of the high technology on the other side of the brane was worth the risk, they said. And if that, too, failed—well, there was always one more sample, if a less promising one. He had, of course, pushed back.

Then the threats had started again. He remembered the hacks, the blackmail, the murders. They'd even gotten to Slade, a potential outcome they'd both feared and prepared for. He'd at least found a way to keep Nisha safe, if a less-than-ideal one. And he's sent the children off to the Academy and infiltrated it with people to watch over them and keep them safe. But he knows it isn't enough, that none of them will be truly safe unless he finds a more permanent solution. There has to be something more than this endless stalemate.

He's spent months poring over the data, the fraction of a second of information captured at the moment of displacement. Every sensor in the facility had been running. There has to be a clue somewhere inside it. Something he can see. Something he can use.

One day he finds it.

■ ■ ■

She remembers it all—James, Lizzie, Jack, the Displacement Engine—everything. It's been two years, she thinks, depending on how long she was really in that tank. She's told Emi everything. Almost everything. There are things she can't say, things that don't have anything to do with her past.

Things that, if she gives voice to them, will only make Emi's life harder.

The messages come when she's sleeping, images of a great shining sea to the west, a town nestled in the crook of a bay. There's someone out there, something with incredible power. A mind so big it's beyond imagination. It calls to her at night; it whispers. It tells her that her family is in danger, her real family, from her real home, from the other side. It says she needs to go, in order to find them. To help them. Soon.

She writes the goodbye note before bed, then hides it under her pillow. Two changes of clothing are all she can fit into her school bag, so it's what she'll have to work with. A water bottle and a pack of nutrient wafers stolen from the pantry fit into the front pocket. In her head are the directions; she won't need to get the whole way on her own.

In the hours of the day that are still too early to be morning, she slips down the stairs of the house she's lived in for months and months. She avoids the bottom stair and its faint but characteristic squeak and pauses for a moment at the door.

Hana and Toran. Emi. Her friends from school. Her stomach twists, but she knows what she has to do. She silences the notifications on the entrance panel, then slips out into the night.

A quarter-mile from the house is the research orchard where she's helped out Toran so many days now she can't even begin to count them. Three rows in, another fifty yards along, there's a small, round, metal plate in the grass, no wider than her shoulders, maybe narrower. She pulls out the long handle and twists it, undoing the latch, easing the plate out of the ground and leaving it nearby.

She lowers herself down into the hole, sticking at the shoulders until she forces her way in, leaving a layer of skin behind as she does it. She winces, sliding further down between the irrigation and waste pipes until her head's below the level of the ground, then hooking her elbow and hauling the lid back in place above her. When it latches, it lets out an almighty *clank* that she's certain will have someone running over, but after a minute passes in silence, her panic subsides. She flicks on a flashlight and pushes on.

Six feet down there's a T-joint where the access shaft meets the mains, and she slips her feet backward into one side, arching her back and easing herself in until she's fully horizontal. After that, it's just a matter of sliding forward into the tube ahead of her, one inch at a time, in the direction of the wall. It's two hours before she makes it the half-mile to the grate, her knees and elbows scraped and bloody, her back and neck screaming with the abuse. The metal lattice isn't there for security, and with a shove it falls to the sand below with an almost-noiseless *puff*.

There should still be two more hours of darkness. She hopes it's enough.

■ ■ ■

She spends two days and two nights under the camouflage fabric as the drones fly overhead. They're hot days, sweltering even under the solar swarm that provides the extra power for Greve that its wind turbines don't. As the sun beats down on her fabric roof, she's both glad of its shade and almost suffocated by it, the way it kills the breeze and makes her own body heat cling to her like a miserable, sweaty blanket. She curses her nearly empty water bottle but takes solace in the existence of the hideaway. Until she'd found it, she'd still had her doubts.

But now she knows, if she can wait long enough, they'll come for her.

There's a voice in the distance, calling her name. The drones haven't been able to find her, so they've sent out search parties on foot. She hardly thinks they'd do all this for a simple runaway, so the ones looking probably know exactly who or what she is.

A defector, of sorts.

"Alice!" she hears the call. The voice sounds familiar.

"Alice! Are you out here?" Closer now. It's the scientist, from before. The first person she'd seen. The one who'd asked her all the questions about home while she'd tried not to throw up and cried about her missing hand. She looks at it now, the hand—a seamless replacement—and wonders about a place with so much technology that still has so many problems.

The voice comes closer still, saying that if she can hear her, she needs to come back. That they need her. That it's not safe out in the Wastes. That she could die out here. She drinks the last of her water, and waits.

The voice recedes again. Eventually even the drones stop flying overhead.

It's another day before the machines find her, parched and dizzy, and carry her on their backs as they run through the night.

■ ■ ■

"I'm only agreeing to this because of the funding," the woman says.

"I'm well aware of that, Dr. Sullivan." Patton puts down the large cardboard box in the server room. In it lies the experiment that will prove his theory.

"And I certainly can't guarantee that Betza will find anything with it." She opens the box and reveals the contents—half a dozen boards, plus spools and spools of composite and metal wires for the 3D printer, topped with a ream of paper and a thumbdrive. Materials and blueprints for a communication device. The first of its kind.

"You'll need only to hook it up and present it to Betza as a resource," he says. "Even if it doesn't prove useful in achieving this 'optimal outcome' it's aiming for, I'll be satisfied."

Arms crossed, she eyes him with even more suspicion than usual, the brilliant young woman who'd used his money to build this—a better chess player than Patton would ever be. And maybe his only hope.

"And if anyone comes knocking?"

"You tell them you work for the highest bidder," he says. "It'll be true, after all."

She shakes her head.

"This is ridiculous. You're ridiculous," she says, but after he doesn't react, she concedes. "Fine." She looks at him and unfolds her arms.

"Don't come back here again." She fishes in her pocket for a small note-card and hands it to him. It's blank except for an eleven-digit number, scrawled in pen. "Use this number the first time. Like I said before, you'll get a new one each time you do."

He nods.

"And whatever you do, don't chicken out. I don't know if any of it will work, Goldmark, but I know it definitely won't if Betza has to course correct all the damn time because you won't do what he says."

"I know."

He stops at the door, then looks back. She's got her arms folded again, but she's smiling.

"You still think we were worth the money?"

"I do," he says. "Now go prove me right."

■ ■ ■

It's been almost a year since she arrived in Chee, carried on Sanna's back because she was too weak to walk. She'd insisted, even dizzy with heatstroke, on seeing Herald right away—and to their surprise, Herald had agreed. She'd gone to sleep in the meeting chamber and had vivid dreams of home. When she'd later awoken in Sanna and Milza's house, wrapped in soft sheets while the sea breeze blew through their open windows, she knew she'd done the first, most urgent part of what she needed to do.

Herald had learned the first half of what they needed to.

They'd spoken English after that, some of them, adapting to her the way she'd been made to adapt to the people in Greve; but she'd made changes, too. She'd learned to speak their language from Milza, who'd taught her new words daily. She'd learned to work on the monitoring boats, taking samples of seaweed and algae for testing back on shore. She'd worked in the greenhouses growing seedlings for planting in the new redwood groves to the north. She'd even gone way out to the maritime plantation offshore, taking dispersal loads from its vast plankton farms out into the deep ocean, where the waves rolled like great dark monsters beneath them, slowly coming to life with every passing year.

She'd spent time taking care of the children, too, on the days when Ange wanted to steal Arn away for a while and sneak off to the eastern plantations, where the mud runs red like rust and the fields of silver-green sedge stretch as far as the eye can see. She'd taught Lith and her brother Salu to sing songs she knew from when she was their age, and had even had Tek show her how to use the fabricator to print up a swing-set for them.

But now the time has come for her to do the harder part, the second part of what she has to do.

The emissary had arrived in the night and watched her while she slept. Both Milza and Sanna had seen it, and, knowing what it had meant, had let her sleep as long as she could. When she'd awoken to its cold, dark gaze, she'd known, too.

She follows it up to Herald and its great metal fin, its darker-than-black skin soaking in every drop of light that strikes it as the sun starts to climb in the sky. It looks like a hole in the world, like you could fall into it and never return.

In Herald's depths is a familiar sight—a perfect reproduction of the bridging room. A raised bed lies off to one side, like the amplification bed years ago, in another life. She knows what to do without being asked. The signal begins to reverberate, to cascade within her. It isn't the exact same signal as before—her defective nanomachines are gone, and with it the last copy of the true signal in this universe—but it'll be enough for what Herald needs from her.

Lying there, she remembers her Poppa's words, that every human being needs someone to take care of them as they grow, and she worries about the others the way she's worried every day since she arrived in Chee.

There's a shifting sound, like rain on leaves, and a humanoid figure is standing beside her, waiting to help her across the room to the machine as the familiar dizziness builds.

"Why are you doing all this, Herald? I respect what you do, what you're doing to repair this planet, but helping me—well, it doesn't seem like it'd be the top of your priorities."

The figure seems to speak as it guides her, nauseated and in increasing pain, to the interface. She realizes it's the first time she's heard Herald's voice out loud. It's a chorus of whispers, a distant song, coming from all around her.

"There is someone with whom we share a mutual interest," it says.

"A friend?"

There's a pause as the figure attaches the harness. A considered answer follows.

"In the absence of a more precise word. You'll understand soon."

It's been three years, but Alice remembers her training from the calibration drills. She closes her eyes and lets her mind go blank, feeling the soft hum of the grips slowly working its way up her arms. This time, there will be no screeching in the chamber, no panic as she's torn from one universe to the next. This time, the lasers will fire, and she'll begin her journey.

The hum of the machine reaches the back of her skull, seeps down her spine, follows her veins and arteries down to her toes and back up to her heart. When the sound of thunder echoes off the buildings of Chee, she doesn't hear it.

She's already gone.

■ ■ ■

It isn't like the Displacement Engine at all, she thinks.

If she had to compare the two, it would be like the difference between being a human trapped in a diving bell as it rapidly descends, and simply finding yourself transformed into a dolphin, swimming in an almost boundless ocean.

In the frozen, terrifying moment of Displacement, you're surrounded by nothing, by the bone-cold horror of unbeing itself. It's not the space between worlds, but the sight and the knowledge of the sheer pressure, pressing in on Being from all things Not. From that timeless frame, you become forever aware of the onion-skin of potential separating everything you know and love from the purest form of annihilation.

But from the Potentiate, she can see everything. Not all at once, of course, but in the Potentiate there's time enough to see it all. It's not as though time doesn't pass, but there are currents to follow, from moment to moment, and you can always swim back to the present.

At least, if you can find your way.

And she *can* see it—everything that's happened, both in her own world and in the one from which she's come. She sees her own funeral, sees her father trying to protect everyone, and how they all push each other away when she's gone. She sees the people working in the shadows and all their selfish desires, sees Brenner's plans formulating and those behind him pulling his strings. She sees all the things she's missed, and more besides, as though she were there for it all.

But those moments are all upstream now, past the slowly-crawling boundary of the present, and though she can view them, she can't get back to them. She can't swim up to a place where she can help, where she can fix them, no matter how hard she tries.

Downstream she can see all the futures they could have. There are so many choices—and so many ways it could all go wrong.

She realizes now that this is what her father had found in the data. Not this, exactly—not these beautiful, branching paths of possibility, not the stream of near-infinite potential futures—but the existence of the Potentiate itself. The signal in the noise; the answer to his search.

He could see that there are waves like ripples bouncing in the stream, finding their ways into various futures and winding their echoing ways back into the past. She can see the brilliant mental leap he made, his hypothesis—knowing of the existence of nanomachines in the Primeverse, seeing the signals from when she was taken, inferring the possibility of a being like Herald.

She can almost feel his hand reaching out toward her, the working of his mind.

All this time, Herald has been listening to the stream, listening for the echoes of the future that it seeks, and every day correcting its children's course, little by little.

But Betza isn't like Herald. Betza sees the present and compares it with all it knows. *Is this what a winning board looks like?* it asks. And if the answer is no—if it's more no than yes, or even less yes than it would like—it changes the board's configuration. But Herald doesn't play games like Betza. Herald listens to the sound of the future and tries to steer a course toward it.

And now they're whispering to each other across the Potentiate, working together, all because her father had given them a way to talk.

Betza tells Herald about the present, and Herald tells Betza about the future.

Herald was right, 'Friends' isn't the right term, but there may not be a more precise one.

This is what Herald needed her to see—this, and the knowledge cradled within it. She can't go home. She has to wait here, in the Potentiate, has to guide her brother across it when he comes. Has to catch him as he passes, and show him what he needs to do, who he needs to talk to, what he needs to say.

But there are so many futures, so many streams. She has to explore them, has to see them all before he arrives. Has to follow all the branching possibilities to find the one that will take them all to the right place. To the best future.

Even if it's one that doesn't include her.

■ ■ ■

Brenner stumbles down the long tunnel and finally out into the night. He's out on a large, cultivated lawn, stretching for hundreds of yards. He must've walked a mile since that damned booby-trap dropped him to the floor below. He's lucky he didn't break his damn neck.

There's a low wall around the lawn, made of the same stuff as the tunnels, and the breeze makes the tall grass beyond it hiss. It gives him the creeps.

Better get this done and get back.

He crouches down and pops open the case, pulling on latex gloves to keep the sample clean and pulling out what looks like an e-reader with a thermometer attached by a long, coiled wire. After turning it on and calibrating the sensor in the air, he drives it into the soil and waits.

He doesn't get anything the first time, or the second, or the third.

He curses to himself and climbs over the low wall. Maybe he'll have better luck in the creepy whispering grass. Nervous about what might be living in it, he pulls out tufts of the stuff and tosses it to one side, before jamming the sensor into a clear patch of dirt below.

"Gotcha," he says out loud when the results come in. He twists a small tube into the ground, pulls a vial out of its slot, and drops the narrow dirt core into the glass, filling it. He plugs the top and puts it back in its place, then repeats the process until all half-dozen vials are full.

This dirt is going to make him a millionaire. Hell, maybe a billionaire.

He packs up, throws the gloves into the field, and heads back to the bridge.

■ ■ ■

"All right, Sullivan, shut it down." Faye turns around just in time to see Brenner step back through the bridge—alone.

"Where's the girl?"

"Hell if I know. Don't much care, either." He's smiling.

"What?" she says, incredulous, but all he does is give a shrug.

"We got separated. I'd tell you to go look for her yourself, but I think my employers would all feel so much better with this particular door closed behind me."

"Well, I don't know how. At least, not safely."

"What are you talking about? All we gotta do is turn the damn thing off. Pull the plug." He walks over to one of the large coils and looks about to give it a yank when she stops him.

"Are you kidding me?" she shouts, grabbing him by the shoulder. "You ignorant hobgoblin, who knows what that'll do?"

He shoves her away and pulls out his gun, aiming it first at her, then at the device suspended above the bridge.

She keeps talking, trying to make sure he doesn't pull the trigger. "Listen, the device isn't keeping it *open* anymore, it's just keeping it *stable.*"

"And what happens if it becomes unstable?"

"I don't *know,*" she says. "I'm a *programmer,* not a *nuclear physicist.*"

"It'll be fine," he says. "Here, I'll show you—"

"August." The cold, familiar voice comes from behind her and freezes them both in their tracks. She turns to see Patton Goldmark standing on the stairs, a hunting rifle at his shoulder, aimed and ready to fire.

Brenner chuckles nervously and starts to turn.

"I wouldn't recommend any sudden movements, August. You standing still is the only thing keeping a bullet on the outside of your skull just now."

"Let's not be hasty about this," Brenner says.

"Indeed. Hasty is the last thing you want to be at this precise moment. Now, I'm going to tell you what to do, and you're going to do all of it—and I can't stress this enough—very slowly." He continues, voice calm like a bomb, ready to explode at the slightest provocation. "You're going to face away from me. Then you're going to gently put the gun on the ground. If you do anything other than those two actions—again, slowly, and in that precise order—I am going to shoot you. Do you understand?"

"Sure. Sure thing," he says, doing as he's told. The gun makes a hard clatter as he puts it down.

"Take off your coat."

"I don't have another gun."

"Your coat and your shoes. Put them next to the gun."

Brenner grumbles, but complies.

"Now I want you to leave this place, and to never, ever come back."

"Yep, okay. Can do." He pats the briefcase on the side. "Got what I came for anyway."

Goldmark just stares at him and Brenner's smile slowly dissolves and drips from his face.

"Leave. Now."

Faye watches as Goldmark escorts him up the stairs, out through the door, and into the elevator, not lowering the gun—or even seeming to blink—the whole time.

"Well, this has been a real pleasure, this reunion," Brenner says.

"Never come back to this place," is all that J. Patton Goldmark offers in return.

Brenner taps the button for the first floor and lets the doors slide closed.

Patton finally lowers the weapon, flipping the safety up as he does. She watches as he lets out a breath that ages him five years. He wanders back into the server room, dropping the rifle on the top of the nearest stack with a clatter.

She jumps at how hard he puts it down.

"Don't worry," he says, an almost sheepish look on his face. "It's not loaded."

"What are you *doing* here? I told you not to come back!"

He fishes in his pocket for a cellphone and shows it to her. It's an email from Betza telling him to come, and to bring a gun. It also says to make sure Brenner leaves with everything he came with, except his coat, shoes, and gun, which they're supposed to toss back through the portal. Goldmark follows the instructions to the letter.

"So what now?" she asks. "Your kids are still on the other side of the bridge."

He heads toward the stairs.

"Now, we wait," he says, "and find out just how good your chess player really is."

■ ■ ■

They let Jack lead the way as the six of them—three from one earth, three from another—follow the emissary back through the dimly-lit tunnels inside Herald. It had been waiting for them at the doorway when they made their way to the top of the hill, and now they're walking behind it as it takes each quiet, rustling step deeper into the living structure. At a certain point they reach a dead end, and the creature—really just another part of Herald—dissolves into the floor.

Then the cul-de-sac unfolds and a great shining light fills the space.

It's the bridge—but it's different. It's no longer the silent, almost mundane warping of space that she'd come through to get here. Instead, it's got the brilliant shine and dimpled, mirrored surface that it had displayed in the hour or so before it fully opened. It's like it's closing again.

"Oh no," Lizzie says. She approaches it, but it's hot up close and she draws back.

"What is it?" Jack asks.

"The bridge, how I got here—" But then she stops. Also in the room is a lot of equipment that hadn't been there when she arrived. It had just been the strange, quiet anomaly in the room here before, but now there's a platform above and below like the one in Faye's building. And the lasers are here, too. How—?

"Do not concern yourself," comes a voice from all around them. A humanoid figure, made of the same material as the walls and floor, slides around and into sight. "This is not the path you followed to arrive here. That remains open and secure."

"Then what is this? And who're you?"

"This is Herald," Jack says.

"Oh! Uh, right. Thanks for earlier, with Brenner—that was you?"

The figure inclines its head in acknowledgment.

"What did you do with him? Is he here?" Jack asks.

"The one you call Brenner has been returned to your universe. He is of no concern."

"Then...okay, what's this? If it's not our bridge, then...?"

"A transuniversal bridge requires two points of synchronicity. This has only one," it says.

"So then it's...half a bridge? What's the point of that?" Lizzie asks.

"Half a bridge is an inadequate metaphor," it says. "We have called the space that the bridge crosses the Potentiate. A bridge uses that space, but does not provide access to it." It pauses, seeming to consider. "Consider this: while one may find utility in a bridge passing over a river, this does not mean that others may not also find utility in a path down to the water's edge, or indeed, in swimming."

Lizzie shakes her head, not really getting it at all.

"This is not a bridge as much as it is a lifeline," it says.

"To what?" Jack asks.

"To *whom*," Tina corrects him.

Jack swivels around. "You don't mean—"

"Indeed," Herald continues. "For the past three months, Alice has been in the Potentiate."

"In...*that thing*?" Sanna can't take their eyes off it. "For three whole *months*?"

"Beyond it, yes." The mannequin folds its hands. "Sending her into the Potentiate was necessary to achieve the optimal outcome."

"You sound like Betza," Lizzie says.

"Yes, Betza." It pauses. "We are collaborating with that existence. For all its limitations, it has taught us much."

"What for?" Lizzie says. "And why would you send Alice into that?"

"To aid us in achieving the optimal outcome. Let us explain. Approximately seventeen years ago, a spatial disturbance was observed within the city of Greve. Based on the gravitational waveforms detected, it was understood to be an interuniversal displacement, an event unlike any previously observed, and one supporting previous hypotheses concerning the possibility of greater access to the Potentiate. Further, in conferring with those who created us, it was inferred that the chances of a random event were too insignificant to be probable, and that a focal resonance must have been involved."

"A focal resonance? ...you mean Alice, don't you? And the rangefinder signal?" Lizzie asks.

"That is correct, though at the time we required more data to confirm. Several years ago, other humans from this world began a series of experiments in interuniversal displacement, returning the existence known as Alice to this world. Though brief in duration, the signal she emanated allowed us to extrapolate the possibility of access to the Potentiate in a more complete fashion than that of which we were capable. All outcomes may be charted from within the Potentiate, and more perfect knowledge of outcomes makes our chances of ecological restoration greater, but we have until recently had only imperfect access to it, relying upon remote sensing capabilities to determine the benefits of potential present actions. We therefore required the assistance of Alice."

"You mean she could go into that thing, but you can't?"

The figure nods once again.

"Furthermore, as we predicted, once the ability to create interuniversal displacement events was achieved in this universe, it became necessary to actively work against the potential for the destruction of your world, in addition to our own. In order to achieve this outcome, a greater knowledge of the potential futures was required."

"Why tell us now?" Tina asks from behind her. "How does that help your outcome?"

"Upon tracing its progression through the Potentiate, we have concluded that the existence known as Alice has chosen a suboptimal path, and altered events in an imperfect manner. We believe she has imparted faulty information to the other similar existence, the one known as Leigh, and that the latter is planning to act upon that information."

"Sorry, what?" Lizzie says.

"We believe that its limited human intellect has not allowed it to fully realize the most optimal possible outcome, and that it is planning to sacrifice itself unnecessarily."

"Sacrifice? You don't mean—" but Herald doesn't let her finish.

"We believe that unless steps are taken to convey more precise information to the existence known as Leigh, that the existence known as Alice will prematurely cease."

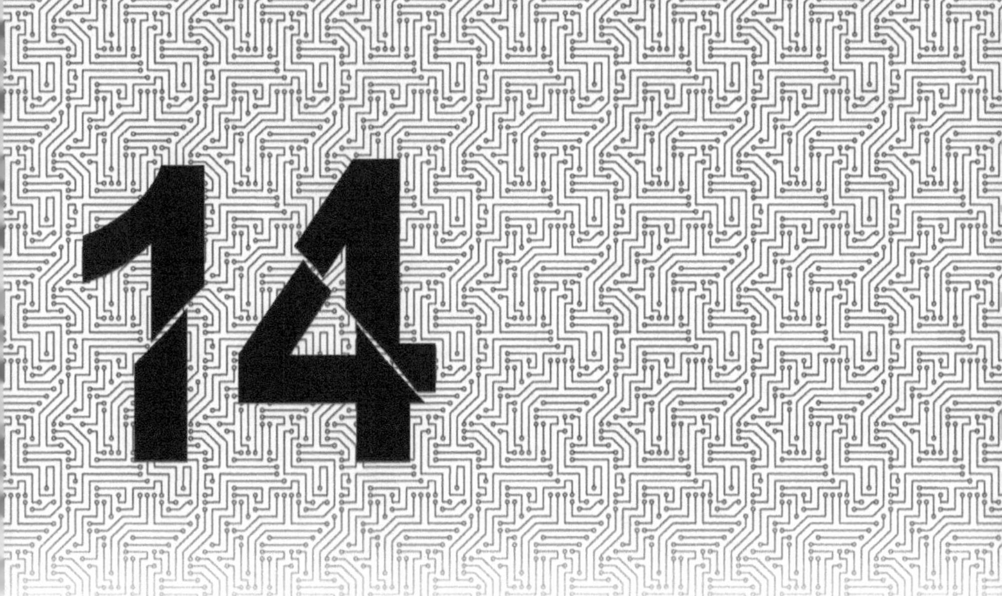

14

"**HOW FAST CAN WE GET THERE, AND HOW DO WE GET IN WHEN WE** do?" It's the next morning, and even though Herald had said there was time and that they should sleep, Lizzie's still exhausted from tossing and turning all night. Her hand is wrapped tight around a small metal cylinder with a clear, glassy cap. Herald had called it a 'nanofluid autoinjector,' but really it just looks like one of those needles for kids with peanut allergies. They just need to stab Leigh with it, Herald said, and it'll take care of the rest.

The problem is getting to him.

"The swarm prevents fast arrival by air—at least, if we want to avoid detection, which we do," Ange asserts, leaning against the counter. The six of them are standing in her kitchen, which somehow looks both futuristic and old fashioned at the same time. Maybe it's the complete absence of wood, Lizzie thinks.

"And you are not equipped to run at the speeds we are capable of," Tek adds.

"On the other hand, they don't know we're trying to break in, so security shouldn't be as tight as it was last time, getting out with you," Sanna says.

"Do you have anything like a dirtbike or a four-by-four?" Jack asks. "Could we copter in to the perimeter, then ride in on the ground?"

Ange shakes her head. "If you'd only leave it to us—"

"No. Sorry," Lizzie says. "Thank you, but no. Leigh's family. We're not about to leave him to be someone else's responsibility."

"That's a problem then," Sanna says. "Because there's no way even two copters can take six of us plus the weight of enough ground transport for six."

"There is another option." Tek's usual stoic face is borderline mischievous.

"No," Ange says, a little too quickly.

Sanna's eyes light up.

"Absolutely not," Ange repeats, but Lizzie can already tell she's lost whatever argument they're having.

"We split the difference," Sanna says, smirking. "We hit the tripwire on the way in, but we do it so fast they don't see us coming anyway."

"What do you mean?" Jack asks.

Sanna's grinning now. "How do you feel about heights?"

■ ■ ■

Brenner pops the case open on his lap as the small jet taxis down the runway and toward the unremarkable building in the Nevada desert. Six vials of high-tech dirt that'll let the human race skip whole stages of technological development. And, of course, make him fabulously rich.

He pulls one out and stares at it in the daylight coming through the window. He hadn't taken a good look since collecting the samples, and it had been night then. In the sun, he can see the finest of silver threads tracing its way through the soil.

He puts it back and snaps the case shut as the plane comes to a stop.

It's time for an auction.

■ ■ ■

"These are the locations I'd like to transplant," the professor shows him, poring over a table that's effectively a giant touchscreen. Maybe five hundred or so crisscrossing the globe.

Leigh wishes he'd spent more time studying maps back home. "I don't think that would be a good idea, there," he says, pointing at a spot on the east coast of North America. "I think there's a city. Maybe here?" he shifts his finger north. "I think this is mostly trees here."

Zee makes a note. "You'll be able to see once you're attached to the interface. While it's running, you should have the time to more accurately adjust the borders of the transplant areas to best avoid accidental human stowaways. It's not likely that humans from the other side would survive long enough to become a problem, of course, but we wouldn't want to take the chance."

Leigh nods.

"And we'll want to avoid any of the other surviving states. I'm sure you're aware of them now, even if you weren't taught in school. Here, here, and here as well."

Roughly a dozen points on the map light up red. They're all so small. Is this all that remains of humanity on this Earth?

"How many are left, do you think, in total?" he asks, adding, "The machines weren't interested in sharing that kind of information."

"It's hard to say," she says. "Without satellites, we can only go on the reports of our spies. Fifty thousand here, another hundred fifty thousand there." She points to a small pocket in Asia. "A hundred in the Wang Tian Empire. Our best estimates place the human population at around two million." She looks up at him, then, thinking. "How many are there in Apex?"

"Seven point five, seven point six? Billion, that is. And counting." A hell of a lot fewer if your plan succeeds, he thinks, but when he looks up, she's just shaking her head in disgust.

"Humans that can't learn to self-regulate their civilizations have whatever's coming to them," she says. "We should know."

He doesn't say anything in response, and she flips off the screen.

"I understand how you feel, but *this* is your *home*, Alice. An infinite number of universes exist with an infinite number of possibilities. That means there are an infinite number of worlds that have been destroyed and an infinite number that won't be. The only difference this will make, in the grand scheme of things, is that this world, your true home, will survive."

Leigh just nods.

"Everything is simpler now that you're back." She squeezes his shoulder and motions for him to follow her as she walks down a hall that's all windows on one side, letting the sunlight stream in. "Come on, let's go introduce you to the team."

■ ■ ■

"You've got to be kidding," Jack says. "A HALO jump?" He gestures at Lizzie and Tina. "They're—technically we're *all* civilians. I don't have that kind of training. They call it *Military* Free Fall for a reason."

"Don't worry, you'll each be strapped to one of us," Sanna says.

"We're going to jump," Lizzie says. "Out of a perfectly functioning plane. From many *miles* in the air. And open our parachutes under six hundred *yards* from the ground."

"Closer, if we can time it right," Sanna responds.

"At night, the swarm is thinnest over the center of the city," Tek says, "because it's only used for perimeter defense at that time. At terminal velocity, it will take us four seconds to pass through. A static field should further disrupt the swarm's communication and reduce the number of impacts as we pass through. It is possible that we may even go entirely undetected."

"Terminal velocity is something like 160 feet a second," Jack says.

"Perhaps faster in tandem," Tek corrects him.

"Do you know how little time that gives us to open the chutes?"

"Roughly eleven seconds, though the opening of the parachutes will quickly slow our descent."

"Exactly how many times have you done this?" Lizzie asks.

"Ange has done it twice," Sanna's almost bragging. "Me and Tek have done it once."

"It'll be cold," Tina says.

"We'll fabricate the necessary suits and tanks, don't worry."

"You keep saying 'Don't worry,' but I have to point out—"

"Not helping, I know," Ange finishes. "I don't know what to tell you. It really is the best way into the city with you three. This is why I said you shouldn't come."

Jack scowls, but doesn't budge. "We're coming."

Ange sighs. "I was afraid you'd say that. Fine, we go after dark. Tek, start fabricating the things we'll need. Sanna, teach them how to use the stunners." She gets up and wanders over to the door. "I'll go get us a ride."

■ ■ ■

Tomorrow. That's what Zee had told the team. They're going to be executing the plan tomorrow. They'd spent all afternoon calibrating the device, and tomorrow they're going to expose him to the hand and perform the displacement. They'll use him to destroy one world to save another.

He has to act tonight.

The bedroom isn't like the one at Hana and Toran's. It's almost clinical, spartan like a hospital room, but lacking the bags, wires, and telemetry readouts you'd expect. There's just the bed, the desk, and a series of drawers all filled with the same sterile clothing everyone else in the facility wears. There's a small washroom attached, too, with a shower that's more like a foggy day than a rainstorm. He waits until late, until all sound has died away in the hallways, then slips out of bed.

The shoes they provided along with the clothes are soled with something hard, some kind of heavy plastic. It's just fine on the industrial carpeting, but every step on tile makes a loud clopping sound that echoes down the halls, bounces off the windows, and fills the atriums with noise. He leaves them behind in the room, instead creeping out in the running shoes he'd borrowed from Emi.

He needn't have bothered. As soon as he takes his first steps he knows there's going to be a problem. It's not that there are guards, it's that the place itself doesn't need them. The little snitches in his blood tell the building where he is at all times, lighting the halls ahead of him as he goes. But he steels himself for confrontation, because he's got to try anyway. All he can do is hope that the sensors are like the security cameras in the subway back home—always on, but rarely watched, at least not in real time. Not unless someone wants to go back and take a look.

He closes his eyes and extends his senses, feeling for the hand. He knows it's here, somewhere in the facility, and if he concentrates really hard, he's pretty sure he can even tell what direction it's in.

There's no-one about the place in the middle of the night. There's a little sound that mumbles out from the occasional door when he first sets off, but as the halls start to look less and less like residences and more and more like vacant labs, he starts to feel like he's in some kind of zombie movie. Like he's waiting for one of 'The Infected' to jump out at any moment, to feast on his flesh.

But the place isn't full of monsters like that. The ones here smile and laugh and talk about working hard to save their way of life.

Even if it means the murder of seven and a half billion people.

He'd felt its presence earlier that day, when they were calibrating the machine. It shouldn't be far off. He's walking past a large set of windowless doors, almost next to the lab he'd spent the afternoon in, when he feels it—a twitching at the edge of his perception, like something's tugging at his brain. The hand is in there.

He wonders if they've managed to get the signal-cancelling program working again in the stasis cylinder, or if it's going to get progressively less and less comfortable to approach it. He remembers the painful resonance with his own nanomachines when they first disabled the program. They'd turned it back on, though, he thought, it just hadn't had much of an effect once he'd been exposed. He wishes he understood better how it all worked.

The doors aren't locked and the room is lit, but he can't see or hear any signs of life. He sneaks in as quietly as he can. The room is a huge space, occupied by at least a dozen enormous glass cylinders that stretch all the way from the floor to the ceiling. They're dark inside, and filled with some kind of bluish liquid. At the sound of footsteps from the far side of the lab, he silently ducks behind one of them and holds his breath. Is someone working late? He'd waited until he thought nobody would be around, but he supposes it's not even midnight yet, and he has to admit he doesn't really understand the place's schedule.

His heart thumps against his ribs, but he refuses to breathe. Thankfully the footsteps don't pause, they just tap their way past him and out into the hall where they fade out into the distance. He holds his breath as long as he can, then lets it out and gasps for air in the empty room.

The hand is close.

■ ■ ■

"Won't they hear us coming?" Lizzie shouts over the engine noise before remembering the mics in their masks. The jet is tiny, at least the part for them is. It's about as wide inside as two people standing next to one another, and they're seated in knee-to-knee pairs in the cargo hold. The whole craft seems purpose-built for the operation, except for the noise of the engines behind them.

"We're almost six miles up," Ange's voice comes to her through the earpiece. "And the jets are on the top of the wings to deflect as much noise upward as possible. It's only this loud because we're basically right next to them."

She nods, but it doesn't make her feel much better. The plan, at least as much as they've said out loud, has so many holes. They have a pretty good idea of where they're keeping Leigh, to the point where there's a good chance they can even land on top of the right building. According to Herald, there had been signals emanating from it all that afternoon that suggested they were doing some kind of displacement research. But from there, the plan is basically 'run around looking for Leigh and don't get caught doing it,' which really doesn't seem great. Herald had been able to pinpoint the location they'd been keeping Tina and Jack, but apparently Leigh's more mobile, and therefore harder to nail down. They'd said to focus their search on the second floor. And they're all just supposed to trust Herald.

Ange stands up in the narrow hold. "Okay, get up and turn around."

Lizzie does as she's told. A second later she feels a sudden pull backward as the magnetized clamps in their suits lock them together. Turning her head to the side, she can see Sanna and Tek doing the same thing with Tina and Jack.

Ange's voice comes over her earpiece again. "Okay, the hold is going to open up in a second. We'll do just as we practiced. Cross your arms in front of your chest. Three sideways steps, and then you can just fall. Close your eyes if you need to. Take a few deep breaths. I'll say out loud when you should brace for the opening, but I can tell you it's going to come a lot later than you're going to want it to. Try not to panic; you'll need to have your head screwed on tight when we land. Got all that?"

Lizzie manages a half-swallowed, "Yeah," and then the door is opening, revealing a vast expanse of stars and blackness. She stares out into it, but Ange is already counting.

"On three," Ange says. "One, two—"

Her heart leaps into her throat as she ignores every survival instinct she has and falls ungracefully out of the plane.

The wind screams past her helmet as they spin—black ground and starry sky, black ground and starry sky. After a few nauseating revolutions, they stabilize face-first. She hugs her crossed arms to her chest as they speed down into the darkness, willing herself not to panic.

And then she sees it—the city. It's not like the cities she's seen before, in the photos from space, long lines of twinkling lights stretching out like spiderwebs, organic and almost random-seeming on darkened terrain. It's different here, faint, probably to save electricity, and not random or organic at all. It's concentric circle after concentric circle, small arcs of blackness interspersed with geometric shapes and lines radiating out from the center. It looks like a gossamer mandala stretching out below them in all directions.

"It's beautiful." She says it out loud, for a split-second forgetting her terror at the fall.

"Yeah," comes Ange's response. "But so's an active volcano, from far enough away. And we're about to get pretty damn close."

The city continues to expand until it fills her whole field of view, closer and closer, until the dim lights and dark patches resolve themselves into buildings, streets, and fields. Strange circular patterns turn out to be wide silos—for some kind of manufacturing, maybe, or industrial farming. And then they pass through the swarm, sand-sized particles rattling off her faceplate and toughened jumpsuit like gnats on a summer windshield, almost turning into a hiss through the densest parts of the cloud.

By the time they're through it, the buildings are dangerously close. There aren't many tall ones, not many skyscrapers like the cities back home, but there's one especially tall spire in the center of the city that, to Lizzie, sure looks like it's stretching higher up into the sky than they happen to be right then.

"Hey, aren't we a little too—"

"Opening parachutes in three, two—" Ange interrupts, and then she's being yanked upward so hard it almost knocks the wind out of her. She squeezes her arms together to stop them from flailing away downward, then forces her eyes back open to watch the darkened rooftops still quickly approach. The roofs are flat and nondescript, save for what look like air conditioning units and ventilation pipes. She doesn't have the time to get much more of a look at them before they're beneath her feet with an impact that passes up her legs and into her spine.

They're down.

■ ■ ■

There are shadows in the tanks.

He looks up at them as he passes them, peering into their dark interiors. Out of curiosity, he reaches forward and touches one. The moment his hand makes contact with the cool glass, the cylinder illuminates from above, and he jumps back in surprise.

There's a person inside.

She's got long, dark hair that forms an irregular halo around her head, drifting in the liquid. Her eyes are half-open but unseeing. There are thick tubes feeding into her mouth and into a plastic collar that seems fused to her neck and spine. Fluids, dark like blood, circulate through them.

These must be reconditioning tanks like Emi had told him about. At least half a dozen of them are occupied. Are these all people from other universes?

Why is the hand here of all places?

He taps the glass again and the lights inside begin to fade off. The tugging is stronger now, and he turns to the back of the room where a wide white door breaks the symmetry of the otherwise featureless wall, its outline cutting into it like a seam. It's behind there: the hand. He puts an ear to its cold, smooth surface, but he can't hear anything except the rushing of blood in his head. Well, it's this or nothing, he thinks, and opens the door.

To his temporary relief, it's dark inside, but only for a moment. Sensing his presence, the lights come on and reveal a smaller lab space. It has more stainless steel—platters, countertops, instruments—and there's a smell that gets stronger with every step he takes into its interior. Something sterile and sharp—not bleach or ammonia, more like biology class on dissection day.

There's a table in the middle of the room, and a wall of what look like enormous pull-out drawers. There's a drain in the floor.

Oh, no.

He's only guessing based on the junk crime shows he's seen on TV, but even the possibility leaves him unnerved.

He walks over to one of the drawers. They have little lights on them; most are blue but a few of them are red. He pulls on one of the latter. There's an obscuring puff of white clouds as the contents slide out.

It's a body.

This is an autopsy room.

The pieces come together in his mind, then—the tanks, the bodies, the proximity to the hand, which is definitely in the room somewhere.

They've been experimenting. They've been exposing the kids from other universes to the signal. They've been trying to make it replicate inside them.

And it's been killing them.

He can feel a weak echo of the signal even now from the body before him, even as he's just standing over it. He stares at the great Y-shaped autopsy scars carved into the body's chest—no, not 'the body's.' *Their.* Their chest. This was a living, breathing person, maybe earlier today.

And he'd been the one who let these monsters have the hand. He'd been the one to take it out of the mausoleum. He'd been the one to turn off the shielding and let them summon it along with his friends.

He hadn't known; how could he have known? He hadn't even known what the signal *was.* There's nothing he could've done differently, he tells himself, but his throat tightens. A wave of guilt so heavy it nearly crushes him settles on his shoulders and drives him down into a crouch, gripping the side of the drawer like a drowning sailor grabs a lifeline. But this is just the opposite.

After a minute he realizes nothing is going to change. He'll be crouching there forever. No-one is going to come and tell him it's going to be all right, because it won't be. It's up to him now.

He pulls himself back up and stares down at the body. They look like a girl, but then, if they were in each others' places, so would he. They look relaxed, maybe a little sad. He can't imagine it, what their last moments must have been like. Maybe like his, right before the bridge opened. Maybe they saw their life flash before their eyes, too. Maybe they found a way home.

"I'm so sorry," he whispers, and rubs his eyes with his sleeve.

Then he grits his teeth and pushes the drawer back in.

This has to stop.

■ ■ ■

Brenner mills about the auction room, holding—but not drinking—a complimentary glass of champagne. He's probably the worst-dressed person there, despite wearing the nicest suit he owns. At least half a dozen of the men there are wearing tuxedos, including the ones who 'hired' him.

This is a Consortium auction, after all.

A man slides up to him, smiling as the auctioneer reminds them all that, while they are showcasing the items individually, the bids themselves will be silent and are due in to the desk fifteen minutes after the showing of the final item.

"August," the man says with a smile. The warmth of his voice is at odds with everything Brenner knows about him. This is Lyman Fahrenthold, a man whose job seems to be appearing in photographs next to the rich and powerful—usually months to years before they're discovered to have funded a terrorist organization or have been involved in some private, vicious, and highly profitable war. He's a dangerous man, and one for whom the words 'plausible deniability' aren't so much a defense as a creed.

"Lyman," he says, smiling and shaking the man's hand. "It's been some time."

"And yet you wish it were longer still." He chuckles, and Brenner smiles uncomfortably. "I hear you've at long last brought us what we've been asking for. I was beginning to worry about you, August."

"Ah. Yes. Quite." This time he takes a long draw of champagne while surreptitiously scanning the room. In addition to Fahrenthold, he can also see the four other 'members' of the Consortium slowly circling like sharks—Kamensky, Xing, Evering, and Finch. Five people whose individual net worths dwarf the GDP of several developed nations combined. Even if you didn't know who they were, you'd recognize them as the only ones clearly there to bid, yet who at the same time didn't feel the need for armed guards.

That's because they don't need them. These are the people who'd pulled the strings behind pretty much every unsavory deal in the past two decades. The ones whose personal histories are a better deterrent to violence than any personal arms. The ones whose desire for power and competition had demanded every ounce of his hard work up to this point.

And who, now that he had delivered, would presently be trying to outbid one another for sole control of this universe's first taste of militarized nanotechnology.

"I don't suppose you'll just agree to share it with one another, hey?"

Fahrenthold smiles like a snake. "Now where would the fun be in that?"

Well, whoever wins is fine. It'll be over tonight. They'll get their prize, Brenner will get paid, and then maybe he'll buy a little island somewhere that the Consortium has never even heard of. Somewhere with sandy beaches and palm trees and folks who'll serve him drinks in half coconuts with those little paper umbrellas.

If he never sees any of the faces in this room again, it'll still be too soon.

It's not that he was forced into it exactly. He'd brought it up to the right people—people who knew people, who knew people themselves—but once word got to the top, he'd started to regret it. Striking a deal with the Consortium is nothing but a series of ever-more-dangerous escalations. At first you think you're out there fishing for a prize marlin, then you think maybe you've made a mistake and you're really fishing for a whale, and by the end you realize maybe you weren't even the one doing the fishing at all. Maybe you were just the bait, and the ones holding the rod are more dangerous than whatever shadows are circling you in the deep. Fahrenthold pats him on the shoulder and he tries not to recoil.

"Looks like you're up."

The time for the final item's introduction has come.

But as the auctioneer holds up one of the vials in his white-gloved hands, Brenner can't help but feel there's something different about it, something off. He slips from Fahrenthold's now inattentive company and wanders to the front of the purchasing crowd for a better look. As the auctioneer drones on about the nanomachines as though they're a Renoir or a Monet, the vial catches the light.

It's entirely full of silver.

He starts to panic. Has someone swapped out the vials with something else? No, that's not possible. The security is perfect, and the auctioneers here are beyond reproach—their lives depend on neutrality between the factions. But if those really are the same vials, the ones he'd been looking at just hours before—

He hears the sound before anyone else, but only because he's listening for it—the faint high-pitched creaking, grinding, crinkling sound of glass under great pressure.

By the time the vial bursts, he's already sneaked his way to the back of the room. The glass pops with a faint *pinging*, and showers its powdery contents over the gathered crowd like a plume of wispy, silver smoke. At first, the noises from the attendees are ones of surprise and annoyance, but as he slips out into the hall he can hear them quickly turn to fear and pain.

The nanomachines are replicating, and they're using everything— *everyone* they've just landed on as raw materials.

■ ■ ■

The hand has to be in one of the other drawers. He heaves one out, then another, but they're either empty—the ones with the little blue lights— or they're full of more bodies. As he's staring in horror at the fourth, one who looks uncannily like Lizzie, he hears a voice from behind him.

"Looking for this?"

It's Zee.

He doesn't say anything.

"I thought you might come back for it. I knew you wouldn't help us out so willingly." Her face turns cruel. "You've been corrupted, just like them."

"Corrupted?" The fact that she has the nerve to call her own victims 'corrupted' kindles a fire in his chest.

"Not one of them could see our need," she says. "Not one could see that *this* world needed them more."

"They weren't even *from* this world!" he shouts.

"Which is why I had so much hope for *you*, Alice. So much hope. Surely, if they were so motivated to save their *own* worlds, then you could be motivated to save *yours*."

"This *isn't* my world."

"This is what I mean. Corrupted." She shakes her head and takes a couple of steps toward him. "This is the world that gave you *life*, Alice. This is the world that they *stole you from*. And you want to let *that* one *live* and *this* one *die*?"

"I don't want *any* worlds to die, but if one of them has to, maybe it should be the one that destroyed *itself!*"

"Seven and a half billion people and counting!" she shouts. "That's what you said. You think your world is any better than this one? You think it's any less doomed? They're just doing what we did in slow motion, consuming it inch by inch instead of all at once. But by helping me, by helping *this world*, you could at least save *one*. Think about it, Alice. We know the value of conservation. We know how to live within our means. We've learned the lesson that the people who stole you from us never could. They'll destroy themselves either way, but *we survived*. With a functioning biosphere, we could live in balance with this world forever. Apex has fifty years, at best."

"That's fifty years to change, Zee. Fifty years they won't have to change *in*, if you send this world's contaminated land over there. Can't you clear the transplant sites first, the way you cleared this city?"

"It would take decades!" she snaps. "We don't have that kind of time. It's us or them, and I choose *us*." She taps a pad on the side of the hand's container and throws it to him.

He catches it instinctively, half a second later realizing the mistake—she's deactivated the shielding, and the proximity of the signal is sending his own nanomachines into the same feedback loop as before. He drops the hand and falls to his knees, the shrieking in his cells reaching fever pitch. Every inch of him is on fire.

"Turn it off!" he screams.

"Now, you're going to help me to save this world," she says, as the symphony of pain roars louder and louder.

"Turn it off, *please!*"

"Not until you agree. Not until you know that I will do *whatever it takes to save my world!*"

He wants to peel off his skin, to pull off his ears. In his frenzy, he falls the rest of the way to the floor, writhing uncontrollably. Somewhere in the distance he can hear her footsteps approaching. He thinks she's picking up the hand. Are there more people now? It feels like an age of burning and knives. He manages to force himself to his hands and knees. Somewhere behind the wall of pain, the blinding color and deafening, screaming sound, she's there, he knows it. If only he can get to her—

He falls to one elbow as a great wave of nausea passes over him, forcing him to spill the contents of his stomach all over the floor in front of him. He tries to back away from it but can't. He's going to die. He's going to be the next one on the autopsy table.

He'll say it. He'll say he'll do it. Anything to stop this.

Someone's grabbing his hand.

And then the pain is starting to fade away, the tide of searing, boiling water receding from his skin. He's curled up on the floor. His eyes are weeping, nose running, he's choking back the bile between heaving, shuddering sobs.

"Leigh," someone says.

Leigh.

Not Alice.

He forces his eyes open and tries to look. The world's still spinning.

"Who...?" he gurgles out, gagging on his own words.

He sees it then, it's the body from the last drawer, come to take him with her. The last victim come to take the next. He feels cold, but it's nice. He'll be cold in the next drawer over, lying there with the rest of them.

"Leigh," the voice comes again, and he squints harder. Something's not right. It's not a body. It's a living person.

It's *Lizzie.*

■ ■ ■

At the sound of screaming, they break into a run in the darkened halls. A hundred yards ahead there's a lit section, and to the right, through a room filled with enormous tanks of blue liquid, is a lab where a woman in a white lab coat is standing over her brother's body.

But not for long.

She doesn't even get a chance to speak before Jack shoots her, the green bolt of energy dispersing into her body the moment it strikes.

"Who—?" is the furthest she gets before two more shots from behind them take her down.

"One shot won't take them out," Sanna explains.

Tina runs over and picks up the hand, which seems to be in the same container as before, but with a small touchpad attached. It won't light up at her touch, so thinking fast she ducks down and grabs Leigh's hand while he writhes on the floor, using his finger to turn the signal down again.

Leigh's spasms slow, his tortured choking easing into the rhythm of sobs. Lizzie says his name a few times, but he doesn't come out of it anything like as fast as he had before. Ange starts going through a set of steel drawers and cupboards along one wall, emerging with a hand towel to gently wipe his face and arms.

After a minute, he blinks and finally stares more at her than through her.

"Lizzie," he says. "It is you?"

"Well, who the hell else would show up to save your butt in another universe?"

He smiles, closing his eyes again.

"Hey, hey—! Don't pass out, okay?" She sits him up and leans him against the wall.

"Not passing out, just very...dizzy." He hiccups, burps, and makes a face. "I think the extra exposure to the hand...extra signal...further along. Get to the control room...now."

Lizzie manages to follow along. The woman had been exposing

him to the hand to get the signal to replicate in him, but the longer exposure had not only tortured him, it had amplified the rangefinder even further than it had gone when they'd opened the bridge. At this rate, they might not be able to stop it.

"We have to reset his nanomachines," she says to Ange. "If we don't—"

But he grabs her wrist. "No."

"But—"

"Only chance...keep trying otherwise." He opens his eyes again and stares at her. "Going to destroy our world...kill everyone. Stop them."

"What?"

"Wants to displace...all over the world. Seed this one." He burps again and groans, eyes closing, then opening again, never really focusing. "Nano...things...all over ours."

Ange's face turns to horror, the full realization of what he's saying becoming clear. She explains to the rest, about the dormant machines in the soil, and what the scientist is trying to do.

"Give him the injection," Jack says.

Lizzie's still against it. "Look at him, Jack, he's in no shape."

"You heard what he said. He's the only one who can stop them now."

Leigh looks over at Jack. "What...injection?"

"Herald says you met Alice," Lizzie says, "but that she gave you bad info."

He turns and confusedly looks her way.

"If you're going to do this..." She looks around, and everyone's faces are saying the same thing. "Damn it. If you're going to do it, you need to do it with this."

■ ■ ■

There's a spike of pain in his neck, and a rush of cold that passes through his body. At first he's not sure what the injection is supposed to do, but within moments images start flooding his mind—places he's never seen before, people he doesn't know. Layer after layer of information form in his head like memories, like learning a wordless new language.

He has them haul him to his feet, but he can't walk in this state. Two of the new people, who're really strong, it seems, carry him one arm over each shoulder while he directs them. He barely has to open his eyes, just gives them a right and a left when needed.

They don't say much as they go. He tries to say he's happy to see them, Lizzie and Jack and Tina all together, but the words get harder and harder to put in the right order. The nausea has passed, but there's something else that's taken its place, something quiet, creeping, peaceful, cold.

He thinks again of the bodies in the drawers.

They take two long escalators down, to a long hall that ends in a wide steel bulkhead. Behind it is the hangar-sized room where, he now realized, Jack and Tina must have arrived in this universe. In front of it are two very surprised guards that Jack and one of the new ones make quick work of.

They wedge the door open, slip through, and then crank it shut behind them. Jack says something about locking it and one of the others shoots a panel to the left of the door.

Leigh motions to the strange interface that's planted in the center of the room, and they help him over to it. It's like a kneeling chair, but with holes for his hands and feet to fit into the steel cradle on which it sits. It responds to his touch—it has to, he's the only one that can use it—and causes all sorts of lights and sounds to come to life around them. A deep, familiar humming starts up behind the far wall. A set of ten black obelisks light up to one side, and a series of workstations turn on, in front of chairs where Zee's team had sat that day.

Zee had planned for this, he thinks. She'd expected to be able to operate it herself, after torturing him into compliance. That's why she'd been alone. That's why they'd calibrated everything that day—so all Zee would have to do was slot him in like a cog in the machine. The design of the interface doesn't even technically require his consciousness.

But it can handle it.

He points to one of the stations, and they half-carry him over. He closes his eyes, thinking of all the things he's seen. They won't have to change much.

Two windows to the left, he sets a couple values to 'Full Manual,' and changes a few other things to match, still not totally sure how he knows what to do, then has them take him over and strap him into the machine.

An alarm sounds then, piercing even the ringing in his ears, and setting off a pair of orange strobes by the door. A moment later there's a loud banging on the bulkhead itself.

"Looks like they're awake," Jack says. He puts a hand on Leigh's shoulder. "We'll take care of them. You do this."

Leigh nods. He looks at Tina, who still has the hand wrapped in her arms, and motions for her to set it down in front of the interface.

Then he closes his eyes.

"Back," he says. "Get back."

And then the humming gets so loud that the thumping and shouting from behind him, the pounding on the bulkhead, even the angry whistle of the rangefinder signal shrieking in his ears, are all drowned out by its low, almost seismic rumble.

He can feel the vibration in his arms and legs travel up his spine to his skull.

He opens his eyes and takes one last look at them, at Jack and Tina and the others barricading the door, and at Lizzie who's shouting something at him in the impenetrable noise.

"Bring her back," she's saying.

He's going to try.

■ ■ ■

Brenner scrambles out of the building and into the cool desert night, nearly tripping over his own feet in the process. His mind is racing. Why had they become active? The other world was stable. It had *looked* stable.

Damn that bucket of bolts, it had gotten something wrong, and not a small something, either.

Cross the bridge, look for the samples in the soil. Get the samples. That was all Betza had said to do. It hadn't said a damn thing about the nanomachines coming to life and devouring the damn planet, starting with him.

He takes a step toward the tarmac, and the snapping twang of a bullet ricochet stops him in his tracks. He lifts his hands over his head.

"BRENNER!" comes the shout from behind him, about thirty feet back. He turns around to the most terrifying thing he's ever seen.

It's Lyman Fahrenthold. Or what's left of him.

His entire left side is deformed, too small. A thin layer of nanomachines clings to the remains of him, eating him from the outside in, preventing him from bleeding to death as it does so. A silver footprint spreads from each place his left leg has stepped behind him. Another, only vaguely human shape has collapsed in the doorway, motionless, and is dissolving into a pool of silver that's slowly radiating outward. Brenner can hear the sound of windows breaking in the distance as the contagion escapes.

Fahrenthold's face is contorted in horror and pain. And anger.

"You think you can get *away?*" He fires a shot, but it goes wide. He takes a labored step, his teeth starting to show in melting quicksilver through a now-missing cheek. "You think you can *turn* on us and be *free?*" He lisps through half a mouth. He fires again, this one much closer to the mark. Brenner starts to back away.

"*You set us up!*" He drags his almost skeletal leg forward another step. "NO-ONE double crosses us. NO-ONE DOUBLE CROSSES THE CONSOR—"

And then he's gone, his voice lost as a cool wind blows across the desert.

Fahrenthold hasn't died; he hasn't fallen to the ground or been eaten away.

He's simply gone.

Everything, beginning two feet ahead of Brenner and stretching off well beyond where the far side of the building had just been, has been replaced with an orchard, heavy with fruit, and ready for harvest.

■ ■ ■

The sound builds until Lizzie's sure it's going to shake them apart, loud enough to be deafening and low enough to squeeze her heart between her ribs. She covers her ears but of course it's no help, and she shouts at the top of her lungs to her brother, on whom all their hopes now rest.

"Bring her home," she shouts. "Bring her—"

The silence hits her like a punch in the chest, the terrifying oppression of sheer nothingness reaching out for her like an icy hand. It mercifully releases its grip, allows them to pass into reality once again, but only for the briefest of moments. For less than a second, she's sure she can see the outline of home, of the Goldmark Estate set against the distant snow, and then they're being dragged backward into the void again, thrown within a precious bubble of is-right-now through the unending emptiness of forever-wasn't and never-will-have-been.

And then they're standing in an open, well-trimmed yard, the silhouette of Herald's gargantuan fin stretching into the starry sky above them. Beneath her feet is a small circle of concrete.

"—home."

They're all there—Jack and Tina, Ange and Sanna and Tek, all looking confused. A number of the devices have come along for the ride, too. Black obelisks and workstations and a long row of things she can't identify. Six of the tall, blue-liquid-filled tanks are arrayed off to one side as well, perched neatly on their own foundations. The woman in the lab coat is lying beside them, unconscious.

All that's missing is Leigh.

■ ■ ■

It's starting to rain.

The dark spots appearing on the playground gravel start to overlap and find one another, until it's hard to tell if there's more dry stone than wet. The smell of fresh water and dust fills the air, like at the end of a long drought.

"Come to say goodbye?" Alice is sitting on a swing. It's a little too small, but that's okay; they've grown a lot since they were last here.

Leigh's sitting on the next one over. The hand is sitting on the ground between them.

"Kind of," he says, feet tucked beneath him, slowly skirting the ground with his toes.

He stands up, walks around to face her.

"You really do look like me," she says. Her lopsided smile is the mirror image of his own.

"You know, I could say the same thing."

"Yeah well," she says, "I looked like this first."

"You'll get to again," he says. He reaches forward and grabs her hand, pulling her up and off the swing.

"What do you—"

"You're going back, Alice. You've spent enough of forever in here. Out here. Whatever this place really is."

"No." She shakes her head. "I can't. Because there's only one way—"

"You asked me what you were thinking of, before, when I was last here. But I know. I knew. And I didn't need to be psychic, either." He pokes her forehead as he says it. "It's obvious from everything, from everything that you've done from the start. The way you've always been. It was us. Lizzie, Jack, Patton, even me."

"That's not—"

"I know it's not the answer you were looking for, but it's true, isn't it? You were always thinking of us. Always us. Never yourself."

She goes to speak, but he just wraps his arms around her.

"Thank you." As if words could ever be enough. "But it's my turn now."

He squeezes her tight, and then wills her back the way he came, through the brane, through the boundaries between worlds in the fragile bubble of a diving bell, back into the real.

And then she's gone.

His arms close on nothing. He's standing there alone, as the rain starts to fall in earnest.

He takes a deep breath and looks around the empty playground, then down at the hand in its little container. He picks it up.

"Looks like it's just you and me, now."

■ ■ ■

There's a shift in the air behind her, and Lizzie turns around to see Leigh sitting up in the interface, looking confused and more than a little distraught.

He gets up and walks over to her, unsteady on his feet.

"Lizzie?" he says.

It's only as she's hugging him that she realizes the differences.

The clothes. The hair.

"Leigh?"

She pulls back. Tears are streaming down her face. She shakes her head.

It takes less than a second to figure out what her brother had done. In the weeks and months to come, she'll look in the mirror and blame herself for her last words to him, and blame him for listening.

He'd done just what she'd told him to do, back in the control room, shouting over all the adrenaline, the noise and the chaos. For the first time in his whole damn life, he'd actually listened to her, and even as she hugs her sister and celebrates her return, she curses herself for saying it.

He'd done just what she'd said to do.

He'd brought Alice home.

Epilogue

LIZZIE ROLLS OVER ON THE BED AND STRETCHES. THE MILD, SALTY breeze blows through the open window like a gentle ether for her heart. The morning fog has already burned off, and the silence that filled the streets is now a gentle rustle of footsteps and conversation, punctuated by the laughter of children—probably Lith and Salu up to their latest mischief. The late September mornings have grown cool back home, but they've figured out that Chee is somewhere equivalent to San Francisco, climate-wise, and the calendar doesn't even seem to line up, so there's not a lot to worry about as far as the weather's concerned.

She sits up and hangs her feet off the side, looking over to the other bed in the room, where Alice is still curled up, cocooned in her blankets. She's a pretty sound sleeper these days, though she hadn't been at first. She says that working double-time to catch up back at the Academy has taught her the value of a good night's sleep.

They've left the bridge open, between Chee and Doc Sullivan's building in New York, and they've settled into a pattern where Lizzie and Alice visit one weekend in every four, so Herald can tune up their nanomachines and keep general tabs on their health. In return, they bring samples of things that have gone extinct here, mostly bugs and plants, but every now and then something bigger. God only knows where they come from. They just show up and Doc dutifully passes them along. Betza seems to have a new 'optimal outcome' in mind; this time they'd brought a dozen birds' eggs in an incubator.

And of course, a couple of shopping bags full of tea and coffee.

At first it had seemed like a terrible idea, leaving a permanent bridge between their worlds, but with all the equipment spirited away, with the lead scientist behind this world's displacement project under lock and key, and with Betza and Herald both affirming that those behind the plot in their universe had been 'taken care of'—a phrase so cold it unnerved rather than comforted Lizzie—they'd decided to leave it be. The truth was, they weren't even sure it could be closed, and the only ones who knew for sure, Betza and Herald, weren't inclined to say.

The 'powers that be' in Greve, it seemed, had turned their focus back inward after that night, probably in the assumption that, when it came to other universes, discretion was the better part of valor. They'd even managed to get messages in and out to Alice's friend Emi, who'd said that, on the night of their escape, a neighboring orchard had been replaced by a giant mound of silver dust and desert sand, which their tight-lipped authorities had excavated and removed without a single word—at least not to her. Perhaps they'd taken that as a warning not to meddle with other universes anymore. They can only hope.

She slides out of the bedroom and closes the door in silence, heading down the stairs to where she can smell breakfast cooking. Tina's sitting quietly at the table with a cup of coffee.

"Morning, Tina. Morning, Dr. Mallik," she says, sitting down at the table next to her friend. The woman standing at the counter rolls her eyes at her.

"Look, as much as I appreciate the respect," she says, "how many times do I have to tell you, it's just Nisha. I changed your *diapers*." She shakes her head. "'Dr. Mallik,' for crying out loud."

Lizzie smiles. "Sorry. It's still weird calling adults by their first names."

The first thing Pops had done, after finding out they were all safe

and sound, was to get Nisha over to Chee to help out. He couldn't bring
her back from the dead in their own world—he'd done too thorough
a job for that—but he did happen to know of an opportunity for a
trained exobiologist in a location where supporting paperwork was...
somewhat less required.

"Jack and Tina don't seem to have a problem with it."

"Well, Jack's not here, is he?" Lizzie says. He'd just left for college,
said he'd be back in time for the next trip, but it's not exactly imperative for him, not having machines in his blood and all. "And Tina's
Tina."

The girl sitting next to her just nods. She's gotten really comfortable lately, and doesn't force herself to speak when she doesn't feel
like it. The quiet smile into her coffee is all Lizzie needs, to know that
things are going okay.

"Yeah, yeah," Nisha says. "Anyway, what colleges are you going to
apply to? And for what?"

"Nuh uh," Lizzie shakes her head. "No career path conversations
before coffee. Besides," she puts an arm around Tina, "I don't want to
leave this one behind."

Tina blushes, which just makes Lizzie grin.

"Well, the coffee I can help with. Even if I still question the wisdom
of wasting caffeine on the young." Nisha laughs and pours her a mug.
"You have to get off your tush to get it though, we don't do table service
in this establishment."

Lizzie grins harder, just as a bleary-eyed Alice appears like a shadow at the doorway.

"What time is it?" Alice says. "Why are you all awake?"

Lizzie does a double-take. Even though Leigh had only looked that
way for three months, she'd gotten so used to it that she still catches
herself thinking he's somehow, finally come home. But he hasn't.

"It's eleven in the morning," Lizzie says.

"Oh." Alice frowns, then sleepwalks to the coffee and grabs herself
some. "Good," she says, yawning. She sits down at the table and rubs
her eyes.

"You sleep okay? We're going out on the boat this afternoon with Sanna. Don't want you to fall over the side or anything."

"Mmm. Weird dreams."

"What about?" Nisha asks.

"I'll give you three guesses, but you'll only need one," she says around another yawn. Whenever she has weird dreams, nine times out of ten, they're about Leigh.

Herald had said there were instructions in the syringe Lizzie had injected him with that night, a map Leigh might be able to use to find his way home through the Potentiate. Alice thinks she's in contact with him when she has her dreams, like he's asking for directions. Lizzie doesn't tell her what she really thinks, because nobody needs to deal with that kind of guilt. She's got enough for all of them.

It's been nine months, and they're still waiting, hoping. She'll force herself to hope forever if she has to.

"I think he's getting close," Alice says.

■ ■ ■

The waves are smaller than usual today, not even the size of small cars, but Lizzie holds on tight, all the same. She still marvels at the way Alice moves around on the boat, like she was born for it. She walks across the rolling deck and casually leans over the side, releasing a suite of sensors on a line and counting out the depth as the spool unwinds.

When Alice had first returned, she'd been so very quiet. They hadn't gone home, not right away—Alice had been adamant in her refusal to leave Chee, in case Leigh came back. She didn't want to miss his arrival. But she'd seemed ill at ease, all the same, closed in on herself and anxious. She'd wander around the streets with Leigh's headphones on, listening to his playlists, unable to stand still. That's when Sanna had grabbed the two of them and taken them out on the boat.

With every mile from the shore, Alice had come back to life a little more. Eyes closed, face into the wind, she'd started to smile just as the bow had started slamming into the biggest waves Lizzie had ever seen.

Never mind cars, the waves had been the size of city buses, or bigger: trucks, trains—they got to the point where they changed from objects to geography. The boat rode up and over ocean-bound hills at angles Lizzie had thought defied all reason. But what had made it all worthwhile had been the sound of Alice's laughter, pealing into the ocean spray.

Now she's watching her sister from across the small deck, shouting readouts of datapoints to Tina while Sanna steadies the small craft's position over today's particular patch of ocean. She feels a little useless at times, but she knows Alice wouldn't come out without her. That's her job on these trips; it's not the worst thing she could be doing with her time. Besides, she's getting more useful. Sanna has been teaching her how to sail, how to use the wind and waves to her advantage. She feels like, in a way, that's something they've all been trying to learn, since that day.

■ ■ ■

The boat lists to the side as they tack against the wind and pull in toward the shore. Lizzie smiles, a little exhausted, but satisfied. She's been thinking maybe she won't go back and go to college at all, that maybe she'll just stay here and help out in Chee. Maybe she can convince Dr. Mallik—Nisha, that is—to train her in the things she'll need to know.

Or maybe she will go back. Maybe she'll go to school and do what she has to in order to be able to help out here better. She doesn't know. Whatever it is, there's something about this place that draws her in, makes her want to be here forever. Maybe it's the nature of the project, rebuilding a whole world, an entire biosphere. Maybe it's just because it's where she was born. Maybe it's something else.

As they pull closer to shore, she gets ready with the ropes, fishing about in the bow so she can toss them over as soon as they pull up. But as she's sorting them out, Tina starts tugging on her sleeve, hard, and she looks up.

"What?" she starts to ask, but Tina's not looking at her. No one is. Everyone else on the boat, Tina, Alice, and Sanna, are all staring toward the dock.

Perched on the end of it sits a silver, fox-like creature, patiently waiting for them, its dark eyes staring at them from somewhere more distant than the shore.

An emissary.

■ ■ ■

They haven't seen one for ages. It turned out that Herald rarely ever sent for people, and that their brief time in Chee nine months before had featured more interaction with their great and powerful caretaker than most of the city's residents had ever had before, or perhaps would again. And yet here they are, following the strange, scaled creature single-file up the hill to where the entrance to the fin lies open: Alice in the lead, then Lizzie, Tina behind her.

As they near the doorway, she feels a knot of dread twist in her stomach, ratcheting tighter with every step. She suddenly doesn't want to know what Herald has to say, what Herald has to show them. She doesn't want to follow the emissary into the cavern of nanometal scales. In front of her, Alice is certain that Leigh's back, but Lizzie finds herself somehow sure it's the reverse.

It's never been good news before. Why would it start now?

But they wind their way through Herald's interior regardless, up dimly-lit passageways until they're what feels like high above Chee. Lizzie finds herself wishing for a window, suddenly, a way of grounding herself in a reality outside this place. She knows the path they're treading, knows where it leads. When the dust had settled, while Alice had wandered the town, she'd spent whole hours just staring into it: the glowing, swirling ball of light in the second portal room. The hole in the universe that leads to the Potentiate.

It's not like the doorway between their worlds, self-sustaining, stable. It doesn't even look like you could pass through it into anything, its strange opalescent surface shimmering in its own light, hiding whatever lies beyond. What if Alice is wrong? What if the portal into the Potentiate has closed, leaving Leigh adrift in that strange half-place forever? For the last year, Herald has held their foot in the door to eternity. What if they've finally decided it isn't worth the resources? What if they've decided to pull their foot back out, and this is just the formality of letting them know?

As they round the final corner, she can tell from the light that something's different. It's darker. The familiar flickering glow that used to bathe the hallway in its strange shadows and reflections is missing. The only things lighting the hall now are the dim, practical sconces set with clockwork regularity in the walls. In the absence, Lizzie starts to feel a pressure building, a force-field going up between herself and the room, like the air is thickening with every step, making it nearly impossible to go on. Even though it's not really there, even though it's all in her head, she almost comes to a complete stop in the hallway. But Tina's been tracking her slowing progress and steps up beside her to take her hand. Lizzie grits her teeth and walks in.

The portal is gone.

Her heart stops.

Everything else in the room is still there: the amplification table, the platform, the lasers. But where the glowing sphere had once hovered, lighting the room with its transient glow, there's nothing but air. Nothing but dark, empty space. Herald's mannequin is standing at the far side of the room, facing away from them. Silent.

Lizzie wants to run, to grab Alice and drag her back to the ocean and sail away and pretend none of this is real, that none of this is happening. To keep the hope alive for another day, another hour, even. But as she reaches out for her sister, Alice is already halfway across the room and beyond her reach.

It takes a moment to register what she's moving toward with such excitement, a moment to realize that Herald's form has hidden something from view.

And then they step aside.

Sitting on an examination table at the far side of the room, peeking toward them from around Herald's mechanical robes, is a lone, pixie-like figure, eyes lit up like fireworks, a delirious grin on his face.

Before she even knows what's happening, Leigh has thrown himself across the room, grabbing Alice along the way. He wraps his arms around her, around all three of them, nearly knocking them over in the process, hanging off them like an exhausted swimmer holds a lifesaver, being slowly pulled to safety.

It's only then, in that warm and clumsy embrace, that she finally allows herself to believe that it's real. That he's back. Nine months. She hugs him back with all her strength, finally remembering to breathe again, to let her heart beat again.

Alice is laughing, Lizzie's crying, and Leigh's managing to do both at the same time, repeating the same two words, over and over, like a promise of better days to come.

"I'm home."

THE END

RICHARD FORD BURLEY

Richard is a writer and academic editor who's living proof that abstract concepts like 'impostor syndrome' can be physically animated—not unlike an alchemist's homunculus—and given jobs like 'writer' and 'editor.' He lives in New Hampshire with his wife and cat in a house built in the year the first science fiction film, 'A Trip to the Moon,' was released. *Displacement* is his second novel.

richardfordburley.com